MARIAN WELLS

THE SILVER HIGHWAY

MARIAN WELLS

THE SILVER HIGHWAY

BETHANY HOUSE PUBLISHERS

MINNEAPOLIS, MINNESOTA 55438

A Division of Bethany Fellowship, Inc.

Manuscript edited by Penelope J. Stokes.

Cover illustration by Dan Thornberg,
Bethany House Publishers staff artist.

Published by Bethany House Publishers
A Division of Bethany Fellowship, Inc.
6820 Auto Club Road, Minneapolis, Minnesota 55438

Printed in the United States of America

Library of Congress Cataloging-in-Publication Data

Wells, Marian, 1931–
    The silver highway / Marian Wells.
       p. cm. — (Treasure quest books)

    Sequel to: Out of the crucible.
    1. Underground railroad—Fiction. I. Title.
II. Series: Wells, Marian, 1931–   Treasure quest books.
PS3573.E4927S5   1989
813'.54—dc20   89–17558
ISBN 1-55661-060-2   CIP

Books by Marian Wells

The Wedding Dress
With This Ring

Karen

The STARLIGHT TRILOGY Series
    The Wishing Star
    Star Light, Star Bright
    Morning Star

The TREASURE QUEST Series
    Colorado Gold
    Out of the Crucible
    The Silver Highway

MARIAN WELLS and her husband live in Boulder, Colorado. There she has immediate access to the research and documentation of the historical surroundings of this series. Her research and background on Mormonism provided the thrust for her bestselling STARLIGHT TRILOGY, the *Wedding Dress* and *With This Ring*.

ACKNOWLEDGEMENT

I own an 1883 copy of *The Story of the Jubilee Singers*; it contains their story and a section devoted to their songs. They call them Jubilee Songs; we call them Spirituals, and I have used portions of the rich lyrics.

The foreword of the volume contains significant insight. Fisk University, of Nashville, Tennessee, was established in 1865, fifteen years before the foreword was written. President C. M. Cravath says, "The millions of recently emancipated colored people of the South must be given a Christian education, or the nation must suffer far more in the future than in the past from the curse of slavery."

These people from Fisk University carried their message in song across the United States, into England, and as far as Germany. I understand the volume has been reproduced, and I heartily recommend it.

CHAPTER 1

Olivia Thomas got out of bed and went to lean far out the open window. "Oh, the dogwood is lovely!" Closing her eyes, she savored the mingled odors of Mississippi. "Magnolia is best," she murmured, "and it doesn't bloom so early. But it's all home. I love the smell of spring, but right now azaleas and sleepy afternoons aren't enough. I want excitement! How I wish Matthew were here!"

She began to shake her dark hair free of its braid as she looked over the carefully tended rose garden below. The garden was edged by junipers shielding the house from the stables and slave cabins. Even the cotton fields were beyond her vision. Studying the barrier, and irritated at the restriction, Olivia frowned and muttered, "As if we don't know what's happening beyond our dooryard! But they can't hide the smell of home. There's earth, all moist with spring, and green fields."

Olivia ducked back into the room and turned. For a moment she frowned again, "All frills and flounces, pink and orchid. Just like Mama." Impatiently she kicked at the mahogany bed, draped and bedecked with lace and mosquito netting. She gave another impatient kick, this time exclaiming, "Ouch!"

The door creaked open and a dark face peered at her. "That you, Missy? It's early for conversation." The woman eased her bulk through the door. Smoothing her white-streaked hair, she pulled on the white mob-cap. "Want I should tidy up now? Shall I bring some wash-up water?"

Olivia shrugged impatiently, "No; no to both, Mattie. I'm going out. Those junipers hide the whole world. I want to see the Mississippi River. Do you know it's like a silver highway, cutting down through this land, dividing it in half? How it beckons! I'm aching to travel it."

Mattie chuckled. "Silver highway? More like Big Muddy, if you ask me." She shrugged, "Well, it might be a silver highway, but I don't think you ought to travel today. Maybe tomorrow."

"I'm not teasing," Olivia insisted. "I feel this deeply, even when it scares me to think of it. I want to see where it goes. I want to see the cotton bales piled high on the wharf. And steamboats chugging up and down." She stopped and giggled. "But most surely right now, I'd like to taste hoecake. The smell's coming from the cabins. Why won't you bring me hoecake for breakfast? It smells delicious."

Mattie frowned, "Missy. I know at least a million little chillen who'd gladly give you a taste of hoecake in exchange for your good bread and butter. Know what? You'd regret it. By the time you get the dirt and ash scraped off, it's cold and no good."

Hopping to the desk stationed between the big windows, Olivia rubbed her toe and plucked at the leather covered diary. "Mama is even here," she complained. "Pink instead of crimson."

"Smacked your toe, huh? 'Least at seventeen you're too old for a temper fit." She slanted a look at Olivia and went to flick the tumbled sheets into order.

Olivia picked up the pen and dipped it into the ink pot. *Dear Diary*, she scrawled, *it is nice to talk to you. How I would love to chase the morning like a bird, to fly away on the wind, to escape like Matthew. Or would I? Is this desire a sign of growing up? At seventeen, I must be.*

Olivia settled back in the chair, pulled her feet up and thought about her brother. "Oh, Matthew," she scolded aloud, "It is bad enough that you go away to school, but to not come home when spring is in bloom, at least to see the azaleas and dogwood along the canal! What a false brother you are! Besides, I am never allowed to go fishing when you're gone."

For a second longer she watched Mattie picking up the discarded clothing scattered about the room. Jumping to her feet, she rushed to the closet and dug into the box labeled *Private, don't touch.* Finding Matthew's old dungarees and jacket, she pressed her nose into the fabric and smelled the fields, the earth, and the horses.

"Mattie, I've decided I'm going to be wild again."

Mattie came to peer over Olivia's shoulder. "I know," she groaned, "you're going to disobey your mother. 'Tis a shame you're too old for a switchin'."

"Now, Mattie, you know Father would never switch me, no matter what." Flinging her nightgown across the room, Olivia rummaged through a drawer for underclothing. Tossing aside the petticoat, she returned to the closet and found boots.

Mattie watched as Olivia struggled into Matthew's trousers. The woman gave a gasp of dismay as the girl shoved her hair into Matthew's cap. "You're heading for the fields again! Hasn't your daddy said enough about riding out like this?"

Olivia paused. "Enough? All I want to hear." She studied the anxious face and slowly said, "Mattie, there's something in me; I have to listen to it. Something says I can't be a sweet little girl all my life and listen to Daddy say no, while Mama says yes." Studying the black woman's troubled eyes, for just a moment she wondered at the fear she saw there.

Carefully Olivia opened the door and slipped into the hall. All was quiet. Olivia dashed lightly down the hall and took the stairs two at a time. She didn't stop until she reached the stables. Worming her way between the carriage and the line of tack on the wall, she scooped a light saddle from its peg and slipped through the back door.

For a moment she stopped and sniffed. From the slave quarters behind the stables came a drift of smoke and the odor of hoecake baking on an open fire. Voices, deep with sleep and softly melodious, addressed each other. It was the sound of home—those gentle slave voices. Olivia smiled as she slipped into the stable.

Joe was there. His ebony forehead wrinkled and his eyes squinted into troubled creases. "Missy, your daddy will fuss. 'Tis too early for riding, and 'sides—" He shook his head at the dungarees. "Matthew's? Mighty big. What your mama say?"

Olivia grinned at him, shaking her head, and mimicked her mother's mild voice. "Tsk, tsk, Olivia, we girls don't—"

Joe's frown disappeared as he watched her lead Matthew's horse from the stall. "Exercise she do need, but not at five in the morning."

"You go have your hoecake, and you won't even know." He helped her slip the reins over the mare's head before he headed for the door.

The morning was heavy with moisture and earthy smells. Already the cotton fields were knee high with this season's crop. Olivia rode slowly along the trail edging the fields. She felt her spirits lift as she breathed deeply of the morning air. She watched birds dart across the fields in streaks of yellow, brown, and mottled gray. As she used her heels to urge the horse, she noticed a streak of red. "A woodpecker, and I'm certain I saw a mockingbird."

For a moment she reined in to listen. The trees on the far side of the fields sounded like the tuning of an orchestra. Bird sounds ranged from sleepy lows to raucous highs saluting the morning.

When Olivia reached the gate on the edge of the field, she started to slip from her horse.

"I'll get it for you."

With a start, she turned. It was her father's overseer. "Mr. Burton," Olivia said slowly, "I didn't hear you."

The man touched his hat with an indolent gesture. He eased his bulk forward in the saddle and said, "Surprised to see the little miss out this early in the morning." He leered as he added, "If'n it were night, I'd be obliged to turn you around and head you fer home. But I can't think of any young fellers a hanging around this time of day. Out exercising Matthew's mare, huh?"

She nodded. He continued to eye the faded dungarees as he leaned across his mare to lift the latch on the gate. "Better stay outta the woods. Heard Kebblers lost a coupla niggers last week."

Curiously she watched him settle back in the saddle. "I see ya ain't scared," he added. "But a runnin' slave will do anything to save his hide, including hitting ya over the head."

"Mr. Burton," Olivia stated indignantly, "I can't imagine one of our slaves acting that way. Matter of fact, I can't believe any of our field hands would be running away. We treat them better than most do."

Lifting her head, she watched a cloud fragment break free from the bank of sullen thunderheads hovering over the distant river. Glancing at the silent overseer, she added, "Sometimes I think these stories are made up. Why, I don't know."

He chuckled, "Just don't worry that pretty little head."

He closed the gate behind Olivia and raised his hand. As she rode away she lifted her shoulders and sighed in exasperation.

The warming sun was beginning to release new perfumes. Olivia dug her heels in the horse's side and pushed through the oak and budding magnolias into the stand of pine climbing the hill behind the field.

Using the ends of her reins as a whip, Olivia pushed the mare until she crested the hill. There she slipped out of the saddle and tied the reins loosely around a low branch. As the horse dipped her nose into the tender fern growing around the tree trunk, Olivia stretched her arms above her head.

Before tossing aside the hat she wore, she addressed the horse. "Well, Tag, I guess the two of us will have a lark today. You're getting the ride Matthew swears you need, and I'm doing a daring thing." Even as she spoke, she winced at the memory of the time her father found her riding Tag dressed in Matthew's old clothes. "Oh my, what a scolding! I wouldn't want to meet him now."

The mare lifted her head and studied Olivia for a moment before reaching for another fern. Olivia giggled.

"What would Matthew say? Last summer when he threw these old clothes in the trash, little did he know that I would be right behind him pulling them out! Sometimes being a lady is constricting," she confided to the mare, "and I don't think you like sidesaddles and long skirts wrapped around you any more than I do."

Olivia hesitated, looking around. With a shrug she threw herself into the deep grasses. Pulling a long tender stalk, Olivia lifted her face to the warming sun and nibbled the sweet grass.

She watched the sun rise above the dark line of trees to the east. Turning to the west, Olivia narrowed her eyes, straining to see the Mississippi River from her hilltop perch. "There," she murmured. "I'm certain that's a whistle, even though it's twenty miles to Natchez and the river. Oh, there it is again!" She settled comfortably on her bed of grass and studied the clouds. "Nearly like rain," she murmured contentedly as she watched the tumbling clouds join together and surge inland.

Olivia was still watching the clouds when she heard the sharp crack. With a puzzled frown she sat up. Turning she studied the trees behind her, fully expecting to see a hunter. "Can't say Burton didn't warn me to be careful," she whispered. In quick succession she heard another crack, a moan, and then quick multiple snaps.

Jumping to her feet, she walked to the crest of the hill and looked down the slope to the edge of the cotton field. A movement caught her attention. Shading her eyes, she looked at the center of the field. A dark line of slaves stood motionless, heads bowed. Again she heard the snap, and quickly it was repeated.

When she saw the dark line tremble, her hand moved to her lips. "No!" she whispered. For a moment her feet wouldn't move. "They said this happened; I didn't believe it."

Reluctantly she took a step in order to see what the slaves faced. As she grasped the tree branch to lean forward, Tag stopped her grazing. Her ears lifted and then flattened while her nose quivered into the wind. Olivia watched her stomp and whinny as she tugged at the reins. "This is new to me old girl," Olivia whispered. "But not to you."

The sound of the whip fell silent. Olivia moved a step forward. Below, across the green of cotton plants, fenced by that line of dusky figures holding hoes, she could see Mr. Burton. His stocky figure straightened, his arm lifted, and the whip coiled above his head.

It had found its mark before Olivia heard the sharp crack. As the slaves parted, she watched the dark figure on the ground writhe just as the sound reached her. Powerless to turn away, or even comprehend, she clung to the branch and stared at the growing stain of glistening red on the ground.

Tag snorted, reared, and struck at the tree before Olivia could accept the scene as real. But powerless to move, she continued to stare at its ugliness.

Finally Olivia's numb legs carried her to the horse. She reached for the reins and then realized they were torn loose. Slowly she pulled herself onto the quivering mare and rode in the direction of the awful scene she had just witnessed.

When Olivia reached the gate and the cotton field, the sun was overhead, blazing between the ridge of clouds. She didn't need to urge Tag on past that spot. The trembling horse ran, but Olivia couldn't avoid looking at the dark mat of ruined, flattened plants, stained with blood.

Farther on she saw figures, bending, chopping, lifting, moving; their faces were stony, cast in fear, as if they had been chipped away to nothing. The white man was gone.

Later, standing beside the mare outside the stable, she heard a scream. Throwing the reins at Joe, she ran through the gate toward the cabins. The bleeding figure lay on the ground. A woman hovered over him, her hands like frightened dark birds, dipping, retreating; Olivia turned and ran.

Bursting into the kitchen, Olivia flew between the dark figures and dashed into the breakfast room. She stood panting in the doorway. The room was flooded with sunlight. A curl of steam rose from the silver coffee pot. A nosegay of pink carnations and wild violets lay on the folded linen napkin.

Staring at the flowers, Olivia spoke dully. "Father, Burton must go. I'll not step one foot outside this house until he is gone forever."

She heard her father's growl, felt his grasp. "The beast! I knew I couldn't trust him. Has he—"

"He beat the man bloody! I couldn't believe it! Oh, Mama," she addressed her mother. "How could he?"

Her father dropped his hand. "He didn't touch you?" Color began to move back into his face. Olivia looked from his blazing blue eyes to her mother's bewildered expression.

"Then what—"

"Olivia," her mother touched her lips, "why are you wearing those terrible old clothes?"

"Olivia, what in thunder are you talking about?"

The girl's voice was hoarse as she forced out the words. "I saw Burton whipping a slave. Oh, Father, it was horrible. Please go see to the man. He'll die! There's so much blood."

"Daughter!" His face changed, becoming angry. "You have overstepped every rule of this household. Why have you left the house in such clothing? No daughter of mine—what were you doing in the fields?" Before Olivia could speak, he added, "Please attire yourself properly and come down for breakfast."

As Olivia left the room, she heard her mother's voice. "Cornelius, now you understand. It is imperative that Olivia be sent to boarding school."

Olivia stopped. She moved back to stand in the open doorway as her parents continued to talk.

Her father's heavy voice thundered, "Sally Ann, I'll not have a child of mine attending school in such a place. Shall I read you the article again?"

"No, dear, but I wish you would tell me why you object."

"I received this article at the time you received the information about the finishing school, which is in our beloved South. A fine and dignified school with a good reputation. I just happened to notice this article about that fine school, so richly admired by your friends." His voice was filled with sarcasm as he added, "From the article it appears that one of the professors, mind you, of a girls' school, upon hearing that his brother-in-law intended killing him, took a gun, went to the saloon where his brother-in-law sat, and murdered him. I don't believe I care to have a man like that teaching my daughter.

"If you will allow me to find a decent school close to Harvard—which I suggest for the express purpose of having her brother be responsible for her safety—well then, Sally Ann, I will consider sending Olivia to school."

There was a pause, then her mother sighed. "It is so far—but very well, dear. I know of just such a school. I'll write today."

CHAPTER 2

Matthew Thomas turned from the window and grinned down at the fellow sprawled across the one good chair. "I don't know how you've come to be an upperclassman with grades that put the rest of us to shame. Most of the time you more nearly resemble a bum than a senior law student at Harvard."

"And you, my dear friend, take life much too seriously." Alex Duncan sat up and wiped a hand across his face and hair.

Matthew watched the hand, the amused grin still on his face. "See, you've been drinking all weekend, and you don't have the shakes. It isn't fair."

The door was pushed open and a wary face turned from one to the other. "Fair or not, he'd better sober up quick. I understand Howard's quizzing us on Blackstone tomorrow."

"Blackstone?" Matthew groaned, "What part of Blackstone? And why in the world don't they print books with a type you can see without getting your nose dirty?"

The head disappeared as the fellow replied, "Then you couldn't lift it."

Duncan got to his feet. "If it's a test, we'd better get prepared." He headed for the door.

"Where are you going?"

"The pub, where else? We need to get our blood a movin' or we'll never live through tomorrow. Come on."

"No. I take my education seriously. Alex, run along. Your tidewater pappy has more money to burn than my father does."

Alex turned, for a moment the laughter had faded, leaving his startling blue eyes nearly uneasy. Rubbing one hand across his thick mat of dark curly hair he said ruefully, "You remind me of my responsibilities to the clan. Did my pa hire you to say that at stated intervals?"

Matthew shrugged. "Go on. I haven't had a chance to open my mail." As he shuffled through the contents on his table, Alex reached across his shoulder and picked up the newspaper.

"Garrison's tabloid, huh? Where did you get it?"

"Garrison?" Matthew questioned, dropping the letter he held. "Who is he?"

Alex chuckled, "You're a Mississippi cotton baby and you haven't heard of William Lloyd Garrison and his infamous newspaper *The Liberator?* Man, he's an abolitionist."

Matthew took the paper from Alex. "Is he that fella Professor Matson mentioned—the one who pushed the North to secede in forty-one?"

Alex's smile was sardonic. "Better not read it. These here Northerners are looking for converts. Where did you get it?"

"It was in my mail. I suppose someone's getting in his licks—trying to make me see the error of my ways." He chuckled and shook his head as he broke the seal on the letter he held.

He caught Alex's eye and grinned. "Letter from home—from Mother, and my sister," he added as the second paper tumbled to the table.

"Sister? How old is she, six?" Alex fingered the scrawled sheet crumpled into a tiny square.

"Nearly seventeen."

"Doesn't look like it." Alex poked at the smudged paper.

"Well, isn't this 1855?" Matthew glanced up. "Don't judge her by the letter. Seems you'll get to meet her. My life is being hampered. According to Mother, she will be joining us in a couple of weeks to attend a Miss Arvellion's Female Academy, just outside Boston."

"I can't wait," Alex said dryly.

"Mother's just surrendered her to the care and counsel of a Madame Cabet and her daughter, traveling from New Orleans with the destination of same school."

"Ah, sounds French; now that's more like it. Bet they're Creole. What I know about New Orleans makes the whole situation much more attractive." Alex grinned, flipped his fingers in a mock salute and backed out the door.

Matthew was still grinning as he dropped the newspaper in the trash basket, but the grin disappeared as he looked at the letters on the table. They lay beside Blackstone, and he shuddered.

———

"Olivia, I can't understand why you are going to that terrible, cold place just for school. Even South Carolina is better than the North." Olivia turned to look at her cousin Lynda as she spoke. Lynda rubbed at the perspiration on her forehead and pouted.

"Oh, Lynda," Olivia protested in hard, bright syllables, as she shifted the portmanteau. "You just don't understand; this place is so provincial. Mama says I need to broaden my outlook on life."

Lynda's sister, Alberta, bent a brittle smile toward Olivia. "Olivia, I know you well enough to guess you wouldn't go without being forcefully shoved on that boat." Her smile was mocking as she nodded at the steamboat anchored off shore. "Culture!" she snorted. "You won't get it in the North."

Olivia glanced over her shoulder. Mother was leading the way, and the pile of luggage being pushed behind her made it all terribly final.

She gulped, and turned to smile at Lynda. "I just can't believe my cousins are related to each other," she murmured. "My sweet Lynda, I'll miss you. And Alberta," she looked at her cousin's lank blonde hair, already thready and limp with the heat. "I'll send you a—" Olivia swallowed the word beau and smiled before she added, "a letter right soon."

Mama was breathless as she paused and flipped her fan. "Good of you girls to come. We must get Olivia aboard right now. Oh, dear, what shall we do if the Cabets aren't aboard?"

She beckoned to the porter to lead the way. Lynda blinked and Olivia said, "I'm traveling with them. Crystal Cabet will be attending

Miss Arvellion's Academy, too." Alberta's eyebrows were still cocked high, but she picked up the basket of fruit and followed Lynda to the gangplank.

Olivia tried to hurry along. Her feet tangled in her skirt as she looked over her shoulder at the sun sparkling on the bluff high above the Natchez harbor. Tears blurred together the white mansions and the dark green line of oaks behind them. Even the singing of the Negro roustabouts on the wharfboats seemed far away and retreating.

She tried to concentrate on the words of their song as she blinked at the tears and trotted along the gangplank after Alberta. "Cotton in," they chorused, "the last barrel, the last sack!" She nearly stumbled as one tenor voice lifted and sustained the note until a shiver went down her spine.

The others had climbed the stairs winding around the engine room. By the time Olivia had her portmanteau up the steps, her family was clustered around the door of the salon stretching the length of the boat. Olivia had time for only a glance and a nod of approval at the plush furniture, the crystal, and the mirrors before Mama and a dark, round woman surrounded Olivia with rapid French.

"Mrs. Cabet, my daughter Olivia. Olivia, you stay off the texas deck. She says Crystal has already ruined a frock with embers flying from the smokestacks."

Over their chatter, Olivia's eyes met the dark eyes of the tall slender girl behind Mrs. Cabet. Her tawny heart-shaped face was the only motionless object in the room. Olivia immediately sensed kinship with Crystal Cabet; she watched her eyes twinkle as she looked from her mother to the slave beside her.

Olivia still wondered about that feeling as the day wore on. Late in the afternoon the deep bell began its warning, and Mama, the cousins, and all the visitors surged toward the wharf. Olivia followed the Cabets to the rail to wave. After the steamboat had pulled away and the crowd on shore became dim, they lingered to watch the setting sun throw the shadow of their steamboat against the sun-brightened oaks dipping over the river.

Mrs. Cabet disappeared into the cabin, and Crystal smiled at Olivia. "You need to meet the boat. Let me show it all to you—except of course—" she slanted a glance at Olivia, "the texas deck."

"The texas deck, too. I can smack embers faster than they can burn. We can stand upwind." Crystal's serene smile widened as she led the way.

The boat turned into the channel, trembling as the paddles picked up speed. Olivia thrilled to the thudding beneath their feet as the smokestack threw a shower of sparks into the air. She paused to watch the deck crew swing the sounding pole aboard just as the young man holding the pole threw back his head and yelled, "No bottom!"

"That means they'll really pour on the steam." Crystal glanced at Olivia, "I've traveled this route often since I was a little girl. We have cousins in Natchez, and I live in New Orleans."

"I've only taken a poky slow boat, and I love to go fast," Olivia murmured. "I haven't been on a steamboat for ages. But I hear the new boilers are so much better. Mama says our boat will be in Philadelphia in less than three weeks."

"But we don't travel into Philadelphia," Crystal said. "We'll catch the stagecoach at Wheeling, and later we'll transfer to the train."

"Oh. Well, that's exciting too," Olivia replied. She moved her shoulders impatiently and grinned at Crystal.

"Let's go see the gaming rooms," Crystal whispered, "It's too early for the men to be there, but they're just beautiful."

Quickly they hurried up the stairs to the hurricane deck and Crystal led the way to the ornate mahogany double doors. As she reached for the door she murmured, "There'll probably be some of the women in there, but they won't mind."

"Women?" Olivia questioned. The door was pulled open and a woman eased through.

She turned to face them with a frown. "Are you lost?"

Crystal shook her head. "I—may we look inside?"

Unexpectedly the frown disappeared, and the woman grinned. "Thinking of taking up a new career? Takes a lot of practice to handle the gambling tables. Want me to give you a demonstration?"

"Gambling?" Olivia questioned. "Is that what you do?" She studied the long blonde curls clustered high off the woman's neck. Her bright blue satin gown was cut low and much too tight, but somehow it seemed appropriate.

The woman turned a mocking smile on her. "I'm Amelia Randolph," she explained. "They call me a hostess. You might say I help the fellows have a good time—that includes serving drinks and lots of laughs along with the cards. Would you like me to show you how to deal cards?"

Crystal shook her head vigorously.

With a laugh, Amelia said, "I thought not. Better stay away from this place. Sometimes the fellas can't tell the difference between—" She looked hard at Crystal. "Don't I know you from somewhere?"

Crystal nodded. "I didn't say anything, but I recognized you. Didn't expect you to recognize me, too. I've seen you several times in the past few years. We travel the boats frequently."

The woman nodded and turned back into the room. "Take a quick look, and then be on your way."

Crystal and Olivia went in and looked around, and after they came out of the room, Crystal glanced at Olivia. Apologetically she said, "Doesn't seem nearly as nice this time; I must be getting older. Let's go look at the dining room, and then there's a place at the other end of the salon where we can go to read."

As they crossed the thick carpet, Olivia glanced at Crystal. Their eyes met and Olivia smiled. "You know, I've always wanted to travel, to do something exciting, but when my father finally said yes about school, I nearly had the shivers. I think I'm going to like it."

She paused, "Crystal, why have you decided to travel all the way to Boston for school?"

Her lips turned up in amusement. "You'll never believe this. I'm certain you've heard all kinds of naughty tales about Creole women, but Mama decided on Boston because everything about Boston is *proper*!"

Olivia grinned. "I think we are going to be the best of friends!" Crystal smiled as she turned to wave at her mother standing in the doorway of their cabin.

Mrs. Cabet watched the two girls as they walked rapidly to the reading room. Their swaying hoop skirts gently bumped against each other as they linked arms and hurried away.

With a sigh Mrs. Cabet turned away. "Auntie T," she murmured to the dark-skinned woman beside her, "I hope this won't be a mistake. I trust Crystal, but I wonder what influences she will be subjected to? The North is a hostile environment. In Boston they don't think as we do. Will she be seen as—common?"

For a moment the two women exchanged a long look. "Now

don't you go fretting," Auntie T said. "We talked this out, and you're doing the right thing. Can't keep chillen on your apron strings forever."

Mrs. Cabet's lips trembled into a smile at the metaphor. Her hand reached for the dark arm. "Tell me I'm foolish to worry about her discovering anything about—"

Auntie T's head wagged slowly. " 'Tis less likely that far from home. There's been many tracks laid in Boston since Miss Evangeline was there. She won't find out; don't you be worrying about that."

Mrs. Cabet sighed and pushed her fingers against her forehead. "Auntie T, her skin is so dark. Will they scorn her in Boston?"

Tammera watched her mistress with troubled eyes. Mrs. Cabet said, "You might as well say what you are thinking."

"Sometime I think she has questions, 'specially when you push all those fancy creams at her. They don't do a thing about making her lighter. And if she ever found out by accident who her daddy is, it could kill her."

CHAPTER 3

While the books lay neglected, Olivia brooded over the sullen landscape. Last night's snow had knocked the last of the scarlet leaves from the trees and faded to black and white the gaily colored scene she had begun to like.

There was a tap on the door. Glancing at the door, Olivia noticed the spot where the varnish had worn thin. She wrinkled her nose and shuddered. "Come in," she called as she crossed the room.

Crystal came into the room and dropped her books on the table. "Now tell me honestly, what possessed you to come to this terrible place?" The smile faded from Crystal's face. "Surely you didn't leave Mississippi just because you wanted to come to school where it's cold and dreary. Oh, Olivia, isn't this terrible! Let me guess. You have a dark, secret love affair with a rich, lecherous old man, who lives just around the corner."

"I didn't know the place existed until last spring. Mama and Father sent me here. They've been threatening it for ages."

"Threatening?"

"Well—it feels like punishment. I suppose they both decided I needed some polish."

Crystal's smile barely creased her lips. "I probably fit in the same category. Although at the last, Mama seemed fearful about my coming here. In fact, I had to press her, to keep her from backing out of it all."

"She doesn't seem well," Olivia said slowly.

Crystal shrugged. "That's Mama."

For a moment Olivia watched the shadows in Crystal's eyes. *She is unhappy; but if so why did she come?* Olivia turned with a shrug and added, "I've had a tutor. Both of us got our schooling that way, Matthew and I."

"Your brother?" Crystal asked, nodding. "And I suppose your mother was expecting him to take you under his wing, so to speak."

"I know she did. She investigated all the schools in the Boston area."

Wistfully Crystal said, "I'm an only child. You've seen my mother." She sighed, "At home, life is stodgy, to say the least. I've always wanted a brother. Do you have a special relationship with your brother; is he wiser and older?"

Olivia grinned at Crystal's questions. "It appears that way. Sometimes I don't think either Father or Mama realize how impulsive Matthew is. He's always been fun to be around. But when trouble develops, I get the blame."

"And you're always innocent?" Crystal's smile was amused now.

"You're thinking of last week and that silly prank we pulled on Cassandra. She's stuffy." Olivia returned to the subject. "Matthew and I have always been close. But I haven't seen him since we've come. Just a couple of notes saying he's busy and will come as soon as he can."

"Sounds harassed."

"That's what I thought. Anyway, I don't intend to force myself on him. But I have an idea he's afraid a younger sister will infringe on his lifestyle."

"That must hurt." Olivia glanced at Crystal. "But at least you have a brother."

"And you don't. I'm sorry. It must be lonely, being an only child. Your mother—I didn't mean to pry," Olivia murmured as Crystal pressed her fingers to her forehead.

"It's all right. It's—well, sometime I'll tell you about it all."

The following week in English class Olivia recalled the conversation with Crystal. When she compared the obviously wealthy girl with the drab atmosphere of Miss Arvellion's Female Academy, the Academy seemed doubly dreary.

As Miss Hanson walked up and down the aisles, placing a book just below each inkwell, she explained, "I've chosen a contemporary novel for you to read for discussion next week."

She turned, and Olivia forced her attention away from the knob of hair that seemed determined to shed its hairpins. Miss Hanson smoothed her apron with bony hands and crossed her arms to clasp her sharp elbows. As she continued to talk, her expression caught Olivia's attention. Her lips were pursed tight under anxious eyes.

The words she said began to find a place in Olivia's attention. "*Uncle Tom's Cabin*—certainly you've all heard about it—is one of the most successful writings of the past twenty years. It will be doubly impressive to you, since it was written by a woman."

"Harriet Beecher Stowe," drawled a careless voice from the back of the room. "We all know about it."

Olivia straightened in her chair. Excitement and apprehension touched her at the same time. From the back of the room tiny Annabel Martine said, "I'm from Kentucky, and I don't think my mother wants me to read this book."

As Miss Hanson's eyes widened and her lips formed words, the drawl from the back of the room rose again. "Rather than offend our finer sensibilities by reading such trash, why don't we just ask for a first-hand report on the problem from Miss Cabet?"

Slowly Crystal stood. Her chin lifted. Gently, but with an icy voice, she said, "I beg your pardon, but I don't believe I'm any more likely to have the facts than you are, Miss Chinard."

Curiously Olivia watched Miss Hanson's hands flutter like nervous butterflies. There was the tinkle of the bell, and her face dissolved into relief.

Olivia went to join Crystal. Crystal's smile was stretched tight. Olivia slipped her arm through her friend's, and in silence they walked down the hall to the history lecture room.

That evening, when Olivia went to close the heavy draperies to shut out the snowy scene, Crystal came. She stood beside the tiny fire in the grate and said, "I've burned all my wood and coal allowance, so I freeze until tomorrow. May I bring my books in here?"

Olivia nodded, "We Southerners have thin blood. I hear exposure to Boston is supposed to thicken anyone's blood. I hope it happens before spring."

"I don't have much faith," Crystal said with a shiver. She tugged the shawl around her shoulders. Glancing at Olivia, she took a deep breath and asked, "What did you think of our English class this morning?"

"The book? I'm nearly afraid to open it. Since it came out, everyone's been fussing about it at home. But Mama refused to let me read it. She'd probably make me come home if she knew it was on my desk."

"I mean what Catherine said about me."

"Your skin is dark, but that's no reason to accuse you—"

She dropped her head. "My skin is darker than Mama's and even darker than my father's. Mama will scarcely allow me outdoors. She's bought all of the creams and ointments available for skin, to bleach and make it smooth."

"Why?"

"I don't know. I tease her about wanting to make a good marriage for me. You've noticed my clothes?"

Olivia touched the velvet sleeve of Crystal's frock. "I've never seen such fabrics. I thought my mother particular, but you look like a princess in comparison."

"Olivia, if it weren't for the lavish wardrobe, and other ways they pamper, no, no—shield me from everything, I don't think I would have questions. But then, I have to face Catherine's questions." She lifted her head. "Do you mind my saying such personal things?"

"Of course not." Olivia paused, then whispered, "Do you think that—" Olivia couldn't finish the question.

"That they aren't my parents? I am beginning to wonder. See, a year ago, I found a name in Mama's jewelry case."

"But that isn't unusual. Anything my mother wants to save goes right in with her jewelry. She treats a scrap of paper like a treasure."

"That's the whole point. Mama was angry with me for helping myself to a piece of jewelry from the case. Very angry. Her face turned pale, she was so angry." Crystal sat down on the stool beside the fire and held out her hands. Turning them slowly, she said, "When I returned the brooch to the case, the paper with the name was gone."

Olivia took a deep breath and said, "Crystal, I would be inclined to think you are allowing your imagination to run away with you. I doubt your real mother is the Queen of France."

Crystal laughed. Jumping to her feet, she hugged Olivia. "I think you pushed my head back on straight. Nevertheless, I do wonder."

Olivia crossed the room. "Are you going to get your books? I need help with this silly Latin."

Crystal stood up and sighed, "The only thing I can't forget is the name and address. It was Evangeline Cabet, and the address stuck in my mind like a thorn. It was here in Boston."

"And that is the reason you've come to Boston?"

"Well, not really. On the boat I told you Mama picked Boston because it was so proper. I doubt she would ever have let me come if it hadn't been her idea first."

———

Matthew split open the vellum envelope and stared at the printed message. "Oh the deuce!" he cried. "I'll end up being a nursemaid yet."

A warning bell rang. He dropped the paper and left the room. All of the boardinghouse sounds were focused in the dining room. Quickly he ran down the stairs, smoothing his hands over the light brown curls that refused to stay in place.

"There he is." The voice greeted Matthew as he took his place at the table.

"We thought you were pubbing it again until we saw Alex. Don't tell us you were studying."

Matthew shot a grin at the speaker and apologized. "Sorry to be late again. Realized I hadn't opened my mail. Most unfortunate, I won't—"

"Unfortunate to get mail!"

"Pass the potatoes and stop your groaning. We can't all be a dandy like Matt."

"Unfortunate, because it's a command performance from my sister." He accepted the plate of pot roast.

"How old is she?"

"Just a youngster. She's attending—" He dropped his fork and straightened. With a mischievous grin he said, "Say, would one of you fellows like to meet a nice girl?"

"Ho, ho, ho and a bottle of rum. I distrust the word nice."

Alex Duncan grinned at him from the end of the table. "I'll meet your nice sister if you'll accompany me on a similar errand of mercy next week."

"Man, you have a deal. I'll even copy those briefs for you."

"Is she cross-eyed? Buck teeth?"

"None of the above. It's a tea and reception at a stuffy girls' school. A thing for parents and I have to fill the role."

"How do you know it's stuffy?"

"Because it is referred to as Miss Arvellion's Female Academy."

"No qualification on the female?"

"No qualification."

The groan swept around the table, but Alex was still smiling. "In January, anything is tolerable, even a sister. But I'll have your promise in writing."

CHAPTER 4

Crystal turned to face Olivia. "I've identified the house and I've hired a hack for tomorrow afternoon. Will you go with me?"

"Crystal! You're still fussing about that mysterious name? You really intend going up to the door and asking for an Evangeline Cabet? Suppose she's your aunt, and that she's a—bad lady?"

"I'm certain the information won't utterly devastate me. Anything is better than not knowing."

"This is very important to you," Olivia said slowly. "Is it because you have it in your head that you're adopted? Why can't you just accept Catherine's rudeness and forget about it? Crystal, you are a beautiful person; isn't that enough?"

Slowly Crystal walked back and forth across the room. "I don't know how to explain it. It's a feeling—how do you put words to a feeling?"

Abruptly Olivia grinned. "This is too good to miss! Of course I'll go with you. Perhaps she will be a long-lost cousin or something, someone you'll be able to invite to the tea next week. You know Miss Hanson urged us to invite someone to represent our family. I see your invitation still on the dresser. Tuck it in your pocketbook. Who knows? She may be an old maiden aunt, eager for the least bit of notice."

Olivia paused and frowned, "If only I could hear from Matthew right now, I'd ask him to bring a friend for you."

"A Harvard law student!" Crystal gasped. She began to laugh. "Olivia, to think you chastise me for having an imagination! If your brother comes, it will be a miracle; if he brings a friend, I doubt the tender hearts of these old maids will be able to stand the strain!"

Olivia grinned, "Let's go downstairs and tell them. They are planning the decorations for the parlor; that should be a splendid motivator!"

"I must finish my history assignment right now or I'll not have time for my trip tomorrow."

Olivia watched Crystal turn to the door. "I need to study, too. Until tomorrow, when the conspirators—" Her laughter ended as soon as she saw the expression on Crystal's face.

The next afternoon, after checking the gloomy weather, Olivia selected her heaviest cloak. As she went down the stairs, she recalled Crystal's face. *She's afraid. What could have happened in her past to do this to her?*

Crystal stood waiting for her in the hall. Olivia glanced at her face, then at the hand clutching the doorknob. With a twinge of pity, she realized Crystal was still afraid of what she would find.

For a moment Olivia hesitated, and some of Crystal's fear touched her. She gulped and looked at the melting snow on the floor. "I wonder why the powers that be chose January for a gala?"

Crystal shivered as they stepped outside. "I wonder why the Bostonians didn't just eliminate January from their calendar."

The hack driver looked them over as he helped them into the cumbersome carriage. "Is this all o' them?" Crystal nodded nervously and looked at Olivia, who shrugged her bewilderment.

When the horse turned out of the quiet street and headed for the Boston Commons, Olivia whispered, "Do you have any idea where we are going?" Crystal shook her head. Her eyes were still wide with apprehension.

The driver turned his head. "You ladies are expected?" When they didn't answer he said, "Likely won't find them at home, but if you wanna leave a card, I'll wait. Another six bits to take ya back to the Academy."

Crystal nodded and he settled into his collar again.

Olivia gulped and crossed her fingers inside her muff. The driver was turning down a side road, and it wasn't good. The houses were small, and the dooryards were filled with litter.

She glanced at Crystal, who was chewing her lip again. But abruptly the carriage turned once more, and a smile of relief brightened Crystal's face. This avenue was wide and tree-lined. The driver followed a lane to a big house—brick, and very respectable. Olivia grinned at her friend as the driver addressed them again. "I'll wait."

At the door, Crystal handed over her calling card. Her voice was breathless as she said, "I need to talk to—to explain. May I see your mistress?"

The man's composure wavered slightly. He glanced at the card and his frown disappeared. "Come into the drawing room," he whispered. "Madame is preparing to leave, but I will see if she will spare you several minutes."

When his footsteps no longer echoed, Olivia whispered, "Oh, Crystal, your bluff did it! What shall we find?"

Crystal shook her head and placed her fingers against her mouth. There was a hint of sound, an opening door. In another moment the drawing room door slid open.

An elderly woman stood in the doorway, clothed all in black. She looked first at Olivia and then at Crystal.

"Miss Cabet?" Moving toward Crystal she said, "I understand you've come to make inquiries? How may I help you?"

Crystal caught her breath, hesitated and then in a rush she said, "I'm looking for Evangeline Cabet; will you please tell me about her?"

The woman shook her head, "My dear, you've come years too late. For a short time she lived here until her departure for Europe. I understand she settled in France. Where, I have no idea. I would be glad to give you information, but I have nothing more to offer."

Slowly Crystal moved and caught her breath. "Could you tell me about her? Please, I know nothing."

The woman hesitated. Finally she said slowly, "She was a stranger who was here only a short time. I can tell you nothing I know as fact. Would you care to see a picture of her? There is one poor photograph of the entire group. Come."

She crossed the room and pulled an album from a cabinet. Resting it on a desk she lifted the heavy pages, one by one. While Olivia looked around the room, Crystal leaned over the desk. "There!" The woman exclaimed, pointing to a group picture. "I knew I could find it. It has been a long time." Her voice was musing, sad.

Crystal leaned and peered. Finally, with a disappointed sigh she straightened and smiled at the woman. "Thank you for your time. I—I suppose I'm destined to be frustrated. I don't recognize her."

For a moment the woman paused, opening her mouth as if to speak. Then abruptly, with a brisk wave of her hand, she dismissed them and turned away.

Olivia saw the tears shining in Crystal's eyes as she followed her into the hack. They had nearly reached the Academy when Crystal exclaimed, "Olivia, who was that woman? They acted as if I knew, and I didn't think to ask her name. And what was the significance of the group Evangeline Cabet was with?"

With a shrug, Olivia said, "I have no idea, but then I know little about Boston society. We could return and ask."

"The butler said she was leaving. I'm nearly positive he'll give out absolutely no information—you saw that look on his face."

"I think I agree with you," Olivia murmured.

Matthew was hard pressed to keep up with Alex's long stride. When they reached the Commons and were waiting for the traffic to clear, Matthew said, "Mind telling me a little about this highly secret meeting we'll be attending?"

"Secret?" Alex said slowly. "There's nothing secret about it at all. I simply wanted a Southern gentleman with me while I made the call. You know, a touch of civilization."

"Well, it must be important. We walked past the tavern and you didn't so much as slacken your pace."

"It is so," Alex murmured. There was a break in traffic and he led the way, sprinting between the carriages and lorries.

With a grin he turned to wait for Matthew, saying, "It would be safer to brave the Commons on horseback, but my allowance doesn't cover such luxuries right now."

"And you have to feed a horse hay, not beer."

Ignoring the comment, he waved. "It's down this way. Look for number seventeen. You might know the gentleman. He's from Georgia. Name's Mallory." He stopped to look Matthew in the eye. With a quizzical smile he said, "His job seems solely to keep his finger on Washington's pulse. I've known him for years—an old friend of the family. He was a chum of Father's from school days. Never married, so we sort of adopted him, called him Uncle Charles. I've met him here several times. The first time was after my freshman year at Harvard. Among other things, Mr. Mallory liked the grades I made and some of the fellows I chummed with. Does that tell you anything?"

Matthew shook his head. "Go on."

Alex shrugged. "That's enough for now. Let's go see him. Matter of fact, anything else I might add is purely conjecture."

But his grin was jaunty, and slowly Matthew said, "Sounds to me as if they've an eye to using the curry brush on you. Make you a nice little pony for an unspecified cause to ride."

Alex faced Matthew soberly. "It isn't cause so much as supporting the right to freedom—our freedom."

"The right to have slaves?" Matthew said slowly, studying Alex's face. "Maybe I'm the wrong person to be here."

"I want a critical ear. I figured you to be the most fair critical ear," he added with a grin.

The man who opened the door was decidedly Southern, but he was white and clumsy. Matthew balanced his hat on his fingertips until Mallory joined them. Mallory nodded to them, pointed to Matthew's hat and said, "Ham, you'll never make it in Washington until you mend your ways."

Leading the way into the library, he gestured to the group of chairs pulled close to the fire. "Ham is still in the rough. I must admit our Negro butlers have developed a finesse these mountain men will never learn." He paused, adding, "Perhaps they are more motivated. My father always said the first step in training a Negro is the whip. Nothing takes until he learns who is boss."

He uncorked the decanter on the tray and lifted his eyebrow. Delicately Alex said, "Harvard promotes only a beer budget."

Mallory chuckled and nodded at Ham. "You're a man after his heart." After pouring each of his guests a beer, as well as one for himself, he also sat down. "Alex, I've seen your family during the past month. They are well and send you greetings. Your father tells me you'll graduate this year. What are your plans?"

"To pass my examination and then get on with life. I suppose that will include going home for a few months."

"Ah, that should've been easy to guess. You miss the Carolinas and the water."

Alex nodded, "And Father owns a little rig. Just a small fishing and hunting boat, but she's good. It's fairly new. I need to work over the paddles—it's a stern wheeler. Needs a little varnish, and then I intend to take it up the river for a little hunting."

"Up the river? Where's it docked?"

Alex chuckled. "New Orleans. I forgot to mention that. Father owns a piece of river property down that way. A boat like ours is no job for the ocean. It only draws three feet of water. About a hundred and twenty feet long. Just a family toy."

"Cotton?" Alex blinked, and Mallory added, "You said you have property in New Orleans. I wondered—"

"Yes. Father doesn't spend any time there. He has an overseer on the property."

"I suppose it's fever country in the summer."

Alex nodded and shifted in his chair. Mallory turned his attention to Matthew. "You have another year, I understand. Any aspirations toward politics?"

Slowly Matthew placed his tankard on the table. "Politics?"

Mallory leaned forward. "Certainly. You're from Mississippi, and you are a third-year law student. Surely you realize this interview is more than a pleasant interlude. My job is to make certain the South's interests are suitably represented in Congress." He added briskly, "Right now Alexander Duncan is one of our most promising sons."

He slanted a grin toward Alex and added, "As soon as he gets the play out of his bones, and maybe drags that boat over a few sandbars, it will be time to present him to the people."

Slowly Matthew asked, "Just what do you have in mind?"

"Basically, to keep a few strong men in Washington. The old men representing our interests won't last forever."

"And you want to groom the young ones to think and act in the interests of the South?"

Alex's head jerked up. "Matt, it sounds to me like you're a mite cynical."

Matthew kept his voice even. "I just don't like having people tell me how to think."

"Well, we certainly have no intention of doing that." Mallory quirked one eyebrow as he lifted his glass. Matthew gulped his beer and waited.

Mallory set his glass on the table and leaned forward. "One thing you youngsters didn't seem to get along with your mammy's milk is an appreciation for the years of hard work that have gone into making the South what it is today. I don't intend to educate you this afternoon, but I do suggest that if you're interested in preserving the life, now's the time to act."

———

On the way back to the boardinghouse, Matthew kicked at a clump of dirty snow and remarked, "I know the story; it all started back in about 1827 with the first tariffs. About the time cotton prices were down. Since then, tariffs have continued to cut into the market. I've heard my father talk about it all too often. But the market is still there and getting stronger. Matter of fact, it's the yeoman suffering now. And Piedmont—they've been crying for banks and money for loans to finance their small businesses."

As they headed back the way they came, Alex walked slowly with his hands in his pockets. "I guess I've had my head in the sand. Guess too, that I've known all along it would come down to this."

"What do you mean?"

"My father hasn't come right out and said it, but I know he expects me to make good, and I know he means Washington." He faced Matthew. "I think I'm getting a better feel for it all since I've come North."

"Politics?"

"More than that. Matt, this country is teetering on some mighty big worries right now. I don't think I understood how big they were until I studied Constitutional law. Back home we've been snug and secure with the idea that the Constitution supports slavery."

"But it does. It's a necessary evil. Alex, I don't like the idea of one man holding another in bondage. I like it even less since studying law." He paused, adding thoughtfully, "No, it's something else. Maybe I've started thinking about fairness."

"Fairness is one way of putting it," Alex added, "but I wish I could stop there. How long can you think about fairness until you start thinking about responsibility? And equality."

They were in front of the Harvard Public House. "Matthew, let's go rest our weary brains in here."

Matthew hesitated. Blackstone awaited, along with the stack of notes, on his table. He nodded. "Might as well. If nothing else, we've had a chance to hash over the problem." He quirked a grin at Alex. "If I flunk out, I won't have to worry about whose political horn I'm tooting."

CHAPTER 5

When Matthew entered Alex's room, he dropped off a few letters for his friend and looked to see Alex sprawled on his bed. With his hands linked behind his head, he grinned at Matthew. "Have a seat."

"I hope you haven't forgotten tonight's shindig at Miss what's-her-name's Female Academy."

"No. In fact it just occurred to me that we need to go down to the pub and get fortified."

"Doesn't look to me like you've expended much energy since Collins let us out of class." Matthew eyed the stack of mail on the table. "Alex, how come you're collecting all these newspapers? Besides *Harper's*, which doesn't surprise me, I see Garrison's sheet and another abolitionist paper."

"Which does surprise you. Let's just say that if I'm going to be a suitable representative of the Southern cause, then I'd better know what the other side thinks."

"What do they think?"

"You want me to spell it out? I've collected a number of goodies. Did you know auction houses are called nigger pens, and that the South is seen as wealthy due to the fact that four million slaves were sold at five hundred dollars apiece?"

"I've collected a few myself," Matthew said heavily. "Have you heard of a newspaperman by the name of Elijah Lovejoy? Well, it seems he believed so deeply in the cause of freeing the slaves that he defended printing press number three at the cost of his life. Some who didn't like what his press was putting out ruined the first two. Granted, this happened back in the thirties, so I've learned something that isn't new to you."

"I didn't know. How long has this movement been going on?"

Matthew shrugged. "I only know there's been a bunch working for the freedom of the Negroes since shortly after the turn of the century. Also, I've found these people don't have a personal axe to grind. They're preachers and poor folks—mostly women."

With a sigh, Alex sat up. "So what are you saying?"

"Nothing. Right now I only know that I feel like a jerk. Let's go have that beer or we won't be able to make it through this evening."

"Hey, take it easy—not everyone in the North is supporting the abolitionist movement."

As they headed down the street toward the pub, Alex spoke slowly, "I've found a few facts to add. Your friend Garrison—"

"What do you mean, *my* friend?" Matthew asked.

"Well you started this with his newspaper."

"Alex, I still don't know where that paper came from. And you're a great one to talk. I get the idea you're pretty interested in what he has to say. His latest is in your stack of mail!"

"Yes. That's where I found my new fact. He mentioned an incident that happened a number of years ago. He talked about a trip he had taken to England, and mentioned how well received his abolitionist talks were there. Sounds like he won a great deal of respect. He contrasted that to the welcome he received when he came home. Seems some gentlemen were responsible for beating him and dragging him, nearly naked, through the streets of our fair city."

Alex reached for the door handle and turned to look for Matthew. "Hey, where are you going?" He squinted at Matthew through the bright afternoon sunshine.

Matthew's attention had been arrested by the newspaper boy. He stopped and paid him and came back to Alex clutching a paper. "Didn't you hear what he said?"

"No."

"Something about a senator being beaten in Washington. Come on, let's go have that drink and read the paper."

Once inside, Alex carried tall tankards of beer to the table and sat down next to Matthew who had spread out the paper. "It's date-lined Washington. Says a man by the name of Preston Brooks attacked Senator Charles Sumner while he was at his desk in the deserted Senate chamber. Not only was Senator Sumner beaten senseless, but his life is feared endangered." For a moment Matthew lifted his face, looked quizzically at Alex and then added, "It also says that the South Carolina politicians are making a hero of Brooks, and that all this is related to anti-slavery speeches Sumner delivered on the floor! Alex, surely this is exaggerated."

Alex moved uneasily in his chair. "Matt, you gotta look at it this way. These men don't represent all the South. You have thugs in both North and South. There are also respectable people on both sides of the Mason-Dixon Line."

"Yeah, I know." Matt said, "but let's hope these fellas don't take it out on everyone with an accent." He lifted his tankard. "You and I know that not the whole of the South supports the idea of slavery."

"That's right." Alex's voice was suddenly surly. "One of those papers pointed out an interesting item. In the South, no one can preach emancipation of slaves and live. But back in the thirties, a law was passed outlawing even newspaper discussions and pamphlets on the subject. It is feared such discussion will cause a schism in the South, opening the door to a possible slave uprising."

For a moment Matthew was silent. "Are you saying it would be better if they did know?"

"I've been studying law, hearing about government of the people and for the people."

Matthew nodded, "But we can't afford another Nat Turner re-bellion. Alex, that was bad stuff—both for the slaves and the white people living in the area. Isn't it justifiable to think of the people? To go to any lengths to prevent such an event happening again?"

Alex snapped his fingers at the barmaid, while Matthew slapped the newspaper. "And what's this about slavery being called a good thing *now*? Where I come from, I always thought it was considered so. Try to raise a crop of cotton without slaves."

Alex shook his head. "My father said all these problems started building when the tariffs against exports and imports were passed. I understand Governor Stephen Miller of South Carolina was the one who insisted slavery wasn't an evil, but instead it had a national benefit. He had in mind all the cotton and rice the Negroes were cultivating."

Alex hesitated, glancing down at his tankard. "I'll never forget a conversation I heard. My father was defending his position as a slave owner, and at the same time he admitted that the slaves were dying by the scores every summer. They were down in the swamp raising rice while all the white owners were in the mountains, avoiding the fever."

He continued to slosh the beer in his tankard. Finally he lifted his head and continued. "For years slavery was called a necessary evil. Necessary for them to die, so the plantation owner could live and grow wealthy. Now it seems more and more they are starting to justify slavery. And they are no longer apologizing for being part of the institution supporting it."

"What do you mean *they*?"

The numerous wet rings on the table had stuck the newspaper to the surface. Matthew got to his feet. "We've got to go. Tonight's the big night for Miss—"

Alex got to his feet, reeling slightly as he added, "What's-her-name's Female Academy. Are you certain your sister is worth this?"

Matthew chewed his lip. "Right now I doubt either one of us will make it. You've drunk beer and ale two to my one." He gave up on the attempt to pry the newspaper free and headed for the door.

———

It was past nine o'clock. Olivia glanced at the door again and tried to smile. "Crystal, I fear my brother has forgotten his commitment."

"You did hear from him?" Crystal murmured, at the same time extending her hand to the gray-haired parent in front of her.

Olivia smiled and stretched out her hand, "So lovely of you to come." She nodded at the couple in front of her, adding, "I have a class with Twilda." Mrs. Denison shook her hand and moved toward Crystal.

Olivia heard the heavy male voices and looked up. Her heart sank when she saw Matthew and his friend. *They needn't talk so loud. The rush of cold air would have announced them!* Slowly she crossed the drawing room and lifted her face. "Matthew," she whispered as he pressed his cold cheek against hers. She could smell the alcohol as he nuzzled her cheek.

"Sorry we're late. My friend and I had to fortify ourselves for this occasion." He tugged her close. "Olivia, meet Alexander Duncan." She shivered against his cold buttons and reluctantly lifted her hand to meet another cold hand and intense blue eyes.

Olivia murmured, "Alexander Duncan, how kind of you to come." For a moment she found herself staring into the blue eyes twinkling down at her.

She slipped her hands through their arms. With a gulp she searched for something to say. "You are very late. I expect you both to uphold the honor of the family name now." Her thin attempt at humor slipped past the fellows. She started toward Crystal and saw she was talking to Miss Dobby. *Oh no, she's on the board of directors!*

Olivia led them over to the reception line, uneasily aware of their stiff gait. Miss Hanson and Miss Arvellion seemed at a loss for words. She looked at their stiff smiles and realized the smell of alcohol had extended beyond her. Miss Hanson's face was colored by two bright spots.

Olivia's heart sank. Three more professors waited to be greeted. Deciding Alex was the worst of the pair, she tucked her hand under his arm and steered him quickly through the line and then tugged him toward the dining room.

"Oh, food!" Matthew muttered, taking Olivia's arm as Alex slipped away. "We need this desperately. Sorry for the—it's this way. We started late, got lost, and it was so cold—"

"Any excuse will do," she snapped. "Sit down. I'll bring the plates; I don't believe you are up to carrying them. Where is Alex?" Matthew shrugged, and she continued, "Schoolboys, both of you. Matthew, you know how Father's talked about this very thing. Obviously you haven't been drinking like a gentleman."

"Don't be a scold."

"I'm not—"

"Neither am I," Alex said as he returned. His intense blue eyes focused on her, brightened and came closer. "I am from the South, and we have our honor to uphold. Also, I've just been talking to a very lovely lady. A Miss Crystal Cabet. Matthew, you must meet her."

"You didn't!" Olivia moaned, "Was Miss Dobby there?"

"Yes, but she left. For which I was very grateful."

"I hope you didn't tell her you belonged to me."

"I beg your pardon?"

Shrugging, Olivia looked up into his twinkling eyes. She leaned forward. "Well, I'm from the South too, and I'll tell you, I wish you wouldn't advertise it right now," Olivia hissed. Quickly she walked to the table, loaded the two plates she carried, and returned to the pair.

"Sit down and eat; I'll find Crystal."

"A mug will do," he chuckled. With a sigh of exasperation, Olivia headed for the kitchen. The place was deserted and she rummaged through the cupboards.

Behind her the door creaked. "Please, Crystal, come help me find some coffee mugs. These fellows need coffee badly."

"Ma'am!" Alex's blue eyes laughed down at her. "Forget the coffee. Just come, let's get acquainted. I promised ole Matt I'd be good to his baby sister. Seems to me you're not too much of a baby." He leered at her. "Let's go have a talk."

Olivia resisted an urge to tug at her low-cut dress. Glancing quickly around the room, she pointed to a group of chairs in the corner. "It might be a good idea, at least until I get some coffee in you."

He started toward the chairs. She backed toward the pantry. "I'll look for cups."

He caught up with her as she stretched on tiptoe for the stack of cups.

"Wait. I'll get them down." He moved to reach over her shoulder just as she settled down. She felt her heel crunch into his instep. "Oof!"

"Oh, I'm sorry." She dared not move. The cups were in his hands, and she realized he had carefully circled her with the burden. "Just set them down." Rigid, she held her breath until he had put the cups down.

Grinning down at her, he said, "This is the closest I've been to a Southern belle since I left home. My, you smell as sweet as magnolia blossoms." With another grin he buried his nose in her hair. She tried to push away, but the cupboard was at her back.

"Careful, you'll knock the cups over!" he laughed. "I want another whiff of the magnolia blossoms. Wouldn't you like to be walking in the moonlight beneath magnolia trees right now?"

"You make me homesick!" Olivia caught her breath, thinking of the snow. She murmured fervently, "How dearly I would love that!"

"Let's pretend." Grasping her around the waist, he bent close and whispered, "Hear the violins? They are playing our waltz."

"Mr. Duncan, you are outrageous!"

"But I've never found a girl who didn't like it." He whirled her around the room. "Before I surrender you, I'll claim my kiss." Her giggle disappeared as he pulled her close. The smell of alcohol was overwhelming. She tried to push away, but his lips were on hers, at first demanding, then strangely gentle.

" 'It is my lady: Oh, it is my love! Oh, that she knew she were!' " he quoted.

She pushed. For a moment he stepped back, and then he reached again. This time his lips were urgent and his arms hard. Olivia whirled away, hesitated, and then swooped back. Glaring up at him, she said, "Mr. Duncan, you've forgotten something about Southern belles." She raised her hand and slapped him across the face.

"Now take your coffee cup and go. And in five minutes, if Matthew isn't standing beside the front door, I'll push him there."

CHAPTER 6

It was only a brief lull between winter storms, but to Olivia it seemed like spring. As she walked to her room she thought about home. In Mississippi, the heavy spring rains brought the overnight miracle of blossoms.

Closing her eyes momentarily, she murmured, "First come the dogwood, the redbud, and laurel. Oh, how I love the azaleas, the primrose, and wisteria. I suppose by the time I get home the magnolias will be brown nubs on the trees."

Magnolia. The memory of Matthew's friend rose unbidden to confront her. She snorted with disgust and tried to not think about those intense, laughing blue eyes, and that kiss that still chased her through her dreams. She pressed her fingers to her lips. *That isn't the first kiss I've had; why must it be burned into my thoughts?*

She had just reached her room when the door opened. Olivia turned to see Crystal, her eyes red with tears. "Oh, Olivia, will you please come to my room? I'm leaving and I need to tell you about it."

"Leaving!" She rushed up the stairs after Crystal and entered her room. The usual tidy room was a jumble of clothing, books, and open trunks. Olivia turned to look at her friend. "Crystal, I can't believe it! Of all the students here, you have won the highest honors. Why go now?"

"It isn't my idea." She pushed a paper at Olivia. "It's a letter from my mother. She's ill. My father has left New Orleans; he's coming to fetch me home. Oh, Olivia!" For a moment she buried her face in the handkerchief she held. "I'm sorry. It's just such a disappointment. Despite everything, I've really loved being here."

For a moment Olivia thought back to that ugly scene when Catherine had made the remark about her dark complexion. "Oh, Crystal, how am I going to exist without you? Do you realize you still haven't met my brother, Matthew? That night—it was terrible. Now," Olivia patted Crystal's shoulder. "Crystal, this can't be the end of it. Surely you'll be able to come back next year."

Crystal dried her eyes and looked at Olivia, "That's probably true. It's just such a blow. All I could think about was that somehow our searching for Evangeline had something to do with it. I guess I'm just being emotional." With a smile she turned. "See this mess? My father probably won't be here for weeks, and already I'm nearly packed."

"Well, I suggest we go right now and talk to Miss Arvellion. Perhaps she can recommend studies for you while you're at home." With a quick hug, she added, "That way we'll be in the same class next autumn."

———

Alex leaned against Matthew's door and waved a letter. "We have another appointment with Mallory. He said to come as soon as possible. He has the next three weeks free, and then he will be returning to South Carolina."

Matthew shoved the book across the table and linked his hands behind his head. "I'm not certain I want to go."

Alex's grin was crooked. "Neither am I, but right now I feel this is a command, and there are parents at home who won't like it if we don't. Quoting Mallory, it's the least we can do for the sake of all we stand for."

"What do we stand for?"

"The South, of course."

He came into the room and dropped down on the edge of Matthew's bed. "I've been reading about the election process. The Electoral College. I didn't know it was set up to give an advantage to the states who support slavery."

Slowly Matthew said, "I've heard it was so, but I guess I don't understand the whole process."

"Because of the slaves, the voters have been given additional congressional credit. You know the number of our representatives in Congress are awarded according to population. Naturally the slaves are not citizens and can't vote, but the constitution allows us to count three/fifths of our slave population in determining our representation, meaning a slave state gets more representatives per voter than a free one."

"You aren't chuckling with glee."

"It's occurred to me that the more slaves there are, and the fewer masters, the better we are represented in Congress. Might say it's possible to weigh the balance in our favor. Politically, we'll do ourselves a big favor if we continue to build up the slave population in our state."

"Is that important?"

"Of course. Matt, you weren't born yesterday. Don't you feel the rumbles?"

Slowly he nodded. "I get what you mean. Mallory's hinted at it, too. These United States are lining up on one side of the fence or the other."

Alex finished the thought, "Slavery. Matt, if we want our nice comfortable life to continue, we work for the expansion of slavery. You realize that's precisely what Mallory's saying to us?"

"Guess we don't have a choice." Matthew got to his feet with a sigh. "But here, up North, it's too easy to get a conscience if you're not careful."

Alex nodded. "I have to watch myself. These fellas pushing against the abolitionists leave a bad taste in my mouth. Inside I hear a voice saying in another year or two I'll be just like them."

Matthew said, "You're a slave owner right now, by virtue of your inheritance. Me, too."

"That's so." He jerked his head. "Matt, last night I had a dream. Seems I got to be president of the United States and then I revealed I was abolitionist at heart."

Matthew's grin was crooked as he reached for the book. "I'm glad I'm not graduating this June."

"Are you coming with me—to Mallory's?"

Matthew's grin disappeared. Reluctantly he said, "Might be I could at least listen. But my natural inclination is to just forget about the whole problem."

As they walked across campus, cut across the bridge, and headed for Beacon Hill, Matthew said, "I want you to understand, there's just no way I could fight my father's whole life, and the way he believes. The system."

Alex kicked at the chunk of ice on the path. "Same here. I just hope I don't have to give up thinking in order to be a senator."

"Senator Duncan," Matthew grinned up at him. "That sounds good. Will it be from South Carolina or Louisiana?"

"Probably Louisiana. That's where my boat is docked."

Matthew turned in at the pub. "Let's go celebrate your victory now."

Although it was early in the afternoon, the small room was filled. Matthew glanced around, spotted those he recognized as students, and then categorized the remainder. "Alex, there's lots of workmen here, probably warming their hands, but I don't see any senators. I think between now and then you're going to have to get sophisticated."

"It'll be easier when I don't have to watch every cent," Alex said with a twisted grin as he purchased beer for both of them.

"Well, maybe you drink too much, anyway. Might be you can sacrifice quantity for quality."

The grin disappeared from Alex's face as he carefully set the tankards on the table and slid onto the bench. Matthew watched him take a sip before he looked up with a troubled grin. "Matt, are you trying to tell me something?"

"Not that I'm aware of," Matthew said, his finger tracing the water circle on the table. He looked up at Alex.

Alex concentrated on the chipped tankard as he said, "I think I might owe you an apology."

After a moment Matthew said slowly, "Right now I can't think of anything you need apologize for."

Alex sighed heavily. "That night we went to what's-her-name's school. I was pretty close to being out of it. I can't remember much of the night except I—I wonder, did Olivia say anything?"

"Well, I haven't seen her. Had a note in which she scorched me for being late. But she didn't mention you."

The frown on Alex's face disappeared. "Then you don't think I acted improperly?"

"Well I didn't hear her scream while you two were in the kitchen looking for cups. Matter of fact, I think my sister can handle about any situation. She's got spunk."

"I thought so," Alex murmured, rubbing his face.

"Want another beer?"

"Let's celebrate and have ale. That's supposed to be a little more sophisticated in these parts, I think."

Matthew raised his hand and grinned at the barmaid coming toward them. "Aw, she's already guessed."

Alex ignored the drift of hair and bare arm in front of his face. The woman leaned closer. "You fellas are getting to be regulars here. We like to be good to our customers. How about a couple of pretty girls? Now these aren't common ordinary ones, mind you. We like—"

Alex looked up into the woman's face. "I guess we're getting a reputation coming in here in the middle of the day," he said heavily. "Thanks, but no thanks." Turning to Matthew he said, "Come on, we better get going."

Back on the street Matthew looked up into Alex's face. "You're a good stand-in for a thundercloud. Alex, don't take it personally. I think she was trying to be helpful."

Alex snorted and led the way down the street.

Mallory met them at the door of his Beacon Hill apartment. His annoyed frown lifted when he saw them. "Come in. My man is busy running errands this afternoon, but we can manage to take care of ourselves. What will you drink?"

"Anything but ale," Alex muttered, dropping into the chair opposite Mallory.

Mallory leaned forward and said, "Have you fellows been following the news?" Alex rubbed his jaw, and Mallory continued, "Of course, classwork and studies come first. We old men have more time to follow the election news."

He passed the glass to Alex and continued, "I'm afraid these abolitionists are creating a bit of a storm. I understand most of them are Quakers and won't vote, but it seems they are responsible for this Republican Party rearing its ugly head."

Matthew nodded, "I've heard. It could give our party some trouble. Hear they are uniting with the Free Soil party and a number of the Whigs. You can count on the poor people supporting the Free Soil men."

Alex drawled, "I understand Governor Wise of Virginia is a trifle upset."

Mallory chuckled, "Slightly. Declares that if Colonel Fremont is elected, he'll take the militia of Virginia, march on Washington and seize the Capitol and the National archives."

Matthew said, "Seems the Democrats are bound to win. Do you think most of them are solidly behind Buchanan?"

While Mallory nodded, Alex muttered, "Mighty poor pickings."

"At least we know whose side he's on." Mallory's voice was sharp. For a moment his eyes narrowed as he looked at Alex.

———

When Alex and Matthew left Mallory and walked back to the college, Matthew said, "Alex, you're going to have to step carefully. Three times today I saw Mallory staring at you. I have the feeling you made him a mite uneasy."

"Did I? Sometimes it's hard to turn off the analytical thinking they've been trying to instill in us for all these years. For instance, this debate about slavery. Does or does not the Constitution support slavery?"

"And," Matthew added, "what about the Missouri Compromise of 1850? Some are saying it's unconstitutional."

Alex shrugged, "I can keep some of my thoughts to myself."

"What do you mean?"

"Remember the talk we had around the table at the boardinghouse? Well, you noticed I didn't mention Northern Democrats when I talked about the Republican Party."

"That's right," Matthew said thoughtfully. "I'd forgotten our talk. Might be the drain out of the Democratic party will tip the election. Don't know much about Fremont—do you?"

"As much as I know about Buchanan, and I get the idea he'll go a long way to get a vote, either right or left." Alex fell silent.

"I'm not too crazy about him, either."

They were across the bridge when Alex added, "They're saying the attack on Sumner was tantamount to drawing another hard line between the North and the South. The newspapers are calling it ugly. I agree. Also, they are insinuating there's more ugliness being imported from the South."

Matthew growled, "I don't like that. One bad deed doesn't make us all rotters."

"Might be we'll have to prove your statement," Alex said with a twisted grin.

CHAPTER 7

Spring had come to Massachusetts. When Alex crossed the bridge into Boston he found the Commons alive with birds and blossoms. Slowing his brisk stride, he sniffed the mingled odor of spring and salt air as he watched the people entering the Commons.

He tipped his hat to the covey of housewives coming toward him and noticed the gentle smiles on their faces. Stepping off the path, he watched the aproned matrons stroll the greens, now and then pausing on the path in the warmth of the sun to talk with their neighbors.

Momentarily distracted by spring, Alex, too, turned to stroll slowly. He felt the sun on his face as he stopped to study the halo of yellow-green trees that somehow made the day seem brighter.

He was musing over the daffodils and tulips along the path when he heard his name. "A day when a young man's fancy turns—what say, Alex?"

"Hey there, Tim," Alex murmured. The sprinting classmate slapped him on the shoulder and went on his way, while Alex continued his unhurried walk.

As the fellow began to pull ahead, his voice drifted back. "I'm going down to the wharf; wanna see the excitement?"

Alex shook his head. With a lazy grin he watched Tim lope out of sight. Continuing his slow pace down the path, Alex's mind began to wander, and his thoughts weren't on the flowers.

Funny—one word and I think about her, he mused. *What color was her hair? It's a miracle I even remember her. And seems I recall a kiss, I was deep in the cups. Her hair and her eyes were the same. Smoke-brown.*

He shrugged his shoulders and changed his direction to walk toward the wharf. As he approached a group of students lingering in the path, he looked around and asked, "What's going on?" He waved toward the streets lined with people, "Everyone's heading down to the harbor."

"Hear those shouts?" The fellow beside him took his arm.

"Clemean!" Alex exclaimed as he turned. "You following them, too?"

"Where've you been? Don't you know what it's all about?" Clemean matched his steps with Alex's and said, "Remember the slave who's been making all the news? I think his name is Anthony Burns."

"You mean the runaway who was picked up here?" Alex nodded, "Don't we all remember? Quite a riot, when the gentleman—can't remember his name, tried to take his slave home. Matthew and I were down there in the middle of it all."

"You were? Well then, you know it was a paddyroller who did the dirty work. You know, the fellow paid to find Burns and fetch him home."

"I'd heard," Alex mused. "That was quite a demonstration."

"I'll tell the world. Those abolitionists just about tore the town up trying to rescue the man. There was a deputy marshal shot, but the abolitionists got what they wanted—a trial for Burns. Didn't do any good; his master won out in the end. That's what's going on today. Seems the fella has quite a crowd of sympathizers here."

He paused and glanced at Alex. "Don't let Professor Harrison find out we're trailing along. Might be hard to convince him it's all in fun. He's telling us to learn to be objective. Says rioting won't help our profile as attorneys. Personally, I think he's more concerned about our getting our names on file with the police. Doesn't look good for the school."

"Don't get me wrong!" Alex protested. "I wasn't taking sides. It wasn't planned, we just stumbled into it. Actually," he added with a slight grin, "at times like this, we consider ourselves in enemy territory." He saw the quick exchange of glances and hastily added, "We saw the crowd of abolitionists and hung around to hear what they had to say. Man, they were hot under the collar." Dropping his head, Alex added, "I think I understand how they feel. You can't give yourself to a cause like that without getting caught up in it. I remember the fellow's face. I can't imagine a man condemned to death feeling any worse about it."

Taking a step toward Alex, Clemean added soberly, "You know that deputy marshal who was shot? Well that says something to me. When the abolitionists and the free Negroes stuck their necks out and attacked the building where they had the slave detained—when they take risks like that it tells you something. Every one of them was risking his life."

"I heard he had his trial."

"Yes. Those ugly-mouthed thugs who were paid to pick him up for his master sure spelled out the dirt." There was a slight grin on Clemean's face. "Threw in states' rights and a few other goodies designed to make us feel sorry for the owner. I don't get the idea they were trying to make friends with the A's."

"More like intimidation," Alex agreed. "But I don't think they knew their crowd too well. The abolitionists could have been crying over their long lost brother. Their fervor attracted a good deal of sympathy."

Clemean muttered, "Thing that makes me most angry is those fellows who captured Burns are being so smug about having the law on their side. Number one, we're being backed into the corner to see how much we'll take." He threw a quick glance at Alex and continued. "And number two, they were deliberately trying to see how far they can push that law down our throats."

"The Fugitive Slave Act? But you say *we'll take*?" Alex questioned slowly as he studied Clemean's face.

"Begging your pardon, Alex, I know you're Southern. But at least you act like you got a heart."

Alex's head jerked. "Heart? Clemean, you've got us all wrong. We treat our slaves right." The words died on his lips as he watched Clemean drop his head. Slowly he added, "Clemean, it's strange; for a moment I felt I was standing outside all this. Without any territorial loyalties. After hurting with abolitionists, I found myself wondering what I would have done in that owner's shoes."

"Man oh man, will you look at that!" They turned at the exclamation. The group pointed down the hill. "Clemean, Alex, hurry along. They've got the militia and every policeman in town down the street. I'll bet they're escorting our fugitive aboard with his captors. Would you believe it? I think they are still expecting trouble."

As the students clustered on the path, an elderly gentlemen who had been watching the commotion turned to face them. He tipped his hat, studied their faces and said, "Now you young fellows, don't you be going down there causing trouble."

"Well, they're certainly prepared for the worst," Clemean said pointing down the street.

The gentleman nodded. "The whole county is here, but the marshal has made provisions. He's acquired a large body of aides just for the occasion. In addition, he has a company of marines under his command. Ten thousand armed men," he mused slowly, "simply to escort one runaway Negro slave and his jailer down to the boat."

The man's grin was crooked. "Seems the marshal expected a great deal of trouble." His face clouded. "Not that we aren't capable of giving it to them. But there's been enough bloodshed, enough heartache." He turned and pointed. "What you see here today, young men, is a bunch of well-meaning but very confused people. See, we Yankees have about been set back on our heels."

He paused, then continued to address the silent group watching him. Straightening, he thumped the path with his cane and said, "Some of the most able attorneys of the Constitution are stating we've no right to restrict the confiscation of that black man, even when he is on free soil.

"Men, I tell you, we are confused. Our hands are tied. We have sworn to uphold the Constitution, and while those Southerners jeer in our faces, we are rocking back on our heels—powerless to defend our fellow man. All because of the Fugitive Slave Act." He dropped his head and his voice brooded. "Trying very hard to be law abiding gentlemen, we are. But it's hard to forget that fellow's look of utter dejection." At that the gentleman turned and hurried away. Alex caught a glimpse of his face. The contorted features were wet with tears.

For a moment longer the fellows shifted uneasily, and then one of the group muttered, "We're missing out on the show."

Down on the wharf Alex and the others managed to worm their way through the crowd. They were standing beside the gangplank when they heard the drum, accompanied by the shuffle of feet.

Alex turned to watch the militia moving into position. Silence settled over the street as the black man, surrounded by guns and stern-faced men, walked toward them.

Alex moved closer, compelled to watch even as his inner core rebelled. The slave walked slowly up the ramp. For a moment he paused, lifted his head, and astonishment swept across his face. Alex watched the brief flare of hope as the man saw the streets packed with humanity. But while every face tilted upward, the man's lips moved soundlessly. As a new expression stamped down on the black face, his shoulders slumped. *That fellow isn't expecting anything from the crowd, maybe even from life.*

Under his breath, Alex muttered, "Fugitive Slave Law. That's enough to make any red-blooded human feel like an absolute rotter."

He heard a strangled sob coming from the black bonnet in front of him. The woman turned and lifted a tear-streaked face. "Mister, did you see him? Probably has a family. He's being taken away and will never see them again." She paused and looked toward the ship again. Slowly she regained control of her voice and said, "I can't forget how I'd feel in his shoes. But for the grace of God, I'd be a slave, too." She lifted her face again. "They have just as much right to walk this earth in freedom as we do. This country stands for justice and freedom for all, but that man doesn't have it." She turned and pushed her way out of sight.

The crowd lingered to watch as the steamboat gave a final toot and pulled away.

Wrapped in his thoughts, Alex's head jerked at the blast of the boat's whistle. Was its shrill noise a gesture of defiance? Someone besides Alex thought so. A voice rose above the crowd. "Musta been a boat from South Carolina."

Restlessly the crowd moved, and then as one they started up the hill toward the Commons. Alex heard a lone voice. "Makes a body feel bad, seeing a fellow man treated like that. Especially when his hands are tied by a law he doesn't believe in. Down underneath the skin, we're all the same."

Another voice murmured, "Some say the slaves don't really want to be free. It's hard to believe that."

When Alex and his comrades reached the evening-shadowed grounds, a man was standing on a bench speaking to the crowd gathered in front of him.

He waved the paper he held. Although the people stood close and everyone was silent, he raised his voice and shook the paper. "In January of 1853, Wendell Phillips gave an address before the Massachusetts Anti-Slavery Society. In this speech Phillips bared his soul, calling slavery a sin, making merchandise of men. And while in the process of buying and selling, like cattle for the market, families are separated—husband from wife, mother from infant. 'Daughters are sold for prostitution and taught that they are being honored by their white masters.' "

He paused to shake the paper again. "Do you realize the Black Code of 1724 instructs the masters to give religious education to those in subjection? In addition, the code commands confiscation of slaves not educated or those forced to work on the Sabbath. It also forbids the illicit cohabitation between slaves and white. The code says slaves are to be properly cared for. So how come we so often hear of sickness, neglect, and hunger among these people?" He paused and then added, "In addition, while families are being torn apart at the auction block, how often does it happen that one of our black brethren finds life too wretched to bear, and thus he takes his escape in the depths of the river?" He whispered his urgency. "Gentlemen, am I mistaken? I get the feeling these people would prefer being free." And then he shouted, "Along with Brother Phillips, I say these black people must be free!"

A voice came from the crowd. "Mister! There's still the Fugitive Slave Law."

"Then the law must be changed."

Another voice added, "The law is inhumane. It fails to provide a jury trial. Anyone can be snatched up and labeled slave. I dare say there's going to be trouble. The law compels any citizen to aid in capturing and returning these black men. Some of us would rather die than turn over a fellow man."

A few in the crowd had started to move away when a white-haired man said, "There's a group of us who've banded together and signed a petition. We won't be a party to the law."

Alex's gaze was still fixed on the man's face as the crowd drifted away. "Coming to the pub with us, Alex?" He felt the nudge on his arm and sighed as he turned.

Clemean was waiting for an answer. Alex hesitated. "No, fellas, I'll be heading back now."

———

With head down, Olivia walked slowly toward the residence hall. While she studied the clumps of violets growing along the path and between the stones, quick steps sounded behind her. She turned as Marjorie's heavy voice hailed her. "Missy, come down to earth! Your nose is in the air all too often these days."

"Well, it isn't right now," Olivia said dryly. "I suggest you look down at the violets. Did you see the white ones?"

Marjorie blinked. "Didn't notice. Well, now that your friend has gone home, how about giving the rest of us some attention? Arabelle is having a party in her room this evening. There's cards and goodies. Come." She started to walk away, then abruptly she turned. "I hope we weren't too hard on you and Crystal. See, we have problems with some of your values."

Olivia's back stiffened. "I suppose you're referring back to the Stowe novel? It was an unfortunate choice. After all, America is built on freedom, and we Southerners have as much right to freedom as you Northerners." As she spoke, another girl joined Marjorie. The serious, gray-eyed Annie Dudley was the unofficial tutor of the residence hall.

"Maybe we're more curious than anything else," Marjorie said. "Not many of us come from a culture as rich as yours. We wouldn't know how to treat a servant. Tell me," she added with a slight grin, "How do you handle a butler serving you coffee in bed?"

Olivia lifted her chin. "My servant is female. Mattie has been comforting my bruises and teaching me manners since I was a baby. If I can't go down to breakfast with the family, *she* brings me coffee in bed."

Annie's gray eyes shifted from Marjorie to Olivia. "Marjorie, that is irrelevant. The greater problem is slavery, human bondage. I cannot imagine a comfortable life with outsiders invading my home. Or, with the knowledge these people were being mistreated in order to increase their effectiveness to me. Olivia, now that you've been in the North these past months, can you honestly consider returning to the South?"

Olivia felt her face flush. "Annie, that was a very condescending remark. Of course I shall return. Mississippi is my home and will be forever. Slavery is an unfortunate situation, but these people are unable to support themselves adequately away from our help. We are good to our slaves, and in turn they are loyal and happy."

Olivia paused and took a deep breath before she pushed out the strong words. "Perhaps it hasn't occurred to you that you have a distorted view of the Southern economy. Certainly we are rich—"

"But not all of you," Annie said softly. "The number of slave-holders with a significant number of slaves is very small. I know there's a distorted balance of power in the South, both in the number of wealthy plantation owners and the political control that they hold."

"For a hundred years," Olivia's clipped words slipped in, "my family has been working for the life we enjoy. I would not trade it for anything. Certainly slavery isn't the ideal situation, but our land and economy demand it. It is impossible for us to survive without slavery. We have an obligation to protect the lives of these slaves under our care, and that we will continue to do."

Annie said, "But there is cruelty in slavery. How can you stand to be in such a situation?"

That scene in her father's field flashed across Olivia's memory. She winced. "Yes, beatings do happen, but not a one of us wants it to be. In your society bad things happen and there must be punishment. It is the same with us. I still love the South."

Marjorie stepped forward, "But to stay there forever? You aren't taking into consideration other things. For instance, love. What if you were to meet a Northern man, fall in love, and choose to stay in the North?"

Olivia turned to look at Marjorie. "I can't imagine that happening. I dislike the North intensely, the smoky factories and the poverty I've seen. Your factory workers are pathetic people; I can't believe slaves aren't better off. I hate the cold and dreary winters. I shall not stay in the North one moment beyond getting my education."

"You aren't dealing with the question," Annie said. "Marjorie mentioned loving a Northern man."

"If he would not come South with me, I should not even consider such a marriage."

"The South means more to you than love?" Annie studied her face for a moment and then asked, "You would remain a spinster?"

"Oh, my no!" Olivia laughed. "I would marry. I've plenty of opportunities there. I'm simply saying I'm committed to living in the South first of all. There I will be happy with any man as long as he is Southern, comes from a good family, and has an estate of his own. But then, I suppose I'll not commit myself to marriage for a number of years. I intend to enjoy life first." She paused, adding, "Certainly I would never leave my home for a man, when there are plenty of good men in the South. My intention is to love intelligently."

Marjorie began backing down the path. She reached for Annie's arm, saying, "Well, anyway, we do want to understand you and make amends. See you at the party."

Harriet Tipperman approached in time to hear the last sentence. Olivia turned and looked at her classmate as Harriet said, "Well, wasn't that nice of her. Trying to make up for being snippy. I happen to think you were right to defend Crystal. Of course everyone knew she was Creole, but to insinuate that she was—more than that. She has such a big mouth. Marjorie, I mean."

Olivia moved her shoulders restlessly. "To tell the truth, I'm very tired of the whole situation. Since Crystal's left school there's been a whole catalog of theories as to why she had to go. Why all the attention? Betty Foster didn't rate it when she left. Why can't they all accept the fact that her mother is ill? Now I am beginning to wonder whether she will be happy to return next autumn."

Harriet pushed her limp hair out of her eyes and peered at Olivia. "What about you? Do you want to return?"

"I would be glad to go home right now. I miss the South."

Harriet sniffed, "How come Southerners are so snooty about the South? Take that incident about the runaway slave. Those men just lorded over everyone. Why do they feel it is right to have slaves?"

Olivia tried to keep the annoyance from her face. "Harriet, I do believe it depends on where one lives. I really don't see anything wrong with slavery. I have an idea that neither would you, if you had been born and raised in Mississippi."

Miss Fensin hurried down the path toward them. Harriet groaned, "Old Fensin! I haven't turned in my assignment. See you later." She rushed toward the residence hall.

Reaching Olivia, the woman nodded. "Good afternoon, Olivia. I haven't had opportunity to talk with you since Crystal has left. Have you had a letter from her?"

"No. As a matter of fact, I haven't," Olivia said slowly. "She promised to write, so this must mean she's terribly involved with caring for her mother."

"Do you know what the problem is?"

"No, and Crystal didn't, either. You remember her mother escorted us to school."

The woman nodded, "Yes, I recall. I also recall her mother was attended by a Negro maid." She paused delicately and added, "For some of us who've had to struggle our way through life, it is a little intimidating to meet someone like Mrs. Cabet. However, I suppose it is commonplace to you."

Olivia thought of home and the life she had so much taken for granted. Feeling nearly guilty, she watched the woman's pinched face, replying slowly, "We all have problems of one kind or another, even in the South." Hastily she searched for a topic, "I suppose mothers, most of all. Children never seem to quite measure up to what mothers expect." The woman's eyebrows lifted. Olivia leaned forward and whispered, "I'm a tomboy."

Miss Fensin's face cleared. "We wondered. Your brother Matthew and his friend had us a little concerned."

"Would you believe they were so totally intimidated by the idea of going to a girl's school, that—well, they went to a pub to summon up courage. Mother wouldn't be happy."

Miss Fensin took a deep breath. "But you wouldn't keep company with such a wild young man, would you?"

Olivia thought about those teasing blue eyes, the kiss. "Of course not," she whispered, "I don't think he's quite proper. Besides, I doubt those two will ever be invited here again!" As she laughed, Olivia saw the sparkle in Miss Fensin's eyes and heard her giggle.

She was still thinking about the woman as she entered her room. *Miss Fensin wears shabby boots*, she thought. *I don't even know what it is to wear boots with a split seam letting in all the soggy spring wet.* She fingered the newspaper lying on her table. Uppermost was the article that had disturbed her last night. Could that have caused the dream?

Running her finger lightly over the words, she murmured, "Mister, you sound like a poor white, a complaining man who feels the world owes you a living. I can almost hear you saying that you are poor because the plantation owners with their slaves are making you that way. I can nearly see the way your lip pulls down in self-pity."

She read the words, *They take our land. We dig our own stumps and whack away at the cane.* Silently she continued to stir the words around with her finger as she thought about the dream.

She had been at home, seeing that raised whip again. So often she had recalled the black face and the agonized screams, only this time in the dream, when the whip descended, it struck a tender white back. And when the man screamed and writhed in agony, she saw Matthew's face.

CHAPTER 8

Alex glanced up as Matthew came into the room. He touched his freshly shaved face and studied the sober face reflected beside his. "You look kind of out of it, old man. Change your mind about coming with me?" he asked as he turned around.

Matthew blinked, "You mean to see Mallory? Guess I'd forgotten about it. Think I'll skip it this time. I'm a little tired of the whole subject. In the long run, I suppose I'll come around to Mallory's point of view." His grin was twisted as he added, "Isn't that easier than having to ream your mind of a lifetime of thinking patterns? In addition, my grades don't look too good right now; I need all the study time I can get."

Alex nodded. "I know what you mean. I'm glad this is my last year. Don't have much left to do except meet the gentlemen and persuade them I ought to be admitted as an attorney at law. I'll have my first meeting tomorrow; wish me luck."

"Alexander Duncan, Attorney at Law." Matthew shoved his hands in his pockets. "Sounds good, but it's possible I won't join the ranks for some time. Matter of fact, I'm strongly considering taking a year off. I suppose I could blame it on finances or something, but the truth of it is, I need a break from the routine."

"Tired of it?" Alex questioned. "It's rough all around; gets to be a real grind about now. I can't say I blame you. Just don't forget the studies altogether. Remember Mallory and the things he's had to say about our responsibilities."

When Alex reached for his tie, Matthew met his gaze, saying, "You sound like Mallory, shouting that we need more support from Congress. The same old song: we need our slaves, we can't exist without them."

"You don't buy that?" Alex managed to keep his voice level, trying to deny the urge to question. As he waited for Matthew's answer, he faced his own confusion, wondering what it would take to quell it completely.

"I just don't like feeling manipulated."

"Mallory?" Alex turned back to the mirror and jerked at his tie. "Nevertheless, for the sake of the South, I'll go hear him out. Matt, maybe we've had it too soft," he said quietly. "Maybe we don't appreciate the struggle our fathers and grandfathers endured in the effort to build the dynasty we now enjoy."

"Dynasty!" Matt exploded. "You make it sound like a farce!"

"Sometimes I think it is. Nevertheless—" He straightened his shoulders and the corner of his mouth pulled down as he added, "I'll give Mallory another hearing." Slowly he added, "Guess I'm obligated to do so. I've had a letter from my mother. She let it drop that Father had borrowed quite a sum from Mallory. She indicated it would be best not to mention the letter to Father. I guess he found a deal on land he can't turn down. He's that way."

Matthew said, "That puts everything in an awkward position for you. Kinda makes you feel like you're obligated to Mallory's interests just to keep his friendship with your father on an even keel. I guess I can't blame you for following up with the man. I just hope it works out for you."

As Matthew headed for the door, Alex toyed with the folded newspaper on his desk. "Matt, there's something I wanted to ask," he said as he tapped the paper. "Back home, did you have the impression that we didn't always get the news fair and square?"

"I'm not certain I know what you mean."

He punched the newspaper. "Here everything—good and bad— is printed. I read articles that bad-mouth politics and the complacency of the North, as well as digging at the Southern political picture and the slavery issue. The other day I read a story that raked the abolitionists over the coals. Called them warmongers and said they had their heads in the clouds. Said they were irrational in their call for total and instant abolition."

Matthew's grin twisted. "I see what you mean. Sometimes at home I got the idea newspapers reflected only one careful thought, and it always seemed to come from the same viewpoint. Pretty humdrum reading." He pulled the door closed behind himself.

———

Alex headed toward Beacon Hill, still frowning as he crossed the bridge and turned down the street.

The clumsy white man, Ham, answered the door. He grinned. "Evening, sir. We have plenty of beer this time—even got rid of the fancy crystal." He carried Alex's hat into the library and intoned, "Sir, Mister Mallory, the young gentleman from South Carolina is here, Alexander Duncan."

Mallory strode through the door. In exasperation he waved at Alex's hat as he extended his hand. "Your friend Matthew didn't come? Too bad; he seems a likely candidate. Certainly a polished gentleman, and that's important. Now come have your beer and tell me how school is going."

Mallory took his chair and waited until Ham placed the loaded tray on the table between the chairs. The tankard of beer slid in its foamy nest. Alex couldn't control his grin when he saw the pained expression on Mallory's face.

"Sir," Alex murmured, lifting the tankard, "I am surprised to see Ham. With the advent of the Kansas-Nebraska Bill, I would have expected you to have your black butler with you."

Mallory's smile was grim as he said, "Bently is a fine fellow, but you can never be certain."

"I don't understand."

"Back home Bently seems content with his lot in life. But in the North there's always the danger of undesirable influences."

Alex sipped his beer and said, "Such as the shouting mob the day the abolitionists stormed the building where the slave and the paddyroller were holed up?"

Mallory winced. "Paddyroller! The North has contaminated you.

Your speech has suffered." He paused, looked distastefully at the beer he held, sipped, and then asked, "Have you given any more thought to your future? Wait, don't answer me yet. I just want to unload a few ideas on you. Most certainly I am confident you are a true Southern gentlemen, with the South's best interests at heart."

Alex nodded. "But we may differ over the idea of what is best for the South."

Mallory's face changed slowly. Cautiously he asked, "What do you mean by that?"

Taking a deep breath, Alex stopped. For a moment he thought of his mother's letter and wondered where all his half-formed ideas would lead him. "I've spent nearly four years in the North. I've learned to think in a different pattern."

"Like a lawyer, a politician? My boy, that's what we want."

"I've been exposed to Northern ideas; maybe I'm seeing life from a different dimension."

"That's to be understood. And you needn't worry about bouncing your ideas off me. I'm certain Southern principles are still dear to you. See, my lad, it isn't only that we need all the able young men we can get, but in addition we need fighters—for the right cause. That cause is very Southern."

Alex's smile froze as he placed the tankard on the table. "I do believe in the Southern cause, but that cause must be the very best for every one concerned. Not only for the present and for the tidewater plantations," he added, "but for the future and for all people."

Mallory's face stiffened, "Are you trying to tell me something?"

"I'm not certain. Please don't rush me just yet, Sir. I'm still trying to decide whether I love the old way of life enough to fight for it." He watched the lines on Mallory's face sag. "Sir, is there a possibility that slavery is wrong?" He hastened on. "I'm Southern bred and raised; I know nothing else. For the first time in my life I am questioning, and it started when I didn't know there were such questions to be asked." He reached for his tankard and gulped the beer.

Mallory made a tent of his fingers as he watched Alex. Nodding slightly, he said, "Alex, your father and I have been friends for years. I will grant you that the older generation always ends up seeming like a bunch of fuddy-duddies to you young fellows. I suppose the best thing that can happen to any generation is to have the youngsters cause us to question our values."

He paused and took a deep breath. "Now what about those old fellows, back in the late 1700s—the ones who formulated the Declaration of Independence and the signers of the Constitution? At some point in their lives, they were regarded as old fuddy-duddies too. Tell me lad, what do you think now?"

Alex chuckled. "It would be nice to skip the fuddy-duddy process and just be accepted as wise and notable. Most certainly the Declaration of Independence is a masterpiece."

"And Jefferson was a slaveholder."

"But one of the grievances that was a justification for the Revolution was the infliction of slavery upon the colonists. Jefferson himself recognized slavery as a violation of human rights."

Alex stirred restlessly as Mallory pointed his finger at him. "Slavery—a necessary evil, but definitely an unavoidable one. Alex, don't let your heart run away from your head. We can't exist without slaves. That was the tacit understanding at the time of Constitutional Convention. When there was a move to abolish slavery immediately, both Georgia and South Carolina made it very plain that they would not be part of the union if it were done."

"I know." Alex grinned, adding, "You think any youth raised in South Carolina isn't aware of our special standing? We've never been allowed to forget how important we are to the Union! In the beginning they compromised in order to get us in. But Mallory, you and I both know it was an uneasy truce. Yes, the Union needed us badly, but with the tide of feeling against slavery from the beginning, things are bound to change."

"I don't know why. We've been able to live comfortably with slavery. You know the black people are happy in their situation, as long as a troublemaker isn't in there shaking things up. Let me tell you, lad, if it weren't for the element of fanaticism in this country, we would continue to have slavery without challenge. Unfortunately, with the ill winds blowing against us, it becomes necessary to pull the strings up tight and fight for our rights."

"But still," Alex said slowly, "we are left with that statement, 'We hold these truths to be self-evident, that all men are created equal. . . .' And we believe in the unalienable right to life, liberty, and the pursuit of happiness. Sir, since arriving at Harvard, I've had a hard time getting away from that."

Mallory was speaking, and only much later did Alex realize the man hadn't heard him.

His voice was a low rumble. "By right, we should be able to have things hold steady, but the handwriting's on the wall."

"Handwriting?"

Mallory straightened and looked at him. "Birney. A true Southern gentleman, now a traitor."

"I heard about him. Freed his slaves. Didn't have much of a presidential campaign, but he sent out some signals."

Mallory nodded, "About the time we were trying to get Texas into the Union."

Alex didn't miss the pronoun. "You were working on it? That was one of the topics we hashed over in class." Mallory settled in his collar and Alex, suddenly thinking of his mother, said feebly, "Pretty touchy situation, huh?"

Mallory studied his face and said, "Alex, lad, I might as well be candid with you. Until Birney's campaign, it was starting to look as if the Southern position was gaining acceptance—at least tolerance— among all except the abolitionists. Now it appears there's an undercurrent that will ruin us all."

"Unless there's a compromise," Alex said slowly. "Sir, with your stature in Washington, you have the power to save the South if—"

Mallory nodded, leaning forward in his chair. "That has been our intention, and daily the need is becoming more pressing. Alex, let me read part of the letter Calhoun wrote to his constituents a couple of years ago. I've a copy somewhere, cut out and saved to show you. I may have to look for it."

Mallory got to his feet and went to his desk. "Anyway, Calhoun says we have a duty to ourselves and to the Union to force the issue of slavery upon the North. Can't seem to find it." He returned to his chair. "It was published just after Congress set the limits related to the Missouri Compromise, which had opened the possibility of slavery in the territories, down to Texas.

"At the time, Calhoun stressed the fact that we were stronger than we'd ever been, and action was needed as soon as possible. He wanted a convention of the Southern states, to gain a hearing for his proposal of excluding Northern ships from Southern ports if we weren't allowed to take our slaves into free territory, and to have support in recovering our slaves. But unfortunately there wasn't the backing needed to push the idea along."

Alex's protest boiled out, "But that's in violation of the Constitution!"

Alex let Ham fill his tankard. For a moment he watched the man's eyes. What was in his expression? Perhaps the man was not as clumsy mentally as he seemed with the trappings of a gentleman.

Mallory's eyes had a troubled look as he watched Ham leave the library and close the door behind himself. Mallory leaned forward, restlessly fondling the tankard as he talked. "You know, things are looking up for the South. No longer are we under the domination of narrow-minded men. We're well represented in Congress, and I intend to continue that thrust."

Heavily Alex said, "How long can we hold the upper hand in Congress?"

"This will be determined by the strength of the tidewater plantations." He reached for his pipe and the can of tobacco. His eyes searched Alex's as he packed the pipe. "We must protect our interests. Right now it is to our advantage to keep the number of producing tidewater plantations as high as possible. In order to do this, we must have a clear market for cotton, rice, tobacco, and sugar."

"Without constricting tariffs," Alex added.

"If we lose our big plantations, we lose our advantage in Congress."

"And if we lose our slaves, we lose our plantations. We need cheap labor. Free labor."

Mallory winced at the brittle words.

Alex continued, "But how long can we expect that to last? Back home we heard the Constitution protects our right to have slaves. In Boston they say that isn't so. Back home we believe it is to the Negro's advantage to be under the benevolent hand of a master. In Boston they say the black man would rather starve than be in bondage. Mr. Mallory, right now I'd like to know just what the truth is."

Mallory was still staring into his tankard when Alex continued. His voice brooded out the words. "We studied Constitutional law, and I found it gave me a new understanding, which is making me a mite uncomfortable. At the time the original draft of the Declaration of Independence was penned by Thomas Jefferson, those men were doing a great deal of deep thinking."

"You're ignoring an important detail," Mallory argued, thumping the tankard on the tray. "The necessity of slavery."

"That's the leverage South Carolina and Georgia used at the time the Constitution was drawn up. I understand, from reading history, the necessity of having every colony aligned behind the bid for liberty."

"It was compromise." Mallory brooded, "Both Georgia and South Carolina desperately needed slavery in order to survive. And the need hasn't changed."

Alex slowly said, "I can't get away from the fact that the Declaration of Independence says all men are created equal, and among their rights is one impossible to ignore—liberty."

"Alex, my lad, I know your father. There is no finer gentleman alive." Alex moved restlessly and Mallory hastened on, "I'll never be convinced that he is anything except a compassionate man in all his dealings, including the handling of his black people. Stop allowing your heart to dictate what your head knows isn't true. Those people are far better off than they would be if they were to live in so-called freedom. Not a one is capable of supporting himself away from the benevolent hand of his master."

"Meanwhile," Alex muttered, "in the South, the rich get richer and the poor are poorer. Sir, is that a responsible way for us to run our country?"

Mallory's smile twisted. "Even Jesus Christ said the poor you'll always have with you." Alex's head snapped up as Mallory added, "In addition, my lad, we still have states' rights. We have the right to decide the issue of slavery under the Constitution. We cannot exist without it. Alex, your father will be homeless in another five years without slaves. It is the only way the South can exist. Would you strip that advantage from him, considering the alternative?"

When Alex finally raised his head to look at Mallory, he spoke softly, deliberately. "You make me feel I've no choice. As my father's son I am obligated to support the cause of slavery. Will the obligation be so great I'll never be able to consider my conscience?"

Mallory patted him on the shoulder. "Come back next week, Alex. Idealism is a part of growing up. We all suffer through it until we get our heads on straight."

Just before going back outside, Alex took his hat from Ham as

Mallory added, "Unfortunately we need every true son of the South to be committed to the cause, not only for the South, but for the economy of the entire nation. Remember, our goods support the industry of the North." Mallory paused. "I hope to God I live to see the strain between brothers eased. Right now I have a feeling that were it not for those fanatics, the abolitionists, there would be no gulf between North and South."

Studying the troubled face of the short, graying man in front of him, Alex asked, "You don't sound hopeful, Sir."

"I'm not." Mallory started to turn away, but he stopped and peered into Alex's face. "The handwriting's on the wall."

Alex nodded, "One thing, Sir. I didn't hear about Birney until I came North. Why?"

"I'm not certain it's the thing to do—trying to hide the hard questions," Mallory said, moving heavily. "It seems to be a mistake that will rise up to haunt us."

As Mallory turned away, Alex raised his voice. "Sir, are you in favor of acquiring Cuba? And what about William Walker in Nicaragua?"

Mallory looked over his shoulder, his face twisted as he said, "I'm in favor of doing anything that needs to be done in order to preserve the South, including finding a new home for freed Negroes."

"Even secession?"

"Yes. Come back, lad, we need to talk again."

Those final words kept step with Alex as he left Beacon Hill. The blue sky had disappeared behind a low bank of clouds and a cold drizzle began. Shivering in his coat, Alex paused to ponder the bright lights and laughter coming from the tavern on the corner. He considered his interview on the following day and heard the echo of Mallory's voice: *The handwriting's on the wall.* And he recalled the curious expression in Ham's eyes.

The rain began to soak through his coat. With a shiver, Alex caught the opening door. The laughter and warm air rushed to meet him as he entered.

CHAPTER 9

F riend, come in out of the rain."

 Alex screwed his eyes tight, cutting out the lightning stab of pain. Slowly he pushed himself upright and fumbled for his hat.

 "There, friend, under your hand. Had a bad time of it, I see. Well, come inside; we'll see if we can't find some broth or coffee."

 The supporting shoulder was frail and bony. Even in his befuddled state, Alex tried to lift his weight away from the man.

 "Don't fuss; it isn't the first time I've served as a prop. Now, wait a bit until I get the door open. If you were waiting all night to see me, you should have had something more substantial than whiskey."

 Whiskey. Alex rubbed his hand over his face and opened his eyes. There was a stone step in front of him. An open door released the smell of printer's ink. He groaned.

 "We'll go to the back room. It's a little spot of my own, and the smell isn't as bad."

 Alex stumbled after the man and eased himself down on the cot. The stabbing light moved away and in the shadowy room Alex squinted his eyes while the man poked wood into the stove.

 "Kinda down on your luck?" The gaunt face tipped toward Alex, looked at his clothes; then the man returned to the stove. With arms akimbo he peered at Alex, saying, "You're a student?"

"I am." Alex rubbed feeling into his chilled face and tried to grin at the man. "It appears I didn't make it home last night. Powerful stuff." He considered, looked at the man and said, "I have an interview today. What time is it?"

"Eight in the morning of this Thursday."

"Thursday," Alex groaned. "My interview was yesterday. What happened to me? I've lost one whole day."

"Well, you didn't get the whiskey on my doorstep, and you're a long way from Harvard. Better check your pockets."

Slowly Alex's hand moved over his pockets. "Everything's there. You thought I was mugged?"

"I wouldn't guess you to have wandered this far without help."

"Nothing's missing, so that possibility is out." Alex looked around the room, saw the ink-stained coat hanging on the wall and remembered the odor that had assailed him as he stepped into the building. "You're a printer?"

"Newspaper, *The Liberator*. My name's Garrison. I'm also a Quaker. I'm most famous or infamous for my stand against slavery. From your accent, I have a feeling you may not wish to spend much time here. However, I'll be glad to call you a hack." He carried the mug of steaming coffee to Alex.

Alex took a mouthful of the scalding brew and felt the warmth ease through his chilled body. "Ah! Garrison? Are you the man they nearly killed on the streets?"

"That was back in thirty-five, probably about the time you were born." The man's smile was gentle. He pulled off his spectacles and polished them.

"I heard that back in forty-one you advocated the North seceding from the Union over the slavery issue. Why?"

Garrison sliced bread and carried it to Alex. "Better get some food into you, if you're up to it." He grinned down at Alex. "That is, if you can't handle my words on an empty stomach."

Standing next to the stove he watched Alex. "Because I believed that strongly in supporting the Constitution. President George Washington said in his farewell address, regarding the Constitution, that until it was changed by an explicit and deliberate act of the people, we have a sacred obligation to uphold it. To me it seemed a travesty to say we support the Constitution while allowing human bondage." He paused and then slowly said, "Maybe I had a feeling in the back of my brain that all my stomping and yelling around would somehow get people's attention, and that just maybe a few would catch the fever."

"Of abolition?"

Garrison nodded.

Alex passed his hand over his face, looked up and asked, "Why now?"

Garrison stepped closer, and Alex thought he detected a flash of sympathy in the fellow's eyes. Pulling a stool forward, he sat down and said, "I don't follow you."

"I don't follow myself," Alex muttered. "Head like a bladder of hot air." He sighed. "I've been here nearly four years; now all of a sudden I'm being hit with the slavery issue every time I turn around."

"Well, I'll tell you something." Garrison was grinning with delight. "In thirty-two the New England Anti-Slavery Society was established. They promoted the idea that every slave has a right to immediate freedom. That didn't go over too well; in fact, you might say there was enough of the South in the North that our bunch was mighty unpopular."

Alex rubbed his aching head and murmured, "You were very brave." When only silence met his remark, he looked up.

Garrison glanced quickly at him; with a sheepish grin he said, "This may come across as pompous, but some of us see it as a divine mandate." He lifted his hand as Alex straightened. "Now, don't get me wrong. I'm not judging your acquaintance with the Almighty. You have the same churches down South—Quakers, Baptists, Methodists. From what we hear, most of those churches preach the truth. Maybe even fearlessly."

He paused, shoved his spectacles into position, and continued. "You can't quarrel with the Almighty when He says, 'Look here, this is my plan.' " His voice dropped into a brooding question. "What about the people who are hurt? You can't quarrel with your Maker; you obey, even when you don't understand."

He leaned forward to peer at Alex. "I get a feeling—don't know I'm right and won't know until I have time to search it out in Scripture. But anyway, it might be possible when we make a big mistake, God takes us the long way back to rectify it. That applies to nations, too."

The bang of the door and the voice came together. "Garrison!"

"In here, John."

The man's voice preceded him into the room. "Ten in the morning, and your press is silent!"

"Presses and ink are hard on headaches." Garrison slid off his stool and clasped hands with the slender man coming through the doorway. "Come meet Alexander Duncan."

Alex heaved himself to his feet and held out his hand. "It is my pleasure, Sir."

The man peered at Alex as he shook his hand. "Southern, and in here with the editor of the *Liberator*? You must have very serious business. I'll not bother you."

"Stay." Garrison extended his hand. "I rescued Alex from my doorstep, and it seems he's lost a day of his life. Alex, this gentleman is John Greenleaf Whittier, one of America's serious poets."

Slowly Alex said, "Sir, I've read some of your work. And some of it is salt in the wound down South."

"I'm surprised an abolitionist is allowed in the South, even if he's on newsprint."

"Barely tolerated," Alex admitted, studying the slender man with the arms and shoulders of a farmer. "I don't suggest you follow your papers into the South, but I would like to ask you some questions."

"About my feelings on slavery?"

"No." Alex paused, watching the open, honest face. "Sir, forgive me if my questions are presumptuous. Your poetry seems to reflect an intimacy with God. Is this an art form I don't understand?"

"No, it is reality. I suppose you are referring to my alluding to the light within."

"I gather this relates to your being a Quaker," Alex said stiffly.

"No, it is more related to being human and having the touch of the Divine in our lives, which is what God the Father has planned all along. Through Jesus Christ." John's words reached through Alex's silence. "Look, you're not in condition for much of anything. I have my delivery wagon outside; let me give you a ride back to the college."

Alex dropped his head into his hands. "Right now, I don't feel like I can face the pack. Is there any place I can hole up around here? I need to do some thinking."

"A woman problem?"

Alex looked up at Garrison, grinned, and then clapped his hands to his head. "Ouch! I wish it were so simple. I feel like someone turned the South upside down, shook it, and I fell out."

Out of the long silence, Garrison said, "Just perhaps you can stick around long enough to learn to tolerate the smell of printer's ink. I could use a hand around here. What rubs off on you besides printer's ink might not hurt you a particle. Now come on and have a bite to eat; it'll settle your stomach and maybe your head."

————

Whittier faced the young man dabbing ink on the type. "Alex, you've been here over a week now. You've picked Garrison's mind as well as my own. I have the feeling you're hedging. Why don't you just come out and ask the question you have on your mind?"

Alex stood up, and his head nearly touched the rafters in the press room. His eyes were troubled as he faced the poet. "Sir," he said slowly, "to tell the honest truth, I'm not certain what the question is."

"You've asked about the movement until I think I've about run dry of information," Whittier said. "You've even attended a meeting. How do you feel about all you've heard?"

Alex wiped his hands. "I've been impressed with the dedication of these people, to the point where I am ashamed of myself. I get the feeling they're poor people, and perhaps mistreated because of their fervor to free the slaves. But the question that's stuck in my craw is *Why?* I want to know the *whys* behind their actions. I certainly can't see myself acting like this."

"I thought it was something like that." Whittier folded the stack of newspapers. "You've been asking about the inner light until I've about decided I need to start asking you some questions."

"What kind of questions?"

"Well, maybe I need to tell you what I believe about the God and man relationship."

"I'm not certain I believe in such a relationship."

"That might be why you can't formulate a question." Whittier glanced at Alex. "I suppose you're a church member."

"Of course, but I have a feeling that has nothing to do with the matter at hand. Whittier, I'm more interested in things of the mind than I am in a nebulous faith. I got all the religion I wanted when I joined the church."

Whittier sat down on a bench and rested his arms on his knees, leaning forward he watched Alex's expression as he said, "How do you feel about your relationship to God through church membership?"

Alex shrugged, "The way I'm supposed to feel—secure, comfortable. I'm happy with it. It's just that I'm not content with life."

"Have you considered the possibility that belonging to the kingdom of God may require more than being comfortable? I've had to do a considerable amount of thinking on this. I had to understand that being reconciled with God means being able to live before Him in a straightforward manner."

"Mind explaining?"

"I had to decide whether Whittier's ideas about life were more important than Jesus Christ's."

"That goes without saying," Alex muttered, dabbing more ink.

"There's a difference between saying and doing. Really believing demands action. If I say His thoughts are more important, I'd better make them mine. If His plans have a higher intelligence behind them, then why push mine? Get the picture? As a Christian I feel an obligation to find out what pleases the Lord and do it. Alex, I still must constantly check my desires, ideas, and plans against His."

Alex shook his head. "That sounds like a heavy load. Granted, you make the light within sound attractive, but I can't see myself living this way. Guess I need something a little more—earthy."

"You wanted to know the whys of my life. That's it. I can see this doesn't seem exciting to you now, and I won't bother you with more except to say that a genuine relationship with the Lord Jesus Christ is life changing. I am not the man I once was, and I treasure the change."

Whittier watched Alex continue to dab ink on the type. His head was bowed. Finally with a sigh, Whittier got to his feet. "Might be we can talk about this later; for now that's enough. Alex, you could discuss it with the Lord."

"Thanks for explaining, John," Alex glanced at him. "I hope you won't be offended if I say 'no thanks' to your ideas. Somehow I can't be convinced it's what I need."

Olivia came down the stairs just as the young gentleman turned. "Matthew!" she gasped. "They told me I had a visitor. What brings you here?"

She looked at his sober face and led him into the parlor. "Have you had bad news from home?"

"No," he moved restlessly on the chair, chewed at his lip and said, "I guess this is crazy, but I've come to see if you know anything about Alexander Duncan."

"Alex," she said slowly. "That drunk young man you brought to the reception?"

"Well, he isn't the only one who carried the title that night," Matthew said with a small smile. "Sorry, sister, dear. We deserve your scorn. I suppose it's a question of the utmost stupidity, but since Alex seemed smitten, I thought it was worth a try. You know he manages to ask about you at least once a week. Or he did. I don't know where he is. No one knows."

Smitten. Her hands touched her hot face. *Will I never forget that outrageous kiss?* She concentrated on the picture of the tousled dark hair, the teasing blue eyes. "I can't forget the picture your friend presented that night. It was disgusting. Matt, I've had absolutely no communication with him, nor you since that night." He winced and muttered.

"Now it is nearly the end of the school year," she added. "What do you intend to do this summer?"

"Go home, of course. I don't suppose Father has said anything to you, but I've already decided to step out of school next year."

"You're not going to school?" Olivia looked intently at her brother's face. "I had no idea there was a problem. I did get the feeling that Mother wasn't at all disappointed with me when I told her I wouldn't attend the academy next term. She merely said we would discuss it at home."

She stopped, thought again of those teasing eyes, and the words spilled out, "Oh, Matthew, here we are talking about school, and you don't know where—what ever is wrong with your friend?"

"He was due to meet the scholastic board three weeks ago. I know that he had an appointment with a Mr. Mallory. The gentleman saw Alex, escorted him to the door, and that's the last he has heard of him. Alex was to have seen him later, but he didn't return." Matthew jumped to his feet and paced the room.

"I feel responsible, mostly because I was the last to see him, and I didn't get the idea he was terribly happy. It's been that way recently. It seems we've spent more time in bull sessions than in class. But I do believe he valued passing his exams."

Out of the silence, as Olivia thought back to that night, she asked in a timid voice, "You say he inquires about me? I wonder why?"

Matthew looked at her. "I don't have the slightest idea."

"Matt!"

"Oh come on, Olivia; it's simply because you are a girl." He stood up and sighed. "I've got to go. Final examinations are coming up next week. Mother has asked me to escort you home, so I'll be contacting you after the term has finished."

"What are you going to do about Alex?"

"I don't know. So far, the only action I've considered is writing to his parents. That will involve my going to the dean for Alex's home address, unless I rummage around in his room. I don't relish either. I hope the school has done something."

He picked up his hat and headed for the door. "Will you please let me know what comes of the whole affair?" Olivia asked.

He nodded and clattered down the steps. Olivia leaned against the door and thought of the blue-eyed giant who had swung her around the kitchen and pressed those kisses on her unwilling mouth. Unwilling? Again Olivia pressed her hands against her warm cheeks.

CHAPTER 10

The view out Crystal's bedroom window was of an old and gently settled part of New Orleans. She could see rooftops, gardens, trees, and on clear days, a slice of the Mississippi River. She could hear the hacks passing up and down the cobbled streets, accompanied by conversation in the softened syllables of the South or peppered with impatient French.

She smiled as she recalled the sometimes nasal quality of Northern speech, but her smile ended in a soft sigh. "Dear Olivia," she murmured, "how I miss you, and how I long to see you again!"

As she turned from the window, Crystal glanced at the neglected writing desk, with its gilded feather quill and leaded-glass inkwell resting beside the box of heavy vellum stationery. Her sigh faded to brooding as she slipped her fingers across the paper and touched the pile of pencils.

The door opened and the dark face crinkled into a question. "Missy, you still here? Breakfast is long past. Want I should bring you a bite?"

"No, I don't feel like eating. Has Mama gone to her room?"

The black woman, Tammera, nodded slowly. Her sharp eyes shamed Crystal, and as she turned back to the window, Tammera said, " 'Tis bad it turned out so. Causing you to leave school, it did.

I know you're thinking otherwise, but your mama was desperately ill and the Massa thought it best to fetch you home." Again a fleeting curiosity arose in Crystal as Tammera turned away, saying, "I'll just tidy up now, then I won't have to climb the stairs again 'fore lunch time."

Crystal continued to gaze out the window at chimneys as the slave pounded the pillows and shook the comforter. "Missy Sugar-lam—" The heavy voice cut through Crystal's thoughts, irritating her with the familiar baby name. "You's not helping us with your grumps."

"I'm not grumping."

"That mood's as long as a snake, and the dear Lord knows it probably came from the ole serpent. Haven't we talked enough about how a body's to listen to the good Lord and not to that old enemy? Have your been forgetting the prayers you learned at old Auntie T's knees? Now you just quit your moaning about being lonesome and set yourself down and write a nice letter to Missy Olivia. 'Tis a shame you've waited this long."

"I suppose I just don't know how to say it all. How do I tell her all when I don't understand it myself? Auntie T, when Father came to Boston, we were all frightened. Now how do I say that Mama is well, I am bored, and everything's come to naught?"

"Why you call your papa Father, like he's a priest? Northern ways, huh?"

"I suppose."

"I think he like his girl to call him Papa." Now there was a gentle smile on the old woman's face. She came to pat Crystal on the head and said, "Your mama is having her breakfast in bed. She's feeling poorly this morning. Go take her a rose and she may give you some of her new writing paper for that letter. Now hurry along."

———

Crystal paused in front of her mother's bedroom door, suddenly feeling foolish. Staring down at the pink rose in her hand, she murmured, "Oh, Auntie T, why do I let you talk me into something so childish? I'm a grown woman, not a baby." But a smile started on her lips as she remembered the countless times the slave woman had been there with her hand planted firmly in Crystal's back.

Opening the door cautiously, she tiptoed into the room. Her mother wasn't in bed, but was seated on the floor beside an empty drawer. "*Maman!*" Crystal rushed across the room as her mother lifted her tear-dampened face. Dropping to her knees, she peered into her mother's face. "Have you hurt yourself? Did you fall?"

Shaking her head, her mother pushed aside Crystal's arms and gathered a bundle of papers to her. With the papers secreted in the folds of her gown, she gave a painful smile and said, "Crystal, my dear, you are still to knock before entering."

"Oh, Mama," Crystal choked. "It was Tammera. She suggested I bring you this rose. I—" Crystal stopped suddenly. Spotting the faded ribbon, she realized her mother was holding the same bundle of papers she had seen bearing the name Evangeline Cabet. Catching her breath, Crystal reached toward the bundle. "Oh, I see—" Her mother tightened her grasp on the papers, shielding them under the ruffles of her dressing gown.

Crystal's smile faded as she watched the trembling fingers fumble with the ribbon. Whispering, her mother said, "Just some old things. Don't be *curiosite*."

"Of course, *Maman*." Crystal got to her feet and added, "I'll just put the rose in water. Do you want me to help you?" Her mother shook her head. Crystal watched the short plump woman struggle to her feet. The flushed cheeks and the drift of white through her mother's hair gave Crystal a pang of remorse. "Your hair looks as if it's been left out in a Boston snowstorm."

Impulsively Crystal reached for her. "I'm sorry I've neglected you, Mama. Now that you are better, let's go shopping or have Papa take us out to Uncle Pierre's." She paused, then said in a rush, "Sometimes I wish we still lived on the plantation instead of here in town. I miss the fields and horses."

Mama gave her a quick look. "You are much too old to be playing with the pickaninnies."

Crystal sighed, "No matter. What would you care to do today?"

"I have an appointment with Dr. Oliver again this afternoon." She hurried on, "You'll just have to amuse yourself. Why don't you get in touch with one of your friends? You never see them anymore."

When Crystal walked back to her bedroom, Tammera was still there. The slave lifted an armload of frocks saying, "These all need a mite of stitching or a freshening up." She paused. "Weren't gone long. Was she asleep?"

Crystal shook her head. "Auntie T, I think you need to tell me something. Why was Mama so upset last year when I helped myself to some jewelry from her case? And why wouldn't you tell me anything about Evangeline Cabet?"

The woman threw up her hands. "Missy! Don't you go backing me in the corner. I'll not tell you a speck. Now don't give me no trouble."

"Then I shall be forced to ask Mama, and she was very upset when I found her looking at those same papers today." Crystal watched in amazement as the slave dropped her hands.

With a trembling chin she touched Crystal and whispered, "Missy Sugarlam, don't you go say nothing. I tell you it will kill your mama to know you've been pryin'."

"Then you should know something. In Boston I went to the house—the one whose address was on the papers." At the look of dismay on Tammera's face, Crystal added, "You might credit me with not reading the letters when I found them."

The woman nodded. "I do. But that address. You didn't find out anything." The black chin jutted out. "It's been years ago, and I'm sure the old lady is dead."

"You are wrong. She's very much alive. She kindly took out an album and showed me a picture of Evangeline."

Tammera clutched Crystal's arm. With her face close, she whispered, "Missy, don't you ever let on to your mama that you've been to that place. It was for that reason you had to come home!"

She paused, wiped the perspiration from her face, righted the mob-cap, and then leaning close she whispered, "After your mama come back from Boston, they got to having second thoughts about you being so close to that place. Your mama worried herself sick, wouldn't give your papa no rest until he fetched you home."

"Then why did they let me go to Boston?"

"All these recommends." She shook her head sadly. "Even Father Celeste thought it would be safe to send you there."

"Is Evangeline my aunt?"

Tammera studied her face. The worry lines lifted, and slowly she said, "Then you really didn't find out a thing. And sure enough you won't find out a smidgen more from me."

As Tammera hurried out of the room, Crystal watched, saying, "I know only that the mention of her name is enough to make everyone act very strange."

———

Crystal's father put aside his newspaper during breakfast the following week and said, "The weather is fine enough for you young ladies. Will you accompany me to the plantation? Pierre has asked me to go over the books with him, and I see no reason why we can't make this an outing. Pack a case; we'll be gone at least two nights."

Mama carefully replaced her fork and said, "Oh, my dear husband, I think it is best we don't. I have business to detain me, and most certainly it will be an undesirable trip for Crystal."

"Oh, *Maman*, I do desire it!" Crystal leaned forward to implore her father. "Oh, please! I won't create a problem. Spring in the country! The azaleas are in bloom. I want to walk among the dogwood and smell the wet forest again. It's been so long."

In between her long imploring looks and quick words, Crystal knew she would go. Later that morning, settled beside her father in the carriage, she murmured, "Thank you! I've missed being with the cousins nearly as much as I've missed the horses and pasture!"

He laughed. "Be grateful! I consigned myself to this pace when I could have been on horseback. And don't do anything to cause *Maman* alarm, or I will answer for it."

Crystal smiled up at him. Touching his cheek, she caught her breath, noting the new lines on his face. "Papa, you need this, too. You seem tired."

"Just old." He paused and said reluctantly, "Very old. Sometimes it seems as if there's too much of life to regret. Daughter, live carefully. The French in us leads to impetuous acts."

"Regret? Papa dear, I can't see you regretting anything, you are too sure, confident." He winced, opening his mouth as if to speak, and then merely smiled.

"Nevertheless," he said, "it is good to be with you. Let's enjoy the day. I've already planned to stop at an inn that serves the best gumbo I've ever eaten."

They did enjoy each other's company and when they stopped at the inn, Crystal ordered some of the gumbo and decided that her father's assessment of it was correct.

After lunch their route took them deeper into bayou country. The road wound along the river bank, beside stately trees dropping curtains of Spanish moss across their path.

When they arrived at Twin Oaks, Crystal's happiness was dampened only slightly when they discovered Aunt Belle and the cousins were away from home for the week. Kissing her uncle she assured him, "Never you mind. Just let me have a groom and a horse, and I shall ride to my heart's content!"

In the morning, with dawn only a rosy glow in the east, Crystal tiptoed into the kitchen. The cook blinked in surprise, and then nodded as Crystal said, "Just coffee and *pain beurre*." Carrying her bread to the kitchen table Crystal said, "This is a treat! I don't often eat in the kitchen." She hurried and finished the meal. "Now, tell me where to find my groom, and I shall head for the stable."

The cook widened her eyes and shrugged. "Missy, I'll call someone to take you to the stable."

"Never mind," she said hastily, "I know the way." Flicking the last crumb off her riding habit, she headed for the door.

The dew was still heavy. She observed the last of the spring blossoms drooping under the weight of the dew while the budding roses and azaleas cupped droplets of water. Pulling a rose from the brush beside the pasture fence she went into the stable. The horses were being curried. "Hello!" she called. "Nexus, are you here?"

A dark face peered over a horse in the nearest stall. "No, ma'am, Nexus took a colt down the way. Want I should get him?"

She peered through the gloom. "Uncle Pierre said he would have a groom to ride with me. But you'll do. Will you saddle up for me? My name is Crystal."

He stepped out of the stall, touched his forehead and with a troubled voice said, "Ma'am, miss, I—" His voice faded away, slowly he stepped forward. With a strange expression on his face, he said hesitantly, "If you'll wait for me to ask—"

"Of course," she said, impatiently turning away. In a moment the door closed. Walking to the window she watched the Negro striding down the lane. A door slammed behind her and she turned as a slave hung his tack and asked, "Joseph went to find Nexus?"

"Oh, Tim, I didn't know you were here. Joseph?" she questioned. "That is the slave's name? He's new?"

"No, missy, Joseph's been here as long as I remember. He's been working in the fields until this spring. Had troubles, and Massa say he too old to work the fields any longer." He looked puzzled as he added, "He's your Uncle Pierre's best hand. But I reckon you don't know Joseph belongs to you folks. Yes, missy, he been here a long time." The low voice went on as he moved about the stable, replacing tools and getting out the bridle.

"You want one of them lady saddles? All growed up now, you can't be comfortable on a horse fer the rest of your life." His chuckle was low and easy.

She smiled at him. "Tim, you must admit ladies look elegant sidesaddle."

The door opened. Tim said, "Joseph, what's the matter with you? You look all blowed out."

Joseph shook his head slowly, reminding Crystal of a colt trying to shake off a confining halter. "Nexus says I'm to take missy Crystal riding." Tim turned slowly, and Joseph said, "It's all right; Nexus says so. He needs you for the day."

By the time they rode out of the pasture the sun had dried the dripping flower stalks and set them upright. When Crystal rode ahead, she flipped her reins and called back, "Joseph, I'm heading up the trail; I want to ride into the timber."

He nodded. She noticed he was still watching her in that uncertain way as if he had to memorize every detail of her. For a moment she hesitated, frowning as she bent forward to look at his face. As he rode close he murmured, "Missy, it's all right." Again she saw his troubled eyes and noted the timid touch of his hand to his forehead.

"Yes," she said slowly, wondering both at her confidence and this strange expression on the man's face. "Tim tells me that you are Father's slave; I wonder that I've never seen you before."

"Father?" he said slowly. "You must be Crystal Cabet."

She saw in his face what she had missed in the dusk of the stable. His skin was light and his eyes gray. *Sometimes these kind are arrogant, insolent; the white blood ruins them. They don't know where they belong.*

Crystal hesitated, watching his humble but honest gaze. Somehow confidence that she could trust this man grew in her.

In silence they rode the dim trail beyond the pasture and cotton fields, deep into the timber and on up a gentle rise. She knew from past excursions that the trail led to a bluff overlooking the river, and she turned the horse on to it.

When she reached the bluff, she tugged at the reins and held her mount motionless. Gradually, over the restless chatter of birds and the rustle of creeping things, she heard a new sound.

Finally she whispered, "Joseph, do I hear a steamboat?"

"Yes, missy," he answered. "I hear them all the time from up here."

She turned. "That sound is exciting. It makes me want to go. Do you—" He turned away, but she had seen the haunting desire. "I'm sorry," she whispered, "sometimes we forget."

"That we have those kind of feelings too?" For a moment the timbre of his voice changed. She looked into his face. He turned away, but not before she saw the expression in his eyes.

Trembling, she tugged her horse around, asking in a low voice, "Do you want to be free?" Rushing on she said, "I can't believe it. You Negroes seem content, even happy. Certainly you're well cared for."

He pointed at the small brown bird overhead. " 'Spect if you grab that bird he won't want to be free?" When his eyes met hers they burned.

"You hate us, don't you?"

Unexpectedly the expression in his eyes softened. He held out his hand. For a moment she thought he would touch her. "Missy, no one on God's earth could hate you, and He won't let me hate—" he hesitated, added lamely, "the others."

"You have a reason to hate?"

His head drooped. When she could bear the silence no longer, he said, "Most of us can find a reason."

Crystal flipped the quirt and turned her horse down the trail.

They didn't speak for the remainder of the ride. When they reached the pasture, Crystal reined in her horse. "Help me dismount. I'll let you take the horses in from here."

He avoided her eyes as he knelt on one knee and extended a hand.

Taking his hand, she jumped lightly, barely touching his knee with her foot. "Thank you, Joseph," she murmured, walking away.

Crystal had crossed the deeply shaded veranda and entered the hall before she heard her father's voice, coming from Uncle Pierre's office. As she hesitated, her father's voice, loud but carefully controlled, said, "Pierre, Nexus told me Joseph rode out with Crystal. I've given you strict orders to keep that slave in the field."

"Settle down, Brother," came Pierre's soothing voice. "I expect a little jurisdiction over a slave working for me. Joseph is totally trustworthy. He will not contaminate Crystal by his presence. If anyone is to be trusted around her, surely it will be—"

"I will not allow you to address the subject," came her father's angry voice. "Why were my orders disobeyed?"

"Because Joseph is getting to be an old man. He is no longer able to work the fields and keep up with the younger hands."

"Then keep him there until he drops, and then send him to the manure pile. If he can't lift, he can use a shovel until he dies."

Pierre's voice came, now strangely calm. "This is all out of proportion. Joseph is a good man. If there is blame to be placed, then it is only fair to place it on her."

There was silence. From Crystal's stance with one foot on the stairs, she watched the kitchen slaves melt back into the shadows. Controlled, low, and brittle, her father's voice said, "If you were not my brother, I would call you out for that."

"Then let there be no more said between us." Pierre dragged out the words. "It shall be as you say, although it would seem more humane to sell him now."

"Perhaps."

Crystal came off the stairs and started for the office. There was a firm hand on her arm. "Missy." The cook looked at her with a troubled face. "You say anything to your father, now or ever, and Joseph will die for it."

"For what?" Crystal whispered. The woman shook her head and trotted toward the kitchen.

CHAPTER 11

The late autumn rain had soaked the South Carolina landscape from pine forest to rice fields. As Alex bent his head against the slicing rain, he noticed water puddled in the roads. It spilled over the embankments, drowning the low vegetation miserably beaten by the week of rain.

When he reached home his mind still held that view of nature, powerless and defeated before the onslaught of rain. Handing his horse over to the groom, Alex muttered, "Only rain can successfully dominate thistles. Wonder what Shakespeare had to say about the arrogance of man against nature?"

With a shrug, Alex carried the newspaper and the letters into the library. Dropping them on his father's desk, he hung his dripping jacket by the tiny fire burning for the sole purpose of drying the air.

"How did you manage to keep this newspaper dry?" the senior Duncan asked as he sorted through the mail.

"By resisting the urge to drape it over my head. It rode home under my jacket. I thought you'd be interested in the headlines."

"Without a doubt." Duncan unfolded the paper.

Alex quoted, " 'Republican Convention of 1856 nominates Colonel Fremont as presidential candidate.' "

"So Fremont wants to be the President of these United States," the elder Duncan mused.

"We were getting wind of this before I left Boston." Dropping the paper, his father glared at him. Wincing, Alex murmured, "I know it's a sore spot, but Father, what's done is done."

"You could refrain from mentioning Boston. But it shall be un-done, young man. Fortunately, with your standing in the class, it will be possible for you to return, take your punishment—which will be less work than you deserve—and be ready for your examinations before the New Year rolls around."

"Father, it wasn't a pique. I'd been having trouble swallowing Mallory's line from the beginning. I don't like being coerced into supporting any cause under the semblance of obligation, and in a mindless fashion. And he seemed to imply that I'm one of the boys without enough brains to be able to plot my own course in life."

"Mm," came the murmur from behind the paper.

Alex tried to keep his exasperation under control with a quick pace across the room and back. He addressed the newspaper, "It seemed the only way I could get out of it without hurting you and your relationship with Mallory."

The newspaper came down. The elder Duncan smacked his fist against it and said, "I don't agree with the thinking behind this. Seems Douglas opened a can of worms when he pushed the Kansas-Nebraska Bill through. It was premature. There's been nothing but trouble. First, the Missourians stepped out of line just long enough to give us all a bad name. States' rights must be honorably won."

Alex nodded, "I agree, Father, but on the other hand, perhaps another political party won't be all that bad."

"Well, we soon find out. This convention of the newly formed Republican Party, according to this article, is 'comprised of abolition-ists, Whigs, and every trouble-monger alive.' "

Alex chuckled, "Definitely written with a Southern flavor. Well, a good political fight will probably clear the air." He paused and then leaned forward, "Seriously, Father, for the past two years I've been hearing the Kansas-Nebraska Bill discussed by everyone, from tavern keepers to preachers."

The senior Duncan leaned forward and said slowly, "You didn't mention it to me."

"I didn't know what to think of it."

"Well, what did you hear?"

"That Douglas was oiling his own political wheels. But more important than that is the effect it has had." He paused, picked up his father's letter opener, and studied it. "It's had a significant impact on the thinking of the North." Glancing at his father, he added, "About slavery. They are no longer apathetic. In the final six months I was there, I heard more voices raised, saying 'slavery must go,' than in all time previously. Father, I have a very strong feeling this is going to be an issue that can't be legislated out of existence or compromised in any way."

His father's face was still. Carefully he said, "You appear to have made a decision."

Alex took a deep breath. "I'm not certain. You've known for years that I don't live comfortably with slavery. And I know I'll not let Mallory groom me for a political role for the cause of the South, which is the furtherance of slavery."

For a moment his father gripped the arms of his chair, then he settled back with a sigh and tapped the newspaper. "Nevertheless, the Kansas-Nebraska Bill has opened up the possibility of slavery in all states. That is a plus for us. Each state will have the right to decide for itself. Let those who oppose slavery voice their desires, all fair and square, and we'll see who has his way." His chuckle of glee overlapped Alex's statement.

"You don't think there's a possibility that being pig-headed about it will split the Union?" Alex winced as he said the words. The idea that had dogged his thoughts was out.

He watched his father carefully rearrange the papers on his desk as he said, "Alex, If you've read this paper then you know the sentiment of the South, as well as her power. Take the Charles Sumner incident. He should have known better than to use those inflammatory labels on Southern gentlemen."

"Surely Southern papers have reflected the insolence displayed by our Southern gentlemen," Alex said heavily. "When Preston Brooks was readmitted to the Senate, he was presented with a number of gold-headed canes. But that isn't the end of the inflammatory statements. With the Republican nomination of Colonel Fremont, Governor Wise of Virginia stated that if Fremont were to win the presidency, he would personally, with his militia, march on Washington and seize the Capitol and the National Archives. Father, there's enough red blood in Northerners to get riled over a statement like that."

"Son—" He leaned across the desk and with flashing eyes demanded, "Are you afraid to fight for a cause you believe in?"

"I'm not afraid to fight. I just want to be fighting for the right cause. Right now I'm having doubts."

Alex was nearly to the door when his father added, "The first thing you'll need to do is pass your final examinations."

With his hand on the knob, Alex said, "Not until I'm certain that is the way I want to spend the next year. Meanwhile, until I make up my mind, I'm taking Caleb and heading for Louisiana. I want to put the boat back in running order. Might take it up the Mississippi to see an old friend of mine. I'm ashamed of this, but I didn't get around to telling him goodbye before I left Boston."

Carrying the letter, Olivia wandered through the house and into the kitchen looking for Matthew. At her question, the cook straightened and pointed her knife toward the back door. "He headed out just a few minutes ago. Was wearing his riding togs." She called after Olivia, "Now missy, don't you go riding in that dress."

Matthew was at the stable. There was an ebony face lined along beside his as he lifted his mare's foot. "That shoe is nearly off. Take care of it, Ned." He glanced up at Olivia and nodded. Spotting the letter, he asked, "What do you have?"

"A letter from the cousins. Feel like escorting me to Natchez? You're invited, too." She added, "It's from Lynda. They will be celebrating her birthday with a week of merrymaking. A ball on Friday, proceeded by a trip on a boat, proceeded by a fox hunt on Monday."

"Fox hunt!" Matthew snorted, "Aren't we getting uppity in our old age!"

"Now Matthew, if it were your idea, you would think it grand."

"Don't get me wrong," he said hastily, "I've every intention of going and enjoying myself enormously. It just takes me by surprise, the plain Jane cousins putting on such airs. My guess is they don't want to risk having another old maid on their hands."

Olivia grinned. "Be nice to me, or I'll tell Mother you called her favorite niece an old maid."

"Might add, a sour old maid."

"Matthew, just for that you must devote yourself to her."

"When will all this take place?"

"Not until June, which gives you time to order new finery!"

He gave her a playful shove. "And for you to steal my old dungarees for bareback riding. I heard you fussing about Mother taking the liberty, while you were in Boston, of discarding the last pair you confiscated from me."

Olivia studied the letter. "I can hardly wait. But it's three months away. She must be excited too, writing this early. Also, she said you are allowed to bring a guest if you so desire. I think she means male. Too bad that nice Henry boy is gone for the summer."

She lowered the letter and looked at Matthew. "You've missed school terribly this year, haven't you? What do you suppose happened to that Alexander Duncan? He hasn't even written to you and it's been ages—nearly a year since he took off like that."

Matthew threw a quick glance at Olivia as they walked back to the house. "Why do you care?" he asked, "You've given me a million reasons why you don't like him. Which is strange considering you've met him only once."

"But don't forget, he made a terrific impression on me that one time, with his tie crooked and that terrible ale on his breath."

Matthew's face came close to Olivia's. He lifted an eyebrow. "Hmm, you were close enough to smell that! Olivia, I shall tell Mother."

She poked his arm. "He talked incessantly about himself."

"What did he say?" She shrugged and Matthew added, "Olivia, you've neglected no occasion to ask about Alex. Shall I tell Mother to stop pushing that big, fat, old farmer on you, telling her that you are already in love?"

"Fat! Thaddeus isn't fat, he's—you are baiting me." She stopped in the path and watched Matthew.

"You look very serious," he said soberly. "Tell me, is it Alex?"

"No, I'm wondering about you. Why did you decide you wouldn't return to school this year?"

"I—I really can't say." Glancing sideways at her, he added, "Maybe it had something to do with last year. You know Alex and I had time to do plenty of talking. Maybe we talked ourselves out of every illusion we had."

"Illusion? Matt, say what you mean—I don't understand."

"Well, for one, we saw a completely different version of life. Life the Northern way isn't so kind to Southern ideology, namely slavery. It made both of us shuffle our thoughts a bit. Alex seemed to be leaning more toward abolitionist thinking about the time he disappeared. Wouldn't surprise me if he surfaces in their camp. Me? I didn't want to be indoctrinated, which was nearly the way our talks were leading. Olivia, there's plenty wrong with the system, but it'll take a stronger man than I am to make any changes."

"Oh, Matt, I can't believe you're serious. But anyway, I agree. I can't see you in any role except as a comfortable Southern gentleman. Certainly Father would prefer that."

"Maybe we are no long gullible children," Matthew brooded. "Olivia, when you strip away the illusion, you have to replace it with something. Might be neither Alex nor I could find a replacement." He turned to grin at her. "Now how is that for a lecture from an elder brother?"

"Do you think Alex is dead?"

He shook his head, "No. I think he just got tired of it all and shipped out on a steamboat bound for Africa."

"Why for Africa?"

The grin faded from his face. "I don't know. I think at heart he's a do-gooder. Where else would a fellow from South Carolina go?"

"Matt, you are impossible."

He poked at the grass with his foot. "Livie, honestly, what did you think of all the talk floating around in Boston?"

She stopped in the path. Thinking back, slowly she said, "I was astonished at the things I heard. They said very bad things about the South, but I was even more astonished at the hard criticism they had of themselves. Don't they have a sense of brotherhood?"

"Just maybe in the North brotherhood means being responsible for your brother to the point of arguing, begging, even being certain he's got his head on straight."

"I think you are talking about religion, not politics."

"Is there a difference? Thought is thought."

"Is that all religion is, just thought?" He shrugged and strode ahead. She followed him into the house, calling, "But in the end, I believe we will be seen as right. Certainly we have more compassion for people."

CHAPTER 12

The March rains had given way to sunshine. The warmth of the Louisiana sun was welcome on Alex's bare back as he scraped flaking varnish from the hull of the little sternwheel steamboat. Hearing a step behind him, Alex looked up. His arms loaded with cans and bags, Caleb grinned down at him. "Looks mighty fine. You intend stripping off that pretty name? Who was Sally Belle?"

Alex shrugged. "It was there when we bought the boat."

Caleb reached out to stroke the bare wood. "Found a boiler man who'll come out as soon as we get it afloat. Want I should go to scrapin' too? There's a powerful lot to be done on that boat."

Alex stepped back to look at her blistered length. "All one hundred and twenty feet of her needs scraping and varnish." He grinned at Caleb. "I'm getting anxious to try her out. If the weather holds fair, we should be putting the last coat on her about the end of April. If repairs on the engine are easy, and the boiler doesn't need to be replaced, we'll be on our way soon. Hopefully we can be moving up the Mississippi by the end of May."

Caleb shook his head. "Me? I'm no steamboat man, but I don't like the looks of the paddles. They seem wobbly like."

Alex sighed, pushed his hair off his forehead and said, "Caleb, take that can of grease to the engine room. Careful, don't rock her off the skids."

Alex went back to his work. When Caleb rejoined him, he picked up a scraper and dragged it along the bow. "Does come off right smart." He paused dreamily. "My, New Orleans is pretty—tulips and all just blooming their hearts out." He chuckled. "The young ladies are all blooming out in spring colors too. Alex, you ought to be in town getting acquainted with them ladies instead of sticking out here on the mudflats. It's not like you need to be running your pappy's cotton patch; that Jim 'pears to be a good overseer." As an afterthought, he added, "He don't mistreat the field hands none."

Alex threw Caleb a startled glance and then ducked his head to sight along the curve of the bow. "Thanks for being concerned about my love life, but to tell the truth, I hadn't felt a lack. Guess I'd rather be scraping old varnish."

In a minute, while the scratch of Caleb's scraper spurred him on, Alex asked, "Caleb, are you married?"

"No, suh. Just as well. You folks keep me hoppin' around." He added hastily, "And that's just fine with me."

The morning sun positioned itself overhead and the only sound was the swish of the scrapers as they worked. When Alex straightened and stepped away from the dry-docked boat, he flexed his shoulders and sunburned arms while he studied the line of green separating the mudflats from the cotton fields.

The mudflats had created a border along the western edge of the fields, while its eastern edge was filled with old oak, redgum, and osage-orange. As he squinted into the sun, a rabbit hopped across the high ground and a flock of ducks rose from the marshy pond.

"Man, oh man," Caleb muttered, "that drake would make good eating."

Alex turned to look at the black man, only then conscious that Caleb's words had replaced his contented humming. "Pretty tune you were humming—what was it?"

Caleb ducked his head apologetically. "Was 'Steal Away'—to Jesus," he added quickly slanting a glance at Alex.

"Steal away," Alex said slowly as he flexed the blade of the scraper. When he abruptly raised his head, he caught Caleb's eye. "Is that one of those songs that's supposed to have a double meaning?"

Caleb fixed his eyes on the ground. "Guess so."

Alex shifted his feet. "Look, I'm not down on you for having thoughts like that."

Caleb straightened his shoulders, "I'm not; and suh, I'd rather be slave than cheat. You folks treat me good, and I try to be honorable."

Alex sighed with resignation. Caleb's words uncorked painful thoughts he had been avoiding. He recalled the Boston harbor incident with the runaway slave—Burns was the slave's name. Strange how the man's expression had carried its own message; even now it brought to mind words like *demeaned and hopeless*. Alex examined the sore spot in his own heart, the one that had grown there after exposure first to Mallory and then to the abolitionist, Garrison. At times he wondered if he would ever be able to shake those memories.

Glancing at Caleb's bowed head, Alex took a deep breath and asked, "Don't you have a desire to be free?"

The man shuffled his feet. Finally lifting his head, he said, "Even given all the druthers? Yes."

"What are the druthers?"

His face twisted strangely before a slight smile appeared. "That my master decide I'm the best slave on earth and leave me a million dollars and a big plantation when he die."

Alex tried to laugh with Caleb.

———

On the day they began laying the varnish on the boat, using broad, long strokes, Caleb asked a favor of Alex. Conscious of the rhythm created by their days of shared labor, Alex put aside his brush and turned to face the slave. "You want me to read the Bible to you? Why?"

"I don't know how to read, and I want to learn some verses." He stopped, took a deep breath, and added, "You have a Bible in your room; I saw it. See, back home I heard a brother talk about something, and I want to learn it."

Alex thought about the Bible. It had been a gift from his mother just before he left South Carolina. They both recognized it as her frantic attempt to bridge the widening gulf between him and his father. He recalled the wall of hostility his Northern thoughts had created. *Between the gesture Mother made and the expression on Father's face, I nearly pitched that book in the fire*, he mused, wincing as he thought of all the budding ideas he had tossed away in the angry moment. Garrison and Whittier had generated a lot of thoughts, coinciding with his passion to change the South, starting at his own doorstep.

He visualized his father's face and admitted he dare not consider his desires. In the next moment he thought of Caleb. Where did family loyalties end and this strange responsibility begin?

He looked up and saw the eagerness on Caleb's face. "Caleb," he said slowly, "do you know that the Caleb in the Bible was known as a man of great faith?"

Caleb nodded as he spoke, "Yes, suh, and I think it would do me great good to be like him."

"Then," Alex said, "tomorrow I will bring the Bible with us. It seems more fitting to read it here, with the ducks squawking, the fish jumping, and the wind blowing through the gumtrees."

"And the sun shining on us all." Caleb beamed at Alex, and in a rush of words confided, "I want to learn Psalm forty and have you read to me in Deuteronomy, the fifteenth chapter, about all it means in the Psalm."

"All it means?" Alex questioned, "Are you telling me your brother said Deuteronomy explains the Psalm?" Caleb nodded and Alex pursed his lips. "It could be just his own ideas, but we'll take a look."

The next morning, just outside his door, Alex discovered Caleb armed with bread and meat, tucked in with more turpentine and new brushes. With an eager grin, he waited. His dark eyes darted to Alex's hand. Returning his grin, Alex said, "I didn't forget. Did you remember the coffee?"

"No suh," Caleb grinned happily, "but if you stack it on the turpentine, I can carry it."

By ten o'clock Alex sensed Caleb's fidgeting. Grinning at him over the tip of the bow, Alex said, "Aren't you glad this boat draws just three feet of water?"

"If you going to take it on the Mississippi in the middle of summertime, 'tis best. Otherwise you be spending your life on a sandbar." Caleb paused, adding, "There's less to varnish." Alex saw the question in his eyes.

"Let's rest in the shade. I'm about to have sunstroke."

Caleb sprang for the Bible, saying, "The sun dries the varnish fast." He tried to appear nonchalant as they found a log to serve as a seat and pulled it into the shade.

"Now what was the Psalm?" Alex asked as he opened the black leather book.

"Forty, that's a certainty. Now about the chapter in Deuteronomy, I'm not too clear on that. But it's the one that starts out about having a servant, and poking a hole in his ear."

For a moment Alex watched his slave over the top of the book. Caleb's eyes were honest and eager as he asked, "Would you point out the words?"

Still busy with his thoughts, Alex found the place and read with divided attention as he pondered the effect of the words on Caleb. Nearly halfway through the Psalm, Caleb lifted his hand. "That's it, suh, read it again, about sacrifices."

Alex searched for the words and heard them for the first time. " 'Sacrifice and offering thou didst not desire; mine ears hast thou opened: burnt offering and sin offering hast thou not required.' "

"That's it," Caleb said, leaning forward to touch the print. "That's just what Jam said. It's talking about the Lord Jesus, telling all about Him coming to die for us. Now look over in Deuteronomy."

Alex looked bewildered. Caleb poked at the book. "In the front of the book, pretty close to the beginning." With his head nearly obscuring the page, Caleb's finger moved to the number. "Fifteen. I know my numbers. Now go part way down. What does that say?"

Alex read, " 'And if thy brother, an Hebrew man, or an Hebrew woman be sold unto thee, and serve thee six years; then in the seventh year thou shalt let him go free from thee.' " Alex began thinking about the strange request, but now the words demanded attention. " 'And thou shalt remember that thou wast a bondman in the land of Egypt and the Lord thy God redeemed thee: therefore I command thee this thing to day. And it shall be, if he say unto thee, I will not go away from thee; because he loveth thee and thine house, because he is well with thee; Then thou shalt take an awl, and thrust it through his ear unto the door, and he shall be thy servant for ever. . . .' " Alex lowered the book and saw the tears on Caleb's face. Mystified, Alex asked, "What does it mean?"

"It's the Lord Jesus. He was willing to be a slave, just like we are, only He *wanted* to be a slave, because of us. Now read the Psalm again. I want to get the words out so's I can rightly appreciate the thought."

Alex lifted the book, but his attention was not on the words before his eyes; instead he clung to the words Caleb was saying. "The Lord Jesus comes. When He understand what the Father wants of Him, He say, 'Father, I don't want to be free, I want to do Your will, even if it means going to the cross and dying so all these sinful men, living down here, still can have a chance to make it to heaven.' " He paused and looked imploringly at Alex. "You understand it? See, it's just like those slaves saying 'poke that awl through my ear, and everybody know I belong to you.' That's what Jesus said to the Father; that's what we're to be a saying to Jesus: 'Poke the hole in my ear, so I can't ever run out on you, Lord.' "

Alex closed the book and leaned toward the black face. Tears still rolled down Caleb's cheeks. When he could trust his voice, Alex said, "That's a big thing to you, isn't it."

Caleb looked astonished for a moment, and then understanding crept across his face. "You say I know about being a slave, and you don't. Yes, suh, we all know. When you know what freedom isn't, then somehow it gets to you, more'n otherwise. But I suppose since God knows everything and how everybody feels, then for Him to take up being a slave with no turning back, even to dying—well, that's something. 'Least ways, we still hope," he ducked his head, "about freedom."

Late that night—in the midnight hours—with the night as dark as Caleb's face, Alex knew the story had wedged itself into his heart. Were those Jewish eyes soberly regarding him across time, wondering if he would join the crowd of slaves?

Other eyes he couldn't avoid haunted him as well. Garrison's. The man's eyes had burned a hole in his arguments, shaming him down under his veneer of righteousness. And Whittier. He had said he treasured the change God had made. How that statement challenged!

In the following days, under the light of the blazing sun while the varnish slowly sheathed the boat, Caleb gave a torrent of sermons. The daily words from Psalm forty and Deuteronomy fifteen were not only seared into the man's mind, but were winged to his tongue, demanding daily utterance. Alex dared not stop the flow of one word. It was important. "De Lord say He forgive me all my sins, my thieving and whoring, my gettin' my brother into trouble and causing sin. De Lord say it. But until I say, 'Lord Jesus I believe it,' then no suh, I can't believe.

"Know what repentance mean? Jam heard it from a white preacher. I don't know where he heard it, maybe from the Lord himself. Repentance mean turn around in your tracks and go the right direction and don't never come back the wrong way again."

On that final day, working quickly and in silence, they finished spreading varnish. Caleb regarded the empty spot where the name Sally Belle had been. "Alex, suh, what you want us to put there?"

Alex took a deep breath. Wiping his hands he said, "I think I need to make a quick trip into town. Go over those patches between the texas and the pilothouse. When I come back, we'll be ready to paint on a new name."

Caleb's face brightened. "How about getting some pretty gold paint for the name?"

Alex returned in the late afternoon. The boat, still tilted on its skids, revealed Caleb's heels resting on the texas railing. Tossing his cap, Alex called out, "Matey, all hands on deck!"

Caleb's face appeared, a grin dividing his face as he said, "You got a haircut and a fancy red cap!"

"The cap and the paint are for you. I'll stencil in the letters and you paint them."

He headed for the bow with his stock of rules and a square. Caleb came to lean over his shoulder as Alex lifted out the stencils. "What does it say, Alex suh?"

"Golden Awl."

Caleb backed away, studied the stencil and frowned. "Might be Sally Belle isn't so bad after all. What's a golden awl?"

Feeling slightly ridiculous, Alex leaned forward and lifted his hair away from his ear. "What do you think this means?"

Caleb looked at the tiny hoop of gold in the pierced ear, frowned, and then glanced at the stencil. Now his eyebrows slid up. Taking a step away from the boat, he drawled, "Massa, dat a mighty big awl for the job."

"Might be the Lord thought it would best fit the need," Alex muttered. "I have something else for you." He pulled a folded piece of paper from his pocket and handed it to Caleb.

As Caleb slowly unfolded the paper, Alex said, "It's a legal paper, Caleb. It says that Alexander Duncan does hereby release one slave, May 22, 1857, by the name of Caleb, known by registered number 84771.

"Caleb, you are free, but I need a first mate. So I will offer you a job, paying you the sum of fifty dollars a month plus all living expenses."

For a minute longer, Caleb stared at the paper. Blinking his eyes, he looked up at Alex. "I'm free?" He paused, took a deep breath and as Alex watched, he stretched tall and proud. "Do I have to take the job?"

"No, but I will miss you. If the pay isn't enough—"

Caleb grinned, "I'm proud to be your mate, suh!"

Alex stuck out his hand. "Put it there, partner!"

Caleb was shaking his head in a bewildered way as he hesitated before taking Alex's hand. "Now I'm free and you is the slave. But suh, it's good to be the slave of the Lord Jesus Christ."

"Caleb," Alex said slowly, "I'll always be grateful to you for helping me understand what it really means to be a bondservant of the Lord Jesus Christ. In my mind it lacked glory until I heard you saying it out in a dozen different ways." A moment later, he added, "Caleb, you haven't asked where we're going with this boat."

"Suh, where—"

Alex settled down on the railing. "While I was in Boston I met some men who are doing their best to help escaped slaves leave the United States by going into Canada. Caleb, it's wrong. Legally, if they catch us they'll have a right to put us in jail. Maybe worse. But since talking to some of these men, I can't get away from the idea that it needs to be done. And quickly. Every day that passes makes the going more difficult."

Caleb squinted up at him. "De Lord want you to do this?"

Alex nodded. "Yes. And I know this most certainly. Until last night I wasn't sure." He glanced at Caleb with a crooked grin. "Thanks to your sermons, I began to understand. And you said you have to say the words. When I told the Lord I would become a part of the Underground Railroad, it was like a mountain slid off my back."

Caleb's eyes were wide and shiny with tears. "De railroad. For a long time I hear about it. Sometimes black people disappear, and someone whispers 'railroad.' Now I'm partners in it!" He got to his feet, shaking his head he went to the pilothouse and slowly caressed the new varnish.

Alex wiped tears from the corners of his eyes. Then he stooped and picked up the red cap. "Matey, you can't learn steamboatin' without a hat."

CHAPTER 13

Lithie was a kitchen slave; she was light of skin and as graceful as a bird. She was also insolent, an unappealing characteristic that forced her to be relegated to kitchen work, and of the lowliest kind.

Although Crystal had almost no contact with the woman, she was aware of her existence and had felt the battery of hostile looks thrown her way in their infrequent encounters.

In the six weeks since the trip to Twin Oaks, Crystal had nearly forgotten the incident involving the slave Joseph. But she was reminded one day as she entered the kitchen and heard Lithie's two words. The first was *Joseph* and the second was a derisive *her*. But even at that, the words would have been shrugged off had it not been for the reaction seen on the ring of dark faces around the room. The only one with an indifferent look was the one who had caused the startled look to appear on everyone else.

Crystal's words came automatically as she studied the faces. "I'm looking for Auntie T. She's mending the dress I want to wear today."

"I would think you could be more considerate of the poor old woman," came Lithie's retort. The other slaves shrank away from her, turning aside their dismayed faces. She continued, "You'll get more work out of an old horse if you don't ride it so hard."

For a moment Crystal dropped her head, feeling nearly as if she were the grubby kitchen maid. She studied the tall, slender woman, noted the graceful tilt of her head, the almond eyes, then said, "It's a pity you aren't an actress; you have such airs."

There was a nervous titter of laughter from the others. Lithie lifted her head even higher as she said, "Yes, 'tis a pity, and a pity you are such a mouse with the possibility of being anything you desire."

Taking a step forward, Crystal asked, "Can you read and write?"

"Of course not. That ruins good kitchen maids."

The door flew open and Tammera panted into the room. "Missy, your mama is looking for you." Straightening her cap she addressed the group. "And it's a whipping for the likes of all of you if you don't lower your voices and get this kitchen cleaned before dinner."

Breathing heavily, Tammera followed Crystal. "What lies is that Lithie feeding you?"

"Lies?" Crystal turned to meet Tammera's worried frown, "It wasn't a lie at all. Auntie T, why is she such an uncomfortable person to be around?"

"Because she's never come to task with accepting."

"You mean accepting life the way it is? She's a slave. I recall she was very angry when we went east to Boston."

Tammera's hand stretched toward Crystal. "Did she—say something?"

Crystal frowned over the intensity of the question. Slowly she said, "Auntie T, she was very proper. It is only her attitude, not so much what she says. Please, I feel sorry for her; don't tell Mama she is quarrelsome today."

The door clicked behind Crystal and she turned. "Oh, *Maman!*"

"What is the problem?"

Hastily Tammera said, "Ma'am, 'tis nothing. Lithie is upset today. I think it might be she needs a change of work." For a moment, Crystal watched her mother and Auntie T study each other.

Mama looked at Crystal. "My headache is very painful today. I believe I will visit the doctor instead of keeping our appointment."

Crystal sighed and watched her mother close the bedroom door. "Never mind the dress, Auntie T, I won't need it."

Tammera shook her head slowly. "Your father left lessons on his desk. Might be nice to work in there."

Crystal nodded without enthusiasm. She had turned toward the stairs when she remembered the conversation she had overheard in the kitchen. "Auntie T, is there another slave named Joseph?"

Tammera shook her head. "Where did you get that idea?"

"Lithie said 'Joseph and her' just as I walked into the kitchen. I wondered, because at Uncle Pierre's—" Tammera leaned forward with a frown starting between her eyebrows.

Crystal hesitated. "It's not important." She went back down the stairs to the library.

Tammera watched Crystal walk down the stairs. She pushed at the frown starting just under her mob-cap and murmured, "The dear Lord protect you from finding out the truth about Joseph, cause sure enough, it will kill you."

Conscious that Tammera was watching from the head of the stairs, Crystal stopped to wave her fingers at her before entering the library.

Just as she walked into the room, Lithie turned from the desk at the far end of the library. "Oh," she gasped, dropping her hands from her face. "Just you. I came to dust. I'll just slip out the garden door and do my work later."

"Cassie does the dusting tomorrow," Crystal said. "Why—"

Lithie had disappeared through the open door.

With a shrug, Crystal went to the desk for her books. But at the desk she stopped short, murmuring, "That's Father's family record book. I can't imagine him being so careless!"

As she went to close the book and place it in the desk drawer, she stopped. "A Cabet family history," she murmured. "I wish it wasn't so precious that I can't be allowed to read it." Her hand drifted lightly over the dark red leather cover. Then with a sigh of regret, she lifted the heavy leaves together and closed the book. As she moved the cumbersome volume, a slender piece of heavy paper slipped out of the book.

"Oh, dear! How will I ever know where to put the paper?" she whispered.

The heavy script on the vellum caught her attention. *A legal document,* she thought to herself. She had flattened the single page and was reading it when her father entered the library. But even then the words on the sheet had no meaning until she saw her father's face.

The color surged to his face as he roared, "Crystal, why have you been into my cabinet? You know I've forbidden you to do so!"

"Papa, I haven't opened the cabinet. The book was on the desk and I needed to move it. The paper—fell out." Slowly she lifted the paper. She looked at him and realized the obvious must be said. "Papa. This document. It says that Evangeline Cabet is my mother. And is she your daughter?"

That man she called Papa nodded slowly. Now she saw the strain on his face, the defeat. She said, "You talked about regretting some things in your life. Is this one of them?"

"Of course." He came slowly to the desk and dropped heavily into the chair. "And I regret this. I should never have kept the paper in the house. Joseph, mentioned in the paper, is the slave who escorted you at Pierre's. He is your father, and Evangeline Cabet, our daughter, is your mother."

Crystal tried to understand the words, but the only thing she understood was that this man was not her dear papa. For a moment he was a stranger. Not a grandparent, only a stranger confirming the words she had read.

But in the next moment, while each waited for the other to speak, she comprehended the deeper meaning of the paper.

"This is why my skin is darker than yours. I am half slave." Her voice was growing brittle. "Tell me, why does my father work in the fields, and where is my mother?"

He sighed. Like an old man, he settled deeper in his chair until his chin rested against the stiff whiteness of his collar. "If I were a slave, half-Negro with a white father, and I had an impetuous, lovely young girl throw herself at me, I suppose I would have behaved in the manner in which your father behaved. It is that fact that kept me from having him shot eighteen years ago."

"I heard what you said to Uncle Pierre about letting him work in the fields until he drops."

His face contorted painfully. "You will force me to face the ugliness of myself?" He was silent for a moment and then he added, "I've tried to protect you from knowing. Now you've chosen to disobey me by reading the book."

"That isn't so." Crystal felt her chin go up. With a part of her mind advising her that she was talking back to Papa, there was a moment of astonishment. She took time to wonder if knowing the story had given her courage. She pondered the strangeness of being adrift, separated from the people she claimed as mother and father. For a moment she felt rootless, confused. "The book was spread out on the desk. I tried only to fold it together and place it in the drawer."

With a curious light in his eyes, he asked, "You mean you wouldn't have been tempted to pry?"

Crystal frowned. "I suppose it is more the fact that you simply have said no. It made my curiosity more wrong than the deed. Strange, because I don't feel that way about the letters in Mama's chest. I've pried at Auntie T to tell me about them." He was nodding as she talked, and with a slight smile he said, "I must reward her faithfulness."

"What about my mother? Where is she?"

"She is living in France. We've had no communication from her in the past five years. I suppose that she is happy. She married well. But our long ago action has—"

"Made her bitter?" she asked, feeling set apart from it all.

He shook his head. "It is more. How do you reconcile values? I sense she has absolutely no respect for us. I would neither free your father nor allow her to marry him."

With a touch of his own bitterness showing, he met Crystal's gaze and added, "Of course, that was what he had planned all along."

Crystal reached for the doorknob and he added, "Please, don't mention this to your mother, nor to Auntie T. I will handle the situation with your mother when her health has improved."

As if sleepwalking, Crystal went to her room. Tammera was there stitching the dress with the torn lace. Going to the window Crystal examined the gardens, the budding orange trees, and the hacks passing down the street.

Auntie T said, "Why you sigh like that? Crystal, since you've been back from that ungodly North you don't read your Bible and pray like you did before. Now I know what the priest say. But your Auntie T say if you stay close to the Lord, you listen to Him and let Him listen to you."

Pushing the hurt deep inside, Crystal managed to turn with a teasing grin, saying, "I shall tell Mama you don't listen to the priest."

Tammera shook her needle at Crystal. "Don't you sass me! And don't forget, before I came to this place, I listen to God and pray to

Him every day—sometimes all day long. I don't need any man to teach me how to please the Lord when I already know."

"I'm sorry," Crystal murmured. "I have neglected my Bible, only sometimes it doesn't seem to have anything to do with life."

Tammera shook her head slowly. "Might be. I gets burdened down, the Lord say 'cast your burden, Tammera.' I get fussed up with life, and the Lord say 'remember there's still heaven.' Sugarlam, if you got troubles, the Lord help. If you don't know you got troubles, then thank Him for the blessings. I guess you can't embarrass Him with just talking out the problems. Sometimes the only way He can get our attention is by letting a few problems in our life."

She heaved herself to her feet and shook out the folds in the frock. "Now I go press this. You pray."

Crystal stared at the door for silent, leaden minutes. Finally she said, "Lord, I haven't talked to you for a long time. Will you please help me remember how to pray?" And then in another minute, with an embarrassed catch in her voice, she said, "About today, what happened down there. Please don't let people find out about it. It hurts to know I'm just a slave, or at least halfway."

Strangely enough, getting the terrible thoughts into words seemed to help. She closed her eyes and tried to recall the face of that man, but all she could remember was the curious light in his eyes when he learned her name. *He knows, and I think seeing me made him very happy.*

———

Heavy rains turned the following Monday into a dreary one and turned the roads into yellow rivers of mud. They then spewed their dirty water into the true ponds and rivers, bordering them with a line of yellow as the muddy water poured in.

The restlessness Crystal felt seemed to have spread throughout the whole house. The maids trembled at the thunder and crept silently about their tasks. The cook clanged kettles, and all the savory smells didn't balance her unrest. After prying at Tammera's gloom, Crystal gathered her books and went down to the library.

Uncle Pierre and Papa stood before the dark fireplace with glasses in hand. They turned as she entered. "Oh, pardon!"

Looking surprised and ill at ease, the two murmured greetings.

Papa added, "We are just leaving and won't return until evening. Come, Pierre. We'll gather the papers later." Turning to Crystal he added, "I've left lessons for you on the table. Please read the Sir Walter Scott book and I'll write questions later. Also, avoid disturbing the papers. They are related to business, and I've placed them in the order in which we will use them." He hesitated, kissed her, and hurried out of the room.

Cassie was waiting at the door. As the men walked past, Papa said, "You heard me tell Crystal, do not bother the papers on the desk. They are important and must be kept in order."

Cassie cocked her head, waiting. When the front door closed she turned to Crystal. With a pleased smile she said, "I know where they go. They going to slave market, I hear them talk about getting slaves to replace Joseph and Lithie."

"Replace?" Crystal puzzled over the statement. "Cassie, I saw Lithie just this morning."

"Yes, but they're going. And there's not a one who cares—about Lithie, anyway. I don't know Joseph."

"Joseph," Crystal said slowly. She pressed her fingers against her forehead trying to understand the jumble of emotions fighting for attention. Relief! *Now no one will know. I can be Mama and Papa's girl again.*

But a new thought occurred, stemming from the Bible verse she had read that morning. As Cassie began her dusting, Crystal murmured the words she had read, " 'We then that are strong ought to bear the infirmities of the weak, and not to please ourselves.' "

"I'm not certain I know what infirmities are." She addressed Cassie's back.

The woman turned with a shrug. "Me? I don't know either. Better look it up in that dictionary. Least you can read."

Crystal sat at the desk and watched Cassie. Finally she reached for the dictionary, placed it on the stack of papers and thumbed her way through it. " 'Infirmity. Being feeble, having a failing.' I guess that means old people."

She closed the book and tried to erase the damage the book had done to the neat stack of papers. "I think Father needs help with his papers," she murmured as she lined the edges and thumped the papers into a neat pile. Now she realized what the papers contained.

With a quick glance, she thumbed her way through them. Here in front of her were the documents and bill of sale for each of the slaves. She recognized the names. This one was the bill of sale on Cassie, and this one was Tammera's. The papers bore the numbers assigned to the slave, a description, known background and the date of purchase. Quickly she found the one for Joseph. He had been bought as a child of fourteen. That was four years before her birth! She felt her throat squeeze tight. With a strange sensation of being led where she didn't want to go, she folded the paper and stuffed it into her pocket.

CHAPTER 14

Olivia turned to Matthew and grinned at him. He pulled his horse even with hers. "That's a cat-in-the-cream grin. Why?"

"Oh, Matthew, you know. Mother stifles us when she comes along to Natchez. You know she doesn't like these parties with the cousins, so it's really a relief to have her decide to stay at home."

"What you are really saying is that you've every intention of riding bareback with Lem, which she specifically forbade. But sister dear, Mother took the old dungarees out of your valise, didn't you know?"

For a moment dismay pulled Olivia's face down. Then with a grin, she said, "Lem can supply me; we're nearly the same size."

He shook his head sadly, "Tut, you'll never land a promising husband until you reform. Olivia, who knows? This might be the party Prince Charming will waltz into your life. And where is my esteemed sister? Riding horses in the pasture with her rascal of a cousin."

The road narrowed, Olivia pulled her mount ahead and rescued her riding habit from the clutches of the bramble bush. "Nevertheless," she called over her shoulder, "I intend to have a good time. And if you don't behave yourself, I'll tell Mother."

"Tit for tat," he called with a laugh.

The Newton Thomas mansion perched atop a bluff overlooking the Mississippi River. To the east stretched broad pasture land and beyond that, the wild and heavily forested acres that had given the home the name Tall Timbers. To the west the house looked down its own garden path to an inlet with dock and beach. The seclusion of the inlet and the forest made it easy to forget that the narrow winding road leading up the far side of the hill passed the notorious Natchez-under-the-Hill, which had gained its unsavory reputation during the days of the heavy flatboat traffic on the River. From the front door and garden of the house the shacks and brothels of the area were not visible, and not many people knew the Natchez Trace cut through a corner of Tall Timbers.

It was late afternoon when Matthew and Olivia broke onto the Trace and rode up the hill into the setting sun. Matthew halted his mare and pointed to the River. "It's higher this year than last. Look! The little island has disappeared."

"Oh, I hope we'll have a boat ride," Olivia murmured, shielding her eyes as she studied the broad expanse of water, silvered by the setting sun. She added, "It looks as if someone's taken out all the trees on the bank upriver."

"Flack's land," Matthew murmured. "Can't imagine him farming that close to the River. Probably sold the trees to Jenson."

"That fellow who sells firewood to the steamboats?"

Matthew nodded and turned to point down the road. "There's our wagon."

"I'm grateful we didn't have to ride with the baggage," Olivia exclaimed as she watched the wagon roll slowly up the hill. "Auntie's request for help came just in time. Our people are taking up every inch that the trunks don't."

"Let's get out of here before we have to eat their dust."

When they arrived, Alberta and Lynda were there to greet them, with Alberta standing in the doorway and Lynda racing down the steps. She kissed Matthew and Olivia. "My favorite cousins. Oh, Matthew, you are so elegant!" She reached for his arm as she tousled his light curls. "Too bad you are my first cousin, and that I know what an unbearable tease you are. Did you bring a guest?"

"No, cousin dear, but from the look in your eye, methinks I'll run down under the hill and see what I can find."

"Beast!" Lynda tucked her arm through Olivia's. Her blue eyes sparkled with excitement as she tossed brown curls out of her eyes and said, "Lem has nearly driven us wild with his plans for you. One would think it is *his* birthday. Come, Mother is waiting to greet you."

Voices awakened Olivia early in the morning. Slipping from the bed she went to the window. Matthew, Uncle Newton, and Lem were talking in loud, excited voices as they strode down the path to the dock. "Oh no!" Olivia moaned, "They're heading for the boat."

There was a tap on her door and Alberta peeked through the crack. "Mother needs to pick up a sunbonnet today. Hurry and we can go with her."

Olivia gave a longing glance at the window. "I'll be down in minutes." She quickly got ready and rushed downstairs.

Alberta came to meet Olivia in the breakfast room. "That is a lovely frock," she murmured, fingering the voile and touching the ribbons. "How fortunate you are to have such skin! I look ill in yellow."

Olivia gave Alberta a squeeze. "I'll surrender my skin if you can teach me to sit still long enough to learn petit point." She waved to the sampler on the wall, "Those roses are exquisite."

"Is it a fair trade, Mother?"

Olivia's aunt smiled, "Yes, but knowing that Olivia can't sit still very long, you'd never get the chance—you'd still be waiting when her skin is as wrinkled as mine! Olivia, I'm surprised you weren't down here with the menfolk this morning."

"I think they were avoiding me," she said ruefully. "I saw them heading for the dock while I was still in my nightgown. Are we going to have an excursion?"

Alberta's mother nodded. "Yes. They are going to check out the boat this morning."

"I tried to get Papa to rent a small steamboat. The Larkinsons had one last year, and it was so much fun. He says we can't afford one this year. Mother, is it a bad year for crops?"

"No, it's just that birthday parties for an eighteen-year-old are expensive when they last all week."

Lynda came into the room and stood next to her mother. "Aren't you glad you don't have five daughters like the Morgans?"

Mrs. Thomas rolled her eyes, fanned herself briskly, and said, "Now, hurry with breakfast. We've lots to do today."

———

Matthew glanced at his uncle, Newton Thomas, as the three walked down the garden path. Newton explained, "Thought we might as well check out the caulking job on the boat this morning. Give you fellows a chance to limber up your rowing arms, too."

Lem said, "I wanted Father to rent a steamboat. The Allens have a neat little job. They use it for excursions on the river with the family."

"I checked it out. Peter is going to replace the boiler before he uses it again."

After they reached the boat, Matthew hopped in first followed by Newton, who turned to look at Lem. "I trust you brought enough to eat, because I plan on rowing upriver to Timber Isle. You two are expected to have a few sore muscles by evening; don't disappoint me!"

Lem groaned as he stood by, waiting to cast off. He untied the rope, gave the boat a shove, and jumped in. "If we'd waited, betcha Olivia would have been willing to do her share of rowing."

"The women have their day planned," Newton replied as he leaned into the oars and the current caught the boat. Matthew grunted as the current tugged at his oar. While the men concentrated on the rhythm of the dipping oars, Lem rummaged in the picnic basket.

He was on his third tart when he exclaimed, "Hey, heave to. Is that Allen's boat? It's a steamer, and he's not going anywhere."

Matthew lifted his head and wiped perspiration out of his eyes. "Neat little rig. Uncle Newt, shall we check it out?"

"Well it isn't on a sandbar. Might be engine trouble. Better see to it. Lem, stay out of the lunch and come spell me."

Lem shoved a cake into his mouth, pointed at the boat and said, "A man on board the steamer is hailing us!"

They paddled near the stalled boat and then pitched a rope to the dark, bearded man leaning over the rail who then pulled them close. "Hey, thanks fellows. We've split a paddle. I don't know enough about this rig to trust limping into dock in this condition. We do know what we need for repair."

Matthew pulled off his cap and mopped his face. The stranger reached for him. "Matthew Thomas! Well, if this isn't luck."

Slowly Matthew began to grin. "Alexander Duncan? That beard! Who are you hiding from?" He grasped the extended hand and swung aboard the steamer. "Bet this is the little rig you told me about. Friend, where've you been for the past year?"

He turned to help the other two aboard. "Sorry. Alex, I want to introduce my uncle, Newton Thomas and his son, Lem. Newt, Lem, this is Alexander Duncan. We were at Harvard together." Matthew watched Alex shake hands with Lem as he surveyed the beard and the gold hoop in Alex's ear. "Old buddy, I think we have a lot of catching up to do."

Alex nodded and reached for the arm of the Negro standing behind him. "And Caleb is my first mate."

After everyone had been introduced, they all spent some time examining the problem and then Newton Thomas addressed Alex, "We'll take you into Natchez and bring you back to the steamer. Your biggest need is for the metal housing on the paddle. I think I know just the place to find it. Shall we get going?"

Alex hesitated and then turned to Caleb, "Think you can go after it?" The two exchanged a long glance and Caleb nodded. Alex faced Newton. "I'll have Caleb go. He knows as much or more about this rig than I do. Sir, I really appreciate your helping us."

Matthew touched his cap as he went over the side, "Man, it's good to see you. Hope we get a chance to catch up on talk. See you later."

———

Newton Thomas wiped the grease from his hands after replacing the paddle, and nodded at Alex. "I think that paddle will take you to forever and back. And now that that job is finished, I see you and Matthew have a lot of catching up to do. If you aren't in a hurry, lay over at our place. The Mississippi sweeps through our inlet with just enough water to float you."

Newton nodded at Matthew, "Stay aboard and show him the way."

"Sir, that's mighty nice of you," Alex said. "I'll at least spend the night. I don't take the rig up the river in the dark. I'm a novice, and not inclined to take chances."

By the time Newton and Lem had climbed back on their own boat and disappeared around the island, Caleb had the steam up. Matthew watched the roustabouts shoving wood into the fire. "This is a nice little outfit, just as you told me it was. Alex, my curiosity is about to get the best of me."

"Come up to the pilothouse and I'll bring you up to date." For a moment Matthew studied the serious expression in Alex's eyes. He shrugged and followed him up the stairs.

In the pilothouse he turned to Alex. "All right, give. What's going on?"

"Why did you get the idea there's anything—"

"Just your expression. You aren't the old Alex. Man, you've got the weight of the world on your shoulders! I nearly didn't recognize you. Certainly you aren't the pub-hopping fella from Harvard!"

Alex grinned. "That's right. Well, your uncle's invitation demands an explanation. Let's get this thing docked and I'll tell you."

"It better be good. Why didn't you answer the letter?"

Alex glanced up. "I didn't get one. I should have written on my own. I'd intended to look you up. But there's a complication, and I'd decided to scrap the plan for this trip. Now show me the way into this inlet, and let's find a place to tie up for the night."

"How about cozying up under the trees just beyond the end of the wharf? You can tie on to the trees."

Matthew watched Alex cut the speed and slowly flank the steamboat close to the bank. Alex turned from the wheel. "Caleb will handle the rest of it. Come sit down, and I'll fill you in."

"What happened to you in Boston?" Matthew asked.

"I honestly don't know. I lost one whole day out of my life and woke up on Garrison's doorstep."

"The abolitionist?"

Alex nodded. "Also met John Greenleaf Whittier. Between the two of them, I left Boston feeling like my coattails were on fire."

"I'll bet. You're lucky they didn't give you a good dose of religion—their kind."

"I think they did. It just took a while for it to sink in."

"How come the beard and the earring?"

Alex wiped an embarrassed grin off his face. "Rag me, and I'll push you overboard. Matt, I don't know how to say this so that you'll understand without getting offended."

"Well, then just say it, and I'll get offended."

"Simply this. I got a good dose of religion—just like you said. Took all this time—from the time I pulled out of Boston until just six weeks ago, for me to understand the Lord was trying to get my attention. Matt, I know we've both had exposure to church and Bible teaching. But I came out of it with a smug assurance that God was pretty pleased to get me as a church member. It took all Whittier, Garrison, and Caleb had to say before the veneer was stripped off."

"Caleb—that Negro?"

"Former slave, and now my dear friend and employee. Matt, listening to him talk left me with a pretty clear picture of myself and a big heartache for the kind of personal relationship with Jesus Christ that Caleb had. I discovered that true religion is something you know you have. A relationship with the Lord Jesus Christ makes Him Lord of all of me as well as my dearest Friend."

"So now you're reduced to being one of these blubbering evangelicals."

"Guess that's as good a way of putting it as any I can think of right now," Alex said with a twisted grin.

Matthew got to his feet, shaking his head, "And there goes my pub-hopping buddy."

"One other thing, Matt, and then I'll let you go. I suppose one of my problems in Boston was that I had an inkling this was in store if I really wanted to be a follower of Jesus Christ. Ever hear of the Underground Railroad?"

Matthew's head snapped back. For a moment he compressed his lips and then slowly grinned. "I should have guessed that would be the next step. Seems it's inevitable, looking back on it all. I must admit I'm curious. Mind telling me a little about it?"

"Be glad to." Alex paused. "If you're so inclined, I'd be happy to introduce you to the bunch hiding in the cabin."

Matthew turned slowly. "You mean this boat is loaded with runaway slaves?" Alex nodded. His heart was thumping with excitement as Matt whispered, "Alex, I think we do need to talk."

———

When Olivia and the cousins returned from shopping, Lem was

glooming around the house. Peering over her parcels, Olivia said, "What! You're alone? We could have taken you shopping with us."

He tossed a pillow at her and retorted, "And I would have taken you fishing if you'd stayed home. We made a rescue this morning. A steamboat had stalled. Father had to run into town to buy material to repair a paddle. It split."

"For a stranger?" Olivia's aunt asked as Olivia stepped out of the room.

"Yes, Mama. Matthew knows him from school, but I can't remember his name. Matthew stayed with him and is going to direct him back here. He'll be spending the night." He turned to ogle Alberta. "You would like him just fine. He has two ears, eyes, I think and—"

"He'll do, he'll do," Alberta murmured. "And just for that I'll lock you in the closet for the whole week."

Lem caught up with Olivia in the hallway. "Are we going riding this evening?"

"I need to talk to you about that," she whispered. Glancing around, she led him into the kitchen and said, "You'll have a problem unless you can arrange to lend me some dungarees. You won't want to be seen with me if I have to wear my own riding habit."

"One with ribbons and ostrich feathers, I bet. Sure, I'll give you the clothes off my back."

"Shh, you needn't advertise it. Mothers—"

"Don't understand."

———

Olivia waited in the late evening shadows of her room, but Lem didn't appear. In the morning she wore her riding habit to breakfast. Matthew's eyes were amused. Lem said, "Where's the feathers? Trying to work up sympathy, huh?"

Matthew chuckled and Lem hissed, "I get you, but it'll be just this one time. And right now!" She tried to ignore their comments and concentrated on her meal.

"You and your friend must've had some talk last night, Matthew. I didn't see either of you all night, although I did see your friend's boat so I know you made it back safe. Did you two get all caught up?" Newton asked. Matthew simply nodded.

Olivia finished her muffin and wiped her lips. Lem asked, "Mother, will you excuse us? If we don't get this ride early enough, some of the fellas may see me." Both of them left the table and headed for the door.

"Son," his father warned, "remember, Olivia is a lady. Don't take any fences."

"No sir. In that outfit, I'd never get her off them."

They were outside and halfway across the pasture when Lem said, "Angry, huh?"

"You were the one who didn't show up with the clothes."

"That's why I wanted to ride out early. Boy, do I have a mystery!"

"Give," Olivia encouraged.

"Matthew has been acting strange lately. I didn't see him at all yesterday after leaving him with his friend, but I finally saw him late last night sneaking out of the house about the time I headed for your room with the clothes. He looked so guilty I just had to follow. Headed down to the dock. Halfway there, Livie, this fellow off in the bushes calls, 'Matt!' and Matthew hunkered down like they were buddies. I was curious, but I didn't think too much about it."

He paused to catch his breath and then said, "Livie, there's something strange going on. Now, wouldn't you think a couple of fellows would just sit out there and talk casual like? Well, they were *whispering*. I bellied up through the grass to hear what they were saying—"

"Lem! That is terrible of you."

"Well, I didn't find out much before they heard me. The stranger mentioned something about people. He kept saying *they*. Well, I sneezed, and the two of them took after me." He paused. "One thing, besides what he said to Matthew, he made arrangements to meet Matthew again tonight. Matthew mentioned your name. The fellow seemed interested. Said something."

"What did he say?"

"I can't remember, and because he was talking so softly I couldn't recognize his voice."

"Could it be that he was that old friend you rescued yesterday? After all, he did spend the night here."

"I thought about that, but that guy's boat was gone this morning—so I doubt he's the guy coming to meet Matthew again tonight.

"Oh, that brother of mine! He has something cooked up." Olivia murmured. "They. Sounds to me like it's someone he's planning on bringing to the party Friday night." Olivia leaned across and touched Lem's arm, "You say they are going to meet tonight? I'd give anything to hear what they talk about!"

"I'd settle for your quirt."

"Done. When do we leave? Where did you hide the clothes when you decided to follow after Matthew?"

"They are stashed in the linen closet."

That evening, when Matthew excused himself from the game table, Lem caught Olivia's eye and nodded. As soon as Matthew left, she got to her feet, shielding a delicate yawn behind her hand. "Please, I'm so tired. Alberta is winning, and I know it is because I'm sleepy."

Quickly she changed into Lem's dungarees and headed for the back stairs. The night was clear and the moon bright. As Olivia crept down the garden path, she breathed deeply of the heavy blossom-scented air. She also noticed how the crickets became silent at her approach. Suddenly a hand reached across her path and she gasped.

"Keep still!" Lem's voice muttered in her ear. "They're down on the dock. We'll aim for the bushes and hope they come closer."

Crouching, they slowly moved a step at a time. Heads down, they crawled carefully into the heavy undergrowth along the bank. When Olivia raised her head she could see the two dark figures on the dock. They were talking softly, and as they walked along they came near the bushes. Lem squeezed her arm. Olivia pushed her hand against her mouth and strained to hear.

"Friday night?" came Matthew's voice.

Olivia leaned forward but as she did so a stick beneath her hand snapped. The two dark figures turned suddenly and ran toward the spot where the noise came from. "Oh no," Lem moaned. "Let's go!" With the shout Lem was off, and Olivia recognized Matthew in pursuit.

Olivia remained behind and tried to wiggle further into the bushes for cover—but instead her movement gave her away. Spotting the dungarees, the stranger snarled, "There, I knew another boy was with him." When she knew she had been spotted, Olivia leaped to make a run for home, but two strong arms prevented her getaway.

She gasped against the arm around her neck.

In an instant she found herself pitched over a knee. "Ouch!" The blow landed sharply on the seat of Lem's dungarees. Outraged, she fought against the hard arm holding her. "Oh!" Another smack was delivered. The voice behind her warned her to stay away, and then the man relaxed his hold and she was off, running up the path after Lem.

She didn't stop until she was through the door and up the stairs. Across her bed she gasped, panted, wiped perspiration from her face, and cried.

Standing in front of the mirror, she discovered that the mark of the hand was still there, stinging red. Now her outrage directed itself against Lem, and then she was laughing, smothering her hiccuping giggle in the pillow, as she recalled his flight.

———

When Olivia awoke the next morning, she was angry once again. After she got out of bed, she met a subdued Lem in the hallway. He wilted. "Ya got it too?"

"Was this planned?"

"Cross my heart. I didn't hear a thing and I still don't know who that other guy was."

"You might redeem yourself by finding out." Relief swept across his face, he opened his mouth and then nodded furiously as Matthew appeared, looking tired.

He threw a suspicious glance their direction as he went down the stairs. Lem took a deep breath, grinned, and asked, "Wanna go riding?"

She turned away. "Not hardly. I may not sit down for a week."

"That fella must hit harder than Matt."

CHAPTER 15

While Olivia dressed for the party, she thought about the previous evening. Wincing as she recalled the spanking, she puzzled over the questions the whack had raised.

Slowly she combed her hair into loose, soft ringlets. Wrinkling her nose at her reflection she murmured, "I wonder who that mysterious stranger is? And why are those two so fearful of being discovered?" Then she grinned at the obvious answer. "Of course! Knowing my brother, there's something he has planned that he doesn't want me to know about."

She heard the tap on the door and turned, calling, "Come." It was Alberta's maid. "Oh, Ellie, will you please do something with my hair?"

The woman settled herself comfortably and picked up the brush. "I brought you some pink roses for your hair. Let's lift your hair up and tie it with ribbons. It's too hot for it to hang loose.

"My, that drawing room looks nice. Lewis, he put flowers all over the place." She chuckled until she shook. "If you can't stand flowers, just go to the garden. It's bare; they's all in the house." Backing away, she said, "Miss Olivia, you look just as pretty as a picture. Now you go have a good time. There's a pack of ladies and gentlemen down there already."

Olivia paused at the head of the stairs. She could see Alberta and Lynda standing in the hall below. Their pastel gowns billowed over hoops, making them look like giant blossoms turned stem up.

After admiring the pleasing rainbow of color dotted among the white-clad men, Olivia started slowly down the stairs, enjoying the scene each step revealed. She saw the one dark coat in the crowd. It was a gentleman standing beside Matthew with his back to the room.

As she descended the last steps she studied the man. Black was fitting. His dark curly hair rode his collar like an extension of the coat. With his broad, heavy shoulders, she decided he needed the dignity of black.

Lem came to take her hand and she smiled at him. "You look very handsome!" she murmured, adding with a tiny smile, "It nearly makes me forget last night."

He bowed and pulled her arm through his. "Mother wants you over here." He lowered his voice. "Better not mention last night. I think Mother's wise. Matt cast one burning look too many my direction." He guided her toward the dining room.

When they passed the drawing room, Olivia tugged at his arm. "Oh, that's nearly enough to make me like the waltz," she said, watching the violins and bass viols descend upon the piano.

"But not me," he muttered with a relieved sigh as he dropped Olivia's arm and excused himself.

It was late in the evening when Matthew came to her with his friend in tow. "Olivia, do you remember Alex Duncan?"

She turned. The bright blue eyes were sober and serious now. He looked at her quizzically. Had he forgotten her? She hesitated. *Surely this isn't the drunken lout!* She was caught off guard and filled with uncertainty as the man repeated her name. This gentleman was the perfect, remote Southerner.

She recalled the laughing, tipsy youth with warm, bright eyes and tumbled hair. She couldn't believe this dark, dignified stranger even resembled the youth who had flung her around the kitchen in a wild dance which had ended in that terrible kiss.

Taking a step back, she surveyed the dark hair, noting the beard, and then her glance fastened on the tiny gold hoop in his ear. Caught by surprise she felt her eyebrows rise. But the next moment she blushed at the amusement in his eyes as he bent over her hand.

"The kitchen knave." The words skipped from her mouth.

"Was I? I apologize, and pray that I didn't disgrace my mother."

Abruptly she backed away, conscious of only one hard, cold fact. This was the voice she had heard last night. This was the man who had spanked her like a misbehaving child.

She bowed stiffly. "You will excuse me, please? My aunt is trying to catch my eye."

During the remainder of the evening she avoided the pair, although she studied them from across the room. The slight blond man in white and the hulking figure in black raised more questions. But as she continued to watch them, she became increasingly fearful for Matthew. The man had an obvious charm as he bent over Alberta. And poor Alberta! *That sappy smile; she's being swept off her feet! Is it my duty to rescue the whole family from that monster?* As she wondered, she found herself questioning her violent disapproval of the man. She watched Matthew cross the room to Duncan and Alberta. In a moment Duncan stood, bowed to Alberta, and followed Matthew from the room.

"Lynda, I'll be back in a minute." Olivia hurried after the white and black figures disappearing into the library. The door was open. The music coming from the drawing room covered their conversation as they stood in front of the fireplace with their backs to her. Carefully she slipped inside and stepped into the shadows behind the door.

"Everything is ready. Meet me on the dock," Duncan said. Olivia saw him glance toward the door. He stepped close to Matthew and she could no longer make out the words. The black figure moved toward the door, paused and said, "You need to let them know. There could be problems."

Olivia fought the temptation to follow Matthew. She pondered the sentence she had heard. As they disappeared down the hall, she said, "I think that man has a strange hold on my brother. I know he is up to something, and I don't think it's good."

Finally she left the room just as the clock began to strike. Glancing up she murmured, "Midnight. It won't be long before they all leave." Even as she spoke, she watched guests begin to move into the hall.

As soon as she dared, Olivia slipped into the kitchen and ran up the back stairs to her room. Her hands were trembling as she chose a dark, long-sleeved dress and changed quickly.

Cautiously she crept down the kitchen stairs and slipped out the back door to wait in the shadows. She heard the sound of laughter. Another carriage pulled away from the door.

Taking a deep breath, Olivia ran across to the garden path. Remembering the previous night, she moved cautiously through the bushes. When she could see the water reflecting moonlight, she stopped to catch her breath. Except for the lapping of water against a boat, there was only quietness. Not even a frog croaked.

Water lapping against a boat? There shouldn't be a boat at the dock. Carefully she parted the bushes. There was no one to be seen on the path. Taking a deep breath, she quietly approached the dock. At the far end, nestled in the shadows of the towering oaks, she could make out the shape of a boat. It wasn't the fishing boat; it was much larger. Walking up close, she waited for her eyes to adjust to the deeper shadows.

Now she could see the narrow board bridging the shadows and resting on the end of the dock. Cautiously she approached, testing her weight. Again she hesitated, glancing fearfully around before she ran lightly across the plank.

In the darkness she could barely make out the gleam of polished wood. Above her head a stairway circled upward. She tiptoed forward, with her hand outstretched. "Ouch!" She collided with something that shifted beneath her hand. With her hand still outstretched, she heard a hollow *thunk*. It was a long minute before she dared explore the surface with her hand. *Firewood! Is it possible this is a steamboat?* she thought.

The chuckle started deep in her throat. *A nice, neat little steamboat, loaded and ready to go. Those two! They're planning on giving me the slip, so that they can go off on a lark—just the two of them. Matt, you should know better!* Still shaking her head, she started up the stairs. Holding back the giggles, she imagined their faces when they discovered their stowaway.

She had reached the deck when she heard the whisper of sound, and a distant thump. She stopped and listened. *Could that be Matthew and Alex? Surely there must be someone aboard; it takes a crew to man even a boat this small.* Now the sound came from the dock below.

Leaning over the railing she saw the two figures, and heard their brave steps.

Backing away from the railing, Olivia tried to find shelter. There was a hard object against her back. Fumbling, she discovered a doorknob. With a sigh of relief, she cautiously turned the knob. The door gave slightly and then there was soft resistance. Again she pushed. There was a murmur of voices from inside, but the door flew open. She yelled. Immediately she heard the pounding of feet coming up the stairs, from which she tried to run but as soon as she started she felt a pair of arms wrap themselves around her. As she fought, light flooded the air. "You! Olivia, how did you get here?" It was Matthew, and she flung herself away from him. At his shoulder, holding the lantern high, stood Alex. She could see only his frown. Matthew grasped her left arm and demanded. "Tell me, how did you find out about this?"

"Stop it!" she cried. "You're hurting me! You needn't break my arm. I heard you in the library."

"Everything we said?"

She considered his worried face and took the chance. "Of course. When I saw the boat I realized you two were trying to give me the slip." She jutted her chin at the pair. "If you're going to make such an issue of having a female along on your outing, I'll just take myself out of your presence."

She moved, but Alex's hand blocked her way. His voice was heavy. "Oh no you won't. It's much too late for that. In fact, you've made it absolutely necessary that we take you along."

"Where I'm not wanted?" She lifted her chin as he reached for her arm and turned her around. Holding the lantern high, he stepped forward.

Olivia gasped and took a step backward. The light revealed a huddled mass of people, their dark faces terrified. The eyes shifted to Alex. He spoke softly. "There's nothing to fear. This is Matthew's sister, and she will be making the trip with us."

One man detached himself from the crowd. He was wearing a red cap. He looked from her to Alex, saying, "Don't seem right; maybe it's better we let her go and take chances. Alex, she too gentle a lady; this is a hard trip."

"Not for her. She'll stay with the boat. We'll take good care of her. Right now I can't risk your freedom, even the lives of all your people. You trusted me to get you this far. I won't let you down." He paused, and added, "Her inconvenience isn't as important as your lives."

Turning to Olivia he waved to the man. "This is Caleb, my right hand man, my first mate." He turned to set the lantern on the floor. Now Olivia could see the line of small black faces, watching her fearfully. Unexpectedly she blinked at tears. Alex looked at her and said softly, "Welcome to the Underground Railroad. Olivia, you are now involved in the task of helping move these people on their journey to Canada and freedom."

Olivia just stood there, numb, not knowing what to think.

Turning back to Caleb, Alex said, "In another hour, we'll lift the anchor and drift with the tide. When we get beyond the island, have the men fire the boilers. It should be easy going by then."

"Won't they suspect the quiet engines?" Caleb asked.

"If we are fortunate, there won't be anyone to ask questions this early in the morning." He waved at the others. "Go back to sleep; you're safe." Heading for the door, he turned to face Olivia. "Come along."

He walked ahead of her, across the deck to the stairs leading up to the pilothouse. There he opened a door under the stairs. Silently he stepped aside and waited for her to pass through. Inside he placed the lantern on a cluttered table.

Olivia turned to look at her surroundings. She could see the cabin served as office and quarters. Bunks lined the room. A table with benches and chairs around it stood in the center of the cabin. She was aware that Alex was watching her. Reluctantly she faced him. With a slight smile he said, "Not fancy. I've taken the cookstove out to provide room for the crew. You've seen the rest of the accommodations. At best we can carry fifty in the other cabins. Fifty very crowded individuals.

"This trip we don't have a full house, since it's our first and it takes time to get the word around." He paused, then added, "I suppose being crowded isn't important if there's freedom on the other end."

CHAPTER 16

The paper Crystal had taken from her father's desk rested heavily on her conscience. That night, even with the candle extinguished, she could see the words in front of her. Joseph, age thirty-seven, light of skin, gray eyes. Field hand with one leg injury. Number 9766. Her father had paid one hundred fifty dollars for him.

She tossed in her bed while it seemed Joseph's sad gray eyes followed her. And it seemed she must make some decision. She had nearly decided what to do when the blue eyes of her father appeared beside Joseph's. They blazed with wrath, and Crystal trembled.

Morning was nearly an extension of the night. At breakfast time, Uncle Pierre walked into the room. Crystal saw the hard, white line of his lips and quickly rose to bring him coffee.

Addressing Father he said, "Three slaves disappeared during the night. One was yours." His gaze wandered to Crystal as he continued. "I suspect someone has been passing information. Your Joseph has been a contented man nearly two decades; why does he suddenly choose the life of an outlaw?"

Crystal's hand trembled on her fork. Keeping her head down, she listened.

"I'm not surprised about the other two. I'd heard rumors of a boat in the vicinity, suspected of offering shelter to runaways."

Father's voice was icy. "Did they carry identification?"

"Not a thing. I have their papers, and I've not given them tags for this very reason."

Crystal lifted her head just as her father nodded. "Of course you know I'd feel the same way. Neither does Joseph have a tag. This means the lot of them will either escape to the North, be picked up as runaways and sold by the state, or we'll hire someone to bring them back."

Pierre nodded, "I have a name. A new fellow. Claims to have good success or there's nothing left to be sold. If you'll give me Joseph's paper, I'll be on my way."

"Of course."

Crystal watched her father touch the napkin to his lips, nod at Mama, and follow Uncle Pierre out of the room.

Her mother's words captured her attention. "It is distressing," she murmured. "How I yearn for the old days when we didn't have worries such as this." She handed the jam pot to Crystal and leaned across the table. "Your grandfather trusted the slaves completely, even to take care of his babies. We wouldn't have dreamed of treating them harshly, and they all loved us."

Father returned and was standing in the doorway. Crystal had heard him coming, and his footsteps weren't reassuring. She pressed her back against the chair and waited. He spoke to Mama, but it was Crystal he watched, "My dear, something has come up. I must go with Pierre."

"Whatever—"

"I suspect a conspiracy. Joseph's paper is missing. There were only family members and Cassie in the library yesterday. Of course I will speak to her before I leave."

"Oh, dear," Crystal moaned behind her napkin. "This is unfortunate, but Papa, it's even worse than that. Do you suppose there is going to be a slave uprising?" Silently he watched her and she was conscious of the flimsy drapery of her words.

When he left the room, she was on his heels. "Mama, pardon," she called hastily. "Papa," she caught up with him, "Did you tell Mama—"

"Of course not. Crystal, what do you know about this?"

Slowly she said, "I didn't see anyone in the library, but I did go to my room soon after Cassie finished."

"Tomorrow I was to take Lithie and Joseph to market." He narrowed his eyes as he looked at her. "You must not fight this."

"Papa, most certainly I wouldn't interfere—" Her mind was busy with schemes of getting the paper back with the others. She turned back when he went into the kitchen. Crystal hesitated a moment and then hurried to her room.

Auntie T was there. Crystal stopped when she saw the paper in her hands. Slowly she closed the door behind herself.

With the piles of freshly laundered clothing surrounding her, Auntie T sat on the bed, holding the paper. As Crystal approached the bed, Auntie T lifted her troubled face. "You know?"

"Yes, I know all about Joseph and Evangeline," Crystal said. "And Papa said to say nothing to you. Why?"

Auntie T shook her head slowly.

"Did he think you would encourage me to do something?"

"Oh my! No, your daddy would never think such." She smoothed her apron and looked at Crystal.

Crystal endured the steady gaze as long as she could. Finally she stated, "I see you want to say more. You know where he is?"

Tammera nodded.

"They are going to sell him because he is no longer able to work in the cane fields."

Tammera winced.

Crystal tried to guess her thoughts. Slowly she asked, "What will happen to Joseph if they find him?"

"'Tain't if. It's when. They'll beat him good, and when he's well, they get rid of him. No place around for a slave you can't trust."

"Then take the paper and give it to him. I won't say a word."

Tammera dropped the paper and stared at Crystal. "Me? I wouldn't live through a whipping."

"Papa would do no such thing to you. Why, you're family!"

"Maybe sell me down the river to chop cane 'til I die. Never done a thing like that in my life." She looked at Crystal with troubled eyes.

"Auntie T, I can see from your eyes that you have a scheme all planned. You might as well tell me."

The woman's face crumpled into troubled lines as she began to talk. "You know your mama's folks in Natchez, Mississippi, have been inviting you to visit for two years now. Might ask your papa if you can go."

"He won't let me go alone."

"I 'spect most likely I would go along." With an apologetic glance at her, Tammera continued. "You leave home with one nigger, get on the boat with two."

Crystal blinked. "How can that happen?"

"You don't worry; just remember to bring this paper." She handed it to Crystal.

———

The late May sunshine burned with August heat as Crystal and Auntie T hurried from the carriage to the *Mississippi Queen* docked at the New Orleans wharf. Crystal's father led the way.

Auntie T was puffing by the time they reached the first deck. As they stopped at the railing to wave at the distant figure in the carriage, Auntie T said, "It's a good thing your mama stayed in the carriage. It's too hot for her to be walking like this."

Papa turned from directing the porters, saying, "I only wish she were able to make the trip with you. It must be cooler in Natchez." He left the railing, nodding toward the pilothouse as he said, "Come along. The captain is also signaling his distress at the heat."

He checked the slip of paper in his hand and led the way up to the next deck. The porter was there, smiling and nodding as he opened the door for them.

Crystal saw the quick glance Tammera used on the two small rooms. That glance sent Crystal's heart to beating slow and hard. She watched Papa tip the porter, inspect the bouquet of flowers, and then come to kiss her. "Have a good summer, and don't forget to write to your mama." Turning to leave, he looked at Tammera and said, "I'll leave your bag here and leave it to you to get it down to your room."

When Tammera closed the door behind him, she wilted. Staggering to a chair, she dropped and fanned herself vigorously. Abruptly she sat up. With a quick grin in Crystal's direction, she said, "Me? I saw that look, Missy. I don't go around hiding things from Monsieur Cabet."

She fanned harder. "I 'spect he'll wait until we're headed upriver, and then he'll appear with a nice cool drink."

Auntie T was right. Crystal watched him back into the room with his little cart. He was dressed in spotless white. Only his quick, bright glance at her revealed the conspiracy.

She waited until he had served her. His hand trembled on the goblet of fruit punch as he arranged the napkin on the table beside her. Avoiding his eyes, she murmured, "Joseph, will you please serve yourself and be seated?" From the corner of her eyes, Crystal saw Tammera's pleased smile.

The goblet wafted coolness against Crystal's skin, but she dared only touch her lips to the rim as she tried to swallow the lump in her throat.

Finally she realized she must break the silence. "I saw Papa's record of family history. My birth was listed. This is the first I knew— I mean, I didn't know they weren't my parents."

He was still silent. She added, "Last year, before I went to Boston for schooling, I found a letter. It was very old, and the address contained the name Evangeline Cabet, and a street address in Boston.

"I suppose I wouldn't have tried to find her had it not been for the fact Mama was so very upset with me when she found me holding the letter."

The gray eyes were watching her intently. She knew the question. "She hasn't been in Boston for years. Father told me she's married and lives in France. They haven't heard from her for a long time." *Is that pain or relief in his eyes?*

Crystal sipped her drink and mused over the situation. *It is very romantic, except—she looked at his dusky skin and bowed head—I am the one who must suffer. How do I act toward him when I am filled with anger? Why did my mother do that; why did she leave me?*

As if he sensed her thoughts, he stood and moved quietly around the room, gathering the napkins and goblets. Then he spoke. Facing her and lifting his chin, he said, "This is bad for you, yet you are good. I will not embarrass you. You must not admit—" He couldn't say the words his pleading eyes revealed. There was pain in their depths and that pain only puzzled Crystal.

He had rolled the cart to the door when she asked, "What are you going to do?"

"I think that is up to you. Tammera said you have the paper. You could sell me, or you can let me escape. I would go to Canada."

Tammera gasped. "The freedom road. Joseph, it is long and hard. I don't think your poor leg would take you there."

He shrugged. "Missy, it is worth a try."

As he closed the door behind himself, Crystal sighed heavily. Tammera fanned and watched her with a thoughtful expression on her face as Crystal paced the room. Finally she asked, "Will we see him again?"

"Of course." Tammera took a deep breath and said, "He's listed as your slave, and will be sleeping with the servants below. I'll just bed down on the daybed here."

"But I thought you were sleeping below?"

"No, don't you understand? When I was signing up for a room with the other servants, I was actually registering for Joseph." And then Tammera started to chuckle, "Which is why Joseph has a room with the female servants!"

———————

Joseph served their meals and tidied up after them. And Tammera enjoyed being waited upon. Her large frame shook with merriment as she ordered him about and allowed him to place pillows at her back. After the first day, Crystal began to see the humor in the situation and chuckled along with Tammera.

One afternoon, as Joseph tidied the room and gathered the luncheon dishes, Tammera settled herself for sleep. Crystal rose and restlessly walked around the cabin.

As she turned, she saw Joseph watching her. Quickly the light in his eyes faded and he averted his head. But the expression reminded her of the day at Uncle Pierre's. She said, "That day we went riding at Pierre's, did you know who I was?"

He shook his head. "I'd seen you once when you were a tiny child, but they did their best to make certain it didn't happen again." He lifted his face, and she knew that for the moment he had forgotten his role. "I was proud. Such a beautiful woman and my—" Abruptly he turned away.

He started for the door. "Joseph." When he turned, she saw the glint of tears in his eyes.

"Missy, I guessed. For a minute when I first saw you, I thought I was looking at your mother."

Over the lump in her throat, she whispered, "Thank you for caring. I'll try to do what is best for you." He was nearly out the door when she asked, "Why didn't you and my mother run away?"

He dropped his head. "I am a poor foolish slave. How could I care for her and for you? I would not go. Maybe she hates me too."

"What made you decide to run away now?"

"Cassie got word to me what your father was planning to do. I got scared."

CHAPTER 17

Olivia turned from studying the line of bunks as Matthew entered the cabin. Although the light from the swinging lantern was dim, she could see the serious expression in his eyes. "Sis," he said slowly, "You've really done it this time. Can you see?" He gestured helplessly, adding, "This is serious business."

"Matthew," she said lightly, letting her smile encompass the two of them, "I can't imagine you and Alex being involved in anything other than very serious fun." As she chuckled, the two men silently watched her. Sobering, she shrugged, "Well, give me one good example of a serious moment. My observations lead me to believe otherwise."

Matthew blushed. "I suppose we haven't a good reputation. But give us a chance."

"Olivia, is that fair?" Alex protested. "You've met me once; how can you judge?"

"Easily," she retorted. "That time made quite an impression on me." Thinking of the previous night, she winced. *Impression!*

He looked puzzled, then his crooked grin surprised her. "I'd appreciate another chance. And if you tell me my failings, I'll apologize." Staring frostily at him, she didn't answer. Abruptly he said, "Let's get back to the problem at hand."

He paced the low-ceilinged cabin while Olivia and Matthew

waited. When he finally came back to them, his face was grim. "I'm sorry, but I just can't think of any other way to handle this. Olivia, if we were to leave you, there is a possibility you would be subject to unpleasantness."

Matthew and Alex looked at each other. Slowly Matthew said, "Alex thinks there's a chance the river patrol suspects us."

Olivia watched her brother's face as he talked. "What do you mean, 'Us'? Matt, you're pretty excited about this. It seems to mean a great deal to you, yet I didn't know you and Alex were involved in anything. Why did you hide it from me? Why are you being so clandestine? I heard you saying the most alarming things. It was only a few words, but it was enough to frighten me! You were fortunate I didn't have Uncle Newton after you."

Matthew looked sheepish. "I wasn't so much concerned with keeping secrets from you as I was in just protecting the—"

"Slaves," she nodded, adding, "who are possibly the Thomas' slaves?"

"Possibly—one or two."

"How long has this been going on?"

"Olivia," Alex's commanding voice brought her around. "Please, one of these days I'll personally tell you all about this venture, but for right now, you'll just have to trust us. Matthew didn't know anything about this until he and your uncle rescued me two days ago."

"And you pay my uncle back by running off with his slaves?"

Alex winced. Turning, he said, "Look, I've got to get upstairs. Let me explain this—" He waved at the bunks. "I can't shove those people into one cabin; there're too many of them. It isn't fair. So unfortunately, we'll all have to share this cabin. I'll bunk in the pilothouse." There was a slight smile on his face as he added, "After all, it will only be for six weeks or so."

"Six weeks?" she cried as he hurried out the door. She turned to Matthew. "Why did you let him talk you into this?"

"He didn't really talk me into it," he said slowly. "I pushed him to tell me what was going on. Remember, he skipped out while we were in Boston. I hadn't heard a thing from him, and probably wouldn't have. He said he'd scrapped his plans to visit me when he started to pick up runaways." Matthew paced the cabin. "His excitement just—Olivia, I've never been taken by an idea in quite the way

I feel about this one. I'm beginning to think, as Alex does, that there's some divine mandate in the whole thing."

"Divine? Oh, Matt, how could you?" she cried.

"Cut it out! Obviously I've done a little thinking. Do you think I would be involved in such a project if I weren't struggling with the problem of slavery myself?"

"But what about me? I can live with slavery." Her voice wavered, "I mean, I haven't spent much time thinking about it. But this situation has me most concerned. Matt, I honestly can't say I support the project. After all, it's like stealing horses or something."

She saw the expression in his eyes and felt like squirming. "Support or not," he said, "you'll have to endure it." He headed for a bunk. "Better crawl in; it could be a long, hard day tomorrow."

With the first morning light, Olivia became conscious of the motion of the boat, the pounding paddles, and the soft passage of feet. She turned and slept again. Later, once or twice she raised her head to listen, but it was nearly noon before she left the cabin.

She wondered what she would find as she cautiously stepped out the door. Squinting in the midday sun, she looked down the passageway. It was bordered on one side by the deck railing and by cabins on the other. In all she counted three doors down the length of the steamboat. Behind her, outside the door leading to her cabin, was the stairway curving up to the pilothouse.

Down the corridor she could see the door she had forced open last night. The door was closed and the deck deserted. At least, at first glance it appeared so. As she moved toward the bow of the boat, she noticed a figure under the stairs. Walking forward she peered cautiously through the steps. Behind a coil of rope, Alex was sprawled in the sunshine, with one arm draped across his face.

She noted his neat beard, the boyish curve to his lips, and the ridiculous earring. *How does he expect to be taken seriously with that silly earring?* She watched him until he moved restlessly on his hard bed. Sympathy conquered. Going behind the stairs, she nudged him with her toe and leaned over him. "Go sleep in the cabin; I won't bother you. Where's Matthew?"

He heaved himself to his feet, rubbed his eyes and muttered,

"Down below. They cook next to the boilers." As he entered the cabin, she went downstairs.

"Good morning, ma'am." The black woman met her by the woodpile. "There's porridge."

"I think I'd rather just have fruit."

Matthew came out of the shadows by the engine room. "Olivia, you'll have to settle for common fare," he stated. "There's porridge, period. Come see the arrangements." He led the way. "This boat is a sternwheeler. As you can see, the rear of the boat is given over to the paddlewheel housing, with the engine room and boilers in front of it. The woodpile and these levers have us hurting for space down here.

"You probably noticed up above the bow is the pilothouse. Alex and Caleb pilot the boat. Right now I'm helping the roustabouts and teaching some of the men how to stoke the firebox. This thing? It's the speaking tube, but Caleb tells me Alex yells his orders down."

She turned slowly, looking at the remainder of the space. "So here's the cookstove. I suppose that's the best place for it, but it's funny to see a kitchen in the middle of a woodpile."

He chuckled. "It isn't the best of accommodations, but it works."

She nodded, pointing, "I'm guessing those funny arm-like poles turn the paddlewheel."

"Yes," he waved at the engine room, "they're connected to the pistons on the steam engine."

"Oh, Matthew, look!" She pointed to the logs lined with small children. They flashed shy smiles at her.

The woman who met her on the stairs came with a bowl of porridge. "I'm Maggie. There's a chair over here. We've been sittin' here enjoying the view. Looks like high water. Musta had a mighty rain; see the water standing in that farmer's field?"

The porridge tasted good to Olivia and when she finished, the line of tiny dark children moved forward. The tallest addressed her. "You escaping to Canada, too?"

"I don't think I'm escaping anywhere," she said ruefully.

There was sympathy on the small face lifted beside her knee. "I'm sorry." But the child's face brightened as she said, "We all go. That way Daddy won't be sold away from us." The child pressed closer. "Mammy say up there we learn to go to school."

"Naw," another voice chimed in, "That ain't right. We go to

school to learn. My mammy say when we grow up we do what we want to do, live where we want to live, and have jobs with money."

Another face pressed close. "Can you read? Do you have picture books with stories?"

Olivia nodded. As the faces brightened with hope, she added, "But I don't have the books with me. Perhaps when Master Alex is awake we can ask for paper to make our own book."

"Not *Master* Alex," protested a youth, whose eyes were on a level with hers. "He said there no masters here; we are all friends."

"Could you put writing on the book, too?"

Olivia looked down at the eager face. "You seem too tiny to learn." The face clouded. Hastily she added, "But if you wish. Now come tell me your names."

Olivia was still surrounded by children when Alex came downstairs. She was unaware of him until Maggie clapped her hands and said, "Now you all get yourself on the log. It's time for Alex to read to us."

Olivia stood up as the children scrambled for the logs. Alex gestured toward the crude table surrounded by stools. She looked up, wondering at the questioning look in his eyes.

Opening the book he held, he said, "Olivia, every day about this time, if there aren't boats close enough to give us problems, we read and pray together. You are invited to join us."

She knew the astonishment was showing on her face. For a moment more he looked at her, and that expression stayed with her as he began to read. Busy with her thoughts, the words slid past her without meaning, but a deep curiosity about this man began to grow in her.

When he closed the book, she discovered the familiar words had flowed into her mind with new meaning. " 'Comfort ye, comfort ye my people, saith your God. . . . The voice of him that crieth in the wilderness, prepare ye the way of the Lord; make straight in the desert a highway for our God. . . . And the glory of the Lord shall be revealed, and all flesh shall see it together.' "

"The mouth of the Lord is speaking, we shall be free!" came the response. Another voice resounded, "Everybody say, Amen!"

Olivia bowed her head in the midst of the dark heads and listened to Alex pray. And when he had finished, she knew a different side to this man. She watched him walk up the stairs with the Bible tucked under his arm.

Thinking of the laughing youth, tipsy and bold as he danced her around the school kitchen, she realized part of her understanding of him had crumbled. This new Alex left her uncertain and shy.

By the middle of the following week, the children's book had grown to three pages. The penciled pictures they had drawn were worn with smudges, but at the same time, the big block letters beside them were beginning to be familiar to the students.

But even before that, on the second day of school the crowd of youngsters had been expanded by a timid but eager line of parents mouthing the letters and forming the words.

By the time the third week came, the trip no longer felt like an excursion. A routine had been established, and for the first time in her life, Olivia was part of the work force. Meals of the simplest kind were cooked. Laundry was done, with lines strung around the boilers for secrecy and heat. Part of the routine was vigilance. Everyone had become accustomed to disappearing into the cabins when the pilot shouted, "Ho!"

But just as Olivia was beginning to relax in her new role, another meeting with Alex occurred around the table in the cabin.

One morning Olivia had taken a chair and turned to the young woman leaning against the railing. "Tandy, will you bring my porridge now?"

Alex stopped with one foot on the stairs. Slowly he said, "Olivia, before you begin teaching the children, will you please come up to the cabin?" Glancing at his sober face, Olivia nodded.

After she had finished her meal, she went up to the cabin. Alex stood in the doorway waiting for her. She addressed the dismay in his eyes. "You asked me to come."

Slowly he said, "Olivia, I don't want to say this, but I must. I realize you haven't thought this out, but there's a whole new principle behind what we are doing."

"What is that?"

"Just like the Declaration of Independence says—all men are created equal. The key idea is freedom. Not only from tyranny, but from any reminder of it. Olivia, I find myself walking more gently before these people simply because they have been abused by my people.

And I find myself measuring their wounded spirit with a more strict standard."

He took a deep breath. Turning, he went to place his hand on the Bible lying on the table. "It says here that 'there is neither Jew nor Greek, there is neither bond nor free, there is neither male nor female: for ye are all one in Christ Jesus.' Olivia, please honor this request. Don't ask them to wait on you."

Olivia stared up at him, shocked beyond words. Finally, as he moved to leave the room, she said, "All my life these people have waited on me. Do you suppose it is easy to break the habit? Alex, this is your project. I am your prisoner. I can't believe I am to be forced to conform to your ideas."

"Then you have no sympathy with the plight of the slaves?"

She thought. "I suppose I do. Perhaps not so much as I would if I were also a slave." She flashed a dimpled smile at Alex.

He frowned. "Certainly I won't control your actions once you leave the boat, but for now—"

"When will I be allowed to leave?"

A strange look filled his eyes. "Is it that abhorrent?"

After that scene in the cabin, she made it a point to avoid the black-bearded Alex, and he seemed to make it easy for her. Except for his appearance at mealtimes and the daily Bible reading, she seldom encountered him. She knew that nearly always he was behind the wheel of the steamer or hunched over charts, studying the channels.

Her friendship with Caleb grew, keeping pace with her curiosity surrounding the mysterious activities involved with piloting the boat. Around the table she listened to the first mate's talk about channels and sandbars, steamboat racing and river pirates, and his newest accomplishment—flanking. When her curiosity got the best of her, Olivia made her first venture into the pilothouse. On that occasion she learned how unwelcome a woman was in the male domain.

For days she had yearned for an excuse to climb the stairs, and Solomon's mid-morning pot of coffee gave her the excuse.

"I'll carry it up, Solomon," she said, as she watched the black man gather mugs and lift the fresh pot of coffee from the stove.

He rolled his eyes and puffed out his cheeks. "Don't worry," she added, "you'll not have to take the responsibility for my actions. The worst they'll do to me is throw me overboard!"

Carrying the pot of coffee, she climbed the steps. By the time she reached the pilothouse, a line of males waited, greeting her with silence.

The wind swept through the pilothouse, ruffling her hair. "Oh, there isn't any glass in the window!"

Tersely Alex said, "There isn't supposed to be glass in the window." He turned back to the wheel.

Matthew took the coffee pot, "Look, Olivia," he said carefully, "Women just don't come up here."

"I'm not women, I'm your sister." She looked at the others. "Well, I'm not moving in," she added. "Here's coffee. Answer my questions and I'll have a look and be gone."

"No questions," Alex said heavily, pulling on the wheel. "Just keep quiet, look, and be gone."

Stung by his abruptness, Olivia hastily looked and left.

Matthew followed her down the stairs. "Olivia, we don't know the channels," he explained, "and we have only these charts to go by. We're all scared to death that we'll put the boat on a sandbar. Can you imagine what happens when the river patrol comes past and finds us with a load of slaves without papers?"

"Oh," she murmured, "I see. I'm sorry; I just didn't know. Is piloting a steamboat that difficult? Caleb made it sound like a lark."

He stared at her, "The thing doesn't respond like a horse when you tug on the reins. You've heard enough about steamboat accidents to know there are some problems connected with getting the rig from one port to another," he added sarcastically.

"I thought such accidents had something to do with captains sleeping on the job."

Ignoring the remark, he added, "One reason we don't try to take this upstream after dark is because we're all practically novices."

"Even Alex?"

"He's had a little experience. Enough to make him cautious." He headed back up the stairs.

Early that evening, before sundown, Alex took the boat in close to the bank and tied onto the oak trees. Caleb ran to shut down the engine and in the twilight silence, they all lined the rail waiting for the frogs to resume their concert.

Leaving the table, Olivia went to listen to the gentle lap of water against the hull. Fish jumped with phosphorescent spray arching against the night sky, and Maggie said the words Olivia felt: " 'Tis a picture that makes you believe everything's right in the world."

Late that evening when Olivia went into the cabin, Caleb, Matthew, and Alex were standing around the table. She could see they were bending over the pile of charts. Alex glanced up.

"I'm sorry; I'll go—"

"No, stay," he said. His eyes were unexpectedly gentle as he looked at her. "We don't bite women all the time." He grinned and added, "Just when they come into the pilothouse without being invited."

"Do you ever invite them?"

"Not often." He continued to grin down at her. "There must be a very good reason—such as her being the most beautiful lady on the boat."

Matthew glanced at Alex and then Olivia. Dryly he said, "You notice he kicked you out."

Alex turned back to the table. "Stay. We'll be out of here in a few minutes. One reason we stopped early tonight is that we're getting pretty close to the Ohio River, and there's some charting of channels we need to do in order to get a handle on things."

Shaking her head, Olivia leaned over Matthew's shoulder to watch the pencil Alex drew along the eastern shoreline. "I was talking to some old-timers; they told me to watch this section. There's a light-colored bluff about here. The next landmark will be a small village with a big white church. Halfway between the two spots there's a post box. We'll stop there to pick up information about the Ohio.

"But in addition, just midstream of the box, there's rough water. So we'll have to hug the shoreline beyond the village. There's probably a towhead there." He added.

Matthew glanced at Olivia. "A baby island," he explained.

Alex continued, "We'll need to take a sounding before the bluffs. If it's less than six, we're in trouble."

Olivia backed away from the table shaking her head. "I can't believe progress should make life this complicated." She paused and then said thoughtfully, "Maybe I understand now why there are accidents on the river."

CHAPTER 18

The sounds of Natchez came through the windows, pricking at Crystal's attempt to sleep. With a sigh of resignation, she sat up. "Auntie T," Crystal said as she pulled the light wrap over her nightgown, "I'm feeling terribly lazy this morning. Will you please ask Joseph to bring some juice and perhaps a little fruit? I'll not go down to breakfast."

Tammera wiped the sleep from her eyes, got up, and found Joseph. He began putting together Crystal's breakfast. No one questioned his presence on the plantation; everyone simply assumed that Crystal's father had sent two slaves along with her. When Tammera came back into the room, Crystal turned from the window. "Oh, my, what a headache I have from the party last night!" She added slowly, "But it was lovely, and Natchez is beautiful. We've been here less than a month, and already I love it."

"Don't believe this June weather is as hot as May was in New Orleans," Tammera said, nodding her head as she thumped pillows and smoothed the sheets on Crystal's bed.

"Everyone has been so dear to me," Crystal murmured with a catch in her voice. "Last night's party was very special."

"Your aunt had that look in her eyes. I 'spect she's set on matchmaking. That fellow—" Tammera stopped and rolled her eyes.

something special. All that pretty red hair. My, the girls are a thinking so, too!" She chuckled, adding, "I saw a couple of pretty little things looking as if they wished you'd go home."

Crystal smiled. "I will, but for now, I intend to enjoy every day as much as possible." She glanced at Tammera. "Uncle has promised to show me all of the city. I don't know what he has in mind, but I believe I will see that place called Natchez-under-the-Hill.

"You needn't go see the uglies," Tammera said darkly. "We been discussing it down in the kitchen. Down the riverbank there's nothing good. Bad ladies, gamblers, and thieves. I hear said you don't let a good black man go down along the banks. There's a gang o' men hanging around, ready to grab and sell him down the river, even if he's free." Her dark look was meant to inform Crystal.

And she caught the message. "I understand, Auntie T."

There was a tap on the hall door and Joseph entered the adjoining sitting room. "Missy." He came to the doorway. Crystal turned. The expression in his shining eyes was nearly like an affectionate hug. With a sigh she dropped her head to hide the tears in her own eyes as he said, "Good morning. They say you feeling poorly; so I brought some special muffins in addition to the rest of the food you wanted."

As he spread the table and placed the dishes, Auntie T said, "She had too much party last night."

"Lovely, lovely party," he said, and Crystal found herself admiring the timbre of his deep voice. He chuckled. "We stood in the shadows watching our people dancing in the garden and having a good time. Missy, I saw you with that gentleman, Mr. Boyd Darkinson. My, he's a proud young man! They say he's the only son to inherit his father's plantation. Will be a rich man."

Auntie T nodded. "I been inquiring too," she said. "He already manages the plantation well enough to do any father proud." She leaned forward and whispered, "I'm talking kitchen talk, but they're a bet' he has his heart set on one pretty little gal from New Orleans, " She giggled behind her hands.

l gave a wan smile as she walked to the table. "Don't bet erested."

arlam! I see you smiling up at him. So do all the others. by hung around all last night, waiting to snap up the t loose of him once. Personally, I don't think he knows another lady is in the place."

"I don't believe that!" Crystal protested, accepting the glass of juice from Joseph.

Joseph nodded his head emphatically. "There were some pretty fond looks going around." With a pleased grin he added, "Don't you be shy. You're every bit as good as the best of them, and a beautiful mistress you'll make of his wonderful home."

Hastily Crystal got to her feet, "Please! I must lie down." She tried to shield her face as she rushed past Joseph.

Tammera followed Crystal. "Sugarlam, why are you crying?"

"Nothing, nothing, Auntie T. My head aches so. Please let me rest now."

During the day Crystal was aware of Tammera's dark face bent over her. Once the warm brown hand rested against her forehead. But Crystal kept her eyes closed tightly as if her eyelids could close out the memories of the previous evening. *I would have had a wonderful time if it hadn't been for the expression in Boyd's eyes and that whisper as he left.* Even behind her tightly closed eyelids she could recall his face again. With a teasing grin, he had informed her the magic charm was working, that he would be back to see her again very soon. It had been the expression in his eyes, coupled with those words that made her think of Joseph. *If only I had met Boyd Darkinson a year ago, if only we had married not knowing anything about Joseph.*

It was late afternoon when Crystal finally surrendered. She slipped out of bed and went to the door of the sitting room. "Auntie T, I've heard you shuffling around here all day. I've also heard that door creak a dozen times. Please, go downstairs and visit there."

Tammera came out of the rocking chair with a snort. "I'm standing guard. You'da had all kinds of pesteration if I didn't shoo them off."

"Libby and Ann?"

"No, your aunt and uncle. It's Joseph; he's been causing problems. Missy, before I say anything more, I want you to sit right down here and tell me something."

Crystal frowned, "Auntie T, why are you acting this way?"

"It's important." Tammera waved to the chair beside hers. When Crystal was seated, she leaned forward and said, "We got a problem, and you must answer me directly, 'cause your answer will stee course."

Crystal rubbed her forehead and nodded.

"You been cryin' all day. I 'spect it's because you like that Boyd Darkinson more'n you want to let on. I also 'spect you been crying all day 'cause you know when he finds out Joseph is your father, he'll run the other direction but fast."

Crystal bent double and buried her face in her arms. Through sobs she murmured, "I'm sorry. I know it's terrible of me. Selfish, but I can't help it."

"That is why Joseph left." Crystal continued to sob. Finally she sat up and scrubbed at her eyes. Tammera leaned forward. "Did you hear me?" Crystal blinked and shook her head. "I said, that's why Joseph left. He guessed. He told me so, when I chew him up one side and down the other for running off again."

"Oh dear," Crystal moaned. "I wouldn't hurt him for anything. How did he know?"

"Your face give you away when he talk about you being as good as anybody."

"And he's gone."

"He's back. Now you have to go claim him."

"I wish I never had to face him again."

"You spoiled baby! Now it is time for you to act like a grown-up person."

Crystal sighed and nodded.

Tammera said, "Now you come in here, and we'll get you dressed so you can go fetch him home."

Obediently Crystal started for the bedroom. Abruptly she stopped. "Auntie T, what you said does not make sense. He's gone, he's back?"

"Joseph didn't get to the outskirts of the city before the authorities pick him up and want to see his papers. Come along, we can't leave him there all night. Your uncle is waiting to take you. Put some cold water ᵢ that face, and I'll find a frock."

ʳᵉss was suitable—a dignified, polished gray cotton with a
ᵒllar. Crystal carried her head high as she marched behind
ᵗₒ the old stone building and out again. Joseph walked
ᵒ of them, his head down, while Crystal kept her eyes
ʰer uncle's back.

The air of dignity was becoming as limp as the heat-rumpled cotton. During dinner, Crystal just barely managed to keep her fork from trembling, her conversation from wavering, and her resolve firm.

After a polite interval in the parlor, she excused herself, saying firmly, "Now I have a matter to discuss with Joseph, and then I'll put my headache to bed. It seems Natchez parties are much more complicated than our quiet New Orleans parties. Hopefully I will recover by morning." With that, she walked off to her room. Tammera was already inside, sitting in the rocking chair.

When Joseph walked into the room, with his head still bowed, she didn't call him by name. Watching him with pity, she said gently, "Please sit down."

Before he sat, he murmured, "I must speak. I didn't do this to hurt you. It seemed the best way. I cannot stand to see you hurt because of me. Also I must say—what has happened in the past to cause all of this problem is not your concern. I want with all of my heart to take myself out of your life. Do you see? When I am gone you lift your head high. You've done so before, no reason it can't be done again.

"Missy, you're as honorable now as—before. Don't you forget that." Crystal had been watching his face as he spoke. Now she saw more than the affection. There was a new dignity on the dark face. She opened her mouth to speak, but he lifted his hand.

"Crystal, you will honor me most by refusing to reveal me as your father."

She gasped and immediately covered her face. *Did he see my relief, my shame?*

He sat on the low stool at her feet. His eyes were imploring. "Now will you just let me slip out of your life? I am willing to risk my life to flee into Canada. Freedom's been gnawing me as far back as I can remember."

Crystal watched him, feeling a soreness grow inside as he talked. "I don't know how much you've heard about me. When I was just a lad your grandfather bought me at auction. I was the son of a slave woman and her master. My half-brother was well-fed, schooled, and happy, and he was all white. I tried to learn to read, and got a beating every time I was caught with a book in my hand."

Crystal continued to listen with half of her mind busy weighing the chances her thoughts were presenting. Finally Joseph's voice nearly failed as he urgently renewed his plea. "Please, forget about me; let me go."

With a sigh, Crystal said, "You think, after being caught so very quickly, that there is any possibility you would succeed in escaping again? Even with the paper, you would not be safe." He hung his head. "In addition, there is your poor leg. How far do you think you can walk in such a condition?" He didn't raise his head.

Crystal took a deep breath and slowly said, "I have a plan. I've been thinking about the problem all evening. As you talked it suddenly became clear to me that my plan is your only hope of succeeding in your endeavor. It will possibly be the only thing I will ever be able to do for you, but I'm not only willing, I insist. Joseph, I've taken a steamboat from New Orleans up the Ohio as far as Wheeling. Now I will make the trip again. When we reach the Pennsylvania line, I will sign your paper, and you will be a free man. Within a short time you will be in Canada, forever free from the fear of being apprehended, either as a runaway or as an attractive piece of merchandise to be shipped South for resale. See, I've heard the stories, too."

She got to her feet. "Tomorrow morning, Joseph, I will begin to make plans for our trip." She turned to Auntie T. "I do believe it will be to your advantage to stay here until I return. It could make your life less complicated in the future, particularly if anyone happens to bring up the subject to Father."

"Missy," Auntie T's voice was heavy. "How do you intend to convince your uncle of this scheme?"

Crystal winced. "That will be the most unpleasant part. I will invent a fictitious friend in Greenville, Mississippi, who is most anxious for my company. It will help if Uncle sees me running away from an ardent suitor, especially if that suitor is Boyd Darkinson, for whom his daughter Libby cares very much."

———

Crystal's uncle was able to arrange steamboat passage, and the following week Crystal and Joseph left Natchez. Their steamboat was a small packet, moving only between Natchez and Greenville. Crystal looked at the less-than-luxurious accommodations and assured her uncle that the length of the trip didn't warrant waiting for the *Delta Queen*.

When they reached Greenville, Crystal went immediately to purchase tickets on the first steamer bound up the Ohio. As she joined Joseph, standing guard over her luggage, she said, "How fortunate we are! There is a ship leaving tomorrow and we can board immediately."

On their second day out Crystal met Amelia Randolph. In the salon Amelia's cascade of blonde ringlets and the tight dress of brilliant blue satin caught Crystal's attention. When their eyes met, Crystal crossed the room. "We meet again," she said simply.

"Going to school?" Amelia asked. "I thought you'd be finished."

Caught unprepared, Crystal stammered, "No, well not exactly. I am going that way."

And then came the next question. "Who are you traveling with this time?"

"I'm traveling alone. That is, except for my—slave Joseph."

Crystal left the salon painfully aware of the questions in the woman's eyes. The encounter sharply underlined the obvious. Crystal's traveling accommodations were not the usual for a young woman raised as she had been. For the first time in her life, she found herself avoiding the social entanglements that might lead to questions or even a questioning glance from an unattached male.

In the days ahead, during the quiet afternoon time she made it a habit to venture into the reading alcove. There she buried her loneliness in a book. Amelia found her there one afternoon. "Sweetie, you sure look sad. Got a problem?" While Crystal hunted for a reply, Amelia smiled and added, "If I didn't know better, I'd guess you're running away from home."

"Well, I'm not running away from home!" Abruptly, as the woman's eyes softened, Crystal was filled with an intense desire to confide in her. She pondered the idea and then rejected the temptation.

Amelia lingered on. Her stream of lighthearted chatter had Crystal relaxing and then laughing. When the woman finally left, Crystal looked at the book in her lap and sighed. Slowly she replaced the book and returned to her stateroom.

Reflecting on the encounter, Crystal shuddered at the thought of telling the dancehall girl her story. But again she sighed over her loneliness and confusion as she carefully put the desire behind her.

Two days later, early in the morning after a sleepless night in which Crystal had tossed and worried over the course of action she had chosen, she met Amelia again.

Leaving her stuffy cabin and moving quickly through the shadow-filled salon, Crystal headed for the door and fresh air. As she passed a cabin door, it opened and Amelia stepped out. A man stood behind her. As Amelia hesitated, he reached for her and claimed a kiss. With a chuckle he said, "Until tonight, sugar." The door closed and Crystal and Amelia were left staring at each other.

Amelia broke the silence. She laughed, "Don't look so shocked, dearie; it happens in the best of families. A lonely man traveling the boats starts looking for a lady." She linked her arm through Crystal's and tugged her toward the door. "I suppose you want a breath of fresh air; come along."

The woman's face was relaxed and cheerful as they leaned against the railing. With the wind in their faces they watched the sun come up. Finally Amelia turned. "Couldn't sleep, huh? Want to talk about it? I have until three o'clock this afternoon."

Conscious of the warm comfort of the woman's shoulder close to her own, Crystal nodded. Finally she said, "I'm taking my slave to Ohio where I will give him his freedom and a train ticket toward Canada."

"That's mighty nice of you," Amelia said dryly, "but I can't imagine it costing you a good night's sleep and the dark circles under your eyes I see all the time. I get the feeling you're lonely. That doesn't have anything to do with him, does it?"

"Might." Crystal gulped and said, "Because of him, I just gave up a man who showed every indication of falling in love with me."

"That doesn't make sense."

Crystal faced her. "My slave Joseph is really my father. Naturally, a person like me doesn't marry a white plantation owner from Mississippi."

After listening to Crystal's story, Amelia turned to look at her. "You don't look like a darky to me. Your hair is as soft and fine as mine, just darker. If fear of being found out is the only thing bothering you, go do your good deed and come back and marry the man."

"You really think I should?"

Amelia hesitated. "No. If you were in love with him, that would be different. But it would take work to get around all the problems you'd face. I think you feel sorry for yourself. Not that I blame you; it's pretty shocking to wake up one morning and discover you're not the princess you thought you were. I'd never have guessed your story. Seems to me that you're a person who could land on her feet. Don't let this ruin your life." Amelia leaned away from the rail, and turning her head toward Crystal, she added, "And for God's sake, don't mess up your life like I did."

"God's sake?" Crystal questioned. "What do you mean?"

Amelia gave a short laugh. "It's just an expression, meant to convey a strong feeling." She paused. "Sometimes when life gives us a good hard shake we go storming off and do something rash. You know, like heading into something you can't back out of." Amelia faced Crystal. "That's what I did. Action without thought. I can't go back the way I came. So I'm caught with making a living the only way I know how."

Amelia backed away. "Go get yourself a good rest now. Think about it. Surely it isn't the end of the road for you. Bet you have a nice family. Your mother—grandmother, seemed kind. Just don't let a thing like this get you all down in the dumps." She paused again, then added, "If you feel too bad about it all, some day I'll tell you my story and really singe your eardrums."

The following afternoon, Crystal came out of the salon just as Amelia crossed the deck in front of her. She turned and studied Crystal's face. "How you doing, dearie?"

Crystal shrugged. "That's a pretty dress. I like the ruffled lace. I—" she stopped and frowned. "Must be rough water; the boat is vibrating badly."

Amelia glanced up at the towering twin smokestacks. "There's an awful lot of smoke; wonder if there's something wrong?" She moved uneasily and said, "Walk with me to the stairs; it's about time for me to get things set up for the evening games." They were nearly to the staircase in the bow of the boat when she said, "You didn't answer my question."

Just then they heard a scurry of feet on the stairs. As they turned, Joseph ran up the stairs. Crystal saw the fear on his face and heard him gasp. He took the last stairs in a leap. "Crystal," he murmured in a hoarse whisper. "I was afraid, you being right over the boilers. Come on!"

"What do you mean?" Amelia caught his arm.

"Don't know. Haven't been on a steamboat before this trip, but something's—"

The vibration became a shudder, and the moment they started to move there was an explosion. Amelia grabbed Crystal, but before she could speak, the second explosion came. This one slammed them into each other and into the railing.

Joseph's body shielded them as the surge of smoke and brilliant heat surrounded them. As they huddled, still afraid to move, they began to hear low moans. Crystal pushed away from Joseph, looked, and then buried her face against him. Amelia trembled as they heard a scream begin and then stop abruptly.

Crystal heard the low rumble. Joseph tensed, and his arms surrounded them both as his body arched against the explosion blasting out from the salon. Over his shoulder Crystal saw red and black clouds sweeping toward them.

Joseph yanked them to their feet. "Boat down below!" He shoved them toward the twisted stairs. "Run—there's more!"

Through the dense cloud of smoke the lifeboat appeared, a white arrow pointing beyond the rope ladder. When Crystal hesitated above the expanse of boiling water and surging wreckage, Joseph forced her onto the rope and shoved Amelia after her.

Joseph then dropped into the boat and faced the man at the oars. "Didn't see no more—" There was a scream overhead and singed people plunged over the railing.

The last passenger shoved at the boat, shouting, "There's another boiler to go—I didn't see anyone on deck. Go!"

The force of the explosion shoved the lifeboat away from the sinking steamboat. With the blast the steamer twisted like a giant in final agony. While burning timbers flew around them, the men grabbed for the oars.

Crystal watched flaming debris hailing out of the black cloud of smoke. Another lifeboat broke free as a column of steam rose from the river, hiding the sinking hull.

"Crystal," Joseph's gentle shake and worried eyes caught her attention. "It's going to be fine. See? There's a boat right here. They're coming to pick us up."

CHAPTER 19

Late one morning, when Olivia went down the stairs to the main deck for breakfast, she was surprised to find Alex and Matthew there. They were the center of attention. With their chairs tilted back and their feet resting on the woodpile, the Negro men surrounded them, listening to the conversation.

Olivia saw the nods and smiles from the black men before she was close enough to hear the conversation. But when she asked, "Politics before my breakfast?" The chairs came down and the men stood. "Who's piloting the boat?"

"Caleb," Alex answered. "And good morning, Olivia. Your porridge and eager pupils are waiting. I picked up more paper when we stopped at Pagoussa."

"You did?" Caught by surprise, Olivia cried, "How thoughtful of you!" She saw Matthew's grin and the flush on Alex's face. Embarrassed, she rushed on, "Well you needn't deny you do have a heart once in a while," she said indignantly. "Must you act so tough? Or is that part of the role of a riverboat captain?"

"Yes, Ma'am," he said with a grin. He waved at the chair, "Please, I'll be just as much at home on a log. Matter of fact, Matthew and I need to check the charts." The two started for the stairs.

Later when Olivia walked into the cabin, Alex was pounding the table. "I know what Wise said about Fremont, but this talk has been going on for years. Back in July of 1850, South Carolina and Mississippi were talking secession. In fact, as far back as the twenties there's been talk. And when the Southerners aren't talking, the Northerners are. It's just simply this: If you scratch the dirt away you always get back to the slavery issue.

"Don't forget, the Republican party was the baby of the abolitionists. But the Kansas-Nebraska Bill did more to split the Democratic party than the abolitionists did by creating the Republican party."

Alex poked the paper in front of him. "The bill threw open the whole country to slavery. Popular sovereignty—the right of states to decide the slavery issue—was Douglas's answer specifically to Missouri's demand that Kansas be opened to slavery."

"It can't truthfully be blamed on the economy. Right now, the lowlanders can't say they are suffering," Matthew said. "It is the Piedmont area that is suffering. Economically it has affected them in numerous ways. Also, it's obvious the tidewater plantations are prospering."

"But they won't continue to prosper if they don't have their slaves."

"Fremont didn't do poorly at all, considering it was a new party," Matthew said. "He won one hundred and fourteen electoral votes against Buchanan's one hundred seventy four. It should be better next time!"

"You think he will run again?"

"Wouldn't surprise me."

"And believe me, the Southern Democrats are nervous," Alex muttered. "They see signs that will have them redoubling their efforts in 1860."

Matthew glanced at him, soberly saying, "Redoubling? I've been hearing enough in the past months to make me think that one more election, regardless of who the man is, will either sink or swim the South. Republican spells abolition, and abolition spells the end of slavery. You know as well as I do that since 1854 the Republicans' cardinal issue has been opposing slavery."

"Douglas wants to be president badly, but the North is starting to come alive, and he's partly responsible, even though it was unintentional." Chuckling, Alex swung around and saw Olivia.

At that moment the boat's whistle began blasting—long, loud, and repeatedly. Alex and Matthew jumped to their feet shouting, "Let's go!"

They charged through the door and up the stairs while Olivia watched. She had taken one step through the door when she heard the distant boom, followed by the smack of air against her face.

"Distress, distress—steamboat explosion!" The cry came from the pilothouse. "Full steam ahead! Attempt rescue; get as close as possible."

Olivia ran to the rail. Against the horizon she could see the plume of steam and the deadly flames reaching out from a black center.

Matthew sprinted down the stairs. His face was grim and colorless. "Olivia, come with me!" He took the stairs down to the main deck. "Men, shove that wood in as fast as you can! Full steam. We're going to attempt rescue."

He turned and waved at the line of black faces. "All of you will have to go to the staterooms. Remember the drill? Build the barricade of cotton bales. And when we stop, keep absolutely quiet, with the portholes closed." He added, "I know it will be uncomfortable, but your lives may depend on it."

Olivia watched the people stream toward the top deck.

Tandy turned. "Oh my, the pot!" She ran back to the stove, shoved the trenchers and spoons into the oven, seized the simmering pot, and headed for the stairs.

Matthew said, "We only have one boat. Prepare to launch it." Olivia caught her breath. At her blank look he impatiently said, "You don't have to do anything except get the trash out of it. Find all the rope you can and coil it beside the rail. There's some in the cabin."

By the time Olivia had finished her task the deck was beginning to shudder. She leaned back to look at the smoke erupting from the chimney. The whistle gave another series of sharp blasts and she turned to the rail. In the distance, another steamboat larger than theirs was headed downriver toward the flaming mass.

Olivia shaded her eyes and studied the wrecked vessel. Was that white spot a boat being lowered? Moments after the boat touched water there was another explosion. In horror, Olivia watched the damaged hull flame anew, twist in the water, and slowly begin to sink.

"Alex!" she screamed. She flung herself up the stairs and burst into the pilothouse. "Do something, oh please, do something!"

Matthew pulled her away. The wall of the pilothouse vibrated under her hand, and the blast of smoke and hot air sweeping through the open pilothouse struck her face. She choked on the smoke and struggled out of Matthew's arms. "I'm—what can we do? Are we slowing down?"

"Yes," Alex said grimly. "The other boat has reached them and they're just standing by."

"What does that mean?"

Matthew looked down at her. "Waiting."

"I think one lifeboat did make it away." Alex's voice was tense. "It's heading this way. Matt, man the rail."

Matthew ran down the stairs with Olivia behind him. When they reached the rail they could see the little boat bobbing through the turbulent water.

Matthew said, "I think the other paddlewheeler has found survivors too; they've changed course."

"Yes!" Olivia exclaimed. "See, there's another lifeboat."

"Alex is changing course," Matthew said. "He's preparing to reverse the paddles."

Olivia exclaimed, "Oh look, the boat is full of people! Where will we put them all?"

"We'll worry about that later." Matthew put the rope ladder over the side. As the boat glided close, Olivia looked down into exhausted, terrified faces covered with grime.

"We've got you; you're safe!" Matthew called as he went over the side to help the scared people in the lifeboat. "Toss a rope and I'll pull them close," Matthew yelled back.

Olivia was able to find one and tossed one end down to Matthew. He worked quickly to get the passengers onto the boat. The first person coming over the rail was a portly gentleman, smudged with smoke but still wearing his bowler hat. "Name's Jamison Henders. Fortunate that you were in the vicinity." He wiped his face with a handkerchief and whacked his hat against the rail. Regarding it ruefully he said, "It could be worse. I nearly came hatless."

Olivia turned back to assist a woman coming over the rail, a bundle of smoke-stained froth. Olivia gasped, "It's a wonder you didn't become a torch!"

The woman tossed blonde ringlets out of her eyes and managed a smile. "I think my voice is gone forever."

Her begrimed companion lifted an identical ringleted head and said, "Amelia, it is your fault. You screamed like screams put out fires. But at least you alerted us." The woman shuddered and lifted her face skyward. "Oh, Lord! You have most graciously smiled on us all!"

A black man crawled over the rail and turned with a hoarse whisper to the last person to come over, "Missy, let me help you."

The woman extended her hand and he lifted her over the railing. She turned, and Olivia gasped, "Crystal! I can't believe it. It's Crystal Cabet!" She threw her arms around her friend and led her away from the rail. Hugging the trembling girl again and wiping the tears from her own eyes, Olivia murmured, "Oh, my dear friend! I thought I would never see you again, and here we are in the middle of the Mississippi River!"

Crystal winced. "You'll never know the reality of your statement. Oh, Olivia, it has been so horrible! The explosion. Some people were blown against the sides of the ship. I saw—" Abruptly she began to tremble.

Olivia grasped her arm. "There, that is enough. Let's go and I'll get everyone warmed up."

The man in the bowler hat elbowed the colored man aside, and with the grimy dancehall girls followed them all.

———

Seated around the crude table close to the stove, everyone except Jamison sagged against the table and waited for tea. Soon another couple joined them and Crystal gave the woman her seat. Joining Olivia at the stove, she attempted a smile. "I need to work anyway. Where will I find mugs?"

Olivia reached for the oven door and paused. She remembered Tandy had shoved the crude trenchers and spoons into the oven along with the mugs. She saw Crystal's puzzled frown. Quickly she moved her away from the door, pulled out the mugs and handed them over to Crystal. "What are you are doing here in this terrible boat?" Crystal asked. "Do you always cook down here in this woodpit? And do you always store your pans and mugs in a hot oven?"

"Oh," Olivia stared helplessly at Crystal. Dropping her voice she said, "Please, I'll tell you later—maybe." Matthew and Alex came down the stairs.

"Crystal, you remember the night I tried to introduce you to my brother, Matthew? Matthew—" Impatiently Olivia turned. Matthew was frankly staring at Crystal.

He blinked, frozen for a moment, then bent over Crystal's hand. "Olivia, you didn't tell me that your Crystal is the loveliest woman on earth. If you had, I would have torn down Miss what's-her-name's hallowed halls to meet her. Miss Crystal Cabet, we are honored. May I bring you the rocking chair and some tea?"

"Not the rocking chair." She tried for a smile. "I've had all—"

She sagged and Olivia wrapped her arms around Crystal. "Matthew, where do we find more tea?"

Alex joined them. "Miss Cabet," he said. "I can't believe my eyes." He looked at the group around at the table. Olivia saw him stiffen and glance quickly at her before moving to the table.

"Mr. Jamison Henders, I believe. I met you in New Orleans a month or so ago. At the office of shipping regulations. I understand you are on the board of regulations for river patrol. A most unfortunate accident. I suppose you will be wanting to return to New Orleans as quickly as possible."

Olivia watched the man while Alex talked. The sharp eyes had grown increasingly alert as Alex spoke. Now the man thoughtfully said, "Yes, I do need to return to New Orleans. Perhaps you can take me to St. Louis."

Alex shook his head. "I'm an independent packet. Headed up the Ohio with cargo. Unfortunately, I can't accommodate you without inconveniencing my customers."

"What's your cargo?"

"Well, I'm carrying some cotton. There're several other miscellaneous items. Care to check it out?"

Henders shook his head. "What's the best you can do for me?"

"Knowing we were overloaded, my mate is signaling the *City of Troy* to come around." Alex turned to address the other passengers. "As you can see, we are very limited in accommodations. There's cargo in the cabins. I will be happy to transfer as many as possible to the *City of Troy*. She is bound downriver. If you feel you must continue on, I can deliver you to Cincinnati within two weeks, the Lord willing. You will need to share very crowded quarters."

"I will pass on the crowded quarters, and transfer to the *City of Troy*."

The middle-aged man cleared his throat. "My name is McAnders. My wife and I appreciate your help. We will also transfer to the *City of Troy*."

"Me too," echoed one of the dancehall girls. She turned to her companion. "Come on, Amelia, there's no money in this dump."

Amelia stirred, looking confused and uncertain. "I—I think I would like to go to Cincinnati."

"Cincinnati, Ohio," Crystal Cabet said slowly, "Why, we're—I'm going that way. If I may, we'll just stay with you."

The whistle gave a long, sharp blast. "*City of Troy* is coming around," Alex said.

McAnders got to his feet. "By the way, what's the name of this ship?"

Alex paused with his foot on the step. "*Golden Awl*." He looked at Olivia, hesitated, and then ran up the stairs.

———

After the final passenger had transferred to the *City of Troy,* Olivia and Crystal stood at the rail, watching the steamboat move away from them. "That beautiful boat is like a dream isn't it?" Crystal said. "Floating along with all those lanterns bobbing and reflecting first off the white latticework and then sparkling off the water." She caught her breath, "That's how our boat looked until today."

Quickly Olivia hugged her. In a moment she said, "And as silent as a dream drifting away." Olivia turned to smile at Crystal, to touch her hand in sympathy. "I'm so sorry you've had such a difficult day; I know you must be exhausted. I think we need to go into the cabin and see what the captain has decided to do with all of us."

"Oh, is that a problem?"

"Yes, and it's all Alex's problem."

"Alex?" Crystal, looked around, and took a deep breath. Olivia noticed a touch of color had come back into her cheeks. "I scarcely recognized him. He seemed such an irresponsible youth that one time

I met him. I remember him tipsy and laughing while all the instructors were perfectly horrified." She paused and said thoughtfully, "Now he seems steady enough. But why does he wear that golden earring? It makes him look like a pirate."

"I don't know. I simply don't understand him at all. He has changed to the point that now he is completely boring."

"And what a strange name for a boat. *Golden Awl*. What does it mean?"

"Mean?" Olivia replied slowly, "I don't know; it's probably just a flight of fancy, like the earring."

"Will you two ladies join Amelia and me in the cabin? We need to discuss arrangements," Alex said, grinning down at Olivia as she turned. She felt her face grow warm.

When they had crowded into the cabin and Alex had found chairs for the newcomers, he took his place beside the smoking lantern. With hands in pockets, and the lantern light making deeper shadows of his beard and striking light from the slender gold hoop in his ear, he addressed them.

"Unfortunately, since Mr. Jamison Henders is chief inspector for the river patrol, I was unable to be completely candid with you while he was with us. I sense that you are all people who can be trusted, if not to participate in my scheme, at least to hold our secret in confidence."

He hesitated. Olivia watched Amelia as she leaned forward. The bored droop to her lips was disappearing as Alex talked. For a moment Olivia wondered if Alex himself interested the blonde woman.

Alex's words sliced through Olivia's thoughts. "The main cargo we carry is slaves bound for Canada. The cotton we carry is a convenient shield if by chance we are stopped for inspection."

There was a slight gasp from Crystal. Alex looked at her and his face tightened. "As I said, you need not be considered a part of the scheme, or even condone my actions. If you are fearful, I will allow you to leave ship at the first port."

He waited. There was only silence. Unexpectedly he grinned. "Now for quarters. Since the women outrank us, we men will sleep either in the pilothouse or on deck." He saluted. "Goodnight, ladies."

The door closed and the three women faced each other. Amelia said, "Olivia, I don't believe you remember me. Nearly two years ago you traveled the boat I worked on. You were going east to school and I—" She sighed. "I guess I worked at a dead-end job which has just finished."

She sat down and pulled off her shoes. "Funny thing. You think it's the end of the world one minute and the next minute life is exciting with all kinds of possibilities. Transporting slaves? Sounds exciting. Guess I'm a do-gooder at heart, like that fella, Alex."

"I don't think you should set your sights for him," Olivia said softly.

" 'Cause you already have? Sister, I'm not blind." She looked down at her grimy dress. "Ugh. Is there water around so I could wash this thing?"

CHAPTER 20

Alex's hands rested lightly on the wheel. The cool morning breeze came through the pilothouse, ruffling his hair, and filling his nostrils with all the mingled odors of the muddy river and the greenery along the bank.

Beyond the line of hickory, oak, and magnolia he could see cultivated fields, with black figures marching abreast through the young corn. The sun glinted off the hoes as they rose and fell in rhythm. He could nearly guess the cadence of their songs as, sweating and hacking, they worked their way across the field. Softly Alex sang, " 'Go down, Moses, Way down in Egypt land, Tell old Pharaoh, Let my people go.' "

Caleb came into the pilothouse. Alex said, "There's enough verses to get them across that field and into the next." He nodded toward the bank.

Caleb grinned and sang another verse. " 'You'll not get lost in the wilderness, Let my people go; With a lighted candle in your breast, Let my people go. Go down, Moses—' "

"You know Moses?"

Caleb shook his head. "I hear about her. Mighty fine woman, that Harriet Tubman. Not many black women brave enough to be Moses to their kind. I hear there's a bounty on her. Thousands of dollars they pay if she's turned over."

"For a white man to lead slaves across into Canada is child's play compared to a woman like that giving herself to the task time and time again."

Caleb nodded soberly. "I 'spect she won't survive to old age. But I admire that woman more'n I can say."

"I pray for her," Alex said slowly. "She is an inspiration to all of us. The hardships she suffers are beyond me, sitting here all safe and sound in my boat."

"So far you're safe," Caleb said softly. He bent over the charts for a moment. "We're nearly to the Ohio."

Alex nodded. "The Harriet Tubman Moses carries a gun, I hear. A no-nonsense woman; she's threatened slaves ready to quit on her."

There was silence in the pilothouse. The sun rose and the air coming through was moist and heavy. Alex saw Caleb glance at him several times. Finally he said, "You want to say something? Out with it."

"Miss Olivia. You a mite hard on her."

Alex looked at him and grinned. "Since you know more about women than I do, what do you suggest?"

Caleb shifted his red cap and grinned sheepishly. "Aw, boss, I'm not telling you about women. It's just that it bothers me seein' you keep her on the boat. Doesn't seem right. I think she can be trusted."

"Mind if I keep her around just because I like her company?"

Caleb's jaw sagged. "If you like that lady, there's no one on this earth, including the Lord himself, who'd believe it!"

"Caleb, does that look like a sandbar to you?"

"Could be; seems the river's a might low around here."

"Did you take a sounding this morning?"

"Yes. We're drawing plenty of water in the channel. I don't trust that strip just ahead. Look how the sun hits it, and how the water dimples."

"Caleb, no one would believe this is the first time you've been upriver this far. When life settles down, I'll push you to get your license. That is, if you aren't sick of the river by then."

"I don't know." Caleb scratched his head. "Me, I'm thinking of getting married."

Alex looked at him in surprise. "Anybody I know?"

"Naw, just thinking."

"Caleb, go have your breakfast, and don't get married before noon; I want some breakfast, too."

"I could send Miss Olivia up with it." Alex pitched his tin cup at Caleb, who clattered down the stairs laughing.

In the silence of the pilothouse, the Presence was undeniable. "Lord," Alex murmured, rubbing his hand across his face. "Is it that obvious? I'm still wishing You'd take all the wanting out of me. Seems she's not fitted for what You have in mind for me." He stopped and grinned sheepishly. "Here I am, trying to run Your universe again!"

The quiet, the sweep of the wind, and swish of water through the paddlewheel had Alex's thoughts drifting again. Finally with a sigh, he straightened and murmured, "As Shakespeare said so well, 'It is my lady; Oh, it is my love! Oh, that she knew she were!' "

Olivia carefully spread the three sheets of paper on the rough surface of the table. She addressed the line of eager black faces. "Today we are writing R. What words sound like they begin with R?"

"Red." "Rich." "Rule."

Her attention drifted. She looked toward the rail. Crystal and Matthew were in the same spot they had occupied yesterday and the day before. Their heads were close together. Matthew gestured and Crystal seemed to hang on his every word. "River." "Rat." "Rufus," her pupils intoned.

"Oh, that's enough! Let's write—"

"Write." "Wrong."

Olivia looked at her pupils in dismay. "Oh, I think we have a problem. "You are right, but write—"

"Riddle's the rule, right now," Alex chuckled beside her.

She caught her breath. "I didn't know you were here. All right, Mr. Captain, you explain the difference between an *R* and a *W*. And we're out of paper."

"No paper? That raises a ridiculous rift in the wreck." He stopped, and they all listened. The grating, grinding noise seemed to sweep along underneath them. Alex leaped for the stairs. "Reverse it!"

"That's a good R," Tandy said.

"Oh, I think we've struck something!" Olivia said softly. Matthew ran past as they felt the vessel shift beneath them. There was more grinding and a shudder. They stopped abruptly.

Olivia ran to pick up the line of small figures on the floor. "Throw on the wood," came the order. The men leaped forward and the steam began to rise.

The children were jumping up and down clapping their hands, but Olivia could see that Tandy and Maggie had guessed the situation. They came to her. "What do we do?"

"Pray," Olivia murmured, moving automatically around the area, pushing trenchers and spoons into the oven, and shoving the simmering kettle back into position.

Crystal came to stand beside the table just as the steamboat shuddered and seemed to settle more firmly. Alex's voice came through the speaking tube. "That's enough wood. Any hotter and you'll rupture the boilers. Keep the monkey rudder reversed."

The boat continued to shudder. "Now throw it straight ahead!"

Olivia could feel the vessel straining. She was ready to clap, when abruptly the straining ceased. Alex flew down the stairs with Matthew behind him. They ran to the paddlewheel housing.

Alex backed out and groaned, "I feared this. We thought we were having paddle problems in New Orleans. I think we lost a gear."

"What'll we do?" Matthew asked, following Alex to the table.

"We'll have to find help." Alex said slowly. "But we dare not." He looked slowly around the ring of dark faces.

"Alex," Solomon suggested, "we could take to the pine forest. It's thick through here. That way no one knows about us."

Alex's face brightened. "Might be the thing to do. Hide until we get the problem solved." He walked to the speaking tube. "Caleb, do you seen any sign of a boat? We're going to have to hail someone."

Olivia turned to the group. Realizing her hands were trembling, she stopped to take a deep breath before saying, "Go to your cabins; gather up everything. If someone boards, they must not find anything that will give a clue. I'll pack food. How fortunate Maggie baked bread this morning!"

"Matthew, prepare the lifeboat. Will you get them all ashore?" Alex asked as he walked toward the stairs. He paused. "We'll need you here. We'll have to keep trying to work it loose even with a stripped gear. We've got to get off the sandbar before we settle in deeper. Lightening the boat may help."

Alex glanced at Olivia and then came to her. "I don't like involving you, but—"

"Because you still don't trust me?"

"It has never been that. I do trust you, I'm only concerned."

She shrugged indifferently. "I've prepared food to take to them. We had vegetables and beans simmering. They wanted a little more cooking." She paused and looked up at him. Alex's troubled eyes made her conscious of the danger to these people. "Please," timidly she touched his arm. "I think it will be—" She hesitated, then said in a rush. "I'll pray that God will help us know what to do."

Unexpectedly he touched her cheek and ran up the stairs. Amelia had been watching from the rail. With a grin she said, "You're soft on him, all right. No matter, he's a nice-looking fella."

Crystal came forward with a perplexed frown. "Olivia, I don't know what to do. Joseph has an old leg injury, and it's very difficult for him to walk rapidly.

"If a problem arose and the people had to run, I am afraid he would hinder them. Wouldn't it be best for the two of us to stay here? After all, he's my slave."

Olivia nodded and Amelia drawled, "I'll stay, too. I'm not fond of struggling through the forest afoot."

"Do as you wish," Olivia said. "We won't be gone long. Oh, there's Matthew with the boat. Please tell the first group to come down. I'm afraid he'll have to make at least three trips."

———

When Matthew returned for the final trip, he came to carry the kettle for Olivia. "Is there just you and Tandy?"

"No. There's her two babies and little Joe. Matthew, there's food on the stove for you all. Amelia and Crystal will be here, too."

"Come along," Matthew said. "I don't like the lay of the land. There's a cultivated field mighty close to the river. I suggest you spread out, walk up river until you're around the next bend, and then regroup."

"How long will we be there?"

"If we're still on the sandbar come nightfall, we'll bring you back for the night, if it seems safe. One of us will keep you informed. Just don't get separated."

Tandy came down the stairs with a toddler under each arm. Handing Sarah to Olivia, she said, "That little Joe is a handful."

"I'll get him," Matthew said sprinting for the stairs.

When he returned, Matthew had the child under his arm, talking seriously to the grinning boy. "This isn't a picnic," he said, holding the child at eye level. "You settle down and be as quiet as possible. No shouting. You get a hold on Tandy's apron strings and don't let go until she says you can. When I come after you, if you haven't behaved, I'll turn you over my knee."

Olivia saw the child's eyes widen, and hastily she added, "And if you are as quiet as a mouse, I'll give you a special treat."

"Hurry! That toot means Caleb's spotted a boat."

They were able to get into the lifeboat quickly, and as soon as Matthew reached shore, the two women jumped out. Tandy carried her baby and a bundle, and Olivia had the kettle of food and a child under her arm. "Quick," Matthew muttered, "into the woods! Caleb's signaling the boat to come around."

Olivia and Tandy ran into the woods, and when they finally sat down to rest, they were surrounded by the deep, fragrant pine forest. Leaning against a tree, Olivia closed her eyes while Tandy nursed her baby.

A little while later she opened them again and stared at Tandy. "Where do you reckon the others are?" she asked.

"I've been trying to guess while you were sleeping," Tandy answered.

"Sleep! I didn't realize. Oh, Tandy, maybe we should look for them. Let's see, we came from that direction, didn't we?"

Tandy shook her head slowly. "I don't know. I can't hear boats."

"Maybe we're farther from the water than we thought," Olivia said slowly. "You stay here with the children while I look around."

Tandy scrambled to her feet. "Then I might get lost, too."

Olivia chewed her lip. "You think we're lost? How can that be? The others must be close."

"All the time you slept I tried to hear something. Didn't even hear a twig break."

Olivia peered through the gloom. "We dare not shout," she whispered. "But what if we really *are* lost?"

CHAPTER 21

By late afternoon the *Golden Awl* was off the sandbar. Their benefactor scratched his head, saying, "You'd have done it yourselves if it weren't for that monkey rudder. I think the gearing is stripped out of it. If I were you fellows, cargo or no, I'd head for the nearest port. You can't go nowhere without having to back up and flank around curves."

Alex finished wiping the grease from his hands and said, "Without a doubt. That's what we'll have to do. Thank you for your help."

The young captain looked around. "Pretty nice little boat. You've taken good care of it." He paused. "Cargo doesn't pay much on a boat this size. Given the condition, I'd expect you to find more passengers. Only way you'll ever pay for it."

"Fortunately I'm not in debt," Alex said dryly. "My father gave me the boat. It was sadly in need of some upkeep, which we've just finished. Thank you again, sir; it has been a pleasure to meet you. I'm going to take another look at the engine, and then we'll take your advice about going into port."

They shook hands and Alex watched the packet boat captain return to his craft. With a final signal the boat slipped back into the channel. Alex turned to Caleb. "See if you can do something to make that rudder hold together. Have Jeb and Tass shut down the engine and help you. Matthew and I will go after our passengers."

When they reached shore, Matthew said, "I told them to head up river and wait for us. Let me shove the boat back in the willows and I'll come with you."

The two headed into the forest and then turned north. Within a short distance, Solomon rose out of the bushes with a grin. "Didn't mean to spook you. We heard you coming and was being just as quiet as we could."

Alex patted him on the shoulder. "Are you all here?"

"All except Tandy and her babes—oh yes, and little Joe."

"Where did they go?" Alex asked.

"Never did catch up with us. We walked up here just like Matthew told us, and we—"

He stopped and cocked his head. Slowly Alex said, "Do I hear dogs?"

"Might just be a fellow out hunting," Matthew said.

"Them's hounds," Solomon said softly, "just like they use to track black people. Ain't bloodhounds—they track without no noise. From the bayin', I'd say it's coonhounds or blueticks—an' comin this way."

Alex looked around at the group of slaves coming up out of the bushes. He saw the fear on their faces. Making a quick decision he turned to Matthew. "I want you to take Jess and head back toward the boat. If Solomon's guess is right, it won't be long before those hounds pick up a scent. Cut through the trail in a zigzag, and be certain that you are there for the hounds to find. When you get back on the boat, head north for the nearest port."

"Bait," Matthew said tersely, nodding his head. "Then what are you doing to do?"

"Head north as fast as we can go. And pray that there's only one pack of hounds out there. Eventually, we'll catch up to you."

"What about Olivia and Tandy?"

"We'll find them. Since we didn't see them, they've got to be ahead of us."

"If not?"

"Then either you or the hounds will find them. Go, Matt!"

He watched the two men sprinting back the way they came laying a wide zigzagging trail. Alex took a deep breath, turned and said,

"Let's move out. Women and children in front, surrounded by you men. Walk as fast as you can, heading straight north. If the children can't keep up with us, then carry them. We'll survive if we shake those hounds.

"Watch the moss on the trees. It should always be behind you."

———

Tandy whispered, "Listen, Olivia, I think I hear hounds."

"Oh, then there's a house near!" She saw the expression on Tandy's face. "That isn't good. What shall we do?"

"Olivia, we've got to catch up with the others. And with these babes, I don't know how we can."

"We can only hurry," Olivia said, picking up Sarah.

———

Alex walked behind the others, constantly listening to the hounds, trying to determine their position, and dreading the prospect of their silence. But just about the time he felt he knew where the dogs were, the silence came. Almost immediately, however, the hounds erupted with frantic barking. Was the barking becoming uncertain? There was a shout. Alex saw Solomon's pleased grin. "It worked!"

Alex released his breath in a sigh of relief. "Keep moving; we've got to find the others."

———

Olivia gasped. "Tandy, I can't take another step. Please, let's sit down for a few minutes."

"Listen! The hounds aren't coming this way now. They found something." Tandy collapsed beside Olivia. Breathing heavily, she said, "Maybe the others heard the hounds and waited for us."

"I hope so. What will we do if they don't find us before dark?" Olivia tried to swallow the lump in her throat. Tandy's eyes were wide with fear as she patted her fussy baby.

"Tandy, do you hear something?"

Tandy cocked her head, listened, and then said. "Sure enough. There's something coming. Let's hide."

As they started for the bushes, little Joe dropped Tandy's apron string. "I hear a laugh; that's Timmy!" He turned and ran.

Within a minute they were surrounded by their group. Olivia watched Tandy throw herself into Maggie's arms, and in the midst of soft whispers, Alex was there beside Olivia. "You!" she said in amazement. "What are you doing here?"

In a terse whisper, he said, "You were missing, and then we heard the hounds. Keep walking," he warned the group, taking Tandy's little boy from Olivia. "We'll talk later."

When it was too dark to see where they were going, Alex moved among them again. "It appears best for us to find shelter in the bushes. We'll have to stay here tonight. If we did find the river, the boat couldn't see us."

"There's supper in this kettle," Olivia said wearily.

"I'm sorry," Alex murmured, taking the pot. "I didn't realize you were carrying something. We need food desperately if we are to keep walking."

They found shelter in the bush-covered hillside and sat down to eat. As quickly and as quietly as they could, they ate their supper and then quieted the children down for the night. Soon, most everyone else had also settled in for a good night's rest.

Olivia's body was crying out for sleep, but her mind was too busy thinking over the events of the past day, so she sat down with her back against a tree, staring wide-eyed into the darkness. She was conscious of whispers, movement. Alex came to sit beside her.

"The hounds?"

"We're safe. We had planned to find you and go back to the boat, but the hounds cut us off. Matthew and Jess decoyed them."

"Oh, that's what happened. We heard all the commotion."

"We thought we'd have to walk to the Ohio before we caught up with you," Alex said. "How did you manage to get in front of the party?"

Olivia shrugged, "We thought we were behind and tried to walk as quickly as possible. What do we do now?"

"Keep walking. The boat is going to limp into port. Matt and I spotted a likely place on the map. Now it looks as if the best we can do is to meet up with them. Hopefully we can spot them on the river. If not, we'll aim for the first good port."

He shifted his weight and she felt the warmth of his shoulder against hers. "Alex?"

"Yes."

"Will we make it?"

"Of course. It could be difficult, but these people are accustomed to hard times. And the Lord has clearly led us this far. He'll see us through. Now go to sleep."

He shifted his position, and his shoulder was warm and comforting under her cheek.

———

She felt his fingers against her face. "Olivia, it is nearly dawn. I think we had better awaken the others and start walking. It's impossible to guess where we are. We'll have to be concerned with keeping the children quiet and moving quickly."

She got to her feet and shook her frock. With a weary yawn, she tried to guess east and searched for a glimpse of light. Alex watched silently. He was only a darker shadow close to her until he murmured, "Did you rest?"

There was a gentleness in his voice that brought tears to her eyes. She bit her lip hard before answering, "Yes. Thank you for the shoulder. There's bread in this bag. Shall we divide it now?"

"Let's wait. If that is all there is, we'll either find the boat or look for a place to buy food."

"Do you know what lies ahead of us?"

"Not completely. According to the map, there are several small towns along the Ohio River. I'm guessing there are also farms close to those towns—which means we'll need to stick to the woods."

Solomon had been moving through the group speaking softly, and now the people were on their feet, preparing to move out.

A young Negro stepped close to Alex, his voice low and worried. "Them babies are fussy. Didn't get enough sleep."

Alex reached for the bread sack. "Then divide this loaf among them, Ralph. Only one," he cautioned. "Our supplies are going fast."

By mid-morning they were walking along the pine forest that bordered one farm after another. Alex summed up the situation when they sat down to rest at noon. "I believe we are in Kentucky now; soon the Ohio River branches eastward. Unless Matthew and Caleb are having trouble, I expect they've passed us. Right now it seems best for us to begin to head northeast."

The statement was met with silence. Alex studied the tired faces. "And, I think I'd better venture into the nearest town for provisions. I'll take Ralph with me, and the rest of you stay together, rest, and keep the children quiet."

The two of them then headed to find some food and soon were out from under the shelter of the forest. The sun scorched them as they walked rapidly down the lane that seemed to veer steadily northwest. Alex mopped his forehead and grinned at Ralph. "Think we can find our way to the river?"

Ralph shook his head. "I'm wondering where we can buy food. I don't think we'll dare have a cook fire."

"That's right," Alex said slowly, "so we'll need things like bread, cheese, maybe sausage."

Ralph grinned. "Turnips, some roasting ears. I can always just help myself to those."

Alex shook his head. "Let's avoid trouble if we can."

"Here's a fella with a wagon," Ralph said. "Maybe he'll give us a ride."

Alex turned to wave. The wagon stopped and the man peered down. "If'n you're going to town, you and yer nigger hop in."

Alex's attempt at conversation was met with monosyllables. But his irritation disappeared when he realized all the questions were unnecessary. Their destination loomed on the horizon.

After they arrived in town, the man dropped off Alex and Ralph and they went into one of the shops along the wharf. Roustabouts slept peacefully in the noon sun. Casually he asked, "Been a boat through here today?"

"Looking fer a packet?" asked the shopkeeper.

"Yes. Have you seen the *Golden Awl?*"

A frown crinkled the man's brow. "Don't know's I've ever heard of that'un. Ain't seen a boat today. Might wait if you haven't a better thing to do."

After purchasing cheese, sausage, and corn, Alex asked the shopkeeper, "Is there a bakery in town?" The shopkeeper waved his hand toward the end of the street and continued to stuff Alex's purchases into the cotton bag.

At the bakery Alex bought four loaves of bread, two cakes, and a tray of cookies. As he and Ralph walked down the street, he said, "I dared not risk raising her curiosity, but four loaves won't go far with us."

Soberly Ralph nodded. "Seems to me we could go a mite hungry until we find that boat. But that's better than having the hounds on our trail again."

By the time they were halfway down the lane leading to the pine forest, Ralph brightened and grinned at Alex. "Sometimes a hungry stomach can make a fella forget there's freedom ahead. Keep reminding us, Alex. When we grump, remind us freedom is just around the next corner!"

"Mister, wanna buy some apples?" The youth had been standing along the lane for several hours selling his fruit to passersby. Now he had come rushing out and planted his feet in the middle of the lane and straightened under his sack. "I see you been into town. Bet you didn't find any nice fresh summer apples. Wanna—"

"Only if I can buy the bag too," Alex said with a grin.

———

After entering back into the forest, they soon found themselves refreshed by the moist, cool air, heavily perfumed with moss and pine. "Almost there," Ralph murmured, shifting the apples to his other shoulder.

"I can see them," Alex replied as the first little black figure ran toward him.

That night, after eating, they walked, keeping well within the forest, until the children whimpered with weariness.

Regardless, when they formed a circle and divided the apples and sausage, there was nearly a festive air to the group. Alex could see Olivia was feeling it, even though her face was drawn with fatigue.

As he studied her face in the waning light, he felt a new stirring of tenderness. Moving impatiently, he got to his feet. "We haven't taken time these past two days to have our prayer and Bible reading. I've been thinking about the words in a Psalm that means much to me. There's hope to be taken from the words, and I want to say them to you. 'Blessed is the man whose strength is in thee; in whose heart are the ways of them. Who passing through the valley of Baca make it a well; the rain also filleth the pools. They go from strength to strength, every one of them in Zion appeareth before God.'

"Now, 'the ways of them' in this Psalm refers to the sparrows who have found a shelter in God's house. A place where they are so much at home that they build nests and raise their young. Right now none of us has a home, but now at this minute we can be at home in God, with as much confidence as those sparrows have in His Presence. Solomon, will you pray for us tonight? But keep your voice down."

Olivia fought sleep as Solomon's whispered prayer reached out to all those around the circle. She heard the strange note of rejoicing in his voice as he said, "Lord, we don't know anything except You have us in the hollow of Your hand. And we don't have to worry about us. We do the best we can. If we die, we die in You. If we get to Canada, You'll be there too."

When the last rustle and whisper quieted, Alex came to her side. As they settled their backs against the tree, Olivia said, "These people have such childish ways. That prayer of Solomon's seems too innocent. He acts as if he's addressing a person, someone with hands and feet who can help him."

"I think he is. It seems to me that Solomon has a clear picture of Jesus Christ sitting right there listening to him."

"You believe that way?"

"Yes." She couldn't think of anything else to say. Tired as she was, she now had trouble getting to sleep as she listened to the rustle of forest creatures and the murmur of restless children. Finally Alex reached for her and held her in his arms until she slept.

CHAPTER 22

While Jess rowed back to the boat, Matthew watched the men on shore. He said, "It was a nasty situation resolved more easily than I expected."

"Are they still standing there?"

"Still watching, but I don't think they're suspicious." Matthew continued, "The hounds picked up the scent of us all, but I'm convinced we confused them. Just hope we can meet up with Alex and the rest of them tomorrow."

Jess nodded. Pulling close to the *Golden Awl*, he dropped the oars as Matthew grabbed the rope ladder and turned to reach for the rope. Crystal came to the railing just as Matthew dropped to the deck. Leaning over, she saw the empty boat. Wide-eyed she looked from Jess to Matthew.

"Did you hear the hounds?"

She nodded.

"Alex and the others headed north. Jess and I were decoys." He grinned down at her. "Tomorrow you have a job. You'll be chief look-out. Hopefully they'll find their way to the shore and we'll pick them up."

"And if not?"

"Then we'll lay over in Paducah, Kentucky, until they catch up with us." He paused. "Where's the rest of them?"

"Joseph is in the engine room getting lessons on how to run a steam engine. He's also been splitting wood for the cookstove. Amelia is preparing dinner for us."

She paused. "Matthew, what will we do if—I mean, this is frightening."

His jaw tightened. "There are risks, without a doubt. These days you just don't go running all over the South with a bunch of runaway slaves on your heels."

"What ever possessed Alex Duncan to get involved in such a project?"

"Right now," he said with a twisted grin, "I could repeat back all the things he's been saying to me for the past weeks. But frankly, given the circumstances we're in, the reasoning behind his arguments just plain doesn't hold water."

Caleb joined them. His face was very sober when Matthew finished speaking. "So they got cut off?"

Matthew nodded. "How does the rudder look?"

"I need another day to work on it. Sure enough, it needs to be replaced, but with some wire and a few holes poked in it, I believe we can make do."

———

The sun was setting when the river patrol boat pulled close. Matthew watched while the captain studied them. Then the man cupped his hands to his mouth and called, "I'm coming aboard."

"Come ahead!" Matthew shouted. Turning to Crystal and Amelia, he whispered, "It's nothing to be alarmed about. He won't find anything."

The officer came over the side with an apologetic smile. "Just routine. We've been petitioned to examine all the small boats moving on the Mississippi. It seems there's been an increase in runaway slave traffic. Will you please escort me through your boat?"

"Certainly," Matthew said, and then took the patrol on an extensive tour of the boat. When the man finally left them, Matthew sat down at the table and said, "It wouldn't surprise me to have at least another check. I don't think he was satisfied."

"I saw the way he looked when he saw the cookstove down here in the woodpile," Amelia said.

"I think he became suspicious when he saw the cotton stacked in the cabins. We would have done well to have all the cotton in one cabin. Too late now; we'll have to expect another investigation."

Matthew got to his feet. "If you ladies will excuse me, I'll join Caleb in the pilothouse. He's going to need all the help he can get tomorrow, and I think I need a briefing on what to do with that wheel and the bells."

As Amelia watched him go, she turned to Crystal. "Life's looking up already, huh?" She grinned, "I'm glad for you."

Crystal felt her face grow warm. "Matthew is a wonderful person, but I've no intention of taking his flirtation seriously." She paused and her breath caught as her words came in a rush. "Please don't say anything to Olivia about—our conversation. I suppose I'll need to tell her sometime, but not now."

"Especially since Matthew is her brother?" Amelia's eyes narrowed as Crystal hesitated, and finally she nodded.

———

When Matthew left the pilothouse, the moon had risen above the trees along the bank. On impulse he went down to the main deck. Crystal leaned against the railing, her face lifted to the moon. Matthew crossed the deck. "I hoped I would find you here. Where is Amelia?"

"In the cabin. I believe she's washing her clothes. There are both advantages and disadvantages to losing all your wardrobe."

"Name the advantages."

"It doesn't take a half hour to decide what you'll wear in the morning." He chuckled as she added, "But you must also do laundry each night. This is the first time in my life I've scrubbed clothes."

"Let me see if it is ruining your hands." He lifted her hand to his lips. "Smooth as silk. I'll recommend you as a laundress." He tugged her close, and she came willingly.

"Crystal—" he hesitated, then spoke in a rush of words. "I suppose I shouldn't say this, but I must be fair. I think I'm beginning to love you more each day. If I'm not to have a chance with you, please say so."

Crystal hesitated, turning in his arms. She looked out over the water. The party in Natchez danced before her eyes. Centered in the picture was Boyd Darkinson. While his ardent eyes had questioned and demanded an answer, Crystal had begun to understand the difference Joseph had made in her life. And that night, with Boyd's proud Southern face bending over her, she realized she must reject forever the possibility of marriage and happiness.

Now, with an ache in her heart, she closed her eyes, wondering if her life was destined to be an endless procession of such temptations. Conscious of Matthew's nearness, she swallowed the painful lump in her throat. *But Joseph said I am to forget—*

Taking her by the shoulders, Matthew turned her around. "You can't encourage me?"

Her eyes focused on him. Trying for a teasing note as she studied his serious face, she said, "How do you know I won't be a butterfly, flitting from you to the next?"

"Because I care enough to fasten you firmly to this stalk before you look for another." His mouth searched for hers.

"Oh, Matthew, this is happening too soon."

"Let me kiss you again, and then you say that." Her arms reached for him. "I knew it," he exulted. "I knew you were for me as soon as I saw you."

Before Crystal and Amelia were out of bed, they heard the clanking and shudder. Amelia lifted her head and worried, "I hope they know what they are doing. I wish they would wait for Alex. Somehow I have more confidence in that young man."

Crystal sat up. "I think I do, too. Perhaps we should get up before we find ourselves in the Mississippi in this state of undress."

Amelia shuddered. "One dip is enough. I'll never forget that as long as I live. The flames—" She paused and looked curiously at Crystal. "I've heard that when you are dying, your whole life flashes in front of you. Did you feel that way?"

Crystal chewed her lip. *Something flashed in front of me last night when Matthew kissed me*, she thought. *And this morning I have a terribly guilty conscience. I suppose I should just tell him now before my resolve flies out the window.* She glanced at Amelia and said, "Dying? No, I was too busy thinking about what to do next. Did your life flash in front of you?"

"No, that's why I wondered. If anybody's would, I'd expect it to be mine." Her face was troubled when she faced Crystal.

Crystal took a deep breath. "Amelia, I know you girls reputedly live a pretty rough life, but my old nurse—I call her Auntie T, well, she says, no matter what your religion is or isn't, the Lord is willing to listen when you just say you are sorry and want another chance to prove it."

Amelia picked at a thread on her blanket. Abruptly the serious expression fled. "So much for Auntie T; I get the feeling I need to prove it and *then* say I'm sorry. Seems I don't have the confidence He'll listen 'til then."

"All hands on deck!" Matthew shouted outside their door. "We're heading out as soon as breakfast is finished."

Breakfast was unusually quiet. Crystal and Matt exchanged quick glances, but said very little to each other. Afterward, Crystal and Amelia were washing dishes when the boat shuddered away from the shore and headed up the Mississippi. Crystal gave a sigh of relief. "At least we're moving again."

Amelia walked to the other side of the boat and gazed at the line of trees on the bank. "Even though I know they're gone, I feel creepy going off without them."

Crystal joined her at the rail. Nodding, she added, "I just hope and pray that they will not have problems, and that very soon we'll all be together again."

———

Caleb had the men cut back on the engine speed. "I just feel better chugging along without the necessity of flanking this thing, or trying to claw her off another sandbar."

Matthew called Leon out of the engine room. "Let's move the cotton from one cabin into another. I don't want any cause for suspicion the next time we're stopped."

"How long will it take us to get to Paducah?"

"Caleb says two or three days. We'll repair the rudder and wait for the others. There's no chance they'll be ahead of us."

Amelia asked, "Will they be able to reach the boat?"

Matthew nodded. "This rig is small enough we can dock it in pretty shallow water."

"We'll need supplies, Matthew." Crystal shook the empty corn-meal tin. Turning to Joseph she said, "If you chop more wood, I'll bake bread—that is, if you can tell me how to do it."

Joseph's face brightened, and with a pleased grin, he said, "Missy, I'll be glad to. Fact is, I'd be willing to do it for you."

Crystal paused, still pondering over the expression on his face. He responded as if she had paid him an extravagant compliment. Feeling ill at ease and deeply aware of their relationship, she turned away saying, "If you wish. I can better spend my time doing other things."

———

Amelia and Crystal sat close to the railing and watched the scenery. They were now in their second day, and could begin to see the broad sweep where the Ohio and Mississippi Rivers joined.

"I remember this," Crystal said. "It seems like the ocean here—water as far as you can see."

Amelia chuckled. "That reminds me of a story I heard. It was several years ago this happened. One of the men on the boat swore he was on the *Belle Air* at the time. Might have been. The *Belle Air* was shipping downriver in flood stage. They'd lost all their sightings and, like others before them, decided to take a shortcut through the flooded fields. They ended up taking their steamboat right down the main street of Chester, Illinois. There was plenty of water, and things were going well until they bumped into a three-story building and knocked the top story off. When they tried to change course they ran into a stone mill, bounced off some brick buildings, and destroyed the jailhouse before they got back where they belonged."

"Oh, Amelia, that's outrageous. No one would believe that!"

"Some of the others claimed they had heard the story."

The smell of baking bread began to fill the boat. Abruptly Crystal's laughter died away. She saw Amelia's face reflected her thoughts. "I hope they have enough to eat, and that—oh dear, where do runaways sleep?"

Silently they watched the forest surrender to cotton fields. They passed a hog farm, full of raucous noise and overpowering smell.

There was a flour mill beside a stream, a school house silent in the noonday sun, and then a tiny village. Amelia sighed. "Without the children around, this trip seems to drag on forever."

Crystal asked the question that had been on her mind for several days. "Amelia, how did you come to work on a steamboat?"

"Mind if I don't answer that?" came the tart reply.

"I didn't mean to offend you. It's just that it seems like an interesting job, and I wondered—" She looked up and caught a swift glimpse of pain in the woman's eyes, reminding her that the woman had mentioned having a story to tell.

Amelia drawled. "You are a pampered, sheltered child, Crystal; you've no idea how life really treats some of us." Her lips twisted. "And for your sake, I hope you are never forced to see it thus."

She rose and went to the table beside the stove. "Joseph, that bread smells wonderful. If you are ever out of a job, I will recommend you to the best steamboat on the Mississippi as head cook."

Crystal saw the shadow in his eyes as he glanced toward her. *He heard everything Amelia said. I wonder what pain Joseph and Evangeline had to suffer?* For the rest of the afternoon, Crystal sat by the railing and watched Joseph and Amelia while she brooded over the strange drift of circumstances in her life.

Later that evening when Matthew came down from the pilot-house with that light in his eyes, her heart responded with a joy she had thought impossible.

CHAPTER 23

Morning came to the forest. Drifting fragments of mist moved through the trees as the weary people rose from their mossy, damp beds. While they stood in silent, sleepy groups eating bread and apples, Alex beckoned them close. Keeping his voice low, he said, "We are farther along than we were yesterday, but each day we must be more cautious. We are now closer to the junction of the two rivers and to a cluster of small towns."

Solomon lifted his head, saying, "During the night I hear all kinds of sounds. Dogs, cattle, even the sound of wagonwheels. It gives me fear. We are threat to them, they are threat to us." He shrugged apologetically, "Some of the people can't move fast, 'specially the chillen."

Alex nodded, "We mustn't take chances. We'll walk only as long as it is safe. If necessary we'll search for a hiding place and then I'll walk into Paducah alone."

His final words left Olivia trembling. She stared down at the bread in her hand and gulped. Impatiently Alex said, "Put it in your pocket, we've got to move out."

Blinking tears from her eyes, she turned to follow Tandy and Maggie. This morning the children were quiet, stumbling along after the adults, content to cling to an apron string.

At mid-morning Alex gathered them around himself. "I calculate we're close enough to the river. We need to head east now. Keep quiet, take to the bushes if you hear anything. About the middle of the afternoon I'm going to leave to scout out our location. Right now we'll look for a likely spot, then I'll leave you there."

There were nods of approval. Olivia watched the slaves press together into a long compact line. Silently they turned east and began to walk. With only the snap of twigs and branches to give away their presence, they moved through the forest. As Olivia walked she pondered the strangeness she felt. Not only was the gloom of the forest oppressive, but the silence disturbed her. From earliest childhood, she couldn't recall a group of black people surrounded in silence. Walking or working they always sang; now the songs were missing.

When they stopped to rest, the sun was overhead. Bright shafts of light sliced down through the pines. Squinting at the brightness Olivia felt strangely isolated, even vulnerable under the unexpected light. Tandy murmured, "Makes you wonder who's watching."

Alex walked among them, "Rest for now," he said, "I have a feeling we'll be pushing on until after nightfall." He settled down close to Solomon and in a low voice said, "We are nearly out of food again. I don't like being this close to people and not knowing what to expect. I think I'll leave you here while I scout around."

"Ought to take Ralph."

There was silence and then Alex spoke slowly, "No, we were seen together yesterday. I'll go alone." Olivia watched him stride away. Turning she crawled into the shelter of a bush, stretched out, and fell asleep.

She wasn't sure how long she had been sleeping when Tandy's urgent voice penetrated her pleasant dreams. "Tandy, what is it?"

"Little Joe, where is he? His mama say he's gone."

Olivia sat up. "Surely he won't wander off! Don't worry."

"Just the same, I'm going down by that creek, see if he's there. Watch Sarah for me."

With a nod, Olivia settled back. But in the midst of her second yawn, Olivia heard the straggled sound. With her heart pounding, she moved cautiously to part the bushes. A flash of blue caught her eye and she leaned forward. Down by the creek the color appeared again. It was Tandy running. A dark figure caught up with her. Olivia saw her struggling with a man. Once again she was free and running.

Olivia had taken one shaky breath of relief when she saw the dark figure kneel, and lift an object. A gun. His slow, careful aim allowed sharp sunlight to strike the barrel of the gun.

In the moment that Olivia tried to scream, she saw a second figure dashing toward the gun. But only for a moment. There was an explosion. The second figure seemed to pause in his stride. He fell and moved just once in a dark damp pool.

Olivia plunged down the path toward Tandy. She had her arms around her before she heard the thrashing and the guttural sounds. Olivia dropped her arms and they turned.

"There's someone else!" Tandy shivered against Olivia as they watched the struggle. The gun was wrenched away. The newcomer whirled and flung the rifle as he rushed to the figure on the ground.

"Alex!" Olivia's cry was a whisper. She heard his ragged breathing as he sagged over the man on the ground. Behind him the white man got to his feet and moved toward Alex. At that moment the bushes beside Alex exploded and a burly Negro crashed through. For one second the white man pawed for his gun, and then he turned and ran.

Still clinging to each other Tandy and Olivia approached. Alex was on his knees. They watched him turn the man over; blood covered the man's chest. Alex looked up at Olivia with disbelief and said, "It's Ralph. There's nothing to feel. That man got him point blank."

She could see the pain on his face but was powerless to do more than shake her head. Tandy flung herself to her knees. She looked up at Alex, her voice was ragged, faint as she slowly said, "He died for me and I didn't even know him."

Later the others crept out of the bushes and surrounded them. Finally Alex lifted his face, helplessly looking around the circle, saying, "We don't have a shovel."

Solomon stepped forward and tugged Alex to his feet. "We gotta hide him somehow. Let's all us gather stones."

As the men worked dusk deepened. Olivia, Tandy, and the other women pulled the children about them and watched.

Back and forth the men walked carrying stones from the stream.

At the point they began singing, their voices were so low and soft the rhythm struck the heart rather than the ears. Olivia wiped tears and listened to words as familiar as her Mississippi home. She heard, " 'I don't care where you bury my body, Don't care where. . . . O my little soul's going to shine, shine. . . . All around the heav'n going to shine. . . .' "

When the last stone had been placed and the song was finished, Olivia was left alone with the memories glittering out of the past. But as she visualized the sights and sounds, recalling faces that had previously filled her with joy, she began to see other faces. They were black ones, caught in unguarded moments, while their faces revealed wrenching pain and powerless anger.

With a sigh Olivia looked back at the group. Beyond the stones the people clustered around Alex. She moved closer and heard him say, "Father, in Your word we hear Jesus Christ say 'I am the resurrection, and the life: he that believeth in me, though he were dead, yet shall he live.' We take hope and comfort. Our brother Ralph is in Your presence now and we must go on without him. Please hallow this ground with Your protection until the day. Go with us as we travel."

By unspoken but common consent they began to walk through the night, and it wasn't until dawn had brightened the sky before them when they stopped on the edge of the cornfield.

Numb with fatigue they stared around. The forest had disappeared and cultivated fields spread before, beyond, and beside them. Solomon lifted a haggard face, "Suh, what we do now? There's no place to hide."

For a moment longer Alex stood with sagging shoulders. When he straightened, he pointed to the distant farmhouse. "That's where I'm going. Get back into the trees and stay there until I come after you. If they aren't friendly, it may be nightfall before I'm back. Stay together."

Olivia watched him march straight across the fields and then she turned and followed the others.

But he quickly returned. Dawn was still pale and pink in the sky above the deeply shadowed earth when he came. He was grinning, "We have permission to sleep in the farmer's barn today. Come along. Stick to the path along the ditch and don't trample his crops."

The farmer waited for them beside the open door. His eyes were curious and kind. He lifted the pail of freshly drawn water. "Mr. Duncan tells me that you aren't hungry, just tired. Here's a pail of good well water. You climb right up to the loft and have a long sleep. I'll see if I can't find a wagon going into Paducah this evening."

The barn was filled with the sweet scent of new hay. As Olivia followed Tandy to the ladder, the farmer frowned. "I'm sorry to offer such accommodations to the missus," he muttered, "Wouldn't you and your wife rather come into the house to sleep?"

Olivia nearly smiled as she climbed the ladder, leaving Alex to answer the question. Later, cushioned in the hay, as she drifted off to sleep she could see Alex sitting beside the one small window.

———

It was dark when Alex came to awaken them. He carried a kettle of steaming food. "That sure smells good," Andy said, making room for Alex in the hay.

He shook his head, "I've had some. Been talking with Mr. Stevens, and here's what seems best. I'm going to borrow a horse and ride in to Paducah—it's less than fifteen miles. I'll have opportunity to check around for the *Golden Awl*. If it isn't there, I can leave a message on the post box for Matthew." He stood up. "So eat your supper and go back to sleep."

The food tasted as good as it smelled, and after they had finished the meal, Olivia carried the kettle back to the farmhouse. The woman who met her at the door took the kettle and shoved a chair forward. "My man says the whole lot of you look chawed to the bone. Been a rough trip?" Hastily she added, "Now don't you go giving us a speck of information. The Lord's laid it on us to help as much as we can, but the information can make liars out of us."

"Do you have that problem often?"

The woman nodded, "We're mighty close to the river. People need to cross somewhere along. Naturally we know the route, what ferries will carry the cargo and what won't." She paused and peered at Olivia, "You and your mister are Southern. Kinda unusual to find tidewater people doin' this type of activity."

Olivia blinked and the woman grinned, "I know what you're a thinking, we haven't much to lose and you do. Well, we're poor people, never had a slave. Could've used extra help over the years."

She set a mug of coffee in front of Olivia and added, "It's always rankled us to see the black folk mistreated. And the worst is seeing they don't get a chance to learn, to go to school. When our young'uns were little there was always a few darky children hanging around, neglected because their mamas were in the fields picking cotton. I'd feed them a biscuit, but the thing they most liked to do was to see a picture book and have someone point out the letters."

CHAPTER 24

Stevens pointed the way to Paducah. "Thank you, Sir," Alex said. "If I can make connections, I'll be back before dawn. It's possible the boat hasn't arrived yet. If so, I'd better stay until it does. But according to my calculations, it should be in dock now."

With a brief salute, he turned the horse down the night-shadowed road. The mare was frisky, eager for the ride, and he found his spirit lifting. Breathing deeply of the comforting odors of the farmland, he settled into the saddle determined to enjoy the ride.

Briefly his thoughts returned to the harrowing experience in the forest. "Father," he whispered, "You know it all, and it's in Your hands. It would be easy to question why, but I suppose that's to say I have a better plan than Yours, and that our suffering should not be. Thank You that I was nearby when the attacker approached. Please watch over these people You've put in my charge. Help me keep them safe. I need Your wisdom."

He slumped in the saddle and thought about responsibility. Finally straightening, he whispered into the night, "I'm a child of the trouble; it's only right that I also be a child of the healing." His lips pulled down at the corners in a wry grin. "Next," he muttered, "you'll be looking up Whittier and taking lessons in writing poetry." He nudged the mare and again breathed deeply of the moist night air. For a moment nostalgia had him in South Carolina, paddling a canoe down the canal beside the rice fields. As he mulled over the familiar scenes, he softly sang the words he had heard the darkies sing. "'Gwine to ride up in the chariot, Sooner in the morning. . . . Ride up. . . . Sooner in the morning, And I hope I'll join the band.'"

Recalling the hidden double meaning in many of the Negroes' songs, Alex chuckled and urged the mare into a run. Before long he could see the outline of buildings against the moonlight. Glancing at the moon, he muttered, "A good night for a fellow and his girl." He thought about Olivia as he guided the horse through the streets and headed toward the wharf. Her frightened face pricked his conscience. Wincing, he recalled his glib statement to Caleb. "I didn't know my selfishness would lead to this."

Three boats docked alongside the wharf, but the *Golden Awl* wasn't among them. Nudging the horse, he rode as far along the shore as he could go, both above and below the town. When he was convinced the *Awl* wasn't in the vicinity, he headed inland. Patting the mare on her neck, he said, "Well, gal, I guess we find a grassy spot— me for sleep, and you for browsing."

At the first light of dawn, Alex bathed in the river, brushed dust and grass from his clothing, and headed back into town.

He stopped at the boardinghouse across the street from the wharf. "Who should I contact to find out about local packets? I need a ride upriver, and I'm looking for the steamboat, the *Golden Awl*." The waitress turned and pointed to a man in a dark suit seated in the far corner of the room.

With a nod, Alex walked across the room. "Sir, I—"

"I heard your question," came the heavy reply. The man shoveled in his eggs. "Never heard of the boat. Might be one that sank around the bend yesterday. Don't know the name. Everybody lost. Wasn't a very big boat, but it hit a snag, plumb square. It appears to have worked hard to hit it that neat."

"Well," Alex said slowly attempting to hide his emotions, "I guess you answered my question. It hasn't come through." Alex managed to keep his voice smooth as he added, "I'll hang around today. Maybe I'll find another vessel heading up the Ohio. You say a boat was lost?" He shook his head sadly.

His appetite for breakfast gone, Alex strolled casually out the door. He paused to study the mare chomping the row of petunias along the fence, and then turned to walk down to the wharf.

A roustabout was sweating over the bales of cotton on the wharf. Alex headed his direction. "Know anything about a steamboat hitting a snag around here yesterday?" Alex asked.

The Negro wiped his face. "Heard there was one. Water's low through there. Too close to the bank. Acted like he didn't have much power."

"Were there—"

The fellow shook his head. "Heard all lost." He squinted at Alex. "Know 'em?"

"Do you know the name of the boat?"

"Naw. Ask that gentleman coming out of the eating place. If anybody would know, he's the one."

Alex turned and saw the man he had met in the boardinghouse. "He doesn't know; I've talked to him. Guess I'll wait around." As he turned away, Alex saw the flash of sympathy in the roustabout's eyes. "Thanks for your time."

It was mid-afternoon when Alex tied the mare to another tree and sat down to rest in its shade. He had ridden all the lanes and roads leading to the shoreline, and he had walked the streets of Paducah waiting and praying a nearly wordless prayer. Now, dizzy with heat and faint from not eating, he leaned against the tree and tried to summon the desire to look for a cafe.

He heard two sharp whistles. "Do I recognize that whistle?" he muttered, turning toward the river. Two steamboats were passing, and he tensed as the upriver vessel came into view. The bow was still shiny with new varnish, and from here he could see the gold lettering. With a grin, he got to his feet and shaded his eyes. "That's it, my lovely *Golden Awl*!" He slapped the mare on her shoulder, "Finish your dinner, we've a good ride ahead of us tonight."

Alex waited as patiently as his racing heart would allow for the *Awl* to move in closer; and when it finally slipped alongside the wharf, Jess tossed the line before dropping over the side. Alex caught the line and made it fast. "Howdy, Mr. Alex," Jess said with a broad grin.

"How did it go?"

"Just dandy. Had a little delay. Tried to help a sinking boat yesterday. We were too late."

"Yes, I know." Alex took a deep breath as Joseph swung the plank down to the wharf. "Let's go talk about that rudder."

As he ran aboard, Matthew and Caleb leaned over the railing. He saw their anxious faces and replied tersely, "Everything is going fine on our end. We'll join you as soon as this rudder problem is solved."

They spent the remainder of the day getting the rudder fixed and sharing what each had gone through since they separated, and also tried to work out details for the journey ahead. At nightfall, just before Alex rode out, he pointed upriver. "There's a sheltered cove. Spent my time searching it out this morning. Look for the live oak and tie on to it. We'll be aboard before morning." Alex then began the ride back to the farm.

It took longer than he expected. Even though the sky was clear, the night was still very black, making it harder to find the way. He arrived quite late, but as he approached the farm, he realized Stevens had heard the mare. The farmer was standing beside the pasture gate and came to meet him. "Looks like we'll need to haul that load of hay tonight."

Stevens said casually, "I can be ready to leave right away."

"Don't like involving you."

"Once in a while a job comes up that makes it necessary," he said in an off-handed manner as he carried the saddle into the barn. Alex stopped long enough to splash cold creek water on his face and drink deeply from his cupped hands before he climbed the ladder.

He could see the pale oval of Olivia's face at the top. He felt her hands grasping him as he stepped into the hay. "The boat arrived this afternoon. Everything is under control." Turning to the others, he said, "As soon as we can get into the wagon, we'll head for Paducah." He grinned when he heard the soft sighs of relief. The people started down the ladder, and he pressed the hands extended toward him.

As the dark line moved out of the barn and into the wagon, Stevens spoke softly. "No need to burrow into the hay unless there's a problem. Most folks are sleeping at this time of night. Just don't talk. We'll go slow and easy, like one old man getting an early start on going to market."

As Olivia started to follow the slaves into the wagon, Alex took her arm. "You in front, missus." She saw the white slash of his grin, but before she could reply, he lifted her to the wagon seat, and he sat down next to her.

After everyone was seated, Stevens slapped the reins along the horses' backs and said, "Get along gals, nice and easy."

The moon had settled down into the western line of trees. Only the road ahead reflected light. Its whiteness stretched in a peaceful, curving path, but Olivia tensed as they passed each farmhouse with its barking dog. Finally Alex slipped his arm around her. Putting his mouth close to her ear, he whispered, "You're only making matters worse for everyone; sit back and relax!"

———————

To Olivia it seemed only brief minutes later when he shook her gently, whispering, "Sleepyhead, it's nearly morning."

She pulled herself away from him and sat up. The sky was pink and turning bright with sunlight. Alex pointed beyond her shoulder and she turned. Through the woods she could see the faint outline of the boat in the shadows of a giant tree.

She glanced at Alex and he nodded, "That's it."

Stevens pulled into the shadows and stopped. Jumping off the wagon seat, Alex lifted her down and then reached into the hay-filled wagon and began prodding everyone out. Just as silently as the wagon had been loaded, the cargo streamed over its side and followed Alex's pointing finger.

When the last child padded after his mother, Alex leaned toward Mr. Stevens and held out his hand. Olivia could hear only the murmur of their voices, but she watched Stevens smile toward her and nod as he flicked the reins, and the horses plodded slowly down the road as silently as they had come. Alex tugged at her arm and Olivia hurried after little Joe and his mother.

Climbing aboard, Crystal met Olivia on deck. Hugging her, she said, "Ugh! You smell and feel like a haystack."

Before the last Negro had entered the cabin, Jess tossed the line on deck and together he and Alex eased the boat into the current.

———————

When Olivia awakened to the gentle motion of the boat, she

smiled and turned to sleep again. Later she heard the rustle of frocks as Crystal and Amelia left the cabin. She snuggled deeper into the softness of the bunk.

It was very late that morning when she went down to the main deck. She blinked when she saw the line of small black faces around the table. Slowly she said, "I can't believe this; it's as if we'd never been gone at all." But she gulped as she recalled the scene in the forest. When she turned and caught Tandy's eyes, her voice gentled as she said, "I suppose we'll never forget."

Little Joe asked, "Did Alex get more paper for us?"

"I'll need to find out."

"He's in the pilothouse. Go ask now. *Please*." Tim remembered the magic word.

She looked around at the beseeching eyes. Again she heard, "Please." Amelia turned from the stove with a laugh. "You've taught them well."

With a shrug, Olivia said, "I shall ask, right this moment." Running up the first flight of stairs, Olivia turned toward the stairs leading to the hurricane deck. She stopped. At the far end of the boat she could see Crystal and Matthew standing with their heads close together. She started to hail them and then realized they were near the sternwheel. *With that water churning in their ears, they'll never hear me!* For a second longer she watched them, and then with an amused smile, she ran up the stairs to the pilothouse.

With her hand on the doorknob she hesitated. The memory of her first trip up these stairs and the reception Alex had given her made her apprehensive. She was still chewing her lip as she pushed the door open.

With his feet braced against the floor and his hands on the wheel, Alex sang, " 'Gin a body meet a body, comin' through the rye; Gin a body kiss a body, need a body cry?"

Slowly she walked round the wheel, hands on hips, and looked him in the eye. When he saw her, she watched his face redden. "You don't like my song? It's Robert Burns."

"Cry?" she said. "I didn't cry. Mr. Duncan, you *were* in your cups, weren't you?"

His hands dropped from the wheel. "What did you say?"

There was a shout from below and he grabbed the wheel. "Snag, I see it!" he shouted.

She left the pilothouse, closing the door very forcefully behind her. Matthew came up the stairs at a run. "What's going on? Caleb thought Alex was going to wipe out that snag."

"He's just not paying attention."

Matthew's voice was cold, "Then I suggest you save your diverting smiles until later. You could put us to the bottom of the river in a hurry!" With a cry of exasperation, she ran down the stairs.

The children were waiting. She studied their big eyes and said, "I don't think Master Alex wants to be disturbed right now."

"Just call him Alex," Tim said very patiently.

Caleb came out of the engine room, looked at her and scratched his head. Apologetically he said, "I thought for sure we'd get to test that monkey rudder right now."

The rest of the day went along much smoother with everyone settling into their old routines. Just as the evening meal was served, the engine was shut down and Alex allowed the *Golden Awl* to glide close to shore. Olivia heard the signaling bell and stepped to the railing to watch.

She heard Caleb's shout as he reversed the monkey rudder and the boat slipped slowly into position.

Alex clattered down the stairs. "Caleb, it wouldn't hurt to drop an anchor. There's a current through here."

He took his place at the table and frowned at Olivia. "I want to see you after dinner."

"Please," Tim prompted.

Startled, Alex repeated, "Please—I beg your pardon." Stiffly he ducked his head Olivia's direction.

———

When Olivia carried the dishpan of hot water to the table, Crystal said, "I think you had better see what Alex wants; he doesn't look very happy. We'll do the dishes."

Olivia searched for an excuse while Alex watched. His eyes never wavered. Finally she shrugged and left the table. "To the cabin," he said, waving toward the stairs.

As she left the group, Tim said, "Is he going to scold?"

Alex followed her into the cabin. He closed the door and said, "We didn't get to finish our conversation this afternoon. Please, let's continue." She smiled at the stressed *please*, and he said, "Will you explain what you said?"

Lightly she said, "That foolish song, and you teasing with your eyes. That's all; forget the rest."

"Olivia, you accused me of, as you said, being in my cups. I don't remember much of that night. I have only an impression of confusion and noise and a very lovely woman. Did we dance?"

"Yes, in the most outrageous fashion all over the kitchen."

He winced, then grinned. "I didn't have any idea what I had missed by being drunk." His grin disappeared. "But I evidently made a very bad impression on you. What did you mean when you said you didn't cry over a kiss?"

She avoided his eyes, wondering what she should say. Hesitantly he asked, "Did I kiss you?" She nodded. He frowned again, and then brightened as he came around the table. "And if you didn't cry, then I suppose it's appropriate for me to assume you—"

"Alex!" she flew around to the other side of the table.

She faced him with her hands pressed against her hot cheeks. "That isn't what I meant. Don't you remember?"

"I remember you felt soft and warm in my arms." He rested his hands on the table and leaned across.

"I slapped you as hard as I could. And—" she moved away from the table. "It might relieve a great deal of anger if I were to do so again."

He straightened and abruptly apologized. "I can see you mean it. Olivia, I'm dreadfully sorry. Believe me, I'd never do anything to shame a woman, and I want to assure you that it will never happen again."

"I will help you," she snapped. "I'll promise you, there won't be opportunity!"

With a stiff bow, he turned and left the cabin. Olivia flung herself on the bunk and buried her face in the pillow.

The door opened. Olivia listened with her heart pounding. "Olivia, may we talk?" It was Crystal.

With a sigh Olivia sat up. "I suppose. I can guess you want to tell me how foolish I am."

"No," Crystal came to sit on the bunk beside her. Finally she said, "Are you talking about Alex? If you've chased him away, I don't blame you. He's extremely arrogant."

"Arrogant?" Olivia echoed, "I—well I guess I hadn't thought of him as that. It seems to me he's just overwhelming. He's so big, and—" She stopped, and added, "and that foolish earring he wears, I simply don't—" She waved her hands helplessly.

"If you feel that way about him, then why did you come with them?"

Olivia searched for a safe answer. "I didn't intend this kind of involvement. It was really a mistake."

"Olivia, people don't make these kinds of mistakes."

"Well, I did. When they found me on the boat, they forced—"

"Forced! Oh, Olivia, if that is so, then you've reason to feel as you do. In addition, it is arrogant for him to make you come."

"Well, to be honest, I was in a difficult place. See, all these slaves were right there. Alex was afraid I'd let someone know about them. You know they're all runaways."

"I'd gathered that," Crystal said slowly.

"So I had to come with them, just to keep the slaves safe."

Crystal was silent a moment, then she said slowly, "You mean they were willing to sacrifice your welfare just in order to keep the slaves safe? I'm glad Matthew doesn't feel that way."

"You are?"

Crystal faltered. "I think I am." For a time they sat in silence. In the dimness of the cabin, Olivia watched her friend's face.

Finally she said, "Crystal, all day I've had a feeling that something is troubling you. If you need a listening ear, I'd be glad to supply it. I realize Amelia will be popping in here any minute, but—"

"No, she won't. She, Matthew, and Alex are sitting on the main deck talking. I got the feeling it was pretty serious, so I just left them to it."

"Is it because of her that you are so unhappy?"

"No." Crystal stood up and restlessly walked to the porthole. She turned quickly, "I need to talk so badly I can scarcely stand it." She hesitated, then the words poured out. "What would you do if you found out that your best friend's father wasn't Creole, as you'd been led to believe. Instead, the father was just plain Negro slave. Isn't that horrible?"

Silence filled the cabin; Crystal looked as if she were ready to cry.

Glancing down at her hands, Olivia rubbed a fingernail and tried to analyze the problem. Finally she said, "Crystal, I'm surprised that you are this upset. Somehow it isn't the way I expected you to be."

"I'm sorry," Crystal whispered. "I guess I've overreacted, but I trusted her so much, and now I just don't know what to think. Am I to accept her as my equal? It isn't just our social standing that concerns me. It's a moral question—relationships."

"I know what you mean. We've lived with these people; they raised us. Sometimes I feel more mothered by my old nurse than I do my own mother. But there's a line dividing us. It seems against human nature to be forced into a situation where we must say we are all the same."

"I've been raised hearing that they are an inferior race. Am I now to admit I'm no better than they?"

Now Olivia's words came in a rush. She turned and held Crystal's arm, giving it a gentle shake. "That's why I am so angry with Alex, it's not—the other things. What his actions are saying to me are simply this: 'Olivia, you are no better than all these slaves, and furthermore, if I must sacrifice a human, it will be you rather than them.' See what I mean?"

Slowly Crystal said, "Yes, I understand."

Her voice was flat, and Olivia said, "I don't think you do. You don't sound as if you agree. Why?"

Crystal caught her breath and her words came in a rush. "Do you really think that is what God intended? Oh, I know we Southerners look in our Bibles and see things that we say explain slavery. But sometimes it seems so very unfair."

Olivia got to her feet. With a tiny nervous laugh, she said, "It is too bad we aren't still at school; we would make such a good debate team—you for equality, and me against."

"I didn't—" Crystal gentled her voice. "You misunderstood; I didn't say I agreed with Alex's forcing you to come along. But certainly the North is the place to draw a crowd with a debate like that."

Olivia giggled. "You wouldn't dare do it in the South; we'd lose all our friends immediately."

"If I had the nerve," Crystal said slowly, "I'd ask Alex exactly what he thinks."

Olivia stood and impatiently shook out her frock. "But with

those eyes boring into you, it would be impossible to disagree with him. And I don't think I would like that at all."

Crystal got up. "So you are telling me that I should just forget my friend?"

Olivia turned away. "It would be awful to turn against a friend, just because she had tainted blood. Isn't there a way to live with the problem?"

CHAPTER 25

Alex returned and sat at the table long after the women had finished the dishes. Tandy eyed him. "You tired? Too bad this boat can't get through the water without being babied along!"

He grinned at her. "Tired, yes. I was thinking of putting my feet on your table, but I'm afraid you'd throw me overboard with the dishwater."

"Not until after you scrubbed the table again," Amelia chuckled.

Alex continued to watch her as she moved around the makeshift kitchen, rinsing towels and hanging them to dry. "You seem to like kitchen work," he observed. She threw him a quick startled glance and he said, "Hey, I'm not offering you a long-term job; it's merely an opinion!"

She hung the last towel and came to sit across the table from him. "Want more coffee?"

"No thank you." He paused, adding, "Amelia, I've no reason to hurry you along, but you know what kind of boat this is, and I think you recognize the danger we're in. Would you like us to let you off at Cincinnati?"

A cloud settled over her face. He studied the sad lines of her mouth while he waited. She took a deep breath and said, "I understand. It's a nice way to tell me I stand a better chance of finding a position in my chosen profession if I get off at Cincinnati."

"Well, I'm old enough to figure out a few things." His voice failed to convey the light touch.

She toyed with the mug on the table, glanced at him and asked, "What would be the possibility of joining your group?"

"Why?" He was startled to see a fleeting expression of fear on her face.

"Maybe I want to feel good about myself again. Maybe I want to help you. I came from a free state. All this has been a shock—to see human beings treated badly enough that they will risk their lives to escape."

"Amelia, I'll be frank. You may not receive the welcome you've had here. I don't know much about these people we will be contacting, but I do know the abolitionists for the most part are Christians, and I think you'd be impatient with the restrictions they place on life. You'll see them as narrow-minded."

She moved restlessly. "Are you wanting to be father confessor? I know all about Christians. Might say I've been around my share of them." Alex waited, and finally she said, "You want to know what makes me tick?"

"I didn't ask."

"And you won't?"

"No, but Amelia, I'm concerned about the people. You can't just take the slaves on because you feel sorry for them. In the first place, what we are doing is outside the law. We are trying to save them because these lives are precious."

Caleb, who'd been standing at the railing nearby, came and sat down beside Alex. "I heard part of your conversation and I tell you, mostly people don't get the itch to help people unless the Lord puts them up to it."

Amelia studied Alex's face. "Are you telling me that you are a Christian?" Hastily she added, "I mean something other than a fellow whose got his name on the role."

He grinned, "Must be, since I don't have my name on the role. I take that back. I was baptized as a baby. But that isn't the motivation behind my life. Amelia, I think being called a Christian implies an encounter with God that is life changing." He paused. "It's sort of a love affair with God, you know what I mean? A moving out of self-preoccupation into wanting to please God more than anything else in the world."

"About now you should have some Scripture to read at me."

"Not unless you want it."

"I don't. But about Pennsylvania—I want to come if you'll be patient. I promise I won't stay around and clutter up your life if you don't want me to."

"You'll conform to the rules of the group?" She nodded, and then with a grin, he said, "I suggest we stop somewhere before we reach Pennsylvania and buy you a dress that covers more and looks a little more utilitarian." He paused and added with a chuckle, "I don't want these Quaker brethren to make a quick decision about my judgment. You know, I've never met any of them. To me, they're only names on paper."

Unexpectedly Amelia laughed. "A dancehall girl leading a pack of escaped slaves to the Quakers."

Alex got to his feet. As he turned, he realized the railing behind him was lined with listeners. "Hello! I didn't know you were here."

Solomon said, "We been listening. We like Miss Amelia, and we're glad she's a comin' along. Could come to the Promised Land." He chuckled as he pointed to her surprised face. "That's Canada!"

"I thought you meant heaven." She frowned and then glanced at Solomon. "Promised Land? Do you really think it is going to be that wonderful?"

"It'll be free."

Tandy, with her hand on Sarah's head added, "Our chillen gets to go to school. When they grow up, they live where they please. Get married, have a family." She paused, and her voice dropped. "I haven't seen my man since I was with the baby. They sold him. We made agreement. If we can, we escape to Canada. Maybe, the Lord willing, I'll see him there." She tilted her face to Amelia. "I love my man just the same as any white lady love hers. Maybe there we get really married—by a preacher man. See why we call it the Promised Land?"

Jess moved forward and lifted his shadowed face. "Alex, we feel you are our friend, but why do you do this for us? If that patrol catches us all, there will be trouble for you."

Another dark figure moved forward. "We been talking. That white man killed Ralph; it could have been you. Don't you know you might die?"

"Yes, I am aware of it." Alex said slowly. "But remember what Caleb said. A person doesn't do something like this unless the Lord asks it of him. Might say I have an obligation. The Lord Jesus Christ died for me so that I will have eternal life with Him. Now it seems like He's asking if I'm willing to risk my earthly life for my brothers."

"Brothers! You call us your brothers. We're black people! Some say we're inferior. Don't count."

"I can prove you are not inferior, and that you do count just as much as any man who has ever lived."

"How's that?"

Before Alex answered he lifted his head to the whisper of sound. Olivia and Crystal were seated on the stairs with their faces pressed close to the railing. It was obvious they were listening to him. He looked at the black man in front of him. "Andy, Jesus Christ died for your sins, just as He died for mine."

"You can't prove that," the yearning voice protested. "I know that some folks say so, but you can't prove it."

"Yes, I can. The Bible tells us that when we become God's children He sends His Holy Spirit to live in us. Look around; you know some of these brothers of yours live like men with the Holy Spirit inside."

Caleb touched Andy's shoulder. "That's right, brother. I know without a doubt in me that the Holy Ghost lives right inside of me. I know it, and I know when I die I go to be with the Lord Jesus." He paused and added, "And I know Alex is born again just like me. I was there when he decided for the Lord. It's a difference. Better than night and day, the Lord makes a difference in a body. 'Sides, I know he isn't fibbing about the glory comin' down on him. I know because he got the call of God, and just like the Word says, I'm seeing it manifest in him."

"Don't look like nothing except an ordinary man to me," Jess said.

"He got a verse that just brings you down to your knees," Caleb insisted.

Suddenly conscious of the listeners on the stairs, Alex said, "Caleb, don't you think we ought to save that sermon for another time?"

"No, suh," came a voice at the rear of the crowd, "we want to hear it all. Speak out the verse, and then we'll say good-night."

Alex said, "It's from the book of Isaiah, a prophecy concerning the coming of our Lord Jesus Christ. When the words began to sink down deep inside of me, He reminded me that as Christians we are called to represent Him on this earth."

He paused and then quoted softly, "He hath sent me to bind up the brokenhearted, to proclaim liberty to the captives, and the opening of the prison to them that are bound . . . to comfort all that mourn . . . to give them beauty for ashes, the oil of joy for mourning, the garment of praise . . . that he might be glorified."

Crystal and Olivia, still listening to Alex, made their escape. Back in the cabin, Olivia leaned against the door. "Well," she said dryly, "there's your answer. You just found out how Alex feels about the whole situation of racial inferiority. Can you live with his verdict?"

Frowning, Crystal stared at Olivia until she moved uneasily. "Olivia, you're not happy. Just perhaps you are the one who needs a private conference with him. Let him change your mind. Father Confessor, that might be a good name for him. Why should the things he says make you angry?"

Olivia frowned and then carefully said, "Crystal, I don't believe I'm angry, it's just that he sounded so sanctimonious. I find that offensive. He's not one speck better than the rest of us."

"Well, he did say he had to be willing to die; I suppose that would make a person a little above anyone else."

Olivia snorted as she got ready for bed. "I'm too tired to stretch my little mind any more tonight. Besides, I need to wash this dress. I'm getting so very tired of wearing the same thing every day."

"It is too bad they didn't at least allow you to pack some clothing."

Thoughtfully Olivia said, "Right now I'm more concerned about our parents. What can they be thinking of us? Matthew and I've done some things that have merited us a good scolding, but we've never before just disappeared from home." She looked at Crystal and added, "I told Matt we need to write letters, but he said we should wait until we've reached Pennsylvania."

As Crystal removed her shoes, she declared, "As soon as we get there, I'm going to turn around and go right back home."

"Crystal, I can't understand you. Why don't you just have Alex put you on a boat for New Orleans right now?" When Crystal didn't answer, Olivia impatiently said, "Oh, I'm being nosy. I know you've talked to Alex about this, and I'll respect your silence, but I can't help being a little disappointed, especially since we were such close friends at school."

There was still no answer. With another shrug, Olivia went back to her laundry and Crystal crawled into her bunk.

In the morning Olivia yawned her way out of bed, only to discover that Crystal had left the cabin. Fighting sleep she staggered across the room, bumping into the table in the center of the cabin before she dropped into a chair.

She opened her eyes and stared at the table. "What a strange man! I am more confused than ever." She recalled Alex's teasing eyes as he pursued her around the table. Moving her shoulders impatiently, she said, "But one thing is certain—I'll do my best to stay out of his way."

Even as she said the words, she remembered the children and the paper. "Oh, Olivia," she scolded, "if you want to avoid another trip to the pilothouse, get yourself downstairs immediately!" She ran to gather up her clothing.

"Ugh!" She bent over and picked the wet dress off the floor, muttering, "My clothesline collapsed. This frock isn't only soggy, it's soiled!"

Still holding the wet garment at arms length she remembered Matthew's clothes. Dropping the dress she pulled open the cupboard and tugged at Matthew's bag. Inside she found an extra shirt and pair of trousers.

Quickly Olivia dressed. She had the door open when she thought of the last time Alex had seen her dressed this way.

She gave a shrug as she clattered down the stairs.

She could see the people clustered around the stove having breakfast. "Sorry, sleepyhead as usual," she said flippantly as she sat down.

"Going riding bareback?" Matthew asked.

"No I washed my dress last night, and the clothesline broke. It's as wet as it was when I hung it."

Glancing up she caught Alex's puzzled frown. Quickly she jumped to her feet. "No, no, Tandy; I'll wait on myself."

With arms crossed on his chest, Alex continued to watch her as she sat back down at the table. "You're no bigger than a little boy," he said slowly.

Olivia held her breath to avoid choking. Carefully she said, "I'm tall for a woman, and one of these days, when I've nothing to do, I'll sit around eating bon-bons and get fat."

He grinned. "Don't bother; I like you the way you are." He left the table and Olivia glared at her porridge, furious with her wildly beating heart. Suddenly she jumped to her feet. "Joe, run up to the pilothouse and ask Alex for paper."

Alex spoke behind her. "I remembered you needed it. Is this enough?"

Embarrassed, she snapped, "Must you dole it out piece by piece?"

"It's chart paper. You needn't justify your use of it, but it's all I have." Again he grinned at her, his blue eyes teasing, and she was left not knowing what to say.

She swallowed hard, and in a timid voice she said, "Thank you. Students, we are in business again. Back to the books."

Caleb came downstairs, his face puckered with worry. He addressed the women around the table. "See that big sycamore tree there? It marks the beginning of bad water. Alex says the river is filled with rocks, and water's shooting over, making dangerous currents. He say you keep the babies close to you and pray until we get out of the rough water."

————

It was late evening when Alex came downstairs. His face was lined with fatigue. Dropping onto the bench beside the table he said, "According to the charts, this is the worst of the falls. Caleb is going to take us upstream another mile or so. We need to find a place we can tie up for the night."

Tandy brought him a bowl of rich gumbo. "Amelia made it especially for you."

Olivia watched him smile across the table as he picked up his spoon. "Amelia, thank you! For that good deed, I'll buy you another load of wood, just so that—"

"I can make more tomorrow!" she exclaimed with a teasing laugh. "How about catching some fish, too?"

"I hear little Joe and his mama do a good job of hauling them in." Alex patted the little head close to his arm, adding, "You two just make certain you duck out of sight when the boats come along." He took a bite and said, "Tomorrow we'll be getting into Cincinnati."

Little Joe peered at Alex. "Is Miss Crystal going to stay there?"

Alex paused and then said, "No, everyone will stay with the boat until we reach Pennsylvania. Does that make you happy?"

"Yes, but I 'spect it makes Matthew more happy!" With a joyful laugh he ran for the stairs.

Olivia saw the surprise on Alex's face. He glanced at her with a question in his eyes.

Shrugging, she said with a laugh, "Ask Matthew. I refuse to be held responsible for my brother's flirtations. Knowing him, it won't be serious." There was a frown on Alex's face. She said, "How can anyone—"

"Olivia," his voice was soft but commanding. They both heard the footsteps and turned.

"Crystal," Alex said, "join us?"

"I—was wondering if you would be talking about the Bible again tonight," she said. "At breakfast you didn't have time for questions."

"If you wish," he said slowly.

"One thing," Olivia said with a short laugh. "If you wreck your boat, you can always go to preaching."

"Thank you for the compliment," he said with a mock bow.

"I—" Olivia swallowed the retort and went to lean against the rail, feeling uneasy.

"I'll be back in just a moment," Alex said, and he went forward to help tie onto the tree, as Caleb brought the boat near the shore.

Through the trees Olivia could see fireflies pricking the darkness with light. She could hear Alex as he returned and began talking again with Crystal. Olivia turned to lean back against the railing.

A circle of dark faces surrounded Alex and Crystal. As he talked, Amelia and Matthew came down the stairs and stood beside the rail.

Olivia heard Alex say, "This morning we read the Bible verses from Matthew where Jesus criticized the scribes and Pharisees. Crystal, what is the question you want to discuss?"

Hesitantly she said, "You read the verse in which Jesus told the people as they observed the scribes and Pharisees, to not do as these people were doing, because their actions were different than their teaching. Jesus mentioned them putting heavy burdens on the people, and having a demeanor that labeled them superior to those around them. Also he said they were to call everyone brother, and no one master except Christ."

She paused. "You also said the way we keep God's word reveals whether or not we are really followers of Jesus Christ. I find that very troubling. Isn't this an impossible standard?"

"In what we are able to do all by ourselves, yes," Alex replied.

Shaking his head, Caleb said, "But not when we ask the Lord Jesus Christ to help us, Missy."

The words began to slip past Olivia, although she was aware of the clamor of more voices.

She turned back to study out the pattern of fireflies blinking their way inland and thought about Crystal. *She's beautiful and wealthy, but that strange unhappy expression seems to have become a part of her. And now she's searching out religious ideas as if she's an old lady about to die.*

With a bewildered shake of her head, Olivia turned away to watch the fish jump. Beside her, Matthew and Amelia were talking earnestly, but it seemed to have nothing to do with the discussion involving Alex.

She gave them a curious glance as she hesitated beside the railing. Looking toward Alex, she saw more hunched figures and earnest faces clustered around him. All the black people and Crystal seemed very anxious to hear what he had to say.

With a shrug, she fluttered her fingers at Matthew and Amelia before she climbed the stairs to bed.

CHAPTER 26

On the day the Ohio River turned south between Kentucky and Virginia, Olivia sat at the table with the children. Crystal came to sit beside her, quietly listening to the children as they said their letters.

Surprised by her silence, Olivia glanced at her. Crystal's shoulders drooped while she listlessly toyed with a pencil. Olivia could see Crystal was deeply troubled.

Before she had opportunity to speak, Tandy and Maggie, who had been watching at the rail since shortly after breakfast, turned from their post.

With an anxious face, Maggie pointed to a small packet. "I don't like that boat; he's been keepin' right even with us. 'Spect we better go to the cabins."

Crystal went to the rail. "It is close," she said thoughtfully. "In fact it's just ahead of us. Olivia, should we ask Jess to cut the speed?" Without waiting for an answer, she faced Tandy and said, "When he moves ahead, then you all run fast, otherwise someone might see you go—" The gong rang. "Alex is signaling a slowdown," Olivia said, quickly gathering the pencils and paper.

Matthew charged down the stairs. "Get to the cabins!" he ordered. "Shove the cotton in place; there could be an inspection—that boat's riding too close."

He watched them go. "Alex has been expecting this for a couple of days." He looked at the pile of papers on the table. "Better get rid of the book; that's a giveaway."

Amelia came down the stairs. "Guess I'll put on a pot of coffee."

"There, we've dropped behind." Matthew turned, "Run, children!" He casually walked to the rail to stand beside Crystal.

They watched the packet slow down and ease close to the *Golden Awl*. Caleb came out of the engine room, eyed the row of spectators, and gave them a quick warning glare before he went up the stairs.

The whistle shrilled three sharp blasts, and Matthew muttered, "That fellow will get the idea he's stepping on our toes."

The blast was returned, and Matthew said, "Prepare for company."

Alex clattered down the stairs. Olivia saw his grimace one moment before he assumed his welcoming smile. With a shiver, she hugged herself and waited.

"Stop being a baby, Livie," Matthew muttered, moving toward Alex.

Olivia glared at him and went to clear the table. Amelia gave her an amused grin, saying, "Picky brothers! Carry this coffee up to Caleb; you need something to do."

She nodded gratefully and took the coffeepot. When Olivia entered the pilothouse, Caleb said, "I just hit the dead slow bell; they'll be aboard in a minute. Missy, you need this coffee worse than I do. Never saw a lady get the shakes as bad as you."

"And the taunting I get makes me want to shake this coffeepot over your head," she cried. He grinned and eased out of her way. Pouring coffee for the two of them, he settled down to wait.

—————

The pilothouse was the last stop on the inspector's tour. He shook his head over the offered cup. "Just a routine check. The traffic in runaway slaves is picking up. With the rumbles coming out of Washington, these Northerners are speeding up their activity. Seems they're bound to get all the slaves out of the country.

"Mark my words, the abolitionists will pull the whole country down around our ears. The South can't take much more of this loss. When you figure a slave is worth more'n five hundred dollars, one boat load could bleed the South of fifty thousand dollars worth of property."

"Fifty thousand!" Olivia gasped. "That's an awful lot of slaves for a boat to be carrying."

Matthew, Caleb, and Alex glared at her as the inspector left the pilothouse with a brisk salute toward Alex. Matthew followed the man.

Alex turned to Caleb. "I intend to keep going tonight. The sooner we get out of this river, the better I'll like it."

"I suppose we could," Caleb agreed, "but we'd have to keep it slow and right in the middle of the channel." He paused, adding, "As long as you want to risk another sandbar or hitting a snag." He shrugged. "Me, I'm not sold on the idea. Doesn't seem the risk is worth it. Right now, we're traveling sixteen hours a day."

Alex nodded thoughtfully, saying, "Maybe it is best to stick to our plan. Push hard during daylight hours and not risk travel after dark," Olivia's breath came out in an explosion of relief. He grinned at her as she hurried out of the pilothouse.

At the bottom of the stairs, she met Crystal, who asked, "What makes you so happy?"

———

After the evening meal, nearly before the last dish towel had been hung, Crystal went upstairs.

Olivia saw Matthew looking after her with a puzzled expression on his face. After a glance at Crystal, Olivia asked, "What have you done to her?"

"I've scarcely said a word to her today," he said, sounding lonely. "I hoped she'd stay down here for the evening."

"Shall I tell her so?" she asked, starting for the stairs. He brightened and nodded.

When Olivia entered the cabin, she found Crystal sitting at the table. A small candle burned in front of her and her hands were folded on a black book.

"You'll ruin your eyes trying to read in the dark," Olivia said as she pushed the door open and braced it with a rug.

"If you've come to talk, I'll not ruin my eyes," Crystal retorted.

"Where did you find a book to read?"

"It's Alex's Bible."

Olivia chewed her lip and pondered the statement, wondering what it implied. "Matthew was hoping you'd stay down with him tonight." Crystal looked up, hesitating. Olivia added, "You two seemed to be getting along very well. Has something happened to change that?"

"No," Crystal said slowly. "It's just that things—aren't what they seemed. Matthew is nice, but—"

"I understand," Olivia touched Crystal's hand. "Nothing clicked. Too bad; it would have been nice to have you for a sister-in-law. But then, Matthew is terribly immature."

"I don't think he is," Crystal protested. "I'd thought him rather sophisticated."

"Why the Bible?"

"Oh, I borrowed it. I've been asking questions until either Alex was bored with them or just plain confused by them. He suggested I read for myself."

"What did he tell you to read?"

"The book of John."

"In the dark?" Olivia snorted. "Reading the Bible in daylight is difficult enough, and impossible after dark."

"Is that so?" Crystal faltered. "I haven't read much of the Bible except for occasional verses. And I'm afraid I didn't get much help at home. See, our church doesn't encourage Bible reading. All I've known is what Auntie T has told me."

"Your nurse, the slave who traveled with us to Boston?" Crystal nodded and Olivia asked, "How did she learn to read?"

"She can't read, but she has a good memory." She smiled up at Olivia. "For a week after she's heard a sermon, I listen to the whole thing, over and over." Moving restlessly on the chair, Crystal said, "Well, if I can't read this, perhaps you can tell me about it."

"I doubt I know more than you," Olivia drawled. "My mind wanders when I hear sermons." She paused, curious. "What do you want to know?"

"I'm not certain how to put this, but after listening to the Bible verses Alex has been reading to us, I have a whole stack of things piling up in my mind. Olivia, I've been raised to believe that once people are baptized into the church, if they continue to go to Mass and say their prayers, God is pretty much pleased with them. I've tried to be faithful, but the more I listen to Alex the worse I feel. Surely there can't be truth in what he says."

"Well, I guess I haven't been listening too closely, but I think I've been hearing much the same thing all my life, Crystal." Olivia sat down and studied her sad features. "What amazes me is that this is all making you so unhappy."

"I simply don't understand. Alex says we become Christians by accepting Jesus Christ as our Savior and Lord. And then he talked about faith. You have to believe, and you must pray and tell God you are serious about being a Christian. But more than that—" She shrugged.

Helplessly Olivia lifted her hands. "I can't understand what the problem is. Either you are a Christian or you aren't." Dropping her hands, she leaned forward. "But then if you have a guilty conscience— you know, feel bad from lying or some such, that is a different matter. In that case I think you need to confess—"

"But I can't; there isn't a priest around here. Olivia, what would happen to me if we had an accident and I died? See, I've been thinking about this since that terrible explosion. It was the Lord's grace that I didn't die then. But now—what happens when there isn't a priest around?"

Olivia shrugged and took a deep breath. "I guess you'll just have to hope God will listen to you without a priest." She saw the dejection in Crystal's face. "That doesn't help? I can't understand. If I can pray and feel good about confessing my sins to God, why can't you do the same thing?"

Abruptly Olivia jumped to her feet. "Oh, Crystal, this is just terrible. I don't know what to tell you to make you understand. But wait here; I'll go find Alex and have him talk to you."

Crystal had her face buried in her hands as Olivia ran from the cabin. She looked up at the pilothouse, but there wasn't a glimmer of light. Neither was there a hint of light coming from the open cabin doors down the hurricane deck. Going to the head of the stairs, Olivia leaned over and peered at the deck below.

By the glow of the lantern on the table she could see Alex and

Amelia. They were looking intently at each other, but their voices were only a murmur set against the lap of water on the hull.

As she hesitated, the two got to their feet. Amelia stepped around the table and gave Alex a quick hug. "Thank you, and good night," she called, starting toward the stairs.

Her mind in a confused whirl, Olivia slowly began walking down the stairs toward the two. She mentally searched for words to say, words that would sear away the hurting memory of Alex's arms around her, Alex murmuring in her ear.

Amelia had started up the stairs. "Oh, Olivia! You startled me. I didn't see you—nearly ran you over!" She stepped aside, touching Olivia's arm as she did. "Are you looking for Alex?"

Olivia stopped. Taking a deep breath she said, "No, I'll settle for you. Crystal needs someone to talk sense into her head. I think she's afraid this steamboat is going to explode too."

"Oh dear, I'll go," Amelia said. Stepping around Olivia, she hurried to the cabin.

Still wondering about her strange reaction to the scene around the table, Olivia sat down on the steps. She watched Alex walk to the railing and lean over the side of the boat. She pondered her reluctance to go down the steps. Over the ache that scene had left in her heart, she searched for safe anger and felt a sensation of betrayal.

Still brooding, she thought about the way the pale glow of light from the lantern touched his shoulders, drawing an intimate circle around them. That was the shoulder she had slept against in the forest. Olivia, why are you jealous? He is nothing in your life except a brutish friend of your brother.

She heard a door open and close as Caleb came out of the engine room and went to stand beside Alex. For a moment they talked, and then Alex turned toward Caleb. Olivia blinked her eyes in disbelief. Alex put his arm across Caleb's shoulders. They talked for a moment more, and as she watched, the two men hugged each other, spoke again, and then parted.

Olivia scrambled up the stairs and flew into the cabin.

Amelia was on her knees beside Crystal's bunk. As Olivia watched, Amelia brushed Crystal's hair away from her eyes, patted her face, and stood up.

Turning aside, Olivia prepared for bed. Her mind was full of strange pictures: Amelia and Alex, Alex and Caleb, and Crystal. What was the meaning of all she had seen? The pictures puzzled and irritated her, leaving her more baffled than ever.

———

In the morning when Olivia clattered down the steps, she found Alex beside the table with the Bible in his hands. Crystal was also standing. She faced Alex and then turned to the others.

Olivia slipped into her seat as Crystal said, "Amelia told me that Alex had helped her understand more about God. He asked her how she would approach God if she were the only person on earth. And then he said that is the way any person is to address God." She glanced at Alex and waited.

He said, "I told her just speak to Him. When we get desperate we toss out all the rules and rituals. Looking at the world around us, and measuring the beauty of His creation against our own little selves, reminds us that He is a loving God. He wants us to approach Him and give Him an opportunity to make His love known to us."

His voice brooded. "Although we may not know anything about Him, He knows everything about us." With a smile he added, "His Word provides the link we need—it tells us God loved us enough to die so that we can live. He did it through Jesus Christ." For a moment Alex's gaze rested on Olivia, and she saw the question in his eyes.

Caleb said, "Alex, you make it sound too simple. There's repentance to do and a right way to live."

"But in the beginning," Alex countered, "there's just God and me. He has done His part, and now He waits to see if I will do mine."

Matthew clattered down the steps. He stopped, looked from Crystal to Alex, and then approached. "Your part? What is that?"

For a moment Alex dropped his head. "I suppose Shakespeare said it better than I can. 'We do pray for mercy: And that same prayer doth teach us all to render the deeds of mercy.' "

"I like that," Matthew said as he picked up his bowl and went to the stove. "I'll remember it."

"Only, Matt," Alex reminded gently, "doing the deeds of mercy is impossible without the Lord of mercy helping us."

"Deeds of mercy," Maggie said, nodding her head with a pleased smile. "I think we know Alex has the Lord of Mercy living in him."

CHAPTER 27

Holding the dripping gown in front of her, Olivia hurried down the stairs.

Maggie turned from the stove. "I see you're wearing Matthew's britches again."

Carefully smoothing the wrinkles out of the dark cotton dress, Olivia nodded. "I didn't wash this last night. But then it wouldn't have dried. The rain was cold, wasn't it?"

"We're getting into fall. I been looking at the trees every day, and I see them changing color. Worries me that we won't make Canada before snow. I ain't been in snow, but they tell me it's miserable."

Olivia nodded. "Crystal and I spent a winter in Boston. After beautiful Mississippi, it was horrible. I'll never live in the North again. Snow and cold, and then more of the same."

She heard a chuckle and turned. Caleb shook his head. "Don't say that, Missy—could be just what'll happen to you."

"I intend to leave for home just as soon as this trip is finished."

"You're not goin' to stay and help up North?" Maggie looked shocked. "Here I thought—"

Hastily Caleb said, "Maggie, will you make some coffee for us? Send it up to the cabin by Livie." He went upstairs and Maggie carried the coffeepot to the stove.

"Must be something going on up there." She jerked her head toward the hurricane deck.

"Could be," Olivia murmured. As she continued to smooth the wrinkles out of her wet clothing, she recalled the way Caleb had interrupted Maggie.

Going to the stove, she asked, "Maggie, what made you think I would stay in the North?"

Maggie rolled her eyes. "Missy, we've just been conjecturing. Seems we all thought you and Alex make a good pair. He sure enough seems to want you around."

"Because he forced me to stay on the boat? Maggie, that's simply an indication he doesn't trust me to keep my mouth shut."

"The coffee's done. I'll put the whole load in this box for you. Might be someone'll want a piece of fried bread with it."

Olivia picked up the box. "Are there mugs, too?"

She climbed the stairs to the hurricane deck and found the cabin door was ajar. Olivia pushed it open and went in. Charts and maps were spread across the table. Alex was seated in front of them, busy writing. He looked up. "Thanks for bringing the coffee. Caleb must've forgot."

"No, he told me to. Where is he? I saw him go upstairs."

"Pilothouse. He's staying with Matthew. There's a tricky section coming up."

"I'll take coffee up," Olivia said. Alex nodded and bent over the charts. Quickly she filled the mug and left the room.

In the pilothouse she found Caleb sprawled on the bench with his red cap over his eyes. "Sleeping! I thought you wanted coffee," she taunted.

He shoved the cap aside and grinned, "Alex did. You're neglecting your job. Thanks for the coffee."

"My job is to carry coffee?"

Matthew eyed her. "You wear out my trousers, and then what do I wear?"

"Brother dear, by then you'll be buying clothes for both of us, and it had best be soon."

"We're getting close to Pennsylvania."

She looked at Matthew. "Are you going home with me?"

He grinned. "Not unless I can convince Crystal she should come, too."

Olivia frowned. "Don't push. I have the distinct impression that Crystal wishes you would stop bothering her."

"Off and on she feels that way. But I'm winning. You've noticed she didn't get off at Cincinnati."

"You know as well as I that she's committed herself to seeing that Joseph gets into Canada."

Matthew nodded and leaned forward to peer at the river channel. "Caleb, come tell me what you think about that dark line I'm seeing. Is it a snag?"

Olivia slipped out and closed the door. For a moment she faced the wind. Feeling the prickle of cold against her skin, she shivered. "Maggie is right; fall is coming."

She stopped in the doorway of the cabin. "More coffee?" Alex shook his head. She lingered.

Looking up he said, "Why don't you come in and close the door; it's getting cold."

"What are you going to do during cold weather? You can't keep this up all winter can you?"

"No. But I'll be able to get in another trip before ice jams the rivers." He threw her a quick teasing look. "Want to come?" She snorted. He chuckled. "Just thought I'd ask."

He continued to make notes while Olivia walked restlessly around the room. She discovered he was watching her. "You could read a book or something."

"Your Bible?"

"If you want."

"No, thanks."

"Know it all, huh?"

"You are insufferable."

"Maggie thinks we make a great pair."

"Oh, she's told you, too. Matchmaking. I happen to feel differently. You realize, don't you, if I'd any idea what I was getting into, I'd never have listened to Lem." As soon as she said the words, she put her hand to her lips.

She caught her breath as he dropped his pencil and leaned across the table. "Lem? What—" She watched dismay change to comprehension. Slowly he stood up. Studying her from head to toe, he said, "The youth with your cousin! I thought you were a b—" He sat down and wiped his hands across his face. "I really walloped—"

"Me." Her voice was icy, and suddenly she began to enjoy his embarrassment.

"Olivia," he came around the table and she faced him with her chin tilted. "I honestly don't know how to apologize. It isn't enough to say I'm sorry. My dear," he begged, "I've never struck a woman in my life."

"Until now. I shan't forget it."

"Then you won't forgive me?"

"Not enough to get within six feet of you on purpose." She turned and walked out of the cabin.

———

After the evening meal, Alex addressed the group. "We are getting very close to our destination. At the moment we don't know enough about the situation ahead of us to make hard and fast plans, but I want to tell you what we hope will happen."

A ripple of excitement swept around the table. Looking at the bright faces, Olivia felt her own heart lift. Tandy got to her feet. "Alex, we will never in our lives be able to say what you mean to us. But thank you for what you've done."

"Don't thank me yet," he said with a tight grin. "We may be approaching the hardest part of the whole trip. And don't forget, I'm as new at this as you are.

"One of the first things we will do is divide the group and place a leader over each group." He paused to take a deep breath before he continued. "The reasoning behind this is that there is a possibility we will be separated. I hope this won't happen, but in the event, we want to be prepared."

"Leader? What's his job?"

"Be father and mother and lover." In the silence, Alex continued, "Whatever must be done for each other, must be done within the group. We will have to depend on each other and stick together. If one reaches Canada, we will all reach Canada."

"Alex, are you going, too?"

"Certainly. I can't rest until the job is completed."

"And the ladies?"

"No. They will either stay at a station on the way, or they'll be free to leave."

"Station? Is this part of the Underground Railroad, Alex?"

"It is. The most important part. In Mississippi, we dared not admit this, but in Ohio and Pennsylvania—"

Caleb chuckled. "We stick out like a sore thumb. Except at night, then they can't tell whether we are black or white."

"We don't have to go underground."

"To the contrary," Alex said slowly. "There is still need for the utmost caution. We'll move at night and not consider ourselves safe until we've reached Canada."

Jess turned to Alex. "Are you saying they still catch slaves in Ohio and Pennsylvania?"

"I'm afraid so." Slowly Alex added, "The Fugitive Slave Act is still in effect. In order to be law-abiding citizens, the Northerners are obligated to turn runaway slaves over to the authorities."

"We'll never make it." Jeb stated flatly.

"You'll be surprised," Alex murmured, "how colorblind some Northerners are. There's only one problem; you don't know which ones are colorblind and which aren't."

Alex got to his feet and spread a map on the table.

"I want you all to study this. Those who can't read, ask questions. See these circled spots? Every spot represents a station. I've written landmarks, towns, and names around each spot. These are your life-lines."

He paused, and in the dusk, Olivia watched him look into each face. Pointing to a dot on the map, he said, "We are headed for this place—it's called The Willows. The family name is Cooper. This is just off the Ohio River, in Pennsylvania. Now this little town is New Castle, but if it is impossible to reach this place, we can go to any of the other points and be assured of help. Now, come. I will divide you into groups with a leader. You are now a family group with responsibility for each other."

Taking a shaky breath, Olivia got to her feet. "Crystal, I think this is the end of the trip for us." She added, "We might as well go to the cabin and make plans of our own. Coming, Amelia?" As they started up the stairs, Olivia looked back. The excited voices and the huddled figures made her sharply aware of her solitude. For just one second, without willing it, her eyes sought out the figure of the man at the head of the group. Despite the darkening shadows, she saw the gleam of a golden earring, and again she wondered.

Olivia, during the following week, observed the change in the people and commented on it. "Tandy, it's as if there is a whole new adventure starting."

" 'Tis. Just like Alex say we are to do. We're becoming family, and we're learning to look forward and make plans." Looking at Olivia she said softly, "For the first time in our lives, we make the plans. Sure, we are told to stick together and help each other. But that's good. See, not a one of us has ever been alone before."

Humbled by the woman's excitement, Olivia said, "We're the ones who will be the losers. We will miss the good times, the children. I suppose even the worry of each day."

Wisely Tandy nodded her head. "It's a wrenching. People just don't part easy. And we know it's going to be hardship ahead. That's part of freedom. Alex tells us sometimes the hardest part of life is learning to not expect all easy times. He calls it creating our own heaven on this earth."

"What does he recommend?"

Tandy frowned. "Livie, why don't you ask? You all the time come around saying, 'What does Alex say?' 'What does Alex think?' Go ask him."

Amelia finally reached through Olivia's jumbled emotions. Coming into the cabin one evening she stated, "Alex says we'll be in Wheeling by noon tomorrow. He showed me the map. The fellows are talking about finding a place to dock for a day or so. Said something about spying out the land. I declare, they're starting to sound like Joshua's men."

"Joshua?" Olivia questioned, turning from the porthole. "Who is he?"

Amelia paused, pursed her lips, and said, "For a churchgoing Christian, your Bible education has been sorely neglected."

"Oh, that one. Bible." She moved restlessly around the cabin. "Amelia, have you made plans?"

"I'm going to stay in Pennsylvania for the winter."

"What are you going to do? Oh, I shouldn't be so nosy."

Surprisingly Amelia laughed. "Alex says he'll put in a good word for me. See, I decided to give the straight life another try.

"Crystal—" She turned a mocking smile on the girl as she walked into the cabin. "You aren't the only one who's learned a lesson by the steamboat explosion. You're all looking at the reformed dancehall girl. Think God will be impressed if I start by helping the slaves get into Canada?"

Olivia frowned. "I don't know. Somehow that sounds like all the wrong idea. But then, if you've talked it over with God, like Alex says, well, I suppose it's all right."

Abruptly the smile slipped from Amelia's face. "I wasn't serious. But I do feel I need time to plan my life a little better. I'm too inclined to jump into things." She winced, and Olivia waited. Looking at her, Amelia said, "Jump—you know, like off burning ships."

"Oh, Amelia," Crystal said with a catch in her voice. "Please be serious."

"More problems?" Amelia asked slowly.

"Yes," she said with a sigh. "It's Joseph. I've planned this trip just for the purpose of taking him as far north as possible and then giving him his freedom. Now he doesn't want to go into Canada. What shall I do?"

"Given all we've been exposed to during the past two and a half months, this is unbelievable," Amelia said slowly. "Crystal, why doesn't he want his freedom?"

She shrugged and turned away. "I guess you could call it faithfulness, or laziness—I don't know," she mumbled as she began to pull pins out of her hair.

After a moment Amelia looked at Olivia. "What are you going to do?"

"Take the first steamboat south. I'll go home." Olivia paused as the picture of home washed across her mind. The gentle, lovely picture seemed dim and far away. She strained to feel the familiar tug of family and friends, but the backwash left her moving restlessly around the cabin. "Imagine," she said dryly, "having to decide what dress to wear!

I'll even have my choice at breakfast instead of porridge, porridge, and porridge. I'll go for a walk, and I won't fall in the water when I step out my front door." She stopped.

Crystal said, "I don't think you are any more interested in returning home than I am."

"Right now it does sound boring," Olivia admitted. "Even too secure and ordered. But I don't have anything else in mind."

Amelia pulled off her shoes. "Well, you don't need to decide before morning. Do you object if I go to bed now?"

CHAPTER 28

A new ritual had been added to the breakfast time. At the conclusion of Bible reading and prayer, Alex would spread the map on the table. Daily his pencil marked out the course ahead of them, and always there was one dark head nodding at the map. "Alex, we getting closer. Will we see the big rocks today?" And from the back some anxious voice would say, "How will we know there's someone to lead us on?"

Olivia found herself admiring the unending patience of the man as Alex explained, "We don't know. We have only the promises to go on. We know they have provided in the past. And if they had failed to do so, I believe we would have been told."

"Tell us again what is going to happen."

He pointed to the largest circle on the map. "This is our destination. But at any point marked on the map, you can be assured of help."

Solomon's thick finger traced up into Canada. "A mighty long way up there."

"Don't matter," Jess said, "That's freedom. I could walk near forever if that's where it would end. Might be my family is there already."

One day, Alex's pencil rested on the Pennsylvania state line. He said, "There's no reason we can't be right here by mid-afternoon today."

"In the middle of the day?" Jess questioned. "Is that good?"

"No," Alex replied. "And I don't intend to push in there today. This means we'll be cutting our speed just about noon. Hopefully we'll find a place to dock soon after. I'm going to scout around, get the feel of the land, then after dark we'll move on up the river."

"Don't you think we should let them know we're coming?" Olivia asked.

Alex looked at her. For a moment his eyes warmed her. She blushed and looked away from him. Slowly he said, "We've considered doing just that. But we don't want to raise suspicion. Remember, we mustn't bring danger upon these people."

True to his statement, when the sun was overhead, the women around the table heard the gong signaling reduced speed. Tandy cocked her head. "Only one gong; that means we won't be going too slow." She hugged herself and shivered with excitement.

Feeling the excitement too, Olivia stood up and restlessly paced to the railing. Crystal said, "You had better find something to do." When Olivia turned, Crystal's eyes flashed a warning.

Tandy said, "That pot of coffee is ready; why don't you take it up? There's bread and ham in the box, too."

Olivia looked into the box. "And apples? What are we celebrating?" She saw Crystal's dismal look and Tandy's grin. With a shrug, Olivia picked up the coffeepot and the box and started up the stairs. Thinking of the women's expressions, she measured her own lack of emotion and could only feel bewildered by her friend's expression. *Fear? Yes, of course I'm afraid for them. Only God knows what lies ahead. But Crystal, why are you looking as if this is the end of the world?*

As she walked up the final flight of stairs Matthew came down. He looked into the box. "Have you seen Crystal?"

"She's sitting at the table." Matthew started past her, and she said, "What's wrong between you two? I've seen her avoiding you."

"I only wish I knew," he muttered. "Olivia, put in a good word for me."

"Fight your own battles. Might be she's guessed your wild past."

He snorted, "That's an exaggeration, and you know it. Please, Olivia, this means an awful lot to me."

"What about our parents? How will they feel?"

Impatiently he said, "Crystal is from one of the most influential Creole families in New Orleans. How can they possibly object?"

"Well, I still think you should fight your own battles." She relented. "But I did tell her I'd like her as a sister-in-law." He chuckled and kissed her cheek.

When Olivia walked into the pilothouse, Alex gave her a brief glance, nodded, and turned back to the wheel. Caleb, who was prone on the bench, shifted his red cap and groaned. "Coffee and food," she explained.

"Not ready yet," Alex muttered. "Just leave it."

Caleb sat up and grinned at her. "Want me to leave?"

"Why?" she asked astonished.

He glanced at Alex and shrugged. "Thought you'd come up to talk."

She shook her head, "Nothing to talk about. I was restless and the others too comfortable, so I'm the maid today. Shall I pour coffee for you?"

Caleb's eyes sparkled as he chuckled and nodded. Alex asked, "Please, what is there to eat?"

"Bread and meat," she said, surprised at Caleb's amusement. With a puzzled frown, she watched him and waited.

"You go ahead and prepare it for him," Caleb said, his eyes still twinkling. Silently Olivia poured the coffee, wrapped the ham in the bread, and carried it to Alex.

She saw a reflection of the amusement in his eyes. "Don't mind Caleb; he's practicing being a free man."

She looked at Caleb and asked, "Are you going to Canada?"

Without waiting for an answer, she turned to Alex. "How will you manage without Caleb?"

He shrugged, "Guess I'll have to hire me another pilot. Too bad you didn't learn steamboating. I'd give you the job."

"You're teasing," she said slowly. "You'd never give a woman a chance at a job like this."

He signaled half speed and looked at her. "I was teasing, but as of this minute I'm not."

"That's astounding; I can't believe that you are anything except the perfect Southern gentleman as far as women are concerned."

"Believing that they are beautiful toys, to be pampered and enjoyed?" His eyes glimmered, but behind the teasing there was a sober question that pushed at her.

"With all that implies, you think I'm only a typical Southern woman?"

He balanced his coffee against the wheel and took a bite of the sandwich. She studied the earring and watched him gulp coffee before he finally said, "Yes."

She walked to the door. "Caleb, you can bring the box down later."

The door closed slowly and carefully. Caleb said, "Alex, you didn't do so well."

"And you, my friend, set me up for that." Alex finished his sandwich.

"You know," Caleb said around his mouthful, "I have a very strong feeling that Missy likes you much more than she pretends to."

"Then I'm a mighty poor judge of the Southern woman."

Caleb chuckled. "She'd be a mighty poor Southern lady if she couldn't keep you guessing."

Alex handed his mug to Caleb. "Now, to important matters. I'm feeling the Lord is urging caution."

"I guessed that," Caleb said. "It makes sense to believe that big house on the hill could be watched."

"And we can't go charging in there with all these slaves."

"Those officials would have a lapful," Caleb chuckled. "But they wouldn't stand a chance. Them black people would scatter in fifty different directions."

"Fine, as long as the men don't have guns," Alex answered soberly.

———

Crystal looked up as Matthew came down the stairs. He tipped his nonexistent hat. "Mademoiselle, will you stroll with me in the park?"

He came to her with a quizzical smile and his hand was insistent under her elbow. She sighed, "Matthew, you are—"

"Impossible to resist? I'm willing to get grass stains on my knees for you." Tandy giggled, and he added, "At least come take fresh air on the hurricane deck."

With a sigh, Crystal allowed Matthew to lead her up the stairs. When they reached the bow, Crystal faced into the wind and asked, "Matthew, are you going to continue to work with Alex?"

"Is that upsetting you?"

"No, most certainly it isn't. You know I've become increasingly sympathetic to the plight of the slaves."

"But not committed?"

"I suppose that's the only honest way to look at it. But in addition, Matthew, I don't think you have this same burning zeal that Alex seems to be driven by, do you?"

"No. At the present time, I have only one burning zeal, and you know what that is." He pulled her away from the railing. "Let's sit on the ropes, out of the sun. There." He paused. "Alex has become nearly fanatic about the whole situation. I can't say I'd give my life for the cause."

"Then you are still very Southern." She hesitated. "Our values are most important."

"If you mean I recognize the need for slavery in order for our way of life to continue to exist, yes. But do we have a right to expect life to continue on in this manner for as long as we please?" He paused and added, "No society has existed without change. Perhaps, rather than being against slavery, I am instead in favor of change. For the good of the black man as well as mine. I also sense that a revolution of moral thought is necessary. I believe enough in God to sense He won't continue to bless us if we choose to ignore human suffering existing under the glaring light of our selfish desires."

"Well said," Crystal murmured.

"Enough that I rate a kiss and an explanation for your distance?"

Crystal sighed deeply. "Matthew," she began carefully, "I simply can't say I care enough for you to continue to encourage you."

"You know I don't believe that." He tilted her chin and bent close. Crystal felt the cabin wall behind her shoulders. Finally she pushed away from his kiss. "Matthew," she whispered brokenly, "please don't force me to be angry with you."

"Don't be angry; just be my love, forever."

"No." Giving him a shove, she jumped to her feet and went to the rail. With the cool air against her hot cheeks, she said, "Matthew, I refuse to listen to you any longer. Be gracious enough to stay away from me and allow me time to think—"

The gong sounded twice. Matthew's voice was heavy as he spoke. "Alex is preparing to tie up for the night. I suppose this marks the end of our beautiful time." She didn't answer. He turned to run up the stairs to the pilothouse.

———————

Olivia heard the signal. She lifted her head and encountered the row of dark eyes watching her. "Alex is docking the boat for the night." Slowly she stood. "I think our time together is just about over."

"What are we going to do with the book?" little Joe asked.

"For now I'll keep it," Olivia said as she gathered the papers. "Then, when you are grown, if you come to visit me, I shall give the book to you, or you, or you. Whoever comes to see me first," she added, pointing to the children watching her.

"How will we find you?"

While she hesitated, Abby piped, "That's easy. We will find Alex, and he will know where she is."

They looked up as the men clattered down the stairs. Alex came to the table, and as he spoke, Olivia was conscious only of his overwhelming presence. His smile was reassuring as he said, "We're going to have our supper, and then I'm going to ask you to go to the cabins and be very quiet."

"Why?"

He looked surprised by the question. "Because yesterday you were children; today you are learning to be grown-ups. Today you begin your real journey to Canada, and each of you is responsible for your partners. Silence will buy freedom, noise will—"

"Bring the bad men, like the one in the forest." Jeb's oldest son spoke up, then turned. "Little Joe, this time you won't run away. I won't let you."

As Olivia moved away from the table, she saw Alex rub his thumb across his eyes, and her heart tightened with fear.

Quickly and quietly Tandy and Maggie served the meal, and it was eaten in the very same fashion. Afterward, as the people started up the stairs, Alex reminded, "Don't forget to put the cotton in the doorway."

He moved restlessly around the deck while Matthew and Caleb sat at the table with mugs of coffee in front of them. Olivia was uneasily conscious of the roustabouts lounging in the passageway to the engine room, whistling tunelessly.

Amelia washed dishes while Crystal and Olivia dried them. Crystal looked at the poor collection of trenchers and asked, "What shall we do with these?"

Alex stopped beside her. "Save them for the next group." He frowned at Olivia's wide-eyed astonishment.

Twilight turned to darkness. Light from the one lantern attracted insects, but when Olivia moved to extinguish it, Alex murmured, "Leave it." The frogs began their homey chorus, and as Olivia leaned over the railing she felt nearly comforted. She studied the cattails and marsh grasses lining the river as she listened to the frogs and the soft voices behind her.

Crystal came to stand beside her. "It's almost cold, isn't it?" Olivia nodded and Crystal added, "I can scarcely stand—"

Abruptly Matthew and Alex left the group around the table. As Matthew pulled on a jacket, Olivia said, "What—"

Coming close, Alex murmured, "He's going to check out the house. We need to know what we're getting into before we unload. You ladies might as well go to bed; it's going to be a long night."

———

Olivia awakened to the sound of the paddles swishing in the water. She heard footsteps on the stairs. Getting up and pulling the blanket around her shoulders, she went to the door. Matthew spoke softly. "We're heading upstream; the house is close, and they're expecting us."

Crystal appeared behind her in the doorway. Olivia watched Matthew touch her face before he went back to the pilothouse. "Olivia," Crystal said slowly, with her hand against her face, "I've been thinking about these people. Why do they risk so much?"

Amelia murmured, "Better come in. Who knows what is going to happen." They stood close to the porthole and watched shadowy trees pass. They also saw the faint hint of light to the east begin just as the swishing of the paddles slowed. Soon, on the deck outside their door, they could hear the padding of bare feet.

Olivia pulled the door open. A warm hand touched her and then was gone. Trembling, she rubbed at the tears on her face.

Straining her ears, she heard a gentle scraping noise, a shudder, and finally only the lap of water in the silence. Matthew came into the room. "They're gone; let's go."

Quickly they disembarked. As they walked slowly up the hill toward the house outlined against the lightening sky, Olivia began to feel peacefulness reaching out to her. The wind moved gently through the trees, rattling drying leaves, while the grass rustled beneath their feet. Beyond the fence, cows lifted mild faces as they chewed contentedly.

They finally reached the house, but before she stepped through the open door, Olivia glanced over her shoulder at the dark boat.

The round-faced woman who greeted them smiled with the same serenity. "Thee are welcome," she murmured.

Olivia hesitated in the doorway. She whispered, "Where are they?"

"Safe. Now go to sleep; thy work is done."

CHAPTER 29

When Olivia awakened she was alone in the room. Stretching in the depths of the feather bed, she rolled over and blinked in the bright sunshine. She squinted against the beam of sunlight, sat up, and looked around the room. She had slept in a trundle bed. The tumbled four-poster across the room indicated that Amelia and Crystal had shared its ample comfort.

"I can't believe—a real bedroom!" There was a washstand with a big pile of snowy towels and a rocking chair draped with a pink afghan.

Getting out of bed, she padded across to the windows. The *Golden Awl* was still at the wharf. Sighing, she snuggled her toes into the thick braided rug for a moment longer. The boat had been a reminder, and she couldn't help wondering if Alex had gone with the slaves.

The water in the pitcher was cold. She shivered and scrubbed hastily. As she pulled on the badly-worn dark cotton, she sighed, "Now I want to go shopping."

When Olivia stepped out the bedroom door, she realized how little she had noticed of her surroundings when she had entered the house in the early morning.

At the top of the stairs was a tiny alcove devoted to comfortable chairs, a writing desk, and a bookcase. Beyond a tall bank of windows she could see blue sky and distant trees. Turning, she discovered another flight of stairs rising at the end of the hall. Olivia walked slowly to the head of the stairs, enjoying the effect of light and color. Sunshine on light polished wood made the vast hallway come alive with warm color. As she started down the stairs, she identified touches of rose, blue, and cream in the rugs. They were threadbare, but clean.

When she reached the main floor she could hear voices coming from the back of the house. Crossing the hall and walking down the long parlor, she followed the sound through a dining room and into a keeping room opening into the kitchen.

Several women, dressed in gentle gray, worked around the large table beside the stove. The room was filled with the aroma of fresh bread. "Oh, what a wonderful smell!" Olivia exclaimed as the round-faced woman she had met earlier came around the table.

"Hungry? 'Tis no wonder; it's after noontime." She nodded toward the table where Crystal and Amelia sat. "They've had refreshment, so come."

"Where are the others?"

The woman slid a loaded plate in front of Olivia and placed a mug on the table. "I'm Sadie Cooper. This is Katy; she's come to visit today, and I've put her to work. The others? They've business to do before nightfall."

"Are—they still here?"

Sadie nodded, pursing her mouth in a prim smile as she went back to the stove.

Crystal said, "Alex is making arrangements for them. Something about wagons."

"They're getting warm clothing for them." Sadie bobbed her head with satisfaction as she moved around the room. "That's one thing we've discovered. These people have no idea of the weather ahead."

She stopped and eyed Amelia's flimsy dress. "Looks like you're not prepared any better than they are."

Hastily Olivia said, "The steamboat went down. We fished them out of the water. They didn't save anything except what they were wearing."

The woman's shrewd eyes brightened, "Steamboat, huh?"

"Fire," Crystal said with a shudder.

"Better fix you up, too," she said, adding, "No sense advertising to the neighbors."

"Then they don't know?"

"Not much. Decent people. The less they see and hear the better off we are." She paused. "Olivia, I'll offer thee a dress until thee can go shopping." There was a question in her eyes, but she said no more as she hurried out of the room.

Throughout the day Olivia enjoyed a peace that she hadn't experienced for some time; Sadie's gentle presence touched her spirit in a way that caused her anxieties to fade away. That evening Olivia wore to dinner the new frock that Sadie had lent her. It was deep rose, cut low in the front, and with a bustle. When she walked into the dining room, she saw the expression on Alex's face. "Some dear black woman will love it," Sadie explained, "but for now, Olivia is borrowing it. She looks good in rose—howbeit, not that cut," she added hastily.

Alex's eyes were twinkling as he said, "I doubt it will keep our Canadian friends adequately warm."

Sadie peered at Olivia. "Oh, dear. I suppose I can find a scarf for your shoulders."

"I'm not the least bit cold," Olivia said, glaring at Alex, "and I don't consider it *decollete*."

———

During the night Olivia heard the clink of a harness outside and footsteps in the hall. Kneeling beside the window, she strained to see through shadows. Finally, when she was thoroughly chilled, she whispered, "Goodbye; good luck." As she wiped a tear from her cheek, she wondered if Alex had gone too.

———

The next afternoon Matthew borrowed a buggy and drove them into town. He stopped in front of what looked like the most promising shop and helped the three out of the buggy. Handing the wad of banknotes to Olivia, he muttered, "Since suitable clothing will help hide our covert activities, I suggest you women all come back adequately attired." He bowed stiffly, and with a teasing grin, headed down the street.

Olivia called after him, "My darling, you'll be a true gentleman if you volunteer to come carry our parcels."

A woman passing by eased her bulk around and said, "Just like a husband." For a moment she looked from Olivia, to Amelia, and then to Crystal. With a puzzled frown she nodded and went on her way.

Finding the right dresses took the better part of the afternoon, but they were happy with what they bought, and couldn't wait to get into some new clothes. When they had finished, Matthew came by in the buggy and drove them home.

That evening, while Matthew and Olivia were talking, Alex came into the parlor. He hesitated and Matthew beckoned to him. "Come settle a problem for us." Watching him, Olivia wanted badly to ask about the slaves.

He sat down beside the two and Matthew asked, "Will you solve our dilemma? Olivia thinks we need to write to our parents. I say we should wait, because of—"

Alex nodded. "I see what you mean, and I appreciate your waiting this long. Go ahead and write. The people have left, and in addition, I've seen a couple of fellows nosing around the boat. I'll need to be on my way as soon as possible. If you refrain from mentioning names, it'll help." Without a glance toward Olivia, he got to his feet, bowed and left the room.

Olivia watched him go, her eyes following every move. Matthew grinned. "It's your fault—you've hardly encouraged him." He paused and added bitterly, "Why are the Thomas chillen such failures in the romance department?"

"Things not going well between you and Crystal?" Olivia asked, but Matthew looked so miserable she dared say nothing more. She left the room, saying, "I'm going to start a letter tonight."

When Olivia entered the bedroom, Crystal turned from the mirror. "Alex told me he will be leaving day after tomorrow."

"Leaving?" Olivia drew in a breath. "Where is he going?"

"South again. He said there's another load of slaves waiting for him. Also, the Coopers have arranged a business deal. He's to carry freight—merchandise of some type. It will help pay his way, as well as provide an excuse for the trip."

Olivia went to sit in the rocking chair. She asked, "Pay his way? I supposed him to have plenty of money."

"He does, but seems reluctant to use his father's money in such an operation." There was a wry twist to Crystal's lips, as she added, "Does seem ironic, doesn't it? Using his father's rice and cotton wealth to destroy the whole system."

In a moment, Crystal added, "I want to go with him as far as Cincinnati. He won't take me any farther; says it's too dangerous."

"Then it's all over with Matthew?"

She nodded. In a rush of words, she added, "Olivia, I have a problem. Last week I signed Joseph's papers giving him freedom, but late today I found he's still here. Even worse, he's hanging around, wanting the Coopers to hire him." She added hastily, "I think he's afraid to be out on his own. I find his attachment—offensive. This is another reason I'm anxious to go as soon as possible."

For a few minutes, Olivia contemplated the situation. She sighed heavily. "Yes, I feel the end of it all, too." She looked up and smiled. "I'll travel with you. But what are you going to do about Joseph? Surely there's some obligation. You can't just leave him."

"Oh, Olivia, that hurts! But how far do you let former ties entangle life? I don't want to abandon him, but on the other hand, he's well able to take care of himself. I've provided him with sufficient funds." There was an amused twist to her mouth as she added, "I used some of the clothes money Matthew gave me. His generosity allowed me to have extra funds for Joseph."

Olivia frowned. "You really do worry about him." In a moment she said, "You should insist he go to Canada. Sadie told me there's trouble with paddyrollers. They apprehend runaway slaves and take them back to their masters, and some of them have become so brave that they are even catching freedmen to sell back into slavery!"

With a sigh Crystal turned away. "You're making it very difficult for me. Particularly since—"

"What, Crystal?"

"I'm sorry, I just can't talk about it."

Finally Olivia said, "You can tell Alex I'll go along too."

"Why don't you tell him yourself?"

Olivia gave a short laugh and turned away. "I'm certain it doesn't matter who tells him. I just thought, since you've discussed this, you might as well say I'm going."

———————

After dinner the next evening, Alex followed Olivia to the parlor. "I need to talk with you for a few minutes."

"Yes?" she lifted her chin.

As the others came into the room, he said, "Let's go upstairs to the alcove."

"Is there—" she began.

"Yes, and I don't want an audience."

Avoiding his eyes and his hand she nodded and marched toward the stairs. When they were seated, Alex said, "Crystal tells me you will be traveling to Cincinnati with us."

"If it is convenient, I prefer being with Crystal to going alone."

"Matthew has indicated he'll come along, too," he said. "You know I'm disappointed you are going home."

"How can you be disappointed? After all, I was practically kidnapped."

"But where were you when you were kidnapped?" he asked with a chuckle. His eyes still twinkling, he added, "I had hoped you would stay."

"It's out of the question," she murmured, shaking her head. "Our parents will be upset enough as it is. Incidentally, I haven't written yet, so your operation won't be exposed. Besides, what could I do here?"

"Well, I have a few ideas. Want to hear them?"

"No." The retort was sharper than she intended. Olivia studied his face, wishing she could snatch back the word. Lamely she searched for conversation, wondering why she lingered. Finally she asked, "Did Caleb go to Canada?"

He shook his head, "He never did intend to go. He'll be traveling with me." She saw the question in his eyes change to amusement. With a grin he asked, "Why did you ask? Are you reconsidering the offer to learn steamboatin'?"

"Of course not!" She started to rise and he took her hand.

"Please stay. I won't have much time for talk later; we'll be going down the Ohio much faster than we came up." He paused, frowning.

"I still feel as if I owe you an apology, and I've chosen this way of doing it."

He hesitated again and finally admitted, "I guess what I'm trying to say is I've been looking for an opportunity to give you this." He pulled a small book out of his pocket and handed it to her. "It's a Bible."

"A Bible!" Astonished, she looked from the dark blue leather to him. "Alex, this is beautiful, but it is a strange gift."

"Yes I know. Something a mother gives a child or—" he stopped. "It seemed the only way I could find an opportunity to explain—"

"About what you did? Don't trouble yourself; it isn't necessary." She started to rise.

His hand was firm on hers. "It is necessary. Most friendships start out with a clean slate; ours has been cluttered with the past."

"I don't really consider it a friendship."

"At the very least I would like it to be that." His grin was crooked, and hastily she looked away from him.

"I might never see you after this trip."

"That's possible. If I may, I'll tell you about the Bible."

She hesitated, looked at the gold earring, and said, "Perhaps later."

He nodded and stood up. "Tomorrow Caleb and the fellows will be helping me make some modifications. The stove is coming back up to the cabin where it was originally. One of the other cabins will be prepared for you and Crystal. The cabin down on the end will carry cargo."

She nodded, "Crystal said Mr. Cooper had found merchandise for you to transport."

He grinned. "Some rope, lots of glassware, even a barrel or so of good Ohio cider. It will be late Wednesday before we get away." With a jaunty salute, he said, "See you then; good night."

After he left, she continued to sit in the alcove, staring down at the beautifully bound Bible. Running her finger along the gold-edged pages, she brooded over his easy acceptance of her rebuff. *The problem is, Olivia, you're afraid of exchanging one personal word with him. The teasing is fine, but—what are you afraid of? Surely it isn't anything to do with that silly earring.*

CHAPTER 30

Early in the morning Caleb came into the cabin. Alex turned from the cookstove. "Slowpoke. We couldn't wait for you. I had the fellows haul the stove up here first thing. Help me get the stovepipe in place."

Caleb rubbed the top of his head. "I kept waiting for you to come to breakfast."

"Got to thinking of all that needed to be done over here."

"Miss Olivia was down early. Did you give her the Bible?"

"Yes, but your plan didn't work; she wasn't much interested in hearing anything I had to say."

Caleb tugged at his ear. "For being a lawyer, seems to me you get tongue-tied mighty easy. What did you say?"

Alex jerked the stovepipe and soot sifted onto the floor. Caleb went for a broom. Roughly Alex said, "I didn't ask her to marry me—is that what you're fishing for?"

"Good thing you didn't—suh, I think she'd be more likely to pop you over the head with something. I don't know when I ever seen a fellow with a good mind being so much on the short end when it comes to handling a female." He shook his head. "Why didn't you just tell her about the Bible and the earring, about like you did the rest of them?"

"She wouldn't give me a chance."

"Did she keep the Bible?"

Alex nodded.

"Well, then that's a good sign. You have this whole trip to get to talking."

"If I can get my tongue unstuck," Alex said gloomily, thumping the stovepipe. "I don't know why it's so hard to come up with the right words."

"You do good on humor," Caleb observed looking around the cabin. "About as good as you do on putting up stovepipes. Might be there's some way you can learn to say the serious things in a humorous way."

———

The next afternoon Matthew carried Crystal's and Olivia's new valises into the cabin. Looking around he said, "Alex and Caleb did themselves proud in this cabin. Be glad you don't have the old one; there's soot all over the place."

Backing toward the door he added, "Did you two draw straws for the job?"

"What job?" Olivia asked, straightening the scrap of a rug with her toe.

"Cooking. I'm not a cook and I don't think Caleb has volunteered."

Olivia sighed. "I knew this was a fairy-tale trip." The door closed behind Matthew. "How are you in the kitchen?"

"What?" Crystal looked bewildered.

"Didn't you hear what Matthew said?" Olivia questioned as she frowned at Crystal. "You seem—don't you feel well?"

"I'm all right." Crystal rubbed her brow. "Just tired. Now what is this about cooking?"

"Not only tired," Olivia said slowly, "but there's something bothering you. I don't believe you've heard a thing I've said for the past two days." She stopped and cocked her head.

They could feel the throb of the engine, and a moment later they heard the swish of paddles through the water. "I guess we're leaving," Crystal commented. "The trip has begun. I suppose we should go talk about that kitchen."

Caleb was on his hands and knees in front of the stove. He glanced up. "The fire's doing fine. I'll get the soot mopped up."

"We're to cook?" Olivia questioned, as she entered the kitchen. Caleb shrugged.

She added, "And that means yes if we want to eat. Do you know how to cook?"

"Of course. Fatback and greens, biscuits and flannel cakes with eggs."

Olivia stared at him. "And I suppose Alex is going to hide out in the pilothouse and ignore the whole situation."

"Well, he and the roustabouts have to keep the boat a headin' downstream. Where's Matthew?"

"Matthew can't cook."

Matthew came into the cabin and dropped his bag. "What can't Matthew do?" he asked. Olivia watched his eyes seek out Crystal, who carefully sat down at the table and folded her hands.

"Did you know that Tandy and Maggie and some of the other women did all the cooking?" Olivia said slowly. "I stirred the porridge once in a while and I sliced ham." She straightened. "Do we have ham?"

They heard the whistle. Matthew muttered, "Boat to starboard. Guess I'll go see what's going on."

———

Olivia complained, "Dishes, dishes, and then food to prepare. I didn't dream vegetables could take so much work."

"And sister dear," Matthew said with a smile, "I didn't dream it was possible to ruin a potato."

Caleb grinned at them both. "Cincinnati comes up in two days."

Olivia smiled back. "And then who cooks?"

"Don't mind flannel cakes myself," Caleb said with a grin, and then looked out at the evening sky.

———

Crystal placed three lighted candles on the table in her room and waited for Olivia. She looked up as Olivia entered slowly and said, "Two days; we have only two days before we reach Cincinnati. Olivia, I need to talk to you. And I must admit, I lied to you."

"Crystal, is this why you've been a walking ghost all this trip?" Crystal nodded, "We've all felt terrible, thinking it was somehow related to us."

Quickly Crystal said, "It isn't. But the real reason I need to talk is that I need help. Even just talking. Somehow it will make me strong. I know it will." She gulped, and Olivia could see the tears running down her face.

She handed Crystal a handkerchief and sat down. "Please—it can't be that bad. Besides, you are my best friend, regardless of what you have to say."

Crystal buried her face in her hands and sobbed. Olivia came over and put her arms around Crystal.

Finally Crystal straightened and dabbed at her eyes. Settling back on her heels, Olivia opened her mouth to speak. Abruptly Crystal seized her shoulders. "Olivia, please, please promise me something before I tell you. Promise that you will never tell Matthew. I must have your promise before I can confess, and if I can't, I think I'll just die right here."

Olivia pulled back from Crystal's frantic grasp. She searched the girl's face, "Crystal I can't imagine—" Crystal began shaking her head slowly while the tears flowed afresh. "All right," Olivia murmured, giving her a hug, "I promise, I truly will keep my silence until you give me permission to speak."

Olivia went back to her chair and waited. One of the candles gutted and went out before Crystal began to speak. With a sigh of resignation she began. "Remember when I told you about my friend; the one whose father is a slave?" Olivia thought for a moment, then nodded. "Well, it wasn't a friend; it's me." She waited for Olivia's reaction. Olivia sighed gently.

Crystal said, "I just couldn't admit it. And Evangeline Cabet, remember? She's my mother. After I was born she left and hasn't been back since. The woman we visited in Boston said she lived in France." Crystal paused, then added, "My parents are actually my grandparents."

"And your father?" Olivia asked, beginning to guess.

"Joseph is my father."

"Why are you helping him flee to Canada?"

"Because he is nearly crippled from injuries to one leg. He's no longer able to work in the fields, and I found out that he was to be sold—sold to someone who would work him to death in the fields."

"Oh, Crystal! Don't talk like that. You know we are more careful to our slaves than that. Who would do such a thing?" Crystal slowly shook her head. Olivia stopped to listen.

"It wasn't my idea to bring Joseph here. Auntie T convinced me that Joseph would be sold and the rest would happen. Of course I had to do something."

"You ran away. Do your parents—I mean grandparents—know where you are?"

"No. I left Auntie T in Natchez. As far as they know, I'm still there, and will be until later this month."

Olivia went to the bunk, settled back and pondered the situation. Finally she sat up. "I understand. It is because of this that you've broken off with Matthew, isn't it?"

"Yes." Crystal lifted her head. "Please, say no more about Matthew; just relieve my guilty conscience for lying to you. Olivia, I feel so ugly for sneaking. I wish there were someway I could undo it all."

Olivia came over and once again wrapped her arms around Crystal. Hugging her close, she chose her words carefully. "I know how I would feel, and it isn't good. But Crystal, I don't feel like that toward you. Surely it isn't the end of the world for you! To be honest, I thought you'd stolen money or you were pregnant or something equally as bad."

Crystal straightened and shook her head slowly. As she waved her hands helplessly, Olivia continued, "I can guess how you feel right now. Confused. But I think you'll adjust and everything will fall into place. Now, about Matthew—that's another problem. I'm certain he'll never be able to accept that part of your life."

"Of course this is the end for us," Crystal said slowly, twisting her handkerchief.

Olivia nodded. "He's just too Southern, and even more than that, he has pride." She stopped, seeing that Crystal's face reflected agony beyond her ability to understand. "Shall I get Alex?"

Shaking her head, Crystal stood up, removed her shoes, and crawled into her bunk. Before she pulled the blanket over herself, she said, "The unforgivable part is that I refused to think about what I was doing to Matthew. It was too easy to shut my eyes to the past, and now we're both hurt."

Olivia blew out the candles and crawled into bed as well. Neither enjoyed a very restful night's sleep. By noon the following day Olivia wondered how they could endure another day together. Matthew avoided them completely, while Alex turned a puzzled frown from one to the other.

———————

They reached Cincinnati in the middle of the afternoon. Alex docked at the wharf. Coming out of the pilothouse, he smiled around the silent circle, saying, "Good thing this craft is small; otherwise we'd be anchored midstream. This is a busy port."

Caleb came out of the cabin with their luggage, ready to carry it off the boat. He looked from one to the other. "Want me to find a hack?"

Olivia gave herself a mental shake and crisply answered, "Yes, please. We'll have to concern ourselves with finding passage tomorrow." She turned and looked around the group, from Alex's long face, to Matthew's frown, and decided, "Crystal," she said, "we might as well follow him."

With a wan smile and a limp handshake, Crystal went down the stairs. Olivia watched Matthew hesitate and then clatter down after Caleb. With a sigh and shake of her head, she pulled the shawl across her shoulders and reluctantly followed, wondering why her feet felt as heavy as lead.

Alex was standing by the gangplank, waiting for her to come down the stairs. The misery in his eyes stopped her. She touched his arm. "Please, this problem doesn't involve you at all. Thank you for bringing us this far, and—" she choked.

He took her hand and tugged her close. "I appreciate your telling me. To say the least, I'm relieved." Soberly he added, "I thought I'd ruined everything by giving you the Bible."

"The Bible," Olivia said slowly. "I'd forgotten all about it. Didn't you mention explaining something?"

He nodded.

She said, "We've done nothing except cook and wash dishes the whole time." She saw the regret in his eyes, but before he could reply, she tried for a light note. "About a job. I may come to you yet for a reference. Might just go west and hire on as a cook, if the parents toss me out."

"Tell them to toss you my direction. If you aren't interested in learning to be a steamboat pilot, at least come cook for me."

His attempt at humor left her with an unexplainable misery. Olivia blinked at tears in her eyes. "Alex, I'm glad you and Matthew forced me to come along; it's been an experience I'll—"

Abruptly he lifted her hand to his lips, pressed her palm to his cheek. As she tugged it away and hurried down the gangplank, she heard him mutter, " 'Oh, that she knew she were!' "

With her hand still warm from his touch, she flew across the wharf; Caleb and Matthew helped her into the hack beside Crystal. After a brief goodbye, the two were off. They were nearly to the hotel before Olivia noticed the two bright spots of color on Crystal's face.

She sat up straight and took a deep breath. "Sorry," she said with a bright smile. "I've been wondering about a phrase Alex used. Sounds familiar. It must be a quotation, but I can't remember all of it."

The bright spots were still on Crystal's cheeks when she said, "Matthew wanted me to tell you he will come to the hotel this evening. He wants to bring a letter for you to give to your father."

"Oh, yes," Olivia murmured. "The letter we both intended to write and never did. Poor Matthew; what will he say?" She paused, thought a moment, and added, "Poor me! I'll have to face them in another two weeks."

CHAPTER 31

I t was nearly dusk when Matthew knocked on their door. Olivia opened the door, but Matthew looked past her and addressed Crystal. "Come stroll with me for a while. There's a park across the street; we'll be back in time for dinner."

Olivia watched the trapped expression grow on Crystal's face as she looked from Olivia to Matthew. While she hesitated, Olivia opened her mouth to speak. She saw Matthew's bleak face. "Oh, Crystal, do walk. It will be good for you."

Crystal stood motionless, the hurt in her eyes equaling the pain in Matthew's. "Go, both of you—at least part friends." Impatiently Olivia gave Crystal a gentle push. The two of them walked out the front door of the hotel after promising Olivia that they'd be back in time to eat.

As dinnertime approached, Olivia paced the lobby waiting for Matthew and Crystal to return. The words Alex had said kept running through her mind. *Oh, that she knew she were!* "Why does that phrase come back to haunt me?"

Matthew and Crystal hurried through the entrance. Just a moment before Matthew released her arm, Olivia saw their faces and had to turn away. The pain she felt must not show.

As they crossed the lobby to join her, she found herself questioning her reaction. Was it pity, or a hidden envy?

The three of them walked together over to a dining table and sat down. Olivia smiled at them and said, "It must have been a beautiful walk; you both look much more content with the world."

"It was a wonderful walk," Matthew murmured, seemingly absorbed in the menu.

Hastily Crystal said, "Preferable to promenading the same two square feet of deck." Quickly she flipped the menu open and added, "What are you going to have for dinner, Olivia?"

———

As Olivia finished her hair and turned from the mirror, Crystal said, "I don't believe I will go down for breakfast with you. I just don't seem to want any this morning. Will you please go without me?" She added, "But come up here before you make travel arrangements."

Without waiting for an answer, she turned away. Olivia shrugged and said, "As you wish. I'll hurry, I didn't realize it was so late. I think I'm beginning to be a sleepyhead."

Olivia finished her breakfast, eyed the croissant and considered taking it to her friend. "Crystal, you said no," she murmured. "I'll refrain, and you can be angry at my heartlessness."

With a teasing smile still on her face, she returned to her room. A frown replaced the smile when she opened the door. Crystal's belongings were no longer spread across the room. Her valise was missing, and a note was propped against Olivia's case. It was from Matthew, and Crystal had scrawled a sentence across the bottom: *Please don't be angry with me.*

Olivia read the lines in Matthew's hand. *Truly we are sorry for leaving this way, but it seems best, quickly before we manage to talk ourselves into being logical and levelheaded. At least the parents cannot say we are partial even to you. Crystal and I will be married this morning. By the time you have decided which steamboat we are on, we will have departed for New Orleans. Naturally we will be back; we've left unfinished business here.*

Slowly folding the paper, Olivia whispered, "Joseph is the unfinished business. Could she possibly have told Matthew about him?"

For a time, Olivia paced the room. "They're insane—don't they know the problems they have created?" Finally with a sigh, she rubbed her forehead wearily and cried, "What can I do? How can I go home? It would have been bad enough to face the parents with a clear conscience, but this is beyond my ability to handle."

As she stood in the middle of the floor, she heard a steamboat's whistle. It was a shrill, defiant blast, and it made her think of Alex and the *Golden Awl*. She whirled and dashed to the window, hoping for a glimpse of the boat.

"Impossible!" she whispered. "This room is on the second floor and too far from the river. Still, it could have been the *Awl's* whistle. It's past noon now, time for him to be gone."

The thought stabbed her with loneliness, and she contemplated the emotion with a lump in her throat. Closing her eyes, she imagined Alex standing at the wheel of the *Awl*. His feet would be braced against the movement of the boat and he would be singing that silly ditty.

As she paced the room she thought of the song and began to sing softly. " 'Gin a body kiss a body, Need a body cry?' "

Curling up in the chair beside the window, she thought about Alex. "Alexander Duncan, you are a strange man, with your golden earring and *Golden Awl*. I wish I could understand why you are as you are. Why did you kiss me that night in Boston? Why have you treated me like a pesky sister now, and why did you give me a Bible? Of all of the inelegant gifts a man would give, that is the most—"

The thought was born whole in her mind, and she contemplated it with trembling excitement as she admitted, "There's no reason to go home now. No more than Matthew am I obligated to carry the news home to the parents. He follows his pleasure; I shall follow mine."

———

The thought seemed right and good, and it remained so until the stagecoach deposited Olivia in front of the very dress shop where she, Crystal, and Amelia had purchased their new wardrobes. Now she looked down at her travel-stained blue serge and muttered, "Olivia, what do you do now?"

She turned on the boardwalk, looked at the crust of dirty snow, and picked up her valise. "Hack, ma'am?"

He was a fresh-faced lad with big eyes and a battered wagon. "Yes, please. Do you know where the Coopers live?"

"Amos Cooper?" he nodded. "Let me get your bag."

The ride to the Coopers' farm was familiar, and when they arrived Olivia noticed that the house was circled with a rim of drifted snow; in the barren landscape not a vestige of color remained, but to Olivia it seemed warm and peaceful. She was paying the lad when Sadie Cooper came down the steps. Her eyes were full of concern, but she smiled and picked up the valise.

Inside Olivia avoided Sadie's probing look. "I've come back. May I stay?"

"Welcome, thou are. Come." Olivia took the valise and followed Sadie up the stairs. In her old room, with Amelia's belongings still spread across the bed, Olivia faced Sadie and said, "I have an idea you won't ask questions, but I must tell you. As planned, Crystal and I left the boat in Cincinnati. But before we could make arrangements to travel home, Crystal and Matthew left me. There was a note saying they were being married and would travel without me."

Sadie wrapped her ample arms around Olivia, "Abandoned! Tut, there child, it's good thee came back." Olivia was surprised by the comfort in the soft shoulder. Her tears made puddles on it.

When she backed away she was able to laugh as she dabbed at her eyes. "I didn't expect to be such a baby about this all. Do you mind? When I started thinking, this place seemed more appealing than going home. I'll do all I can to help."

"We'll find a place for you. Now, supper is nearly ready. You take care of your valise and then come down."

Olivia thought about the last time she was in the same bedroom as she arranged her belongings. She had just finished when Amelia came into the room. She stopped; touching her throat, she slowly whispered, "Has something happened?"

"Oh, Amelia—" She shook her head. "No. I didn't mean to alarm you. There hasn't been an accident."

"Then why have you returned? I didn't see the boat."

"I, I'm not certain why I came back; it just seemed to be the thing to do. Crystal and Matthew eloped."

Amelia's eyes widened. "But you can't elope when you've nothing to elope from."

"Well, I guess it was from me."

"Left you alone? Where was Alex?"

"I suppose he went on. I wonder if Matthew told him about his intentions?"

Amelia shrugged. "Well, that's a strange state of affairs." She slanted a curious glance at Olivia. "I'd have expected you to go home."

"Mostly I didn't want to face my parents with the news, and in addition, I doubt that they will be very understanding about our leaving in the first place."

Amelia grinned. "I've wondered. You just took off?"

"It was something like that." Amelia's eyes sparkled, and Olivia said, "We seem to be in the habit of doing and then thinking."

"I—know what you mean," Amelia murmured as she began to move around the room, picking up clothing and setting the room in order. Olivia watched her, becoming aware for the first time, of an underlying sadness in the woman.

Searching for a safe topic, Olivia asked, "What are you finding to do here?"

"Not too much right now. There was a group here the day after you left. In fact, Mr. Cooper found them. He'd been told Negroes were seen in the woods, so he investigated. It turned out they were looking for him. They had heard about the place from others. They've been helped on to Canada." She paused. "There's always mending to do and such. Sadie's friends pass on clothing, and she spends time getting it in condition for the people."

"Should we go down and help Sadie?" Olivia asked as Amelia smoothed her hair.

She nodded, starting for the door. "One thing I should warn you about." She faced Olivia. "There's been a horde of guests. A constant procession of preachers and people working in the abolition movement. Hope you don't mind being preached at constantly."

Olivia shrugged. "I don't mind; does it bother you?"

"I didn't realize it did." Amelia touched her cheeks. "I'm trying my best to be a good Christian; what more can they expect?"

Olivia followed Amelia downstairs and into the kitchen. The stocky farmer came to meet her. "Mr. Cooper," Olivia murmured, "I'm grateful for your hospitality, but surely this is a burden."

Probing her with eyes that seemed to see far too deep, he said, "Burden? No. We will make good use of thee. Has Sadie told thee of the uproar going on?" She shook her head and he added, "From now until spring when all of us farmers will need to get down to planting and hoeing, we're going to be having the biggest bunch of people rolling through here that you've ever seen."

"Why?" Olivia asked, astonished beyond good manners.

"For a starter, politics." He nodded toward the fireplace. "Now come and meet Brother Lane. He's a good Quaker and interested in saving souls and bodies; thy soul and the black man's body."

She heard the chuckle behind her and turned. Although dressed in somber Quaker garb, wearing the demeanor of a parson, he was tall and thin and seemed very young. "Miss Olivia Thomas," he said, bowing over her hand with eyes teasing and joyful. "I am indeed happy to make thy acquaintance. A lovely young lady always adds interest to the occasion."

"And Brother Lane leaves a string of broken hearts behind him. I've noticed him walking quickly enough to avoid the noose of matrimony which his glib tongue lays." Chuckling and shaking his head, Mr. Cooper led the way to the table.

Sadie placed the bowl of chicken and dumplings in the middle of the table, adjusted the plate of squash and said, "Now just take Amos's talk with a grain of salt. Jerome Lane is a nice young man."

Olivia took her place at the table, waited for the young parson to pray, and then asked, "Mr. Cooper mentioned politics. What else brings people out in the winter?"

Jerome Lane broke a dumpling, surveyed it, and said, "Perfect, as usual." He addressed Amelia, "You know, she's the best cook east of the Mississippi; west I know nothing about. You should take lessons." He nodded toward Olivia.

She winced. "How did you know?"

Amos Cooper laughed while Jerome's eyes twinkled. "Know the best way to find out what kind of cook a young lady is?" She shook her head, and he added, "By making a statement like that."

"And I fell into your trap, and now you know."

Amos was still laughing when Jerome asked, "Thou art Southern, aren't thee?"

"Again my tongue gave me away."

"Now I will answer thy question. I am an abolitionist at heart. A great number of the brothers are."

"From the manner of your statement," Olivia responded, "I see I'm judged and found wanting. And I know that statement comes out of the Bible. What you Northerners can't understand is that we Southerners aren't heathen."

"Olivia," Amelia protested, "he didn't accuse you of being heathen."

Her voice overlapped Amelia's. "I've spent two-and-a-half months traveling with runaway slaves. I am as compassionate as any-one who has regard for their freedom. And for those who really want freedom, for those who have been mistreated, I will work for freedom. But coming from the South and having lived with contented Negroes, I must say I can't support the idea that everyone wishes to be free."

Jerome Lane finished his piece of chicken and looked at Olivia. "Hast thou considered the possibility that perhaps some of these peo-ple have never been taught to value themselves? With the contempt of their masters echoing in their ears, it must be near impossible to think of themselves as worthy people. Our goal is to teach that their race and color is just as much to be honored as is the white race."

He looked down at his plate. "Perhaps our race needs this message as much as they do."

Amos Cooper leaned forward to look at Olivia, "It isn't to our credit that a so-called Christian nation denies the Word of God, by statute no less, to all these black people."

Sadie shook her head and sighed, "We don't give these people a chance to learn to read."

Olivia stared down at her hands, "All my life I've heard the Bible supports slavery. Certainly I consider myself Christian. Now you are telling me that slavery is wrong. To whom should I listen?"

Amos pointed his knife at her. "Young lady, don't listen to anyone except the Lord. Don't take our word for it. Now if thou aren't in the habit of reading thy Bible and asking the Lord to give thee direc-tion, then we'll be obligated to read to thee and pray over thee."

"And make me change my mind?"

"Never make. The Lord himself won't force thee to change thy mind. Though, could be, someday thou'll regret not knowing how the Lord feels about some of these matters."

While they were preparing for bed, Olivia asked, "Are all these guests as dogmatic as Jerome Lane?"

"Not all," Amelia answered. "And I have the idea some of them are too busy to line up all the reasons you heard tonight. They seem more interested in people than in *why*."

CHAPTER 32

Olivia walked into the dining room as the short, bald man sitting at the table bowed toward Amos Cooper and said, "It's all thanks to the Dred Scott case that this year of our Lord, 1857, will be known as the year of infamy."

The slender man at his side faced him and said, "Please to God that it doesn't get worse; but sir, I fear this is only the beginning."

Olivia whispered, "Has something happened?" The men jumped to their feet. "I beg your pardon," Olivia murmured. "I didn't realize you were having a meeting."

Sadie came into the room bearing a pot of coffee and a platter of pastries. She beamed, "Oh, Olivia, I didn't know thee had returned, did thee find the Tuckers well?" At Olivia's nod, she added, "Come meet our guests. This is the Reverend Nathaniel Barker and Thomas Caffrey. Now, gentlemen, this is Miss Olivia Thomas." She bowed and Sadie said, "Come have refreshments with us, Olivia."

Thomas Caffrey sat down and offered the plate to Olivia. "I didn't intend to alarm you or anyone else. Unfortunately the climate of these United States is as frosty as the weather."

The Reverend Barker explained, "Caffrey is a newspaper man, and a very good one. He could become one of the nation's most influential men if he would keep his mouth shut about the number one problem in the country."

"Washington," Olivia guessed.

"No, slavery. Without a doubt it will pull us into war. Now we are down to quibbling over *when*."

"Not war, secession," Olivia said quickly. "We've been hearing this for years. South Carolina started it over the tariff situation. Sir, surely you know more than I, and it's common knowledge in the South, that the Union will make concessions before they will allow war. The South has economic problems, and we both know how vital slavery is right now."

Caffrey poured coffee for Olivia. "From your speech I assume you are from the South."

She nodded and picked up her fork.

"Then perhaps you can carry a message back to the people. It is virtually impossible to reach the common Southern family now."

She put her fork down. "Sir, why is that?"

"Northern newspapers are suppressed in the South. Anything that addresses the slavery issue is prohibited. Of course, you know freed slaves don't live in the South."

"Sir, they do live in the South. I feel I'm being baited. Surely it's their choice to live where they please."

"Not theirs. In the Southern community, a free slave sends signals saying that emancipation is possible and workable."

"But you said free Negroes aren't living there. I'm absolutely positive they are."

"Then I should qualify my statement. I know that after the Revolutionary War some slaves were given their freedom. This was their reward for fighting in the war. They did continue to live in the South, and their descendants do so today. In addition we all know that there is a group of mixed-blood free men, the offspring of white masters and slave women, some of whom are free.

"But, Miss Thomas, these people, while they are residents in the South, have no real freedom. Education isn't available, neither are they seen as citizens of country or state. It isn't correct to list them as free."

She took a bite. When he turned to his own pastry, she asked, "You said I could carry a message. What is it?"

"That the common Southern man is losing the right to speak

out; he is surrendering his freedom by default. Each day that passes there is less opportunity for recovery of that freedom. At this rate, soon a few plantation owners will be shaping not only the South, but the future of the entire Union."

He leaned forward and peered into her eyes, saying emphatically, "I cannot believe that the South is willing to surrender its freedom. And I mean the South that includes all men, rich and poor. Plantation owners and the common yeoman."

"Surrender its freedom? That is not so," Olivia replied. "On the contrary, Sir, we are demanding the right to preserve our way of life in freedom."

Gently the Reverend Barker said, "Freedom isn't freedom if there's one segment of our people who are not free."

"I am not speaking of slaves now," Caffrey said. "When we finish this delicious treat, I will show you a newspaper clipping, written by a resident of North Carolina—a farmer by the name of Helper. His article addresses that fact that many lower-class Southerners have been impoverished by the institution of slavery. While this saddens me, I rejoice to know there are Southerners who don't support slavery."

Caffrey sipped his coffee before he continued. "The time is passing quickly. Soon it will be too late to reverse the trend of unquestioning compliance. There must be change in ideology."

"What is your objection?" she asked curiously.

"You've a handful of men whose self-interest has dictated the continuation of slavery, contrary to the Constitution. They are willing to pull this whole country into war to serve their interests. Will you take this message back? Ask the Southern women to rise up in protest. If their menfolk will not come to the aid of the country, they must— and quickly, before the minority shapes their lives and orders their destiny to the detriment of the whole nation."

Olivia got to her feet. "Sir, I cannot believe that in this country of freedom, you feel obligated to preach a gospel such as this. The Bible tells us slavery is acceptable, and we know ourselves to be honest Christians."

"I won't quarrel with thee, my dear," the Reverend Barker interjected soberly, "but I will ask thee, for the sake of thy soul and the continuation of this country, be absolutely certain that thee know'st what God is saying through His Word."

"In addition," added Caffrey, "rather than quibble about the biblical support for slavery, isn't it more logical to examine the institution and measure its worth? Aren't the benefits totally for the man who is becoming rich? One way that society creates bad institutions and destroys good ones is through the apathy of its people."

Olivia started for the door and then turned. "You mentioned Dred Scott. I recognize the name, and back home the ruling was welcomed. Why do you object?"

"Because it opened the whole country to slavery. Our goal was a fair plan—sectionalism—and then just allow slavery to phase itself out of existence. But the Dred Scott ruling is handwriting on the wall. I will remind you of the ruling; perhaps you can judge for yourself." Caffrey paused and then continued.

"For a period of years, the slave Dred Scott lived with his master in free territory. Sometime after the death of his master he sued for his freedom. The case finally went to the Supreme Court, where Chief Justice Taney held that no Negro was a citizen of the United States, therefore his suit was invalid. The outcome of the matter is to nullify the Missouri Compromise of 1850. His ruling stated that Congress has no right to limit slavery in the territories. You recall, of course, that the Compromise was an attempt to keep the balance of slave and nonslave states equal."

"So that's Dred Scott. Nevertheless, I am surprised there isn't more rejoicing in the South," she said slowly. "Why their caution?" In the silence she looked up. The men were smiling at each other.

Caffrey looked up at her. "Miss Thomas, thank you. That's the best news I've had all day. If the South isn't rejoicing, then there's a strong reason." He turned. "Barker, perhaps you are right. This man, Lincoln, just might be reason enough to make the South cautious."

———

"Looks and feels like Christmas, doesn't it?" Sadie turned from her work to look at Olivia. She nodded and went back to crimping the crust on her apple pie. Olivia continued, "I keep thinking of Alex and the people out there somewhere. It's so cold."

Sadie shoved the pie in the oven and stirred the kettle of beans. "Thee worries too much. The Father knows where they be, and what is going on." She peered curiously at Olivia and continued, "One of the greatest lessons we can learn in life is to trust the Father to care for His own. Not," she added hastily, "that we aren't to be praying, but instead to remind us even more to pray. Our Lord loves to hear from us, to know we also care about His children."

Olivia rubbed at her roughened knuckle. Gently Sadie reminded, "Thee hasn't shown much enthusiasm for Bible study lately. If you go get your pretty blue Bible and read aloud while I darn this stack of stockings, we might both benefit."

On her way upstairs, Olivia paused to look around the shadowed hallway. With the sun behind heavy storm clouds, the once sunny hall seemed ordinary and dismal. Quickly she mounted the stairs, found the Bible under a stack of papers, and went back downstairs.

"Amelia said she might not return tonight," Olivia reminded Sadie. "If Mrs. Tucker's fever hasn't broken, she will stay."

Sadie nodded and rocked as she plunged the needle in and out of the thick woolen stocking. Olivia watched a moment longer. When Sadie glanced at her, she asked, "Where shall I read?"

Sadie straightened in her chair and cocked her head. "Does thee hear something too?"

"Yes." Olivia got to her feet and walked to the parlor window. The snow had created an early dusk, hiding the wharf and even the road, but the sounds were growing louder. As she listened she decided it was the murmur of voices.

She hurried back to Sadie. "I think it's people coming, I seem to hear voices."

"Build up the fire in the parlor," Sadie said as she heaved herself out of the chair. "I'll get something hot going."

Olivia rushed to the fireplace, poked at the big log, and shoved in more wood. The sound of voices ceased, but she heard a soft crunch in snow. Was that a whimper? Caution discarded, she ran to the door just as the tapping began.

Sadie was behind her and they tugged open the door. A huddled mass of people swayed in the doorway. Olivia began pulling them inside. Shivering, dripping melting snow from scanty clothing, coughing, with babies crying, they came into the hallway and Sadie pushed them toward the fire.

Olivia ran for soft rags and the kettle of hot water. Tossing in a handful of Sadie's herbs, she carried it into the parlor. She looked at frightened black faces, tiny terrified ones, and then the tall bearded man in the doorway. He didn't speak, but Olivia heard him cough. Fighting the desire to run to him, she stopped beside the people and began ladling out hot tea. One black face came close to her, gesturing toward Alex. "Please, for him." Olivia filled the cup and watched the woman carry it to Alex.

Soon, the people began sitting on the floor, moving carefully, and sharing the warmth and tea. The strain on the faces eased, and for a moment one face was slashed by a smile.

But she could see that Alex was still on his feet. With a curious frown he peered around the room before slowly following Sadie down the hall.

The outside door opened again, and Caleb came in. He stood shivering and looking around. Olivia went to him. "Come have some tea and share the fire."

"Alex?"

"Sadie is taking care of him. What has happened?"

"Just a bad trip. We fought ice all the way up the Ohio. Thank God it wasn't solid ice, but it slowed us down." While he spoke, she noticed the question in his eyes as he looked around the room.

Caleb settled down beside the fire, and she brought him tea. "I'm going to get food ready," she murmured, avoiding the questions in his eyes.

Sadie was at work slicing bread, heating more water, and stirring the beans on the stove. Olivia looked around and asked, "Shall I make porridge, too? There are babies."

Sadie nodded. "There's plenty of good cream; use that on it. Might be that's all anyone will want. A mighty poor lot they are. I'm going to open up that barrel of clothes. They need something warm and clean right now."

She started for the door and Olivia asked, "Alex?"

Sadie stopped, looked at Olivia and frowned. "He could present a problem. He's asleep now, but that chest is bad. We need to get something hot into him when he awakens."

I'm beginning to regret this, she thought. Hasty Olivia, as usual. With a sigh, Olivia took up the bread knife and began to slice another loaf.

She heard a whacking and thumping at the back door. Amos

came into the house. "I heard them," he said. "Here's milk, and plenty of it. Everybody taken care of? I saw a light in Mother's nursing room. Someone sick?"

Sadie came into the kitchen. "Alex has a cough and fever. The people are in the parlor. Will it be warm enough in the attic?"

"I'll take up a load of wood for the little stove. The chimney puts a lot of heat into the space," he informed the two women.

Caleb came into the kitchen. "Alex?"

Sadie pointed toward the door. "In there. Want to stay in with him?"

Caleb nodded. "He's had that cough for weeks now."

"Sounds like it. I'll get out my herbs and make him a tonic. Won't hurt to make a mustard plaster, too." She turned to Olivia, "Let's get that barrel and then start the little tykes in here for some food."

After everyone had been fed, Olivia found herself staring down into the dishpan, wondering how many dishes were left to be washed. A timid hand touched her. "Please, Missy, we cause trouble. Let me work on the dishes." Olivia lifted a grateful face and a grin spread across the dark face. " 'Sides, hot water sure feels good."

Olivia stepped aside but helped put away the dishes and straighten the kitchen into its usual order. The black woman talked. "We were getting low on wood, so most of the time we huddled around the boilers, sharing our time down there. Alex showed us how to cook 'tatoes on the boilers and how to keep a pot of meal porridge going. It wasn't too bad until we hit the snow. Then ice slowed us down."

There was no problem putting the children to bed—they were almost asleep by the time they got up to their room. When the last dark figure had disappeared up the stairs, Olivia went to the open door. Sadie was bending over Alex. While Caleb supported his head, she coaxed him to take the herb tea. Olivia lingered a moment longer and then went up to her room.

As she prepared for bed, she recalled the things Sadie had been talking about when the people arrived. Olivia murmured, " 'Prayer,' she said, and something about trusting the Father to take care of His own. And that He liked to know that we care for His children, too."

As Olivia mused over Sadie's words, she recalled the picture of Alex swaying in the doorway. Sadie's words were an arrow, pointing her to pray for him. As she knelt, wondering where to begin, she seemed to sense a strong warm link being forged between her and the tall, bearded man. *Why does it seem the link is God? Does He care how I feel about that man?*

When she slipped to her knees beside the trundle bed, Olivia carefully folded her hands, realizing how long it had been since she had shaped a prayer with any real desire behind it. "Please God, Alex— he is very ill, please, will You help him recover?" And with the question there was the remembrance of promise.

Getting to her feet, she thought about the promise Alex had read to the people on that long ago sunny day. Olivia wandered around the room, looking for the Bible. Most certainly it was on the lamp-stand beside Sadie's rocker.

Quietly she tiptoed back to the kitchen. The door to the nursing room was open. She could see Caleb sprawled in the deep chair beside Alex. They both appeared to be asleep. She hesitated a moment longer, found the Bible, and ran.

Back in her room, Olivia found the passage. *John must be his favorite book*, she thought, as her finger traveled down the page. In the dim light of the candle she read, "Hitherto have ye asked nothing in my name: ask, and ye shall receive, that your joy may be full." She got to her feet, murmuring, "But what is joy?"

CHAPTER 33

Only toward the end of the week did Alex begin to recover. For several days Olivia had been sharply conscious of the growing tension in the house. As Sadie moved back and forth with cups of herb tea and the mustard plasters, Olivia hovered between stove and table, unable to remember the next task to do. At times she found herself desperately wringing her hands and thinking about praying, while the strain mounted on Caleb's face.

On the day Caleb ceased prowling the room and went to sit at the table with the mug of coffee cradled comfortably in his hands, Olivia felt her own heart lift.

Taking a deep breath and looking around, Caleb said, "These people have been here nearly a week; it's time to move on."

"Surely there isn't danger here—or is there?"

"Who knows?" He shrugged. "If we've had someone on our tail, could be there's danger. Mostly we don't want to lose anyone, and Canada is waiting."

He grinned and sipped coffee. "As soon as Alex is awake, I'm going to propose taking them on over to the next contact—maybe tonight. Most certain, he's not going to be up to the job for a few more weeks. Even if I have to sit on him to keep him down."

Trying to keep her voice calm, Olivia said, "It was bad, wasn't it?"

Caleb nodded and got to his feet.

"What do you mean by *contact*?"

"The next station on the Underground Railroad. We're only one small contact. There's a whole group of people out there, feeding and housing until it's safe to pass them on to the next station."

"And no one ever knows when more are coming?"

He nodded. "That right." Turning he said, "Guess I'll go out to the barn and talk to Amos about a wagon." He paused at the door with the perplexed frown back on his face. "How come you didn't go home?"

She hesitated. "Did Matthew tell you anything?"

He shook his head. "He just let Alex know he wasn't going on. We figured he would go home with you."

"He and Crystal got married, and they've gone to New Orleans."

"Hey, that wonderful!" His face brightened. As he started for the door, he added, "Better let Alex know; he's in the dark, too."

Olivia stared at the door, wondering how much longer she could avoid facing Alex. She could still feel that kiss pressed against her palm. And Alex, too, would ask why she didn't go back to Mississippi.

At supper time that evening, Caleb came into the kitchen. "It's warmed up considerable; tonight should be a good night to leave. Have food ready for me to carry up?"

Olivia nodded. "Most of the people have been down here all day. The little ones were bathed and the men spent time visiting with Alex." She went to the stove, checked the stew, and said, "Sadie guessed you'd try tonight. She's cooked extra meat and bread to carry with you."

"I'll be back tomorrow. I'm using the sleigh—minus the bells. Amos has buffalo robes; that will help. In case we meet anyone on the road, there will only be a few well-wrapped figures visible." Caleb took the kettle and headed for the attic.

There was a whisper of sound behind Olivia and she turned. Alex was leaning against the door jamb, smiling at her. "Then I wasn't dreaming." He walked to the table and sat down. "Pardon, please; I don't seem to be up to a marathon."

"Would you like some herb tea?"

He shuddered. "Coffee?" She carried the cup to him and he touched her hand. When she pulled it back quickly, he grinned. "Just making certain you're real. Mind telling me why you decided to come back?"

The door opened and Amos and Sadie came into the kitchen. Sadie unwound her shawl and hung it on the hook. Amos came to the stove, rubbed his hands together, and picked up the coffee pot.

Sadie peered into Alex's cup and frowned, "Tea'll do thee more good. How's that chest this afternoon?"

"Nearly burned all the hair off it with the mustard plaster," he muttered. She chuckled and patted him on the back.

Sadie looked at the stove, and Olivia said, "The vegetables were cooked so I sent them with Caleb. He's leaving tonight."

"It smelled wonderful," Alex said wistfully.

Quickly Olivia responded, "There's more if you want it."

During the meal, Olivia watched Alex eat eagerly for a few bites and then pick at his food with a trembling hand. She could see he was tired; even the lamplight revealed his pallor. She found herself worrying as she watched him. When he shook his head at the offer of apple pie, she blurted, "You've lost weight."

Sadie looked at him. "Either go back to bed or sit by the fire; it isn't warm enough here." He nodded his head and moved to the rocking chair beside the fireplace.

Caleb and one of the women came into the kitchen. She was carrying the bowls and spoons. "Chillens down for the night," she said. "Thought I'd come down and wash the dishes."

"You needn't," Olivia replied. "I'll do them all later."

The woman shook her head, grinning. "Don't seem right for white folks to be waiting on such as us."

Thinking of the conversation with the Reverend Barker and Thomas Caffrey, Olivia carefully placed her fork on the plate and said, "Is that so? You know, even after being waited on for years, I've never thought of how you would feel."

She walked over to the woman. As she looked into her face, she saw the fleeting shadow. Was it uncertainty or fear? Olivia touched the woman's shoulder. "I'm just now realizing, it shouldn't be that way. Now you people are starting a new life. Beginning this moment, to do something for a person is a kindness, and only that. Never again will you be forced to do anything. You were kind to me, and I don't even know your name."

"Ella."

"Ella, when I went to bed that night I thought of it. You had suffered from cold and misery for days, yet you came to me when I was tired and took away the dishcloth. Do you suppose we white women will ever learn to do that?"

"But I will be kind tonight."

"We will wash dishes together."

The two enjoyed a warm conversation that made the chore go much faster, and by the time they had finished, Alex had disappeared and there was only Sadie nodding over her knitting. As she wiped the table, Olivia could hear the people coming down the stairs. She hugged Ella. "Have a wonderful life in Canada."

Olivia discovered she had slept with the blue Bible under her cheek. She also discovered Amelia was home.

Sitting up in bed, she said, "Amelia, you look terrible."

"Mrs. Tucker died. Now that man is alone with four small children. At times like this I wonder if there really is a God," she said bitterly.

"Ask Alex; he has an answer for everything." For a moment Amelia brightened. "You didn't know he's here?"

"I'd forgotten. But in addition I wondered if you would entertain us all by snipping at him again."

Gloomily Olivia looked at the Bible and said, "Probably."

Olivia slowly got herself out of bed, and when she reached the kitchen Amelia and Alex were sitting at the table watching Sadie knead bread. Alex saw her and started to rise. "Don't bother," she said. "I haven't the strength to pick you up off the floor."

He grinned at her and said, "Sadie, I think your patient is going to live; I can tell by the way Olivia is talking to him."

Amelia's eyes were sparkling. As Olivia passed her on the way to the stove, she muttered, "You bring out the worst in me."

Alex said, "You didn't answer my question yesterday."

She sighed. "Did you know Matthew and Crystal are married,

and that they'll be coming back here?"

"No, I didn't." He was silent. When he lifted his head, he asked, "Does that explain why Joseph is still here?" She threw him a startled glance, and he added, "Don't pour coffee on Sadie's bread. Amos said Joseph is working at the blacksmith shop."

She nodded. "Crystal told me he had refused to go to Canada."

Alex shrugged, "His staying shouldn't be a problem. She's given him a paper declaring his freedom."

"It's just that I think she feels Joseph complicates her life."

Alex frowned and continued to stare at Olivia while she ate breakfast.

Sadie thumped her bread into a bowl and covered it with a towel. "There's going to be a meeting of the Female Anti-Slavery Society at the church next week."

"Never heard of that," Alex looked at her with interest.

Sadie nodded wisely. "Thee's Southern and young. 'Twas started back in the thirties. I suppose thee doesn't know the abolitionist group is largely women, poor people, and Quakers? Harriet Tubman will be speaking. She won't be the only one, but she's the one everybody wants to hear."

"Is that so?" Alex murmured, "I'd like to hear her, too."

"Who is Harriet Tubman?" Olivia asked.

"Even I know," Amelia said. "She's a runaway slave who bought her freedom and now is helping other slaves flee the South. They call her Moses."

"I understand there's a big price on her head, upwards to forty thousand dollars," Alex stated. "She's helped scores of slaves in the past ten years, and her reputation is such that John Brown calls her General Tubman."

In a moment Olivia asked, "Who is John Brown?"

"Know anything about the Kansas-Nebraska Act and the fighting that's going on in Kansas Territory?" Alex asked.

She shook her head.

With a wry smile he said, "Well, if you're going to stick around, we'd better get to educating you." His eyes asked the question, but she ignored it.

Sadie said, "Senator Stephen Douglas started it all." Shaking her head she said, "I thought he was an intelligent gentleman. Would have guessed so, since he's Senator from Illinois."

"He's coming up for reelection in 1858 this next year—which will begin in less than a month," Alex added. "And it appears Abraham Lincoln will be running against him for the Illinois seat."

"I heard Lincoln's name mentioned a couple of weeks ago," Olivia said, "but I don't know anything about him."

"He was in Congress for a term back in the late forties," Alex said. "But the most interesting thing is the way he's been emerging as a strong voice in the Republican party. He created a lot of excitement in 1856 when Fremont ran for President."

"Fifty-six?" Olivia said. "That's when we were in Boston." His eyes were asking questions, and she looked away.

He sighed. "Where was I? Aren't we getting off the subject?"

"You were going to tell me about Kansas."

"First the Kansas-Nebraska Bill was written by Douglas, and there's a strong feeling it was penned for the purpose of gaining support for a presidential bid. It set aside the Missouri Compromise of 1850, which placed limits on the expansion of slavery. The Bill allowed each territory to decide for itself whether or not slavery would be allowed by their state constitution. The concept is called Popular Sovereignty."

As Alex got up and moved to the rocking chair, Sadie peered at him. "Thee's overdoing a good thing. Best go back to bed."

"I want to talk to these young ladies, and I doubt they will follow me in there."

Sadie pursed her lips. "Amelia and I will be riding into town with Amos while Olivia tends the bread and cooks the beans. Go to sleep."

"Yes, ma'am," he said, heading for the bedroom.

Amelia looked at Sadie. "He's been very ill?"

"He'll be fine if he takes care of himself now." She turned to Olivia. "Shove the bread into the oven when it's to the top of the pan. Might be Alex will want something to eat later. I hope he has enough sense to stay inside and rest. The lung fever could come back." She peered at Olivia. "Thee won't be too sad, being left?"

Olivia shook her head. "I need to write a letter to my parents while it is quiet."

After they left, Olivia rolled a log onto the fire in the parlor and then went to her room. Gathering up paper and pencil, she eyed the

Bible and quickly pushed it into her apron pocket.

Except for the crackle of the fire, the house was quiet. Pale winter sun had turned the landscape into mother-of-pearl, and the soft light seemed to have wound its way through the house.

Settling into the deep rocking chair pulled close to the fire, Olivia nestled her head against the afghan draped across its back and stared dreamily into the fire. The paper and pencil were lying forgotten on the floor.

She slipped her hand into the apron pocket and fingered the soft leather, musing again over the strange gift and wondering about the giver. A door opened, and the floor boards creaked. Slowly she sat up, dreading the encounter, and yet curious. His question must be answered. He stood in the doorway.

"Would you like some soup?" she asked.

He shook his head and came to sit in the chair opposite her.

She sorted and discarded all the things she could say, and waited. Finally he looked at her and smiled. She held her breath while her glance slid over the gold earring.

"Now will you tell me why you came back?"

"Not until you tell me about the earring."

He continued to stare into the fire. She openly examined his face, seeing the pallor and the lines, and noting new things. There seemed to be a seriousness, and a gentleness she couldn't remember having seen before. As she watched him, she began to feel a crumbling inside, as if some wall had broken down, leaving her vulnerable. Filled with the need to flee, she started to slip out of the chair.

He looked up. "I'll tell you, but I have a feeling you'll laugh." When his eyes met hers she felt a shiver of recognition. *His eyes look the way I feel on the inside, quivering and raw.*

He looked away as he started to talk. "Olivia, I've always considered myself a regular guy. Not too good and not too bad. I was spoiled by life, but not reconciled to life. And I've considered myself a Christian, a guy who kept all the rules and somehow deserved the best heaven could afford, both here and there.

"I'm not certain when the change began, but I can point back to things that happened—like stepping stones, they led me to where I am.

"Did Matthew tell you I dropped out of sight while we were in

Boston?" She nodded and he continued. "I was on a drunk. An ugly, dirty drunk. I don't know where I went or what I did, but I do know that I ended up on the front steps of William Garrison's newspaper office. I'd heard about his paper, the *Liberator*, but how I managed to find the place in my befuddled state, I'll never know. I like to think the Lord cared so much about me that He led me there." His lips twisted in a small grin.

He continued, "I spent some time with the man and his friend, Whittier. That was my first taste of humility. They are great men."

Silently he stared into the fire. Olivia quietly left the room, ladled soup for him, and returned. He looked surprised, but he took the bowl and ate. When she left again and returned with coffee he nodded and grinned at her. His hand brushed hers as he took the cup, she caught her breath, but he seemed unaware.

"The rest happened while Caleb and I worked on the boat. I had it in dry dock on my father's Louisiana plantation. We've always hit it off, Caleb and I. For years he's been more of a friend than a possession—a slave."

Olivia went back to the rocking chair and Alex continued. "After listening to Caleb talking about the Lord as if they were the best of friends, and after being exposed to God's Word—Caleb talked me into reading it to him—I had to face some things in my life."

"What?" she whispered.

He looked up as if suddenly aware of her; his eyes were changing, but she didn't notice. She went to sit on the stool close to him. Her hand on his sleeve urged him on. He said, "That going to church, being baptized, and taking instruction doesn't make one a child of God. Just as Caleb's whole life told me, being a Christian is a love affair with God."

He touched the hand on his sleeve.

"Caleb had me read a passage about servanthood. When a slave had been freed, if he voluntarily chose to stay with his master, he had his ear pierced with an awl and an earring inserted. To me it became a picture of submission to Jesus Christ—belonging to Him for life."

Alex shrugged. "I suppose I was an ignorant youngster, but I had to do something to show God I desperately wanted this relationship with Him. So I had a hole poked in my ear and bought an earring to fill it. It was hideous and visible, but it said what needed to be said.

By then I knew what God wanted of me."

"What does He want?" she whispered, nearly fearful.

"To give the way He gave. Only for me it was to be a redeemer of physical lives. Olivia, do you realize what I am saying? This—what you see now, will never be any different."

"You won't be a lawyer or a plantation owner or anything except—this?" The sweep of her hand took in the pallor of his face, the room, and pointed in the direction of the *Golden Awl* at the wharf.

"That's right." His eyes were expressionless but gentle, and she knew he understood what she was thinking.

When she frowned, he asked, "What is it?"

"I'm wondering what it could be that so convinced you."

"It was that fifteenth chapter of Deuteronomy. After reading it to Caleb and having him act as if the words had set him on fire, I realized what a magnificent thing it is to belong to God."

Looking embarrassed, Alex said, "I decided I had to express to God how I felt about being accepted by Him. Not the act, but the commitment. But after the commitment, I needed the other. The earring. It was the only way I knew to say, 'God I want to belong to You, and I won't trust my weak humanity instead of You.' "

"What do you mean?"

"I needed to take a step that would forever brand me as belonging to Him, a visible sign." He moved uneasily. "I didn't want to leave an open door for backing out of the commitment."

CHAPTER 34

The following week Matthew and Crystal returned. It was nearly Christmas, and Alex was still recuperating. In the kitchen Olivia and Sadie were making preparations for the holidays. Sadie mended stacks of clean woolen stockings while Olivia shaped Christmas cookies. Sadie said, "Not many people would consider a mended stocking a gift, but I know some who would rather have that than nothing."

They heard Alex go to the door. Over the heavy male voices, Olivia recognized Crystal's. "They're here." Sadie gave her a questioning glance, and Olivia hurried down the hall.

Crystal rushed to meet her. She looked hard at Olivia and then pressed her cold cheek against her face. "I'm so happy!" she whispered. "Please, can you accept a sister-in-law?"

Olivia returned the hug, considering the layers of meaning in Crystal's question. "Crystal, with all my heart I wish you and Matthew happiness."

Matthew hugged her. "Forgive us?" The face seemed strangely boyish, and Olivia nodded.

"You are back to stay?" Alex asked.

Matthew hesitated, but Crystal said, "Yes, of course. We want to help."

Matthew turned to Alex. "What's the trouble with you, old fella? You look a little peaked."

"Lung fever," Sadie said. "He nearly didn't make it. Caleb said he'd been sick for several weeks." She turned to Matthew, "Now thee can take the luggage up to the east room, just off the sitting room. And come down and have some coffee."

Alex carried the tray of coffee and cookies into the parlor and Matthew soon rejoined him, asking, "What is happening now?"

Alex grinned. "Caleb is anxious to be gone. He drove the last group over into Canada just a week ago. As soon as the ice breaks, we'll be back in business."

"Had a bad time of it?" Matthew asked as Crystal came into the room and sat beside him.

"Floating ice in the river slowed us down." Alex paused and added, "One thing. Remember the last inspector we had? We ran into him in Mississippi. I'm certain he recognized me. Fortunately, we had legitimate cargo."

They spent most of the afternoon talking about the recent past and going over plans for the future, which seemed to rejuvenate Alex. At supper that evening as they waited for Amos and Caleb to join them, Sadie said, "Tomorrow night we're all going into town. The meetings are starting." She glanced at Crystal and Matthew and explained, "Every year about this time, while the farmers are free, the Anti-Slavery Society sponsors lectures at the meeting house."

"Abolitionists," Matthew said slowly. "We Southerners are uninformed. How old is the group?"

"Before the first tariff was written and the first protest against it by the South Carolina crowd, the society was formed, and people took to the streets to protest against us."

Amos sat down and grinned. "In the thirties the societies were blooming like roses." He added, "No sense in getting riled, Sweetheart, thee said thyself the rest of the country didn't know what was going on here." He looked at Matthew. "My Sadie is sensitive to it all. She's been in the group for twenty years now."

Gentled, Sadie said, "We've had some setbacks. You know, in the beginning the abolitionists were able to take their message into the South itself."

Amos added, "Didn't rile people much in the beginning, even in the South. But since Garrison and his paper came along, the feelings have been running hot."

As Sadie began to serve the meal she muttered, "They burned down the new convention hall in Philadelphia. Nearly killed Garrison—and they did kill Elijah Lovejoy."

"You could go on," Amos said mildly. "Some of the Puritans say Negroes descend from Cain, and the Tappan family were snubbed and mistreated when they aided runaways." He turned to Matthew and added, "Things like this cause problems. Not all the bad feelings are on the Southern side, but when it comes to correcting the situation, we need to work together on both sides."

Alex said, "I understand your sister state, Ohio, had its share of problems with the movement. It's been labeled free but pro-slavery."

Amos nodded. "That's one reason we're here instead of in Ohio. Reverend Rankin has even had his sons holding off the pack with rifles while slaves were escaping out the back door."

Sadie handed Alex the plate of biscuits. "Garrison is a Quaker preacher."

"Yes, I know." Olivia met his eyes, remembering their talk. For a moment, as she thought of his story of the earring, she nearly forgot the others in the room.

————

Late the following afternoon, Crystal tapped and came into the room Olivia and Amelia shared. "I've brought you gifts. And of course it's blue for you, Amelia, and rose for Olivia."

Olivia shook out the folds of the soft knit shawl. "Oh, Crystal, Mississippi watermelon pink. I love it!" She kissed her friend.

Amelia wrapped the shawl about her shoulders and turned in front of the mirror. "It is so—generous, big and soft. I've never had anything this luxurious," she said. "Thank you; it was kind of you to remember us."

"I thought you would like to wear them tonight. Oh, Sadie said to tell you it's time to go." After Amelia had rushed out the door, Crystal caught Olivia's arm.

"Please," she whispered, "I haven't said anything to Matthew about—" She sighed. "I promise I will as soon as possible, but for now, don't give me away."

With a sinking heart, Olivia tried to cover her emotions with a smile. "Let's go, they're waiting."

When Olivia reached the foot of the stairs, Matthew was wrapping his wife in a soft fur cape. Quickly he pressed a kiss on her cheek and Crystal smiled up at him as she touched his face.

Alex, who felt recovered enough to go to the meeting, stopped beside Olivia. "We're riding in the sleigh; will you be warm enough?"

"I have a heavy cloak," she said, turning away from Crystal and Matthew. Alex glanced at the pair, looked at Olivia, and frowned. As he started to speak, she shook her head. "Please!"

Amos explained the sleigh. "There are too many of us for the carriage, and it's too cold to go without buffalo robes. Besides, the sleigh is nice on a night like this."

"Romantic," Matthew said with a self-conscious laugh.

When Olivia reached the sleigh, she felt Alex's hand under her arm and recalled the last time they had been together like this. She had slept against his chest, while farmer Stevens drove them to Paducah. Glancing up at him, she decided he had forgotten.

With a grin, Amos said, "We're going to have moonlight, and I want my sweetheart close!" He chuckled as he helped Sadie into the sleigh.

The ride into town was smooth and swift across the frozen road. The jingle of the harness bells overlapped the hiss of runners and the low hum of conversation.

"Good thing we came early," Amos said as they arrived, nodding toward the stream of wagons and sleighs pulling into the meeting-house grounds. "I think we will be having a big crowd."

"No doubt at all," Sadie said. "With all the rumblings and grumblings going on, there's an interest."

"What rumblings?" Alex asked.

Amos looked around Sadie, "Did thee hear about President Buchanan's latest attempt to settle the war in Kansas?"

"No." Both Alex and Matthew chorused the word.

"Back in 1854, Missouri shoved slavery men over the border into Kansas and they started fighting with the anti-slavery settlers. Been going on for a couple of years before Buchanan interfered. Some say he was trying to keep the South happy and make himself a point for his presidency.

"Buchanan came up with an idea of how to settle it—sleight of hand, it was. He tried to talk his Democratic Congress into admitting Kansas into statehood under the Lecompton Constitution which authorizes slavery. Thee'd better believe we'll be hearing about that tonight. It sure has caused an uproar. They say even Douglas is disgusted with him." He paused and shook his head.

After parking the sleigh, they all got out and trudged inside where the long wooden benches were filling rapidly. Amos chose a bench close to the front of the building, and the others filed in after him.

Harriet Tubman was the first speaker. As the trim woman strode purposefully across the platform, the audience rose to their feet. "General Tubman!" With a slight smile on her face, she waited for the noise to subside.

"You're looking at a woman who is worth forty thousand dollars—dead. I don't know how much I'm worth alive. But I aim to keep on living as long as the Lord wants me here. You understand I am not a brave person by nature. The Good Lord made me that way in order to do His job. The only thing that keeps me going is the grace He heaps upon me."

She paced the platform, saying, "We're all weak people. I carry a gun. Haven't had to shoot a man with it, but it's there. I've threatened a lot of men. Negro men. I says to them: You signed on to go to the Promised Land, and you're going! There's no room for quitters in God's business. You say you go with God, you go. Life's risky, but so's heaven. It's not for quitters. I'd rather miss out on life than to back out of heaven." She paused and looked around the room.

"Now I know you come here to listen to me tell brave stories of where I've been and what I'm doing. I come here to tell you to pick up your cross and get to moving with it. Life's a-wastin', and there's much to be done." She leaned over the podium. "You know we're getting mighty close to having a war over this situation called freedom. If you people get up on your legs and go to work spreading the message that emancipation is the only solution, then these black people can quit sneaking away from home, and the owners will be forced to look at themselves and thank God they aren't wearing the black man's shoes. Because, down underneath it all, men are the same, and they want freedom. Black or white, the good Lord made them all for freedom."

The crowd was on its feet again, and the roar this time was deafening. Olivia looked around. The building was packed, and when they sat down their bench held more people. Alex was forced against her. She watched him from the corner of her eyes, amused at his discomfort as he struggled to find room for his shoulders.

Finally he draped his arm across the back of the bench, muttering, "I would leave, but then someone else would be squeezing you." She grinned and turned her attention to the next speaker.

This sober speaker reminded the audience of the humble beginnings of the abolitionist movement. "Until 1850 we Northerners were caught in apathy," he said. "Since that time, my friends, the momentum has started to build. From a stance of indecision—because in the past we have been taught that godly love is always gentle—we move to decisive action. We are moving forward for God and man.

"I want to remind you, my friends, of the distance we have come in our fight for freedom. Do you all know what the Dred Scott decision means?" He paused, and the low rumble of displeasure moved through the house. "And have you considered the implications of the decision?" Again the sound came, and Olivia shivered with the ripple of strange excitement sweeping over the crowd.

The speaker rattled his papers and continued. "If the decision had been handed down while Garrison was being dragged through the streets of Boston, or when Birney's printing press was tossed into the Ohio, or perhaps when Pennsylvania Hall was set ablaze and Elijah Lovejoy bleeding his life away in the streets of Alton, Illinois—" He paused and looked around the room. "Do you realize what I am saying? I'm pointing to the time when abolitionists were regarded as the scum of the earth because they dared challenge one of America's institutions—slavery. At the time period I have mentioned, the whole of this land was in a frenzy of hatred for these men and women.

"I say, if the Dred Scott decision had been given then, our whole nation would have toppled to the demands of a few. As weak as we were then, it is surprising a few free states did not give in to the demand. But now my friends, we are growing strong. Public opinion is stirring, shifting. The diligent effort of a few who were willing to stake their all for a God-given cause, is winning."

When the final speaker sat down, the whisper swept through the hall. "Sing, 'Swing Low, Sweet Chariot,'—it's Harriet Tubman's favorite." And in the Quaker hall, the crowd stood and linked into a swaying mass, lifting their faces as they sang: "Swing low, sweet chariot. . . . I looked over Jordan, and what did I see, coming for to carry me home? . . . Swing low, sweet chariot, Coming for to carry me home."

———————

Amos was right. The moonlight reflected on the snow, turning the night into a shining white world. Still filled with emotion too deep to understand, and while conversation swirled around her, Olivia sat beside Alex and pondered his unreachable distance. The sleigh bells were keeping mellow time as they rode back to the farm, and Olivia's thoughts drifted from the speeches she had heard to the memory of Alex's arm warm and close around her shoulders.

When they reached the house, Amos stopped at the front door. Alex said, "Want me to take the rig to the barn?"

"Naw, you've been out long enough for a sick fella. Caleb can take care of them." He climbed down and reached for Sadie. Alex jumped out of the sleigh and silently offered his hand to Olivia. Just as silently she accepted and followed Sadie into the house.

"Let's get some hot spiced cider," Sadie said, unwinding her scarf. As Olivia followed her to the kitchen, Sadie added, "There are some fresh donuts, too."

"Sadie, you go sit in the parlor; Amelia can help me. The cider only needs a little warming."

"I'll help you," Alex spoke behind her. Sadie glanced at him, shrugged, and left the room. Silently Alex went after the mugs and Olivia, just as silent, stacked donuts on the platter.

He carried them into the parlor and returned. Sitting down at the table, he reached for a donut and asked, "What did you think of it all?"

"The speeches? They were overwhelming." She stirred the cider and lifted out the spice bag. "I'll ladle the cider here and let you carry it."

They all talked well into the night about the meeting, but when the fire had died down and, along with it, the excited chatter, Sadie stood up, and Amos said, "Last one to bed put on the backlog, and good night."

Matthew and Crystal followed them out of the room and soon Amelia left. Olivia began to gather mugs. Alex followed her to the kitchen with the donuts. Still there was silence, heavy and uncomfortable. As she started for the door, Alex touched her arm. Turning she saw his face. Trying to will her pounding heart steady, she backed toward the door, saying, "I—"

He came close. "Olivia, I want very badly to kiss you, but I must say this—"

"Don't."

"You know how I feel. I'm not playing games. It's marriage I intend."

Her shoulders drooped wearily and she turned away. Thinking of what he had told her about the earring, she said, "It's an impossible burden."

"I know. That's why—"

She looked up at him, blinking her eyes and shaking her head. "Alex, don't—" She rushed past him, then stopped in the doorway.

He tried to smile. "It's all right."

"But I can't stand for you to look like that." She reached out to touch his arm.

He held out his arms. "Don't kiss me," she whispered.

"I won't. But let me hold you, then never again, unless—"

Her arms strained to hold him tighter, feeling the warmth and strength of him, knowing it would never happen again.

CHAPTER 35

The Christmas month slipped away and then two more months were gone. Olivia faced the neglected burden.

"Matthew, I'm writing a letter to Mother and Father, shall I tell them you are married?"

They were in the hallway, standing in the warmth of the early morning sun. Matthew looked at Olivia. "You haven't written that letter yet?"

"No," she shrugged. "It's been one thing after another. I didn't dare write before you came back."

"Yes, I suppose you might as well. Tell them we will be planning a trip home, possibly in the near future."

"When you run out of money?"

He chuckled and pinched her cheek. "You've helped spend it, too. No matter. I might even look for a job if we're here much longer."

They heard a stomping and turned toward the door. Alex looked from Matthew to Olivia. "Well, I thought I was the only one up."

"And I've been tiptoeing around to avoid waking people," Olivia admitted.

A fully recovered Alex pulled off his jacket. "Been down to the river. It's finally starting to look like spring. Matt, Caleb and I will be working the *Awl* over next week. Hopefully we can be out of here the following week."

"Have someplace in mind?"

"Yes, we've been asked to go to the same spot. People are coming up the bayou country, and it looks like the best place is still around Greenville. Amos has more rope and glassware for us to carry down there. He's also come up with some wooden casks. That'll be a lighter load for us. If I can't get cotton in small bales, I'll just hang on to the casks."

Matthew nodded. "An easy move to shield. Have you any idea how many people there'll be?"

Alex sighed, "As many as I can carry. Things are tightening up. For some reason the people are coming out in hordes. Amos says he thinks there's a rumor circulating. It's possible the people are afraid their escape will be cut off."

Olivia started toward the kitchen as Matthew asked, "Are the women coming along? Crystal might object to being left."

"I suppose that's up to them. We could use a cook."

Sadie hurried into the kitchen tying on her apron as she came. "Oh my, I've overslept. Olivia, thee missed a good service last night. 'Twas a special prayer meeting, with the most wonderful news."

"And what was that?"

"The brethren have just come from New York. They are having revival there. It has been going on for sometime. There are indications, Brother Strait told me, that revival is spreading this way. Remember I told thee Garrison has claimed a mighty revival would rescue us from the brink of disaster," Sadie said as she began working on a breakfast of ham and eggs.

"What did he mean by that?" Olivia continued to line the forks beside the plates.

"Oh, thee most likely haven't heard. Garrison, back in thirty-one or thereabouts, when he started up his newspaper, talked hard about the North seceding from the Union. Because of slavery. He fears we'll never all pull together in our natural state."

The men came into the kitchen. Olivia asked, "What do you mean by natural state?"

Sadie lifted sizzling slices of ham out of the frying pan and poured in the eggs. Flipping them, she said, "The Old Adam. Better ask the menfolk, or I'll ruin their eggs. I get stirred on the subject."

Amelia came into the kitchen. She stopped, "Old Adam? Did I miss breakfast?"

Alex chuckled and pulled a chair forward. "No, we haven't taken up theology for breakfast." Feeling very ignorant, Olivia slipped into her place. "Biscuits?" Alex questioned.

Olivia got up again. Alex's eyes warmed her. She brought the biscuits to the table and went back for the coffee.

Pouring coffee, leaning over Alex's shoulder, she noticed his hair curling on the nape of his neck and felt her throat tighten. *Why must it be this way? Just misery. Two months ago I could have teased him over his long hair, and now I'm tongue-tied.*

After everyone had finished, and the kitchen was straightened, Olivia sat down and wrote her stilted letter. Still aching, she wrote happy, reassuring words about Pennsylvania, then she inserted a casual remark about Matthew's marriage. Feeling deceitful, she enthused over Crystal and tried to assure the parents that she was busy, happy, and useful.

As she finished the letter Crystal came into the kitchen. Olivia waved the letter and said, "To the parents. It's full of nothing except that Matthew is married to a wonderful girl and I am happy, useful, and prospering. Oh yes, I told them where we are staying—just in case they'll want to replenish their children's resources."

"Oh, dear," Crystal murmured, pouring coffee for herself and searching for a cold biscuit. She glanced at Olivia and sighed.

"We need to talk, don't we?"

"But not now," Crystal said hastily. "It won't change anything, I—" The door opened and Alex came into the room.

"Sleepyhead," he said to Crystal. "I saw Joseph yesterday. He asked about you, seemed lonesome and very anxious for news of you. I told him you were married."

"You did?" Her voice was taut, and Alex watched her. Hastily she sipped coffee and said, "Does he seem pleased?"

"Well," Alex frowned, "I'd say more interested and satisfied." He started for his room and then paused. "Joseph would be one happy man if you paid him a visit. He works at the blacksmith shop and has a little house right next door. Sadie might even give you some donuts for him."

Alex picked up his tools and left the house. Crystal and Olivia sat in silence.

Amelia came into the kitchen. She looked at the silent figures, shrugged, and poured herself coffee. "Have you got spring fever, too?" She added, "I always get the desire to roam this time of year. Something in my blood starts saying, 'Amelia, it's time to go.' "

"Well, you have your chance," Olivia said slowly, "Alex is working on the boat. I heard him tell Matthew he wants to be out of here in two weeks."

Amelia straightened the sugar bowl and examined the spoon holder. "That wasn't what I had in mind. Matter of fact, that boat scares me to death. If we don't go down, the patrol will get us."

Crystal asked, "Olivia, are you going?"

Thinking of Alex, Olivia shook her head vigorously. "No, I don't want to."

"Then I'll be the only woman with all those men."

"You could stay here," Olivia said, but when she saw the expression on Crystal's face, she hastily added, "I know that's terrible. Maybe Matthew will stay here this trip."

Olivia got to her feet, gathered her letter and pencil. "I need to see if Amos and Sadie will be going to town."

As she passed through the hallway, she turned into the parlor and went to look out the window. The sky was blue and nearly cloudless. She blinked into the sunlight, moving her shoulders in the warmth. Close to the house the snow had melted, revealing a strip of green.

On impulse, she dropped the letter and reached for Sadie's shawl hanging behind the door. Stepping outside, gingerly avoiding puddles of water, she made her way down the hill to the wharf. Only the *Golden Awl* was moored there. Muddy footprints crossed the gangplank and disappeared on the deck.

She followed them. Matthew and Caleb were in the engine room, and Matthew had grease on his hands. Staring at the grease, she murmured, "I can't believe it!"

Impatiently he shrugged and said, "Go up to the pilothouse and give the bell cord a yank. Something is loose."

Dutifully she climbed the stairs. Alex turned as she entered the pilothouse. "I saw you coming," he said. "Is something wrong?"

"No," she stopped to catch her breath. "Matthew sent me to yank on the bell cord."

"I've had it off when I polished the bell. It's working now."

"Polished the bell?" she exclaimed, watching him covertly. After the one miserable meeting of their eyes, he had turned away. *It was a mistake—one foolish hug, and now we are no longer friends. How long will we need to avoid each other before we can act like friends again?* Without being told, she knew and faced the bleak future.

"What?" He was looking at her, waiting for an answer.

"I asked if you are coming with us this trip."

"No."

"Look, Olivia, if it's because of me, I'll stay out of your way."

"I just didn't think it necessary."

"As you wish."

She thought for a minute, chewed her lip, and looked at his profile. "You're inconsistent."

Caught off guard he turned to her slowly and said, "That's the nicest thing you've said to me for two months. Why did you say it?"

"Last autumn you refused to take Crystal and me home. Now you're more than anxious to have me—us along. Why?"

His neck reddened. "It is inconsistent." Abruptly he faced her and shoved his cap back on his head. "One stolen embrace and it's all ruined, huh? You've been avoiding me since."

"It was foolish, wasn't it? The hug." She studied the hurt in his eyes. Slowly she said, "I find myself lonesome for your company, and regretting that we can't be friends."

"It isn't just the hug, is it?" He hesitated and said hastily, "It's all the other. The kiss, the whack. I'd give anything to undo it all, but right now I know of no way."

She nodded and left the pilothouse. As she walked slowly back up the hill she pondered the situation. *Why do I feel the kiss and the spanking aren't the important things? What is?*

At the end of the lane she turned away from the house. The wind was sharpening. Tightening the shawl around her arms, she said to herself, "If only there were someone to advise me. If I could only understand why we are miserable."

And suddenly the whole of it lay before her. She stopped in her tracks and pondered it, then slowly she cut off the road and went to lean on the fence. Sheep grazed in the early grass. The stream coursing down to the river was free of ice, and the clear water chuckled and gurgled as if rejoicing in its freedom.

The peacefulness of the scene reminded her of Sadie sitting contentedly beside the fire carding wool. "Each stroke of the comb, and more of the sticks and burrs are gone. The strands lie smooth and straight. If Alex were saying it," she mused, "he'd say God is speaking to me, and right now I can't deny it. Is that it? And is that why I suddenly see it all—because You make me to see it?" She moved restlessly against the fence, even as she felt the wind pricking through the shawl. She listened to the tinkle of bells and the rustling of contented sheep.

With a sigh she straightened and looked toward the house. *Is it because Alex is what he is, and I don't want that?* she wondered. *He is of a caliber and a determination that I dare not face. I am not woman enough, and I dare not demand he change by stepping down to my level. More than the thought, the earring is a reminder of all he told me, and that makes me uneasy.*

This is no ordinary man; he is one of the called out ones. I can want him with all my soul, but I cannot have him because it would destroy us both. Me? I would be destroyed through the sheer pain of straining to lift myself to his level. Olivia looked up and took a deep breath. Having verbalized the hard words to herself, she knew a painful release. " 'Tis called acceptance." She mimicked Sadie's gentle speech.

————

Her peace lasted a week before it was again attacked. One morning Crystal came into her room as Olivia dressed for the day. Bluntly she said, "We have one more week. I cannot stay here without Matthew, and he says I may not go unless you also go."

Olivia turned from the mirror, and Crystal said, "Why don't you do what Alex always does?"

"You mean—"

"Pray about it. Surely you are being stubborn and—"

"You think God will change my mind." Olivia's voice echoed the amusement she felt. "Oh, Crystal, do you really think I don't know my mind?"

Crystal's face changed. "I don't understand completely, this praying and such. But I can't believe you understand God's will without asking first."

"You are very young."

"No younger than you."

Olivia sighed. "Very well; I shall pray."

"And what will be the sign that God wants you to go?"

Olivia took a deep breath and released it slowly. "Crystal, there's something wrong with this. Perhaps the smartest thing we can do right now is to ask Amos for help." Then she added, "Oh Crystal, this is ridiculous."

Ignoring her, Crystal rushed on, "Better yet, let's ask Alex to give us a Bible study. He and Amelia study the Bible together often; perhaps we can join them."

"They do?" Olivia considered the information and felt the stirring of jealousy. *She's no better than I!* She smiled. "You have the privilege of making arrangements."

Amelia came into the room and looked from Crystal to Olivia. "What kind of arrangements are you making?"

"We're talking about Bible study," Crystal said.

Olivia added, "Crystal has such strange ideas about prayer and God's will." She looked at Crystal. "Where did you get these ideas?"

Crystal shrugged. "Auntie T. She's been teaching me to pray and trust God for as far back as I can remember."

Slowly Amelia said, "Are you certain you remember right? I'm beginning to think most of us twist around our thinking until the good comes out bad and the—well you know." She added, "Alex has been helping me understand more about God. He won't mind if you come and listen, too."

"That sounds like a good idea," Olivia said slowly, considering Amelia's face. *She's old, but would he care, especially now?* Feeling guilty, Olivia smiled and said, "If you don't mind sharing him with us."

Amelia looked startled. Studying Olivia's face, she grinned, "Not at all; I'm certain he'll be flattered! All these females hanging around. Bring your Bibles down after dinner."

Olivia looked at her in astonishment. "You have a Bible?"

"Alex bought it for me."

After dinner, Olivia, carrying her Bible, took her place at the table. She sneaked a glance at Amelia's Bible. It wasn't as nice as hers.

Crystal sat down. "I don't have a Bible."

Alex came into the room, followed by Caleb. He said, "I'm certain Sadie will let you use hers."

Olivia studied Caleb as he sat down beside her. "You told Alex all about God; why are you here?"

He grinned. "I'm learning how to read the words. 'Sides, nobody ever gets to the place where he can quit studying God's Word."

Crystal asked, "What's the difference between Bible study and what we did every morning on the boat?"

"That was devotional reading. Now you're going to be studying it for yourself. This means finding an answer to your questions."

Matthew came through the kitchen. "I wondered what had happened to everyone."

"Bible study," Alex replied. "You're welcome to join us."

Matthew shook his head and continued down the hall.

Alex said, "Open your Bibles to the book of John. Find chapter three. Caleb, you've been reading this to me every night, how about reading the first three verses." He looked around the circle, "The rule is, if you have a question, we stop."

Olivia watched Caleb carefully turn the pages. From the condition of the cover, she guessed the Bible was new, but she noticed some of the pages were beginning to curl.

Caleb found the place and began to read. Olivia concentrated on Caleb's careful reading, feeling the rise and fall of his rich voice. Now the words found their way into her thoughts. "Except a man be born again, he cannot see the kingdom of God."

Next Crystal read, "Except a man be born of water and of the Spirit, he cannot enter into the kingdom of God."

Just those passages sparked a flurry of questions among them all—except Olivia. When the study ended, and the group closed their Bibles and left the table, Alex said, "Olivia, you didn't ask one question. Have you studied this in the past?"

She confessed, "No, at least if I did, I don't remember. To tell the truth, I felt very stupid."

"Then ask now."

Trapped, she thought to herself, *if you run now, you'll never whip this silly attitude.* "Alex, I was raised in the church. Both Matthew and

I. We were baptized into membership at an early age. Now I'm hearing that you have to believe or you perish, that you have to be born again. What does Jesus mean?"

"You sound disturbed."

"I am. I can't believe God is so strict—do it My way or die."

He leafed through the Bible and placed it in front of her. "Does this disturb you?"

"Ask and I'll receive? Of course not."

"And this one?"

She moved impatiently, reading the words his finger touched, " 'I am come that they might have life, and that they might have it more abundantly.' " He found another and pointed. "Peace I leave with you, my peace I give unto you: not as the world giveth, give I unto you. Let not your heart be troubled, neither let it be afraid."

"Is it fair to expect the good things without dealing with the hard verses? And, Olivia don't you want the good ones? You obey the hard ones, and the others are yours, too."

He waited as she got to her feet. "When you want to deal with the hard ones, I'll be here."

As Olivia slowly climbed the stairs, she blinked tears out of her eyes, knowing that all her good resolutions were gone, and that she was as miserable as ever.

She muttered, "Acceptance, my dear Sadie, is out of the question."

CHAPTER 36

Olivia had her hands in the dishwater when Sadie touched her shoulder, "Thou art going on the boat?"

Olivia nodded.

"But thou aren't happy," Sadie continued. "Sometimes love isn't easy."

"You know?" Dishwater dripped on the floor.

Sadie looked at the water and nodded.

Olivia turned back to the pan, "I didn't think—"

"Oh, tut, child." She sighed, smiled. "But one thing if thou decide for the hard life, thee've become good around the kitchen since you've come."

Olivia shivered. "I've decided against. I'm just waiting for the agony to go away."

"That's a lad any woman would be proud of." Sadie picked up the towel and they worked in silence.

Finally Olivia spoke. "I suppose I must go carry things down to the *Awl*. Tomorrow morning is too late for such."

"Did the menfolk move the cookstove to the main deck?"

"No. It's cool enough now; we'll be glad of the fire in the evenings. Matthew and Crystal will have the big cabin; I'll share my cabin with the stove, and the fellows will be crammed in with the cargo until it's warm enough to sleep in the pilothouse."

Sadie nodded. "I've dried fruit in abundance. There's cakes, bread, and pies to get thee on thy way." Abruptly she said, "My, it's like having children leave home; we will miss thee all. But we will be praying for thee every day."

"Praying." Olivia contemplated the word and sighed. "I thought Bible study would teach us better how to know God's will by praying. But now I'm more confused than ever. I'm not certain this trip is a good idea, or even that I should go. Amelia has been studying the Bible all winter, but she seems dissatisfied with her lot. And Crystal—" She stopped to think about the shadows she sometimes saw in her friend's eyes. "I'm not certain about Crystal."

"I've noticed Amelia." Sadie shook her head. "Seems she's struggling with a big problem. But then fighting off the old Adam is never easy. We might say we choose to walk with the Lord, but the steps are hard."

———

Amelia carried the tin of pastries down to the *Golden Awl*. Studying the sturdy craft, she shuddered as she walked up the gangplank. Alex turned. "Food? That's generous of Sadie. Mind putting it in the cabin?"

When she came back to the main deck Alex was seated at the old table with a greasy object in his hand. "Did something fall apart?" she asked.

"It's an extra gear casing. I'm just cleaning it. Who knows what might happen." She shivered, and he looked at her. "Got something on your mind?"

"Alex, last night you said that repentance means a change of direction, even going back the way we came. But sometimes that is completely impossible."

"Are you absolutely certain?" His keen eyes studied her. She nodded. He added, "If it is impossible, be assured God will not hold you to the impossible. But Amelia, there's room for growth in every life. Sometimes what seems impossible is just extremely difficult. God expects even that of us." Without looking at her, he said, "The greater the sin, the more agonizing the cure. I've proved this in my own life."

"Is God really that way—making it difficult on purpose?"

"I don't think it's God so much as man. I don't know all there is to know about God, but I can look at myself with clearer eyes since I've become a follower of His. I see the struggle a Christian has as similar to being lost in the forest. The longer you've wandered, the nearer death and despair you will be when you finally get out of the woods. And there's no way you can take a short-cut."

"I felt this coming. Say what you mean."

"Aren't you working too hard at being the good little servant of Jesus Christ, and ignoring the real life?"

"I'm not certain what you're saying, but I've always understood we prove our relationship with God by doing things for others. Isn't that what you are doing?"

"I'm very aware of being committed to God's purposes for my life," Alex continued, probing the greasy gear. He looked up at Amelia. "But I'm also aware that there's not one thing I can do to win enough of God's favor to merit salvation. Amelia, that's a free gift."

"Then why don't I feel as if I have it?"

"Because you either have refused to obey God, or you don't trust His promise to forgive our sins."

She got to her feet. "See you when you get back."

"I hope so, Amelia. We love you."

"We?" She looked surprised.

"All of us."

Alex put the gears back together and wiped the grease off his hands. Caleb came aboard with his bag. "About ready to push off?" he asked.

"Just waiting on the rest of them." Caleb hesitated. "Yes?"

"Miss Olivia coming?"

Alex's lips twisted. "The last I knew. But—" he shrugged.

"Now you don't go giving up on her. Didn't the Lord say she was for you?"

"I guess there's a possibility I'm not hearing clearly."

Shaking his head, Caleb climbed the stairs to the cabins.

―――――

The ice on the Ohio had broken. By March the channel was clear, but the air still carried a nip. The crew soon discovered the hours they could keep the *Awl* in the water were limited. Each evening they docked early and gathered about the table and stove in the captain's quarters.

Olivia discovered she had forgotten how circumscribed life was by the boat and their mission. On the first evening, after she had coaxed a suitable meal from the stove and they had eaten, Alex brought his Bible to the table. "We would be most foolish if we didn't take time to honor God by reading His Word and asking His assistance in this endeavor. Until we have guests, we'll take turns reading the evening's Scripture. Olivia, will you please read this passage for us?"

He offered her the Bible and she looked down at the scuffed cover, still warm from his hand. She smoothed the pages and began to read aloud; as she finished, the final verse rose up to confront her. She murmured again, "For where your treasure is, there will your heart be also."

Each day they traveled south the air softened and took on the dampness and perfume of home. One evening as they rode at anchor, Olivia left the cabin to stand by the rail. The moon was full, and the brilliance of the night seemed to have inspired all the frogs in the river.

Caleb came out of the cabin and went down to the main deck. Alex followed and started for the stairs, but seeing her he came back to the railing. "Make you homesick?"

She nodded.

"I feel the same way. Another month and it will be getting hot in the rice fields, but right now, with the rice like emerald water and with the flowering trees at their best, it's wonderful country. Father's planted osage-orange, peach, and apricot trees along the dikes."

"Must be beautiful," Olivia murmured, wondering again how he could choose this present way of life. "Will you go back some day?"

"I don't know. Father won't welcome me when he finds out what I've been doing."

"Doesn't it disturb you to go against his wishes?"

"How do you feel about what you're doing?"

She turned to the rail, with a light, amused air, she said, "With the moon full, shining on the water like this, I feel it's nearly a heavenly scene, a highway ordained in heaven, and paved in silver."

She cocked her head and looked at him. "But seriously, am I trying to justify my actions by thinking so? Or is it possible God places people in situations like this? And do they become a way to fill a role in His scheme of things? Or—"

"Or what?" His voice had deepened and she turned to look at him.

She shrugged and moved down the railing.

"Were you going to add that we fail God? Is that something that concerns you?"

"I—I don't think so. I haven't thought that far."

"But you see the possibility of a situation like this being a holy calling?"

Olivia shook her head and stepped back from the rail. "Of course not. That's nearly sinful, to think we play that much of a role in this world."

"You realize that down through the ages, people have been aware of such a high calling?"

"I can't believe society would regard them as normal people."

"How did you feel about Harriet Tubman, even about Sadie and Amos Cooper? I think they are very aware of their calling. I believe they feel they dare not fail God."

She shook her head and turned away. She couldn't keep the mocking tone out of her voice. "Weighed in the balances and found wanting. Good night, Alex."

———

Rain had battered the *Golden Awl* for most of the week. Each day, as they rode the current and fought to stay in the channel, the Mississippi challenged them and became their foe. On the worst day of the storm, with the clouds boiling black and the lightning flashing, Olivia carried the full pot of coffee to the pilothouse. The rain lashed at her, demanding caution with each step she must take up the slick metal stairs. As the door flew open, she watched Alex and Matthew fight the wheel. The boat was headed into the storm, and the driving rain, coming through the open front of the pilothouse, had drenched them.

"For God's sake as well as ours!" Matthew roared, "Alex, let's dock!" Matthew rushed to close the door.

"Impossible!" Alex shouted over the crack of thunder, "We'll hang it up. There're several sunken vessels through here. There's nothing we can do except ride it out until we get below Greenville." He glanced at Olivia and snapped, "You could have scalded yourself carrying that hot coffee! After this—" his face softened as he quickly turned his attention back to the wheel.

"Where's Caleb?"

"Went below to help stoke the furnace. Need every bit of power we can get." She set the pot on the floor and carefully poured coffee into his mug.

Matthew still paced the cabin in short agitated strides. She offered him coffee and he glared at her. "Matt, stop being this way. There's nothing Alex can do now."

He turned on her. "Do you realize our chances of coming through this are nearly zero? I tried to get him to lay over last night."

"It was too shallow there. We'd have beat the bottom out of this rig," Alex said wearily. "I'm doing the best I can now. If the storm worsens, I'll wreck the ship rather than risk your lives."

"What would you do?" Olivia asked.

He gave her a quick glance, "Run it aground. More coffee, please; I'm freezing."

"I'm going to check on Crystal," Matthew muttered as he went out the door.

Alex glanced at her. "Either put my slicker on or go down."

She shook her head. "I'm already wet."

"And bull-headed like the rest of the family." He chuckled and she felt as if she'd been patted on the head. Glancing at her, he added, "Aw, don't take it that way. Sometimes it's a compliment."

When she went to give him more coffee, his hand circled hers. Later she stood beside him and said, "The storm is easing."

He nodded and grinned. "And I'm going to take it in as soon as I get around this next curve."

She wanted badly to touch his wet shoulder, but instead she asked, "There's another cup of coffee; want it?"

He nodded. She filled the cup and headed for the door. "Thanks, Olivia—for staying."

That evening, after they had eaten, Alex said, "We're right on schedule. This is where I intended to dock. With the rain we may have to stay here for a couple of days. The people will be delayed by the storm. Caleb, suppose we ought to pull out all those spare parts and look busy, just in case?"

Caleb grinned and nodded. "Just in case."

———

The storm ended and once again it was spring on the Mississippi. Another two days passed before the people began to arrive.

While waiting for them, Alex and Caleb had moved to the main deck and had been sleeping on pallets spread beside the roustabouts. During the night the people began arriving, Olivia awakened to the soft shuffle of feet and Alex's low voice. With a strange sense of contentment, she turned, tucked her hand under her cheek, and slept.

In the morning when Alex came into the cabin, she asked, "Porridge?"

For a moment he looked startled, then he smiled, nodded and said, "We're back in business," then he stepped out for a moment to look things over.

Crystal came into the cabin. "Alex is happy again."

Olivia nodded, "Like a mother hen." But strangely, as she said the words, she felt they described her feelings.

"May I help you?"

Olivia turned. The woman standing in the doorway was tall and slender. Olivia nodded, acutely aware of the woman's beauty as she came through the door.

"I'm Bertie. You missus—"

Olivia shook her head as Alex came back into the cabin.

He said, "Bertie, we're pleased to have you here. This is Olivia, and Crystal, Matthew's wife."

For a moment as Bertie looked at Alex and then to her, she seemed puzzled. Olivia said, "I'm Matthew's sister."

Bertie nodded. Just as she turned, Caleb came into the cabin. His usual smile disappeared. He stared at the woman until she dropped her eyes. "I'm sorry," he muttered. "But you are the most beautiful woman I've ever seen."

Olivia turned from the stove, "Yes you are," she said slowly, as her eyes took in the delicate, wide-boned face and almond-shaped eyes. She added, "And Caleb may not survive this trip."

Crystal chuckled and said, "Bertie, if you are going to help us, you might feed Caleb. He shows every indication of being willing to eat out of your hand."

Caleb headed for the door and Bertie said, "Don't think so at all." She ducked her head, but they both saw the twinkle in her eyes.

After Bertie had left, Alex said, "You two, take it easy on Caleb. It isn't much fun to be struck between the eyes with a woman like that. Your teasing makes life miserable."

Crystal pursed her lips, saying tartly, "So now we make life miserable for you men."

Olivia realized Alex was looking at her. Hastily she said, "Until you get the stove down on the main deck, we'll have them eat in their cabin."

Alex sighed, "There's not that many of them. Bertie said two were picked up by paddyrollers day before yesterday."

Olivia looked at him. The disappointment in his eyes was obvious. "I'm sorry," she whispered. "I know how this hurts."

Bertie came into the room with the group following her. Olivia put her hand against her lips. Even the children were thin and listless. She watched three men file past, smiling with haggard faces as they helped two women with their children.

"Please come sit at the table," Olivia said. "I have porridge ready."

Alex sat down and addressed the gray-haired man. "Tim, to me, that foot looks bad. After you eat, let's get some ointment on it."

The man nodded. "Sliced it on a hoe, and can't seem to get it well again."

Later, the group returned to their cabin and Bertie came back. As she walked into the room, Alex said, "I think you must be the leader of this group. Mind telling me how you made contact?"

Her eyes were sober. "John tells Jim, Jim tells Mac, then he whispers it on to Tabby. See? The word gets passed along. The bravest ones get away. I don't know, but I think it's the Lord himself who shoves us all together finally. We just crept out of the woods and found each other. Seems we guessed we were all at that spot for the same reason."

"And such is the story of the Underground Railroad," Alex said. "God willing now, we'll all make it back, and safe to Canada finally."

CHAPTER 37

Olivia leaned against the rail. Tonight the river wasn't a silver highway; it was only a muddy, gurgling stretch of the Mississippi. She stared down at the swirling water and decided nothing would change the dismal aspect, either of the river or her own heart.

The last whisper of sound on the boat had quieted, and she felt as if she were totally alone in the world. She knew it was past midnight, but the haunting hour fit her mood.

Restlessly she moved from the railing to sit on the stairs. Wearily she pushed her head against the hard metal, wishing for the kind oblivion of sleep.

Tonight Alex's Bible reading was responsible for keeping her awake. Her lips twisted with the irony of it. The verse he read was to have given comfort and encouragement. It had done just the opposite. Now the words drummed against her mind: *"Let not your heart be troubled: ye believe in God, believe also in me. . . . I go to prepare a place for you."*

She heard a step and looked up. Alex came down from the pilothouse. He sat on the step above her. "I heard you roaming around. Can't sleep?"

She nodded.

"Want to talk?"

She shook her head.

He waited, and in some strange way she was comforted.

Finally she admitted, "That Scripture you read. It was like giving me a dose of trouble. Instead of my heart not being troubled, it is. Doubly so."

"Why?"

"I don't know. I feel as if life's closing in on me." She turned to look at him. "Alex, Crystal and I came to Bible study to learn more about how to pray. We didn't have much time to study, but the things you said to me that night keep rolling around in my mind. About how I had to deal with the uncomfortable verses if I wanted to have the promises. Do you remember?"

He nodded and she continued. "Tonight that verse was like a sour note. It reminded me of what you'd said." She was silent. Finally she got up and went to the railing. He followed her. She looked at him and admitted, "I'm still not dealing with them. In fact, just thinking about it all scares me. I don't know what I would be getting into."

"Plenty," he murmured. "And don't ever think otherwise. You'll be getting life in exchange for death. Remember the verse in John, chapter five. It says if you believe in Him you have everlasting life. In addition to life, you have a totally new relationship with Him."

"Is that what Bertie was talking about tonight?" Olivia turned to look into Alex's face. "She looked like the happiest person on earth when she started talking about God. But the strangest part was the way the faces of those poor wretched people lit up when she talked that way." Olivia's voice caught as she admitted, "Alex, I felt left out. I was suddenly the poor person."

"There is a man in the book of Revelation," Alex mused, "who thought he was rich. The Lord told him he was actually 'wretched and miserable, and poor, and blind, and naked.' What a privilege it is to know our poorness!"

She shook her head. "Not when you've no way to cure the situation."

"But Olivia, you do. Just tell Jesus Christ you accept Him. Let the Lord of all be your Savior. Remember John three? 'The Son of Man was lifted up that whosoever believeth in him should not perish, but have eternal life.' The real issue is, do you believe God is telling you the truth?"

"Oh, Alex, that's a foolish question!" She dabbed at her eyes.

"You know and He knows you do, but He still wants you to say it." They sat in silence for a long time, and finally Alex asked, "Want to do it now?"

She admitted, "I've thought and thought; I suppose it's time to begin trusting Him with my life."

With her head cradled on her knees, Olivia took a deep breath. "Lord Jesus, I—please, I want You to be my Savior. Please. I'm sorry I didn't understand what it was I should do. But I've been rebellious too, not wanting to know. I need You more than anything else in the world. I want to be like Bertie."

———

With the *Golden Awl* fighting the muddy current, Alex stood at the wheel as the morning air handed out its refreshing touch. He chuckled, shook his head and then began to sing, " 'Amazing grace, how sweet the sound! That saved a wretch like me!' "

Caleb came into the pilothouse. He looked around. "Who's doing the singing?"

"What do you think of a white Southern woman who wants to be like Bertie?" Alex laughed.

Caleb crossed his arms and studied Alex. "Better explain." "That's what Olivia told the Lord last night." He glanced at Caleb's face and added, "I mean it! Olivia accepted Jesus Christ as Savior. I was there when she prayed.

"Furthermore, my friend, I guess the two of us don't make such a hit as a bright, shining example. It was Bertie getting excited about the Lord that capped it all."

Caleb began to grin. "Well, bless my soul, and praise the Lord!" He sat down on the bench, put his feet on the chair and with his hands clasped behind his head, he began to chuckle. "If that don't beat all! So, when are you getting married?"

"Married?" Alex's jaw dropped. "You don't believe in rushing things, do you? I just patted her on the head and said good night." He slanted a glance at Caleb's shocked face and admitted, "We talked about it last December. The next move is up to her, and right now, I believe she'll think hard and long before she accepts this old man."

"That so?" Caleb stroked his chin. "Guess it takes white folks a lot longer to make up their mind. But then Bertie and I don't have much time. If I don't grab her, she'll go off to Canada and marry some rich man."

"Well, there goes my first mate."

"Nope. Just might be I decided I want to get my license. Getting so I'm fond of this boating business."

"Caleb, I think there's a wood boat ahead. Go check our supply. If we can take on wood now, we won't need to stop today."

Within minutes Caleb was back upstairs. "Jeb says get wood."

Alex reached for the bell cord. "The people need to take cover. Want to take the wheel now?" Caleb nodded, and Alex ran downstairs. Olivia's startled face peered out the cabin door. "We're just taking on wood," he said to her as he ran down the final flight of stairs.

The flatboat was pulling alongside. "Okay, let's go!" Alex yelled. Jeb and Pete came out of the shadows, made the flatboat fast, and dropped the plank. The flatboat's crew swarmed over the side with their load.

Within minutes the load of logs had been transferred from the flatboat to the *Awl*. "Good work, fellows." Alex pulled coins out of his pocket. Then he noticed the curious manner in which one of the roustabouts from the flatboat studied the boat.

"Wanna buy it?" he asked dryly. The fellow's jaw tightened and he hurried to scramble over the side.

Alex continued to puzzle over the roustabout's behavior as he started up the stairs. Olivia was still standing in the doorway. He threw her a quick smile and hurried to the pilothouse.

Olivia turned back into the cabin. Soon the boat was buzzing again and she sat down and watched Bertie and Crystal helping the children use pencils. Slowly she asked, "Bertie, do you mind taking the coffee up to the pilothouse?"

Bertie glanced up with a smile. "No, ma'am I don't—"

"Not ma'am, just Olivia. You might want to make sure that everyone has come back out."

When Bertie closed the door, Olivia turned to Crystal. "I never think to ask except when there's people around, but did you see Joseph before we left Pennsylvania?"

Crystal didn't look at Olivia. "No. I'm ashamed of myself. Seems nearly impossible at times to remember why I must see him. We'll be in Pennsylvania in a couple of weeks. I really intend to go then."

Bertie came back into the cabin. "Alex says we have wood enough until tomorrow afternoon. If you want, he'll take you to the market when he stops. Said something about getting some newspapers."

"Newspapers?" Olivia said in surprise. "Why does he want newspapers?"

Bertie said, "The menfolk are all talking about Mr. Abraham Lincoln running for the Senate. There's going to be some debates between him and Senator Douglas. When I went up there, Matthew was talking about finding out what's going on." She started toward the table and turned. "Alex has a spot in mind, and he hopes to reach it tomorrow. We will also be stopping for the night in another hour."

"I'd better do something with the fish," Olivia murmured.

"Want me to cook a fish stew?" Bertie asked. "For this crowd it's the easiest. Good with potatoes and dried corn."

Olivia nodded.

When Alex came into the cabin at suppertime, he gave Olivia a quick, searching glance. She was still wondering about the look afterward when the table had been cleared and Alex took up his Bible. Everyone had gathered for the evening devotion time, and he stood, took a deep breath and looked at Olivia. "When I was a young boy at home, birthdays were an important event. There were gifts and a beautiful cake. I always felt like a prince on my day.

"God's Word tells us that in order to be part of the kingdom of God, we must be born again. As Jesus said, born of the Spirit. That is the most royal of birthdays, the time when we are born into the kingdom.

"Tonight, if I had gifts and a birthday cake, I would give them to Olivia, because last night she was born into the kingdom." With a smile he paused until the excited voices quieted.

"I have nothing to give her except God's Word. Olivia, Jesus said, 'I am the light of the world: he that followeth me shall not walk in darkness, but shall have the light of life.' And, 'Peace I leave with you. . . . Let not your heart be troubled, neither let it be afraid. . . . Ye are my friends if ye do whatsoever I command you. . . . Hitherto have ye asked nothing in my name: ask, and ye shall receive, that your joy may be full.' Happy birthday, Olivia!"

That night, as Olivia lay in her bunk, she thought of the evening and sighed. "Dear Father," she whispered into the darkness, "thank You—for the gifts of Your Word, and most of all for belonging to You. I think I understand what joy is. I still can hardly comprehend all that happened. It was beautiful, only—" She stopped and thought about prayer and the gulf that still seemed to stretch between her and Alex. And in the quietness of the cabin it seemed the question was still there. "If only I knew what the question is," she whispered.

———

When the boat slid into the sleepy river town the next day, Olivia was ready with her list. Matthew, Crystal, and Caleb were lined on deck chairs—on guard, but seemingly only interested in taking a double portion of the long absent sun.

With a teasing sparkle in his eyes, Alex escorted Olivia to the shops like a dutiful husband, then excused himself when she reached the drygoods store. "I'll go find my newspapers and see about refilling our wood supply. Then I'll return for you."

Casually she shopped for needles and thread, a length of bright cloth, and new towels while she babbled on about curtains and chair covers.

When Alex returned, she took his arm and they walked to the boat.

When the *Awl* was safely back in the channel, Alex turned to Matthew and asked, "Well?"

"Not a thing. Except for the people who loaded wood on the boat, that was the most sleepy of sleepy towns. Even the dogs wouldn't bark."

"I hope you're right," Alex murmured. "Every extra day we spend on the river means we're more likely to attract attention—now or any other trip."

"You are developing old lady nerves," Caleb said with a laugh.

"Maybe so. If you'll take the wheel, I'll read my newspapers. Maybe next trip or the one after, I'll know enough about this river to take it during the night."

Caleb nodded. "Wouldn't be so bad when the moon's full."

Alex found the article he wanted and carefully spread the newspapers on the table. Olivia came with coffee and fresh pastries. After she poured the coffee, Alex waved her to a seat. "Listen to this. Abraham Lincoln received the Republican Party's nomination to run for the Illinois Senate seat against the Democratic nominee, Senator Stephen A. Douglas." Alex paused and chuckled.

"He's getting a good start. Already he's forced Douglas to admit the Dred Scott decision didn't overthrow popular sovereignty in the territories. Listen to this. 'Douglas admits communities hostile to slavery could blight and destroy the institution of slavery, simply by refusing to pass laws friendly to it.'

"Here's a report on Lincoln's June 16th, 1858, speech." He lowered the paper. "That's his acceptance speech for the Republicans' nomination to run for Senate." For a moment Alex was silent, then thoughtfully he said, "I think Lincoln is going to be the man for our times. In his speech he said, 'A house divided against itself cannot endure permanently half slave and half free. I do not expect the Union to be dissolved—I do not expect the house to fall—but I do expect it will cease to be divided. It will become all one thing, or all the other.' "

Matthew came in as Alex read. When he finished, Matthew said, "Well said; but Mr. Lincoln, I'm afraid you're just the excuse the South has been looking for."

"Secession," Alex stated. Matthew nodded and Alex slowly said, "Might just be, and it breaks my heart to admit it. But is there another solution?"

Olivia said, "Sadie seems to think if the people would turn to the Lord, war won't happen. Just before we left, she told me about a report of revival starting in New York City."

Matthew's lips twisted as he said, "But my dear sister, you are ignoring one thing. Both North and South think they have God's will all figured out. In such a situation, who's going to give? There is a certain rigidity connected with the dogmatic assurance a man has when he's convinced he knows God's will better than God himself."

CHAPTER 38

From across the room, Olivia watched Alex as he talked. The dark-skinned people pressed closer and seemed to hang on every word he said. Reluctant to cross the room and interrupt the conversation, she focused on his lips and tried to guess his words as she watched the nods and smiles. She heard his low chuckle and turned away with a sigh. *Olivia, such jealousy! Whenever he smiles at anyone, you're wanting it for yourself. Dear Lord, help me!*

Through the open door of the cabin she could see Bertie and Caleb outlined against the moonlight. They were standing by the railing with their heads close together. Feeling alone and forgotten, she sat down on her bunk and picked up the tiny garment she had been stitching together for Martha's child, Ann.

The child watched her from across the room. Olivia smiled and beckoned. "Let's see if it will fit you," she whispered.

With her dark eyes shining, Ann touched the bright cloth and asked, "Will I be your girl and fetch for you?"

"My slave? No, Ann, you will be free. I made the dress because I like you, not because you are my slave."

The child's eyes were still wide with wonder. Olivia put aside the sewing and took Ann's hand. "When you go to Canada, you will learn to read and write. Up there, you will go to school with the rest of the children."

Ann leaned against her knee. "I'll wear the new dress? I've never had a brand new one." Olivia touched the child's cheek, feeling the baby softness as she mused on the statement.

The crowd around the table moved away, and Alex crossed the room to crouch beside the child. She climbed on his knee. "Missy is sewing a frock for me, just because she likes me."

"That's a good reason," he agreed. "And I've come to tell you that Mama wants you to go to bed right now. Good night." He kissed her brown face and she scurried away.

"It's been such a short time, but already the children are beginning to look healthy." Olivia concentrated on the dress, taking quick stitches.

"What were you thinking? Your face was sad."

She looked up. "Just now?"

He nodded.

"Ann said she'd never had a new dress. It made me recall an incident I'd nearly forgotten. Years ago, one of the slave children— my favorite playmate—fell in love with my dress. We traded; I'll never forget the effect—on my mother, on Tissy, and on me." Olivia gathered up her sewing and went to sit at the table. In a moment Alex followed her. He sat down across from her and toyed with the scissors. The cabin grew dark and he lit the lantern swinging from the ceiling. "This light is not very good for your eyes. Can't the sewing wait until morning?"

Slowly she folded the bright print as he said, "I don't mean to pry, but if there's something you'd like to talk about—" She looked up and he gestured toward his Bible lying on the table.

"Oh, I thought—" She moved her shoulders uneasily and tried to ignore her response to his closeness. She said, "Caleb and Bertie seem—happy."

He nodded and got up. "Guess I'll go see if the fish are jumping."

She watched him walk to the door, and swallowed to get rid of the lump in her throat. *Why be so foolish as to think we could be friends now? It is agony, and I am so lonesome.*

He stopped in the doorway. "Want to come?"

She nodded, put away the sewing, and came to him. But when

she looked at him, she thought his smile seemed cold and his eyes remote. She hesitated and turned away, saying, "I think not."

"Is it that bad? I'd hoped we could at least be on friendly terms. Olivia, I—" Abruptly he left the cabin.

———

Closing the door, she dropped the latch and prepared for bed, stopping frequently to press her fingers against the tears on her face.

During the night she awakened, sat upright in bed with her heart pounding. Pressing her hands against her face, she tried to remember her dream. It was gone, but the sense of urgency, the panic was still with her.

In the darkness, she fumbled her way to the table and found her Bible. Pressing it to her cheek, she sat on the bench, murmuring, "Why, Lord? Please help me understand."

The minutes passed. She fumbled for the matches and lit the candle. In the feeble light she turned in her Bible to 1 John and found the verse that had been troubling her. With her finger resting on the paper, she said, "Lord, when I read this verse last week, my mind just flew away from it, but I can't forget the words. Why?"

She bent close to the page. The troubling uneasiness she had encountered the first time she'd read the words in the third chapter was still there. She whispered, "It says, 'and do those things that are pleasing in his sight.' Lord, from the way I feel, I must conclude I'm doing something that isn't pleasing in your sight. What is it?"

Finally she went to her bunk and knelt beside it. Just as reluctantly, she folded her hands and waited. Confusion tumbled through her thoughts. She could no longer stand the strain. "Lord, You understand these broken thoughts I'm thinking. I can't understand. I keep thinking of Alex; am I hearing You? Are You telling me I'm not treating him the way I should? Lord, he's the one who started all this. He kissed me when he had no right."

Abruptly Olivia remembered that night and the words he had said as he swung her around the room. She settled back on her heels. "He said, 'It is my lady; Oh, it is my love! Oh, that she knew she were!' "

She covered her face and the confused thoughts merged, re-shaped, and marched through her mind with undeniable authority.

With a sinking heart, she faced them and admitted, "Love? That is a strange thing. I thought love was to come slowly with friendship and flowers." She sighed and examined the troubling emotion. Finally she whispered, "I am displeasing You because I won't let Alex say those things to me. And the reason I won't is—not because I am afraid of him, but because I am afraid of You." She trembled, and finally whispered, "I think I know what You will say to me."

Olivia got to her feet and went to the porthole. She took a deep shaky breath, looking out at the dawning day. "At least I know *why* I feel this way. And there's a way I can avoid the agony. I don't need to stay here; I can return home, and forget about this place, these terrible problems—and him."

With a yawn, she crawled back into her bunk. Relaxing, she let her thoughts dwell on home. What about Thaddeus? For a moment she winced. Stodgy seemed the word that best fit the man who would never stay rebuffed. Now she visualized herself walking through his plantation home. The gardens, the wide pleasant halls, and the line of dark, smiling faces, seemed to grow increasingly attractive. Strange, how difficult it was to visualize his face.

The fresh morning air swept through the pilothouse. Alex lifted his face to the air, breathed deeply, and grasped the wheel more tightly. At the sound of the door opening, he looked over his shoulder. "Caleb, I think I've finally come up with a plan. See, what you think of it. I'm still hoping this feeling is just a crazy hunch, not the Lord warning me."

He paused, tightened his grip on the wheel, and peered at the river and the change in the water. "Might be a pretty good-sized sandbar coming up; what do you think?"

"Could be," Caleb murmured, following the direction of Alex's pointing finger. "The channel is plenty wide right here—just ease to starboard." They were silent until the shadowed water was behind them. Caleb said, "What about your plan?"

"Won't be long 'til we get there. Day or night, we'll need to be prepared when we reach the Coopers. Without a doubt, if there's a problem, it'll happen there. My suggestion is that you, Matthew, and Crystal be prepared to stay on the craft, even to take it as far up the Ohio as you can. I have names of stations on the Underground, and

I'll give them to you. Even if I'm not with you, the people can still be safely delivered to Canada."

Caleb's brow furrowed. "What you planning on doing?"

"Being a decoy. Olivia and I will get off the boat while you move up the Ohio at half speed. If there're no problems, we'll signal you. Look for a light in the attic. If you don't see it, keep going."

"You still think you're being followed, huh?"

"Might be. There's no sense in worrying about it. We'll pray and trust the Lord to intervene as He sees fit."

That evening, after the meal, Alex faced the people, picked up his Bible and read, "Peace I leave with you, my peace I give unto you: not as the world giveth, give I unto you. Let not your heart be troubled, neither let it be afraid." He closed the book and placed it on the table. Watching him, Olivia wondered about the shadows in his eyes.

As he spoke, she looked around the table at the happy smiles and nods. But the shadows in Alex's eyes gave his words new import. "Peace isn't a condition, it is a gift from Jesus Christ, given when we accept Him as Lord of our life, as well as Savior. This peace is not related to the peace the world gives. It is planted in our hearts in a divine manner. Possessing this gift, we are obligated to obey the rest of the verse, which is a command. It instructs us to be neither troubled nor afraid. Good night, friends, sleep peacefully."

Alex stopped beside the bench where Olivia sat. "You aren't going to have many more days to watch this moon with me. The trip is nearly over, and the full moon is on the wane."

When Olivia lifted her head, she saw Crystal watching with a gentle, peaceful smile on her face. For a moment Olivia found herself envying that expression. Getting to her feet, she started for the door. "Is it cool out?" she asked, ignoring her quickened pulse and the uneasiness she felt. She chided herself. *Olivia, do you ever think of the consequences of your actions?*

Alex stopped outside the cabin door and muttered, "Well, Caleb and Bertie have that section of railing. I don't want to disturb them."

"We'll have a better view from the stairs," Olivia said, pointing to the flight leading up to the pilothouse. She led the way and sat down. Alex sat on the step beneath her.

With his earring nearly on a level with her nose, she studied it and thought of the things he had said about it.

Commitment, he had called it.

His low voice interrupted her thoughts and Olivia tried to recall his first words as he continued. "Matthew seems bored with the whole movement."

"I'm not too surprised," she answered. "I didn't think it was ever a major concern of his."

Alex was silent a moment. He asked, "What do you think it was in the beginning?"

"A new excitement. Nearly everything in life falls into that category. He could have returned to Harvard last year, but most of us at home could see he was simply bored. Matthew worries me. He is impetuous. Knowing myself, I know how badly he needs the Lord. Sometimes I shudder to think where his impulsive nature could lead."

Alex sighed. "I'm sorry to hear that. But at least it takes the burden off me."

Astonished, she leaned forward to peer at him. "Burden! You hold yourself responsible for his actions? Alex, he's a grown man. I hope you don't hold yourself responsible for any other people's failures."

"Only those I feel personally involved with." He was silent and she dared not say more on the subject.

In a moment she said, "Under the moon the muddy old Mississippi is beautiful." He nodded. By moonlight she saw the planes of his face in a way she hadn't noticed in daylight.

"Do you know you have a stubborn jaw?" she asked. He jerked his head and then she saw the flash of his smile.

"How would you know? It's hidden under this beard."

"Is that why you have a beard now? To hide your stubbornness? You didn't have one in Boston."

"Boston," he sighed. "We always come back to that, don't we?"

"I wasn't referring to that time," she snapped. "Alex, I believe you are too sensitive on some subjects. Can't we just be friends and leave it at that?"

"You know we can't."

Olivia stood and Alex came up the step to her. He took her hand and stroked its roughness with his thumb. "I even feel guilty for your dishpan hands."

"Don't." The urge to touch his shoulder was nearly irresistible. She pulled her hand free and stepped away from him.

"You know we should be back to the Coopers' home in less than a week?"

"I've been thinking about that. Alex, I feel bad about staying with them for so long."

"You needn't," he assured her. "I've talked it over with them. They've let me help with expenses; but in addition, I believe they are sincere when they say we've been more help than hindrance. A spare Quaker way of saying they were lonesome and overworked before we came." She listened to his soft chuckle and yearned again to reach out to him.

He said, "Theirs is a life of true commitment, in the deepest sense."

That word again. Coupled with obedience, it is an impossible burden. Alex, my dear, I can't wait to go home and forget you. But one kiss, before I do. He moved down the steps, away from her, and she could breathe easy again. Quickly she ran down the steps and said, "Good night, Alex."

———

Alex turned to look at Caleb. "One more night and we'll be at the Coopers', the Lord willing."

"Still feeling uneasy about it?" Caleb lifted his head from the map and studied Alex's face.

"Not since we've developed a plan of action." Alex looked at Caleb. "What about you and Bertie?"

"We want to get married as soon as possible. Legally Bertie is a runaway. That'll cause problems, won't it?"

Alex grinned at him. "In the United States, yes. Guess you two can't complain if you do have to make a trip to Canada."

Softly, Caleb said, "I was going to bring that up. Suh, I'd be glad to do the job!"

Alex chuckled, "Plan on it. But you will come back, won't you?"

Caleb nodded. His face was suddenly serious. "Did you tell Olivia our plans?"

"For marriage?"

"No, the other ones."

Alex's grin disappeared. "No I haven't. Day before yesterday I had intended to do so. We got to talking about other things, and I guess I must have said something to rile her. Anyway, there hasn't been an opportunity since."

"I'm feeling it'd be best to talk to her as soon as possible," Caleb said soberly.

"Then send her up. And what about the others?"

"No. I don't like seeing them frightened when likely we won't need the plan."

Alex nodded and Caleb left the pilothouse.

Olivia came with the coffeepot. Alex watched her sober face as she filled his mug and brought it to him. "Hey, why the long face?" he asked.

She looked surprised. "Didn't know it was." She smiled, but he saw the shadows were still there.

"Getting tired of traveling?"

"I suppose. Mostly it's the feeling I need to get on with life."

"Mind telling me what that means?"

She sighed, "I was afraid you'd ask, and I didn't want to say anything until I'm ready to go."

"You're leaving again? Like last time?"

"No, I really mean it now. Alex, I'm sorry, but I can't—remember last winter? One morning Amelia said something to you. I don't remember what it was, but your reply was a quotation from Hamlet."

He nodded. "This above all: to thine own self be true, And it must follow, as the night the day, Thou canst not then be false to any man." His voice was rough as he finished. He added, "Olivia, that quotation can be an excuse, or a warning."

"Of what?"

"A reminder of all that God has said to us. Rather than the quotation reflecting a decision to act, it is the natural consequence of all that we are, whether good or bad."

"And you can judge me bad according to your desires."

"I choose not to judge you. If my desires were the only thing that counts, you would have been mine long ago."

She lifted her chin. "And how do you mean that?"

With his heart aching, he breathed, "Any way you want to take it."

She was out the door and down the stairs before he remembered why she had come.

CHAPTER 39

O livia had been gone nearly an hour when Caleb came up to the pilothouse. "How did it go?"

"I didn't say anything to her." Alex glanced at Caleb. "I'd every intention of doing so, but forgot. After she left I started thinking about it, and realized it was a risky thing to do."

Caleb shrugged. "You get off the boat, give your sweetie a kiss, go put a lantern in the window, and that's all there is to it."

"That's what I thought all along." Alex paused, then slowly added, "But now, thinking and praying, I can only consider the possibility of being attacked. I can't take the risk of having something happen to Olivia. My plan, which I will tell some of the others tonight, is for me to go alone. I don't want you to even consider the option of having her along."

"You can't go alone," Caleb protested. "Sure, I know she's a woman. But if you get hit over the head, someone needs to get help in a hurry. As little as Matthew knows about the boat, I still can't get along without him. It's no use, Alex—you've got to use her."

"I know those are good reasons," Alex said lightly. "But old man, I'm the boss. And in addition, I have the right to do everything in my power to protect the woman I love. Give me that privilege and say no more."

It was late afternoon when Alex docked the *Awl* for the night. He came down to the cabin with a grin. "By late tomorrow night we'll be finished with our roaming."

"Wonderful!" Crystal sighed. "I was beginning to think it would never end. How I look forward to a normal life—for a time," she added hastily.

Alex looked at Olivia. She continued to stir the contents of the kettle. Without pausing she said, "What is normal? Crystal, it seems we've lost sight of that."

"True," Crystal murmured. "Not a one of us has had a normal life for over a year now."

Bertie lifted her face and turned toward each one in the cabin. She seemed puzzled. Alex asked, "You're wondering about us?"

"No," she said, "I thought of myself and wondered about normal. Guess I don't know what it is."

When the evening meal was over, and after Alex had read scripture, he closed his Bible, realizing it needed to go in his pack. The thought swept over him with a sad sense of finality.

Olivia was washing the table. Taking a deep breath, he said, "Olivia, Crystal, I need to talk to you. And Bertie, you too. Please come to the pilothouse as soon as you finish."

Seeing the expression on Olivia's face, he added, "I want to see you now."

She followed him up the stairs. Alex closed the door and leaned against it. In a voice high with tension, she asked, "You are forcing me to stay here?" Realizing his position, Alex stepped away from the door, saying quickly, "No, my dear, not at all. I'm thinking about what should be said." He went to the bench, adding, "Come sit here and I'll tell you."

Taking her place beside him, stiffly she said, "It will do nothing for our relationship to have you coax."

"Olivia, I've no intention of ever addressing the subject again. Now listen, the others will be here—"

Bertie and Crystal came into the pilothouse. With a sigh he stood up, took a deep breath and began. "Thank you. It seemed best to be away from the others. I don't wish to alarm them unduly. Now, this is the plan. I want to arrive at the Coopers' wharf tomorrow late in the evening. It will be dark."

He paused, adding reluctantly, "I must tell you, there have been several things that have happened in the past month which have made me uneasy. I don't want to alarm you in any way, but there's a possibility we are being watched. If my suspicions are correct, the slaves are in danger of being apprehended also."

"Also?" Olivia questioned.

"Of course, I'm their target; after me they'll go for the slaves. Caleb, Matthew, and I have discussed the problem and the best solution seems to be for the boat to arrive after dark. Caleb will drop me off, then slowly travel on. If I make it to the house without being detained, we'll place a light in the attic. Caleb plans to stop just around the next bend. From the pilothouse he'll have a good view of the Coopers' attic window. When Caleb is certain everything is under control, he will bring the boat back to the wharf." He shrugged. "That's all there is to it. But I felt you should know before we arrive." He paused, then went on in a rush. "If by chance I am taken, it will be up to the rest of you to take the slaves on to the next station. I've given Caleb the names and locations of other groups who will see the people make it into Canada."

Alex got to his feet and grinned at the women. "That's it. Hopefully we'll not have an opportunity to use the plan, but it seemed best to be prepared."

The women filed out of the pilothouse; only Bertie looked at him with fearful eyes.

That night, Olivia lay staring wide-eyed at the pale oval of light coming through the porthole. Where there should have been a heart was only a numb, tender spot. She considered all the brave words she had said to herself during the past week. Even the decision she had made to return home. *How could I have thought I had a choice? Obedience is either obedience or disobedience. Is it possible for a child of God to disobey and still belong? Her mind shied away from the thought. But there's Alex. It is unfortunate he doesn't have someone to love him.*

Near morning she realized she did have a choice. Whether or not she obeyed was a decision to be made. And as for Alex, it was impossible to resolve that pain. More was involved than just simply loving a man. Loving Alex carried no possibility of compromise, either on his part or hers. "It is impossible for Alex to walk back into the old life, and I won't walk into his new life."

She closed her eyes and dreamed back the childhood pictures of home and family, knowing she could not surrender them. Turning away from the light coming through the porthole, she felt a pang of loss. "Is there a deeper element to life, one I don't understand?" She had a feeling something was slipping away from her, and she knew it by the unmistakable sense of loss.

Still wakeful, she tossed on the bunk and finally sat up. "There is something I must do," she decided. "And it isn't so much related to God as simply that Alex is a friend. Tonight I must follow him when he leaves the boat, not because I care about him, but simply because he is a friend worthy of help." She returned to her bunk and slept.

During the day, Alex seemed as cheerful and pleasant as a youth on a fishing trip. Olivia packed her bag, and Crystal's eyes widened. "But Crystal," she explained, "he doesn't expect the worst; why should I? You will be the one caught without her nightie and toothbrush."

The afternoon and early evening lolled away with dreaming indifference, as passengers and crew took their leisure in the shade of the main deck. Only Olivia noticed the preoccupation of Caleb and Alex. As they dashed around, she guessed their activity in the pilothouse was related to the telescope she saw trained on the forest that surrounded them.

That evening their meal was light and hasty as they prepared to get underway. When the first stars came out, the *Awl* moved back into the channel and chugged slowly up the Ohio.

The children were put to bed and the decks deserted. The hours passed in silence. Not one light graced the boat when Olivia felt her way down to the main deck. Moving quietly to avoid disturbing the roustabouts, she stashed her bag behind the stairs and sat down on the coil of rope.

She slept, but when she awakened, it was without a sense of time. At first she thought there was only silence, and then she became aware of the quiet, rhythmic motion of the roustabouts as they stoked the furnace. Another sound was added, and after listening intently, she knew it was Alex.

Her heart began its slow, heavy thumping. The time had come. Now, with every sense alert, she watched the cluster of houses and dark shadowed barns. As they passed on, the scene was replaced with towering trees sweeping down to the bank.

Alex moved to stand in the shadows, and she could tell he was watching the shoreline. She saw him lean over the railing. Quickly he stepped to the engine house. She heard the slowing of the engine and the paddles. With her heart in her throat, she gathered her bag and waited in the shadows.

Now the boat was scarcely moving; the swish of paddles could have been a school of fish. She saw a shadow merge with Alex's, heard a voice. A roustabout leaped to the wharf and held the boat close. Taking a step forward, she watched the place Alex stood. When he moved, she followed. He turned. "You!" Slipping her arm through his, she tugged him into the path.

The boat moved on, nearly imperceptible in the dark. Olivia trembled against Alex as they started up the hill. They were nearly away from the stand of young hickory when they heard the shout. "Alexander Duncan!"

She felt the tremor go through him. "Right here. What do you want?" From all sides the men came out of the bushes. Alex thrust her away from him. "Run!"

Powerless to move, she watched. With his arms flailing he met the crowd. For a moment he stood. In the dim light she saw the heavy stick rise and fall. She watched him tumble to the ground and hard, cold anger swept through her. Charging, swinging the bag, she screamed, "Beasts! You'll kill him." And when the crowd gave, Olivia threw her head back and screamed.

Amid lights, lanterns, torches, and people, Amos Cooper, who came running from his house, appeared beside her. "Give way!" he roared. "What is the meaning of this, attacking a defenseless woman?"

The torch revealed the face of the town constable. Amos faced him. "McInn," he shouted, "what is an honest man doing sneaking through my pasture in these wee hours?"

The man stepped forward, "An honest day's work, Sir. These men have been charged with the task of arresting Alexander Duncan."

Olivia gasped and stepped forward. "Outrageous! You beat a man senseless and then call it arrest?"

"We're not about to let him escape. Ma'am, he is being charged with the illegal exportation of slaves. Under the Fugitive Slave Act of

1850 he is guilty of theft, seduction—"

There was a moan from the figure on the ground and Olivia whirled away from the constable. Alex sat up. Holding his hands to his bleeding head, he tried to rise. Two men dragged him upright. "Duncan, you'll have to come with us, either peaceably or in bonds."

To Olivia the scene ceased being a dream when she heard Amos' weary voice. "Where are you taking him?"

"For now, to the county seat. He will be arraigned there."

One of the men holding Alex said, "Might be, if you want to tell us now where to find the slaves you carried out of Mississippi, might be, it will go easier with you."

"Paddyrollers!" Olivia hissed. The man turned quickly and Alex raised his head. She went to him, "You can't take him like this; he needs a doctor's care."

"He'll get it in jail." The man nudged Alex with the club he held.

Amos' hand was strong on hers, "Come, child. There's nothing more we can do."

The crowd around Alex moved off, and Olivia wearily stooped to pick up his bag. "Oh, Amos, he's terribly injured."

"I don't think a big strong lad like that will be hurt badly. Tomorrow we will get in the wagon and go see him. It's only fifteen miles." His hand was gentle on her arm, as he led her to the house and Sadie.

By the time she reached the house, the scene beside the path seemed like a bad dream. But that impression disappeared when Olivia saw Alex's blood on her hands.

"Thee has been hurt, too?" Olivia shook her head and tried to find the words to explain.

Amelia drifted close, offering a glass holding a bitter drink.

———

In the morning, Amos, Sadie, and Amelia sat around Olivia, patting her shoulder and listening to the story. She kept pushing at tears with a trembling hand. "I don't know why I am acting like such a baby."

"Well, thee'll just have to get thy gumption in gear and eat thy breakfast if thee wants to go with me," Amos rumbled. "I aim to be on my way before noon. Ladies, pull yourselves together and do some praying. We'll get that young fellow out of there in no time."

"They may seize the boat and find the slaves," Amelia said slowly. "Those poor people will have to face being returned to their masters." She paused. "That seems worse than Alex's injuries." She looked at Olivia and touched her hand. "Now, eat your breakfast so we can leave."

When they reached the jail at Hadenport, the jailer looked at the women. "Only one of you can go in, and I 'spect it oughta be the mister." Amos nodded and went on in.

Olivia paced the floor while the others sat quietly on the splintery benches. Amos returned quickly and rushed them outside.

He nodded toward Olivia. "He's going to be fine. It wasn't a bad wound. He's fearfully worried about those people, and I'll have to search around a bit, see if they need help. They arraigned him under the Act, charging that he's guilty of refusing to support and uphold the law. Unless someone can help him, it looks like six months in prison and up to one thousand dollars fine for every slave he's stolen."

"Stolen!" Olivia gasped. "That makes him sound like a common criminal."

Grimly Amos said, "We need to go home and get a prayer meeting started. Praying for those people to make it to the Promised Land does two things—makes them safe, and Alex too."

CHAPTER 40

Leaving the jail, Amos drove directly home. They stopped only long enough to drop Olivia at the front door. Sadie said, "We're going to the meeting house." Her lips were a firm line and her eyes snapped as she added, "This is one the enemy isn't going to get. Do as intended, Olivia, while we organize prayer for them all."

Olivia went inside and began rummaging through Matthew's clothes until she found dungarees and a faded blue shirt. Quickly she changed. Pinning her hair on top of her head, she said to Amelia who had been watching her, "I need a hat to cover this."

"There's Amos' old straw hat; will that do? What about shoes?"

"I think Sadie's old boots will work." Olivia looked at the mirrored image that closely resembled a young boy.

She followed Amelia downstairs. "I prefer bareback; that will fit the image better, don't you think?"

Amelia nodded. Narrowing her eyes she looked at Olivia saying, "You're taking this pretty hard."

"We've worked hard to bring the people this far."

"I'm talking about Alex. Olivia, it's obvious you love him."

"And it's obvious you don't know what you're talking about," Olivia muttered. "Alex is a friend. I intend to return home as soon as the problem is handled."

"Like you did last time?" Amelia grinned as she shoved the packet of bread and cheese into her hand. "Want a bottle of water?" Olivia nodded and Amelia continued, "I suppose you're not interested in taking advice from the likes of me, but don't make a mistake. I did. Sometimes you can't retrace your steps."

Avoiding Amelia's eyes, Olivia slowly pulled on the straw hat and picked up the bottle of water. "I'll ride as far as I can today. According to Amos' map, I should be able to contact two stations. What I find will determine whether I go on."

Olivia put the bridle on the young mare in the pasture, and led her to the fence. Crawling on her back, she chuckled, "It's a good thing I grew up on horses." She patted the mare's neck.

The July sun scorched through Matthew's thin cotton shirt as she left the pasture. Olivia pulled the shirttails free and settled the hat firmly on her head. "There. I look like a youth more intent on fishing than hunting," she murmured.

Just ahead the road curved into the forest and she welcomed the shade as she urged the horse into a lope.

The first station was at the northernmost curve of the Ohio. Olivia studied the paper she held in her hands. "Jasper is their name. Go straight north of the Duggle wharf. Stone house. There's a red barn with an open hayloft window. The safe flag is hay visible in the window."

The slanting afternoon sun had tempered the blast of heat, and the sun was on her back as she rode up the lane. She found the house and the barn. The window above the barn door was empty. Trying to appear at ease, she tucked her shirt back into the trousers and straightened her hat, and then walked to the house.

The woman who appeared in the doorway eyed her with suspicion. "I know nothing about a steamboat called the *Golden Awl*, nor a man by the name of Matthew Thomas." Her face softened slightly as she looked at Olivia. "Want to come have a glass of buttermilk?"

Olivia said, "I would appreciate it very much. I'll need to ride on."

While she sat at the table and sipped the buttermilk, the woman said, "We haven't had visitors for quite some time." The sharp eyes conveyed the message, and Olivia nodded.

She finished the buttermilk and stood up. "I must go. Thank you."

According to the map she carried, the next station was far north and east of the rounding curve of the Ohio. For some time Olivia contemplated the significance of its position and then touched the point on the map showing the southernmost station, south of Pittsburgh. While the horse moved restlessly under her, she mused, "It isn't logical to consider them traveling south, away from Canada. I'll head for this northern station."

The sun was setting when Olivia arrived at the tiny farmhouse with the big stone barn. She eyed the barn and smiled; it seemed a likely place to house slaves.

As soon as they opened the door to her, the elderly couple led her to the supper table. Olivia hesitated, shrugged, and pulled off the hat. The man's eyes twinkled. "Thought for certain you were a boy. I'm Jake Warner, and this is Isabel. Why are you out wandering around by yourself?"

His gentle question had Olivia blinking back tears in her eyes. Isabel said, "You're tired. Sit here, have your supper, and then tell us about it."

As soon as they finished eating, Olivia explained her journey. Jake shook his head. "There's not been a bunch through here for a month. Seems likely to me that they've headed north before now. People don't linger long on these trails."

"Likely you've missed them. Now, about that steamboat." He stopped and rubbed his forehead, looked up, and said, "I don't know where you'd hide a steamboat in these parts. There's not a waterway connecting with the Ohio that would take a steamboat, even in flood stage. About all I can do is be alert to news drifting this way. Is there a message for them?"

She hesitated, but desperation forced her to say, "Tell them Alex has been arrested. He's been charged with refusing to cooperate with the terms of the Fugitive Slave Act."

Jake shook his head. "That's bad. They'll have a case against him if they find the slaves. Guess about all we can do right now is pray. Now you come get a good night's sleep."

Early the next morning Olivia turned the mare homeward. Her heart was heavy as she thanked the Warners for their hospitality. Jake's eyes were filled with sympathy as he said, "At our age it seems all we can do is pray and keep an open door."

Looking into his face, she said, "You'll never know how important that is."

The long morning and afternoon ride gave her plenty of time to review the past week. She was nearly to the Coopers' home when one inescapable fact pressed against her mind. Rather than Alex's arrest pushing her away from him and his activities, it was binding her closer. With dismay, she regarded the situation and the words burst from her, "God, I don't want to be bound to him. I want freedom."

Freedom from what? She slumped on the horse and contemplated obedience. God, obedience, and Alex seem to be all mixed up together. Does love have no freedom?

After supper, while Olivia dried dishes, she asked Sadie, "If you hadn't married Amos, Sadie, would you have thought yourself in rebellion—toward God?"

Sadie eyebrows arched. "Rebellion! My, no." She frowned, "But then, I never considered doing otherwise. Since we were thirteen, neither one of us could see anyone else."

Olivia sighed and saw Sadie's sharp questioning glance. "He's a wonderful lad. Guess the Lord does concern himself with our marriage partners, but Amos and I didn't need urging." She paused. "What I mean is, if the good Lord directs our paths, isn't it natural He leads us to the right mate? What disturbs me about thee is that I know the good Lord gives love as a guideline. I'd have thought thee two were in love with each other."

———

Olivia awakened that night to find her face drenched with tears. She took her shawl and tiptoed out of the room she and Amelia shared. Sitting in the rocking chair in the alcove, she looked at the stars and let the dream fill her mind again. It was just one scene, but it had revealed a hidden layer of herself: a picture of Alex and Olivia, walking hand in hand. Gone were the dear scenes of home; there were only barren, unrecognizable hills. But with her hand held firmly in his, it seemed beauty surrounded them.

Olivia hugged her knees to her chin and the tears streamed down her face. Where there had been hardness, now there was a blooming softness in her heart.

She got up. Pulling the shawl around her shoulders, she wandered through the house to the one spot most likely to comfort. On her knees beside Alex's bed, she whispered, "I can't be a Christian the easy way, can I Lord? To be honest with You, I must face the hard questions You ask. You deserve—require—all of me. A complete me. That's the only way Christianity really works, isn't it? I see it now. Complete honesty. Not because You are a demanding God, but because you are a perfect God." Finally her trembling and the tears eased and she could face Him, whispering out the confession. "Dear Father, how could I have denied love through my own selfishness? I acknowledge what I should have known all along. It was fear, not trust in You. Where You are, Alex and I will be wrapped in love. Where You lead, we will be safe and at home in Your love." While Olivia sobbed, the desire for home and luxury and freedom from care dissipated.

Finally she was able to say, "Now I've faced myself as you see me, Lord, and it was ugliness. I dare to love and trust You, and that love leads me to him. Father, I give myself to You, all of me. I'll be obedient to You always. I have something deep inside that tells me it won't be easy, but I am determined to allow You to control my life. And I know the first step of obedience."

She crawled onto the bed, and with her head on Alex's pillow, she slept.

In the morning, after breakfast, Olivia came into the kitchen. Sadie looked at Matthew's clothes, Amos' hat, and her boots. Her eyebrows arched. "Where dost thou think thou art going?"

"To tell Alex I'll marry him."

A tiny smile touched Sadie's eyes. "And thou thinkest to impress him in that outfit?"

"No, but that jailer wouldn't let me see him the other day. Dressed as a boy, I'll be certain of getting past him."

"Then take him these tarts and meat pastries. He never seems to get enough to eat. When thou return, we need to have some cooking lessons. I doubt he will provide thee with a servant."

Olivia smiled. "I doubt that also." Impulsively, she kissed Sadie.

"Oh, my! I just recalled. Yesterday before thee returned, I thought I should have said something, since Matthew is thy brother."

"What?"

"There is a letter from thy father. 'Tis addressed to Matthew, but perhaps, since he isn't here—"

"Yes, I will need to open it," Olivia said. "He would want me to. Oh, dear, I hope Matthew and Crystal come soon."

Sadie carried the letter to Olivia, and sat at the table with a worried frown on her face as Olivia read, gasped and with shaking hands, spread the letter on the table. "Oh, my! Father is angry. Sadie, what shall I do? Father is coming to take me home."

"I guess thee goes. Since thou art an unmarried girl, and under the care of thy father, thee must."

Olivia looked at Sadie with a startled expression, glanced down at the letter and asked, "How long have you had the letter?"

"I believe—since June."

Olivia said, "Father's intentions were to take the next steamboat here. Sadie, I'm afraid he'll be here any day." She pushed her hands against her hot cheeks and murmured, "How I wish there was some place to hide."

"Child! That isn't honoring thy father. He will have every right obligation to carry you to home and safety. A daughter is too delicate to be running around the country. I would object also."

"But if I were married he could not force me to go."

"Well, that is correct, but thou art not even engaged."

Olivia studied Sadie's face with narrowed eyes. She said, "How do I contact your Pastor Jennings?"

"Olivia, what dost thou intend?"

"To be married before nightfall."

"With a husband in prison?"

"But still my husband."

"What makes thee think he will agree?"

Olivia took a deep breath. "Sadie, I don't think he will refuse."

Sadie got to her feet. Hands on hips, she said, "Thee can't be married in Matthew's breeches. Get dressed while Amos goes after Pastor Jennings."

They were nearly to Hadenport when Sadie turned to Olivia with a worried frown. "I thought thee didn't love Alex."

"I do!" She hugged Sadie. "I do ever so much."

Amos rode and quickly found Pastor Jennings, whose pale blue eyes sparkled with excitement when told of the situation. "I like a spot of the unexpected once in a while. To think this will help along the abolitionist movement is a joy." The two men then rode into Hadenport and met up with Olivia and Sadie.

While Olivia wondered what conversation had taken place before the men arrived, she watched Amos settle into his collar. Sadie opened her mouth and then firmly closed it.

When all of them reached the jail, Olivia faced the three. She discovered she was trembling. Lifting her chin, she firmly said, "I will see Alex first. Will you please wait in the office for me?"

Her bravado carried her sailing into the office. "I want to see Alexander Duncan, please."

It was the same man. His Adam's apple bobbed, and he blinked nearly colorless eyes. In a monotone he said, "Only one visitor is allowed. One of the men may go in."

"I will go in." She took a step closer, he retreated, and she followed.

"Regulations," he said. She smiled, refusing to be denied, and started for the inner door. "Now, ma'am—" She smiled again, and he opened the door. Olivia hurried down the hall to the room with bars.

"Alex!"

"Olivia," he said slowly, "I didn't expect to see you again."

"Oh, your poor face!" She caught her breath, glanced at the jailer, and said, "May we be alone?"

He shook his head. "Regulations." Olivia took a deep breath and moved closer to the bars. "Stay back!" the man snapped.

"Alex," Olivia said, "remember you said the next move must be mine? Well, I'm taking it now." His eyes were remote, curious. She gulped. "I have Pastor Jennings and the Coopers outside. Pastor Jennings has said he'll perform the marriage ceremony for us now."

Alex paled. "What's the meaning of this?"

The jailer hastily interrupted. "There's no such thing ever taken place here."

"This shall be the first." Olivia lifted her chin. "We must get married now, today." The jailer glanced at her waistline and then at Alex. His jaw tightened and a strange gleam brightened his eyes.

"Don't think much of the likes of fellows such as you. All right lady, I'll go get the parson."

She looked at his departing back and flew to the bars. "Alex, don't say no! I love you. Father is coming to take me home. Please, just cooperate!"

Alex released his breath in an explosion of sound. "My dear! What did you say?"

"Father is—" That wasn't what he meant. Quickly she thrust her hand through the bars and touched his face. "Alexander Duncan, I love you with all my heart, and I want you to marry me right now. Last night I decided I would marry you—before I saw the letter. Will you marry me now?"

He took her hand and held it to his cheek, his lips. "Most certainly, my darling. But I'm afraid I'll wake up!" She heard the sound of footsteps approaching and watched him blink away tears as he thrust his hands through the bars to greet Sadie and Amos.

Parson Jennings held the black book to his chest and said, "In the sight of God and man, Alexander Duncan, do you take this woman to be your wife?"

And then Olivia promised, "In sickness and health, as long as we both shall live."

Alex asked the jailer, "Do I get to kiss my wife?"

The jailer shook his head, nearly regretfully. "Regulations. In six months, when you're out of here."

The following morning, Sadie opened the door to Olivia's father. "Mr. Thomas, come into the parlor. Olivia is washing dishes, but I'll get her."

Olivia hurried into the room and lifted her face to her father. He kissed her cheek, pulled her to a chair, and demanded, "Are you some kind of hired girl?"

"No, I help because I wish to do so. Father, unfortunately Matthew isn't here right now. We've just returned from a trip; both he and his wife are with the boat. I don't know when they will return." She took a deep breath. "Unfortunately, I didn't have time to inform you that I'm married, too."

"Olivia," he sighed. "Do you mean I've made this trip for nothing?"

"I'm sorry, Father, but of course I intend to stay with my husband."

His chin dropped to his chest. "Well, I'd like to meet the fellow. I must say I don't approve of my children rushing into marriage without our blessing. What is his name, and where is he?"

"His name is Alexander Duncan." She paused, resisting the urge to impress him with Alex's lineage. "Unfortunately, unless you feel up to another drive, you can't meet him. He's in jail."

He met her statement with stunned silence. Watching his gray face, Olivia nearly regretted her hasty action. "Father, Alex was jailed for helping slaves escape." Instantly she saw that statement made the matter worse.

"I will have this annulled," he whispered.

"No, Father. I am adult; I love this man, and I intend to share my life with him. The life he has chosen."

Wearily he got to his feet. "Let's go see the young man."

CHAPTER 41

T his time Olivia discovered that occasionally the jailer didn't say "Regulations." He looked from Father's gold-headed cane to his white hair and brought Alex into his office. Amused, Olivia watched the man move chairs.

"Sir," Alex murmured, "I am pleased to make your acquaintance, although these circumstances aren't most favorable. I realize it must be extremely difficult to welcome a jailbird into the family." He paused, "I hope that someday both of the families can be together under better conditions."

Within minutes, Olivia's father rumbled, "I like you, son. Let's get you out of this place right now."

"The only way that would be possible, Sir, is to compromise all I stand for. You could easily buy my freedom, but to do so would force me to surrender to them." He took a deep breath and added, "My father is also a plantation owner—in South Carolina and Louisiana. Olivia and I know we are working against the values both of you hold most dear. But this is a new era, and while you cling to the old traditions, we are recognizing the need for change. Our consciences can no longer bow to slavery."

"You will destroy us all."

"I'm sorry, Sir. My heart aches for you, just as it does for my own father. I don't wish to see either of you suffer. But I can't compromise with God in order to please you or my father."

Cornelius Thomas got to his feet. "Sally Ann and I will be happy to welcome you as our son. But we will pray to God that you get your head on straight. Nevertheless—" he turned his head stiffly. "Daughter, we must go."

Alex's eyes were filled with misery. Olivia blinked to keep from crying. She touched his face. That wasn't enough. For a moment they clung together, and she felt his lips against her hair.

As Cornelius turned away, he said, "Six months is a long time."

"I know, Sir," Alex's voice was husky, "It seems like forever."

Cornelius stayed only until the end of the week. "I can't wait any longer," he stated, carrying his valise down to the hall. "Matthew is likely to be gone for weeks."

Amos brought the wagon around. Cornelius looked at Olivia and said, "I must tell you, a friend of Matthew's requested his address. I gave him information. Since he seemed so eager to make contact with Matthew, you may keep the letter from him. His name is Lucas Tristram, an old classmate."

———

At the first of the week, Matthew and Crystal returned. They arrived by hack, and Olivia could scarcely wait to get them in the door before she began her questions.

Matthew warded off the questions, saying, "Come sit down, all of you, and I'll tell you what has happened on our end. The *Awl* has been run aground up a river flowing into the Ohio. The mouth of the river is just below the north curve on the Ohio. We didn't dare stop before then."

"You knew we had trouble?"

Matthew grinned down at Olivia, "We, you say! I didn't know you had gone with Alex until Crystal checked the cabin later." He shook his head. "One of these days you'll get yourself into a situation we won't be able to rectify."

"I think I have."

He glanced at her and added, "Back to my story. We'd figured that the *Awl* had taken us as far as possible, so Caleb took the slaves and headed for the station up north, pretty close to Erie. He had the name of a man who uses his boat to carry slaves across Lake Erie to Canada. That's the last I've heard of him. Crystal and I had to wait for a ride into Pittsburgh and then for passage back down."

He turned to Olivia. "Now what have you done?"

"Alex and I are married."

He grinned slowly. "Well, that tops anything I can come up with. Why the hurry?"

"Father came after me. We managed to beat him by a day. Fortunately, he never thought to ask how long we had been married."

"Where's Alex?"

"In jail. Paddyrollers. He's been arraigned, and unless there's a miracle, he'll be there for six months. He's going to need money. A thousand dollars for each slave he's stolen."

"Stolen!"

"That's their word for freed."

"Guess I'd better go see him. Want to come with me, Olivia?"

"No. I was there early this morning. Besides, they usually let only one person in at a time—unless it's someone like Father."

Olivia watched Matthew and Crystal as they went up to their room, then with a sigh she turned down the hall. "Sadie, need some help?" she called as she entered the kitchen. She stopped. Sadie and Amelia looked up. "Oh, I'm sorry," she said. "I didn't mean to interrupt your conversation."

Sadie stood up. " 'Tis time to pick vegetables for dinner. My, I dread the winter months when there's not a fresh vegetable outside of carrots and onions." She took her pan and hurried out the door.

Olivia watched her go, saying, "Something is disturbing Sadie."

"She has marriage fever," Amelia drawled. "Had such good luck with you and Crystal, now she's working on me. I had to tell her to back down."

"What do you mean?"

"Remember the fellow who's wife died last winter? Well, she pinned me in the corner and wouldn't let me go until I set her straight. To say the least, I disappointed her."

"Oh. You don't want a ready-made family."

"I don't want any family. Guess I had to get rough with her." Amelia glanced at Olivia. "I'm married. That's why I left home. For me marriage is just too confining."

Olivia went to peek in the simmering kettle. "Sorry," Amelia said. "Guess that's not going to set too well with a newlywed."

"You notice I'm not asking."

"Thank you." She stood up and left the room.

Olivia sighed and went to the door of Alex's room. Her eyes caressed his old jacket, the neat stack of papers on the chest, and the pillow that bore the imprint of her head. "Dear Lord, please keep him safe and bring him home soon."

Crystal came in. "I went looking for you, and Amelia said you'd moved down to Alex's room." She studied Olivia's face and gave her a quick hug. "I'm glad for you," she whispered. "Alex is a wonderful person. Only, it must be so sad—you haven't had a honeymoon yet."

Olivia smiled. "About the best we can hope for a honeymoon will be another trip in the *Golden Awl*."

"Aren't you getting tired of that?"

"I guess it isn't my idea of luxury, but I keep thinking of the people."

Crystal turned away. Olivia touched her arm. "Have you told Matthew about Joseph?"

"No." Crystal shook her head and left the room.

I know what it is like, my dear sister-in-law. The rebellion against the God of the Universe. I pray you find a way to resolve your guilt before it tears you apart, or worse yet—both of you. Olivia sighed and went to help Sadie.

———

Crystal bent over her husband. "Lazy, precious husband," she murmured, nuzzling his ear. "Do you remember? Last night you promised Amos you'd help him shoe that filly."

"Kisses before breakfast, Crystal?" He shoved his pillow at her.

"My dear," she teased, "you sound as if you've been married at least twenty years."

He sat up and studied her with a frown. "Where are you going in that outfit?"

"I'm cleaning house. If you stay in that bed a moment longer, I'll let you shake rugs for me."

With a shudder he left the bed. "Housework! I can't believe the torture Northerners willingly endure."

Later Crystal gathered the rugs and carried them downstairs. As she started for the door, Olivia hurried out of the parlor. "Crystal!" She stopped in the middle of the hall and stared at the woman. "What are you doing? Where did you find that dress?"

Crystal looked from the frock to Olivia's face. "Is it that bad?" she faltered. "I borrowed it from Sadie's barrel. I couldn't clean house in silk moire."

"Bad isn't the word," Olivia said slowly looking up from her examination of the brown print cotton with the too-tight bodice. "Your buttons don't do the job. Oh, well, the men aren't going to be in the house. Wave a dust mop at them and they all take off. Matter of fact, you'll have the place to yourself. I'm going to help Sadie pick beans this morning. This afternoon I'm going to visit Alex." With a faraway look in her eyes, she sighed and started for the kitchen.

Crystal finished cleaning the upstairs rooms and came down to get the rugs she had left airing outside the house.

As she reached the main floor, there was a knock on the door. She tugged at her bodice and hurried to the door.

The man standing there had started to turn away. When she pulled the door open he came back. His impatient frown disappeared as he surveyed her, lingering over the bodice and mob-cap. "I think I like Pennsylvania country life. However, I didn't expect to find such lush living. Is the master or your mistress at home?"

She studied his cocky smile and the spotless white suit he wore. "To whom do you wish to speak?"

He hesitated and something changed in his eyes. "I'm looking for Matthew Thomas. Do you know of him?"

Coldly she said, "You'll find him in the pasture." She closed the door. Snatching the cap from her head, she ran up the stairs. In her room she stopped to look at herself in the mirror for one minute before she pulled off the dress.

"All day long," she fumed, "people have been saying this to you, and you have paid them no mind. Do you have to be hit over the head before you'll accept what others so readily see?" With a shudder she surveyed the mirrored figure dressed only in chemise and pantaloons. It didn't matter that the chemise was the most delicate of lace, the mirror confirmed the earlier impression. "Just a plain old nigger. Oh, God! What do I do?"

Slowly she bathed and selected her most delicate gown. When she went downstairs and into the parlor, Matthew and the stranger jumped to their feet.

Matthew came to her and took her hand. "My dear, I want you to meet Lucas Tristram, a classmate of mine from Harvard."

"Mrs. Thomas—" he bent over her hand. "How delighted I am to find someone has finally taken pity on Matthew and married him!" For a moment, his eyes mocked her and terror filled her heart.

"Mr. Tristram," she said slowly, "do you live in the area?"

"No. The truth is I've come just to see Matthew. His father kindly supplied his address." Tristram bowed toward Matthew. "You may be wondering why I've traveled this far for a social call. It isn't only that. If you'll be my guests this evening, we'll find time to talk about it."

Matthew laughed, "Then you'll need to wait for me to wash the pasture and horses off myself. Crystal, you look absolutely stunning the way you are, darling. Will you entertain our guest while I bathe?" He headed for the stairs, and Crystal slowly faced the man.

"May I offer you some of Sadie's fresh peach nectar, or would you prefer cold buttermilk? The Coopers have a wonderful root cellar with an icy cold stream to keep us supplied with chilled drinks."

"The nectar," he said with a smile. "Now I suppose you must go back to playing maid?"

Without answering him she walked toward the kitchen. Sadie and Olivia came into the kitchen with a basket of dried beans. Their hands were dusty and their hair disheveled.

"We have a guest, a friend of Matthew's. Do you care to meet him now?"

Olivia took in the grandeur of Crystal's gown and grinned. "That sounds like a good idea." She hurried down the hall.

Sadie looked from Crystal to Olivia's departing back. "Oh dear, she's so dirty. Well," she shrugged, wiped her hands on a towel and followed Olivia.

Crystal cocked her head, listened to the voices and headed for the back door. With a smile, she said, "Olivia and Sadie, I think you deserve peach nectar, too."

When Olivia reached Hadenport, the jailer escorted her back to Alex's cell. Turning his piercing gaze on her, he said, "I could spend all my time guarding this fella while he has guests. I've got work to do. I'll leave the door open, and don't you get close to them bars." He marched away. Olivia thrust her hand through the bars, touched Alex's face, and then stepped back.

With a catch in her voice she said, "This is worse than the Female Academy in Boston."

He tried to smile. "Olivia, you'll have me standing in the corner yet."

"I'm sorry," she whispered. "It's been so long—the weeks have been forever—and I just simply had to touch you."

His voice was husky as he said, "Tell me about yourself. I seldom see you alone. Have you been reading your Bible?"

"Oh, Alex, I'm afraid I'm ruining it with my tears."

"I'll buy you another one and write in it the things I didn't dare write before."

"What?"

" 'To Olivia, you are my love.' " Her hand stretched toward him and he shook his head. "He may make you leave."

She bit her lip and looked up, blinking tears. Hastily she said, "Alex, does God always come on tiptoe?"

"What do you mean?"

"I told you about the dream. It was as if God had turned everything inside of me right side up. Life was changed. Alex, I haven't had opportunity to tell you all that happened that night. I'd like to now."

"I've been wanting to know, but sensed it wasn't something you'd care to share with everyone coming through here."

She rubbed a fingernail and looked up. "Alex, I nearly turned my back on God. My selfish desires—" She saw his face and knew he understood completely. "Alex, they're changed. I'll admit I was nearly ready to run away from you, back to security and freedom. Freedom? Strange, now I know it's just the opposite; it's here with God and you. Please don't look like that. I'll never want anything except His will. And I'm no longer afraid of Him; His will is suddenly beautiful.

"But Alex, for a long time God's will was whispered into me in such a gentle, loving way I nearly ignored it. That night I realized what I was doing. This is the God of the universe, Creator, Savior—how could I have treated Him like a lackey, sent to make me comfortable?"

She took a step closer and whispered, "Alex, I appreciated the dream so much. It was as if God lifted me and enabled me to do what I couldn't do for myself—trust Him."

"But you were starting to move toward Him," Alex countered, "I could see the change in you."

"His gentleness and patience with me was nearly my downfall. I expected Him to treat me like a doting daddy. I forgot Who He really is until that night when that gentle finger touched all the ugliness in me and I knew I dared not hold onto one bit of my selfishness. The dream was a door opening my mind. Suddenly my whole being was turned around, and I felt I was started in the right direction." She paused. "You talked about directions. I thought it meant my direction, but you meant God's direction. It's God's way when we follow repentance, isn't it?"

"Yes, my dear. And now our jailer is coming. I must say I love you. I miss you—"

"I pray constantly that soon—" The man was there, and Olivia turned away.

In the early morning, with the sound of birds and the scent of autumn with its fresh hay perfume coming through the window, Crystal pushed her pillow into a wedge and studied her husband's face.

When she could no longer resist, she lightly drew her finger down the plane of his face. Without opening his eyes he moved closer. "Matthew?" Finally he opened one eye. "What does that Tristram fellow want?"

He opened both eyes and raised himself to his elbow. "I don't think you like him."

"I don't. I've seen too many just like him in New Orleans. He's the perfect dandy who—"

"What were you going to say?"

"Nothing I guess. But tell me about him. I know you talked after I came upstairs last night."

"And I'm still trying to put it all together. Your 'perfect dandy' describes the way he impressed me while we were in school." He gave her a quick look. "I know you guessed him to be a good friend of mine, but he isn't. I did form an opinion of him, however, and I don't think it's changed much. Right now, if his words are to be trusted, it seems someone has placed a great deal of confidence in him. He appears to have a fund of information which, if true, comes from someone high in Southern politics."

"What does he want?"

"Bright boys to come home and learn how to support the South with all their talents, brains, and money. At least he was candid."

"Does that appeal to you?"

"I don't know. I'm getting a little tired of this game. There isn't enough going on. And frankly, I don't want to risk spending six months in jail like Alex is doing. But on the other hand, I agree with many of Alex's ideas. This is a time of change for the South. The slaves must be freed; it is the only decent way to treat them."

"Decent? That doesn't sound—compassionate."

He shrugged. "Perhaps, but candid. Crystal, I can't pretend something I'm not. I don't have Alex's call. In addition, without slaves, how does the South continue to support their cotton and rice agriculture? It's a dilemma."

He paused, then smiled and drew her close. "How would you like to be a senator's wife?"

CHAPTER 42

When Olivia had swept her way out the front door, she paused to lean on the broom and blink in the morning sun. From habit she looked down the hill, half hoping to see the *Golden Awl* at dock. The wharf was empty. She watched a flock of ducks circle and drop into the water. "They are beginning to migrate," she said, just then becoming aware of the changes in the landscape.

The grass covering the hillside was drying and beginning to turn brown. The hickory tree had touches of autumn color, while apple trees across the pasture bent under heavy-laden boughs.

"September. Has it been seven weeks since they locked Alex away? How long Lord?" The complaint turned to prayer. "Father, be gracious to him. Yesterday he seemed discouraged and so very lonely. But not more lonely than I. Father—please deliver him!"

Olivia turned her back on the sunshine and carried the broom into the house. Crystal came slowly down the stairs. Seeing the shadows in her eyes, Olivia said, "I can guess. Lucas Tristram is still trying to pressure Matthew into joining his crusade. Why does he think his project can help the South?"

"I don't think he has much of a crusade going. To me it seems he is a small frog making a big splash."

Olivia laughed. "Don't let him know you feel that way; he'll feel obligated to defend his honor and challenge Matthew to a duel."

"He has been saying strong things to Matthew. And if Matthew hadn't been questioning the values he's always known, I think he would be gone in a moment. Thanks to Alex, he's been doing some deep thinking. Maybe he will make Lucas take a hard look at himself." She moved restlessly around the hall. "Olivia, I think Matthew is only half committed to this cause, and partly only because Alex has been so terribly burdened by the condition of these people.

"Matthew is emotionally fragmented inside because he has no reason to decide either for or against. To him Alex seems more like a crusader than simply a man with a desire to help people. Matthew is simply excited for the moment. That worries me terribly."

She turned and sighed. "Right now, Matthew and Lucas are sitting in the pub, going over and over the same arguments. Do you know where Sadie and Amos are? I expected them to be here now. I'm to ride into town."

"Yes, they went to see Alex. Amelia rode with them. I'm not certain what her mission is today."

Crystal started for the stairs and turned. "You'll be proud of me," she said with a twisted smile. "While Sadie and Amos are at the meetinghouse today, I'm going to visit Joseph."

"Crystal, that's wonderful!" Olivia said. "Give him our regards."

She nodded. "I'm going to get a light wrap and meet the wagon out on the road. I'm certain we'll be late getting back," she added, "so don't plan dinner early."

When Crystal left, Olivia finished dusting the parlor and carried her broom to the kitchen. As she poured coffee for herself, she heard the jangle of harness and paused. "Amos is back. He didn't have much of a visit. Poor Alex—he's so lonely." She listened. The wagon paused only momentarily and then left.

The front door crashed open. "Olivia!" For a moment she couldn't move. He rushed into the kitchen.

"Alex!" It wasn't a dream. His arms were holding her tight and in a wild dance of jubilation he swung her around the kitchen. "Oh, Alex, put me down! Let me see you. Are you home to stay?"

"No questions until I kiss you." She touched his beard, and her arms went around his neck. Nearly fainting, she clung and pressed close. While he called her name again and again, he kissed her.

He held her away, looked at her, and touched her face with a fingertip. "My beautiful wife," he whispered brokenly, "I can scarcely believe this. Olivia, I used to be afraid you would never want me to kiss you. Why—back then were you so very angry? I don't remember, did I act—in a way I should not have?"

She shook her head against his shoulder. "Alex, for a kiss it was perfectly respectable. I—I guess it was, but—" She was silent, thinking back. Blushing, she admitted, "But from that moment on, I never again belonged to myself, and that was very frightening." She leaned back to look at him. "I didn't understand for a long time, I knew only that I was disturbed every time I thought of it. Angry? Could that have been love beginning?"

He nodded, "For me it was. I could never get you out of my mind after that evening."

"But you never came again."

"I felt completely unworthy, and underneath it all I was fearful of what I had done to you. See, I didn't forget the slap!"

With a sigh she slipped out of his arms and looked at him. "Alexander Duncan, I'll not rest easy until you tell me why you are here when your sentence was to have been six months."

He tugged her hand. "Come, sit down. I've a great deal to say to you."

Olivia poured coffee for him. When they were seated across the table from each other, he said, "Last week they scheduled a hearing for me. One of the beautiful principles of this country is that it is illegal to hold a prisoner indefinitely without a valid charge against him."

"You didn't tell me about the hearing."

"I couldn't bear to get your hopes up, when I had nothing to offer except a prayer for release."

"But you are released?"

He nodded. "The charges are dropped. The attorney for the paddyrollers can't locate his clients right now. I suspect those men were completely confident that when they had me, they would find the slaves." He paused and added, "I find it strange that they didn't discover the *Awl* when it's aground such a short distance away."

Slowly it began to sink in. Alex was really free! The tears began to roll down her cheeks as she reached for his hand. "Free. Oh Alex, you are free. Never again will you have to—"

Roughly he broke in, saying, "Olivia, that's what I must say. Are you certain you want to be married to me?"

"With all my heart."

"Then if you wish, I'll give up this project and we'll go home. To Mississippi or South Carolina."

She frowned. "Alex, why are you saying this?"

"Because I love you too much to subject you to this kind of life against your will."

"But your commitment to God?"

"—Must include my wife's. If we are to be one, then our commitment to God must reflect this oneness."

"Alex, my dear husband! I dared not love you until I faced God and said, 'Yes—anywhere, and anything.'

"See? For a long time I was afraid of you, and finally I started trusting God enough to understand. A commitment had to be made before I was free to love you with all my heart. Your commitment is my commitment too." Olivia got to her feet and as she started around the table, she stumbled over Alex's bag.

He came around the table, catching her as she stumbled. "My dear! That bag, I'll put it away."

Carrying it to his bedroom, he opened the door and stopped. Olivia pressed her face against his arm. "I've been staying in here while you were gone. I needed—"

He turned to look at her.

"I wanted to be close to you," she whispered, touching his face. Gently he took her hand, led her into the room, and closed the door. "Alex!" She saw the smile on his face, and lifted her arms. "Now you are home with me!"

———

Crystal walked slowly past the blacksmith shop, came back and turned in. The burly man left the forge and came toward her. "Do you have a Negro named Joseph working here?"

The smithy nodded. "Not here today. Leg's been bothering him some." He turned to point. "Lives in that little house over there."

"Thank you." She left the shop uneasily and walked over to Joseph's house, aware that the man continued to watch her.

When Joseph answered her knock, Crystal saw the tears spring to his eyes, and guilt swept over her. She pushed at the door and walked in. "Joseph, your leg is bothering you, isn't it?" Using his thumbs to wipe his eyes, he nodded. "I'm sorry, I've neglected you. There's no excuse. But you do know I'm married, don't you?"

Again he nodded. Limping, he brought forward the only chair in the room. "Missy, you don't need to apologize. I'm just glad to see you. May I offer you a cup of tea?" She nodded and he reached for the can on the shelf.

Crystal turned slowly, taking in all the details of the poor room, with its bench for a bed and a three legged table. Pegs held Joseph's wardrobe, and she could see the fireplace served both for heat and cooking. She watched Joseph ladle hot water from the iron pot hanging close to the flames.

Crystal stayed for an hour. Their conversation was stilted as they avoided the subject that bound them both. Finally Crystal rose. "Joseph, I must leave, but I'm concerned that you need so much more than you have. Please, this is all I can do for you." She pressed the gold pieces into his hand.

He looked at the money and pushed it back. "Please, Missy. If they see a black man like me with this kind of money, they'll think I stole it. I can't take it."

The words were out before she thought. "Then I shall have to spend it for you. Tell me what you need. Is that the only blanket you have? What about a heavy coat? The winter will be cold. I shall buy food."

Lowering her head to avoid looking at him, she left the house. While walking down the main street of the small village, she investigated the shops and finally selected one that seemed to carry a large variety of merchandise.

Besides the coat and three blankets, she added underwear, heavy socks, shirts, and trousers. As she paid for the merchandise, she said, "All this will need to be delivered. May I rely upon you to take care of that for me?" The clerk nodded, and she said, "It is to be taken to the house beside the blacksmith shop. The man is Joseph, a freed slave. Now tell me where I can find a good grocery."

As she turned from the counter, she nearly bumped into the man behind her. "Ma'am—" He bowed with a deep mocking sweep. "We meet again."

"Mr. Tristram," Crystal said, hoping her dismay wasn't obvious.

"So you are shopping, and very generously so. Did I hear you say he is a freed slave? That is most kind of you. Pity more of our friends don't take this responsibility."

Crystal carefully controlled her irritation as she bowed and moved toward the door. The clerk called after her, "And I'm to let Joseph know you've chosen boots for him, and he's to pick them up?"

"That is correct. Thank you." Crystal hurried out the door. As she deliberately slowed her feet on the rough walk, she mulled over her encounter with Lucas Tristram. Recalling his mocking smile, her heart sank. "Mr. Tristram," she whispered, "I have a feeling you're not above using this incident to your own advantage. I've no idea what it could be, but your cynical eyes leave me shaking in my shoes."

Crystal entered the grocery, ordered generously of canned foods, cured meats, and staples. By the time she had paid her bill, Amos was waiting. The clerk carried her order to the wagon and Amos watched in silence as the bundles were loaded. As he flipped the reins along the horses' backs, he said, "Mighty generous of you, Crystal. I hope it doesn't cause a misunderstanding."

Lucas Tristram's face flashed through Crystal's thoughts as she murmured, "I do, too."

CHAPTER 43

At breakfast Amos carried in a stack of newspapers. "Alex, I've been saving these for thee. Thought thee'd be interested in articles about the Lincoln-Douglas Debates. There are some reference to the New York revivals. Gave me goose bumps to read it. Makes one think the Second Coming of Jesus Christ is right around the corner. Did thee know this move toward revival began in 1857? The *Watchman* and *Reflector* helped it on by their articles. From there it started catching fire. Now we're hearing it's moving west."

After breakfast Alex stayed on at the table to read the newspapers. Looking over the top of his paper, he addressed Olivia. "I'm afraid this war talk might foster that very thing. It seems the South is now constantly finding fault with the policies of the North. How I would like to hear Lincoln and Douglas!"

Matthew came into the room and Alex said, "What would you think about giving me a hand?"

"What do you have in mind?"

"Paying a visit to the *Golden Awl*. I need to see what needs to be done before we can move her. Won't have a boat if she's caught in the ice this winter."

He heard Olivia's sigh and looked up. He grinned, "Of course, we need cooks if we stay there for a week or so. Matt, is it level enough to live in?"

"Unless something's happened since we saw it. I think that's a good idea. I've been concerned, but didn't dare consider anything until Caleb comes back. Leaving it there makes it subject to vandalism."

"When can we start?"

Sadie came to the table. "I baked yesterday; there's bread, pie, and cookies."

"Want to come along, too?" Alex asked, grinning at her.

She patted his shoulder and said, "You like my cookies. These women can take care of you just fine."

"Alex, what if we are followed by those terrible men?"

He turned to look at Olivia. "My dear, I doubt that will happen. But even if it did, they wouldn't discover anything of significance. There's no evidence of the people having been there. If anything, being in jail has given me new confidence. I simply need to be certain the slaves aren't apprehended. No slaves, no evidence."

"How about leaving tomorrow?" Matthew asked.

"How about today?" Alex countered.

"I've got an appointment with Tristram this morning. He wants me to come to his hotel." Sadie sighed, and Matthew said, "I'm getting tired of it too. Right now I feel obligated to listen to his arguments. You realize I'm making a choice that may have ramifications for the rest of my life."

"I'd be interested in what he has to say."

"He's leaving this evening. I suppose he may come back. Depends on how the meeting goes today. In addition, I don't think he's going to waste his time on you," Matthew said dryly. "He sees you as having made up your mind."

"Doesn't think his arguments can hold up under pressure?"

"Alex, it's politics. You and I both know how the South feels about this growing tension. According to Tristram, and I must agree it makes sense, the Southern cause can best be fought in Washington."

"How's he going to get you there?"

"He seems to think there's no problem at all. Several times he's mentioned the influence both our families have. Crystal's and mine."

"But it's a gamble." Alex stated flatly. "Tell me, has he aired his view on Lincoln?"

"I don't think he's worried; he doesn't see him as a political threat. Seemed to view him as inept in about everything. However, he has mentioned that several of the strong governors in the South see Lincoln as a threat." He paused, adding thoughtfully, "Certainly Lincoln seems to have an ability to move those who listen to him."

After Matthew left, Alex said, "I think I'll ride over to the *Awl*, take a look myself. If it's feasible for us all to stay there, we can have Amos take us in the wagon tomorrow, with enough supplies to last us a week or so while we get the *Awl* running again."

"Oh!" Olivia exclaimed.

Sadie looked up and smiled at Olivia. "Can't stand to have him out of thy sight for a day? Well, ride along with him."

"I'd like that," Alex said, getting to his feet.

"I'll pack food for us."

Olivia quickly finished washing the dishes. Sadie chuckled, "Stars in thine eyes like I haven't seen before." Olivia blushed, and Sadie added, "Enjoy the good times; life has a way of settling back to normal all too soon."

Olivia sighed and admitted, "I'd hoped this would be normal."

"Seems as long as we're on this earth, life heaps up the work and troubles. Guess the secret to having marriage a little nicer than normal is making our partners more important than hoeing the beans, but not forgetting the beans altogether."

Alex came into the kitchen. "Amos doesn't have a sidesaddle."

"That's fine; I'll wear Matthew's dungarees."

When Olivia came back into the kitchen, Alex solemnly looked her over. "Sadie, there's only one problem that I see. She looks like a little boy. I've a feeling she runs the danger of being treated like a little boy."

He grinned at Olivia. "Come along, lad; you need to carry your share of the load. Might be I can find a hammer and screwdriver for you."

When they reached the *Awl*, Olivia mourned, "I rode within a mile of it! It didn't occur to me that they would leave the Ohio." Alex slid off his mare and went to hobble the horses in a grassy spot. Coming back to the boat, he shook his head, "Caleb was nearly foolish to head up here. But thinking those thugs were hot on his tail was enough to make him attempt this, and it has been proven wise. That is, if we can get it out of here." He held out a hand to Olivia. "Come along, favorite wife; let's look over the boat."

Both of them went in separate directions as they inspected the boat for damage. But at the end of an hour they were together again, and Alex said, "Even the firewood is still here. We have honest neighbors—or perhaps no one has discovered the boat. It's going to take a while to dig the paddles out of the sand. Looks like Caleb tried to flank it and the rear end swung just enough to bury the paddles. Knowing Caleb, he shut it down immediately, so I doubt there's severe damage."

"I've checked out the pilothouse and cabins," Olivia said. "The pilothouse is dirty. Dead leaves and such. Why don't they put windows in the front of pilothouses?"

"Glass cuts down on visibility and the pilot can't hear as well." He added, "Imagine trying to see through a window when the rain is coming at you."

"Are you going to start work today?"

"No, I'll make a list of things we need—like more shovels. We'll eat lunch and head back."

"We need to bring drinking water. Otherwise we'll have to find a well. I suppose you don't want to have too many neighbors knowing about this."

"Right." He faced her. "Makes me want to make another trip; how about you?"

"Whatever you say," she touched his cheek. "I don't care where we go, as long as you take me with you."

He wrapped his arms around her and snuggled her close. "One of the reasons I like the boat is because we've spent so much time here. It's home, and I can close the door and forget the world is out there."

"We have all afternoon," she mused. "Would you like coffee with your sandwich?"

———

The following day, after Amos had unloaded their gear and departed, Matthew surveyed the sandbar and the buried paddlewheel. Shoving his hands in his pockets, he paced the river bank and said, "I'm inclined to do it the easy way. How about using logs to build leverage under it?"

"It's going to make it difficult to keep dishes on the table," Alex said dryly. "Now, if we dig a little and then enjoy a day or so, we could try your method."

Matthew laughed and poked his arm. "I get you, my friend—hey, not friend. Brother." Matthew grinned. "That just dawned on me."

"Well, brother, if you agree, let's go find some coffee and get the pilothouse cleaned up. That ought to be work enough for today. Tomorrow we can check out the engine."

They found the cabin filled with the aroma of coffee while Crystal and Olivia sat with their heads together. Alex grinned at the two while the pink mounted in their cheeks. Chuckling, he took the coffee pot and mugs and headed for the pilothouse.

"Matthew, what do young brides talk about when they are alone?"

Surprised, Matthew frowned and shook his head. "Beats me—probably about how wonderful their husbands are."

"Spoken like a true Southern gentleman," Alex said. Matthew gave him a quick glance. As Alex took up the broom, he pondered the strange expression in Matthew's eyes. *He's confused and more than a little unhappy. Guess this project has the Lord's hand on it after all.*

By mid-afternoon, with the brass and windows shining, Alex said, "Looks top-notch. Might as well sit down and enjoy the place while it's still clean. I'll go down and get us some more coffee."

When Alex came back, he asked, "How did your meeting with Tristram go?"

Matthew sighed. "He passed a lot of words off on me. I'm still chewing on them. Made sense—I just don't know my own mind. Alex, he's given me a pretty heavy load about my responsibility to the South."

Alex poured more coffee. "Mind telling me? I scarcely remember the fellow. I remember a dandy image—slender, wore white most of the time. Got the idea he had a good opinion of himself."

"I guess that's fairly accurate. Remember Mallory?" Alex gave him a quick, startled glance, then he nodded. "Well, he's had contact with him and other unnamed gentlemen. Here's what it boils down to. Southern politicians are getting a little upset with the events occurring across the country. For a time it looked as if the South could at least maintain a balance of power."

"In Washington?"

"There, but also in the territories. I hadn't fully understood the uneasiness caused by all this business with the Compromise of 1850 and the Kansas-Nebraska Act, plus the shakiness the Dred Scott ruling has created. Tristram says the Northern reaction to the ruling made most of the Southern governors sit up and take notice."

"For what reason?"

"I think they are fearful the South is losing out. I feel somewhat that way. Seems if action isn't taken soon, there won't be a South as we know it. You are aware of the uniqueness of our life compared to the North. It's culture compared to—"

"Now Matt, that isn't fair. There's a difference, yes. But I don't believe it's culture the way you mean it, so much as values. The North seems to operate under a completely different value system. Granted, they aren't any nicer than our people, but there's things about the North I prefer."

"Such as?"

"I'll never forget the first time I saw a Negro gentleman walking down the streets of Boston."

"Alex, that word gentleman is an unbelievable contrast with the word Negro."

"Nevertheless, my eyes didn't deceive me. And it happened more than once. Dignified black men—dress, behavior, education, and occupation supported the image. That couldn't happen in the South today. Unless we take action, it never will happen."

Alex and Matthew were both silent. Finally Matthew protested, "You realize you're cutting through all the things Tristram is saying to me? You bring up one fact and, measured against all he says, I am nearly ashamed of being Southern. Alex, this is tearing me apart. The South is home in a way that makes it impossible to consider what you have to say."

"He's really put the load on you. So, you've decided?"

"No, but—" He got to his feet and paced the pilothouse floor. "It's like telling your family you disown them."

"I know; I've gone through the same struggle."

"But you seem at peace now. And you've chosen to turn your back on Southern principles."

"It's because of Jesus Christ. I was confused until I threw out everything except the necessity of having Jesus Christ as Lord of my life."

Matthew's voice was mocking. "You're saying that if you follow Jesus Christ, you'll not have anything to do with the Southern cause. Tell that to all the good people in the South who are convinced they love the Lord with all their hearts and they are living just as He wants them to live."

"I'm not saying they aren't Christian," Alex said slowly. "Not at all. That is between them and God. They know they will need to face God one of these days, and if their conscience is clear before Him now, who am I to say my values are better than theirs?"

"Then why this?"

"I'm not trying to solve all the world's problems. My individual commitment to God demands I follow the call He has placed upon my heart. Freeing these people is my burden and joy. And knowing this is what He wants of me, how else can I live?" He paused and then added, "Thank God, Olivia now feels the same way about this. On this last trip I was starting to see indications in her life that told me how deeply involved she was in the movement. More involved than even she recognized." He looked up with a grin, "But don't get me wrong! She gave me a very uneasy time until I heard her say the cause had become hers, too."

Matthew's eyes were thoughtful, nearly wary, as he said, "That surprises me. It doesn't seem like her. I'd figured you'd just come across so strong she was willing to take the risk. I also guessed she'd try talking you into going home. Maybe I underestimated her. Either that, or she's finally got her head on straight."

"Might be you've failed to understand what the Lord's been doing in her life."

Matthew moved impatiently. In a moment Alex said, "But getting back to your meeting, I am honestly interested in what Tristram had to say."

"Well, for one thing, he pointed out how the political balance was upset when California, Minnesota, and Oregon were admitted to the Union. This has all happened since 1850." Matthew paused, then added, "I don't know whether or not Tristram knows our involvement in the abolitionist movement, but this is one of the things he has mentioned several times as being an infringement of the South's rights. I agree. I don't know how it could be considered otherwise."

"Matt, I have a feeling the movement is causing more alarm in the South than any other single factor. Certainly it's bleeding their resources; how much we'll never know. Also the rise of the Republican party is seen as a threat. You know that."

Matthew nodded. "Events in Boston gave us the clue. Since then their presidential candidate has been defeated." In a moment he added, "But that won't go on forever, and that worries the South." He took a deep breath. "Secession is getting to sound better all the time."

"The North had the same idea for a time," Alex said dryly.

"But the South has some feasible reasons for considering secession."

"Give them to me."

"You've heard them all. But basically, we would be free to maintain our way of life. Tariff problems would be gone. The slave problem would no longer exist."

"You mean the abolition of slavery?"

"Alex, you've forgotten how passionately committed the Southern people are to their way of life. There's the cry for preservation— our forefathers established this culture; do we give up on it so easily? What is to replace it? The North is industrial; that isn't our forte. But you're putting me on the defensive. We don't need to justify our culture. We need to fight for it.

"Every man of us needs to accept that challenge. If the North has their way, we'll become paupers, stripped of voice and rights. The North's poor folk. Alex, we must have what we need to exist, as we have in the past, or it's the end for us, economically and politically."

"I don't think that's true. Granted, change will be necessary, and it might be painful. But Matt, the present direction of the South is disaster for everyone."

"You're mistaken. Do you realize France and Britain are nearly committed to our side right now? If it comes down to a fight, they'll help us."

Alex jumped to his feet and paced the floor.

"Don't get me wrong," Matthew continued. "I'm not in favor of either secession or war. It has scared me nearly to death for several years, but Tristram's changed my thinking on that too."

"Well, then, reassure me."

"The primary consideration is that the North will never allow it to happen. We threaten, and the North will come bowing and begging for our favor. They can't get along without our products any more than we can exist without their factories.

"I think Buchanan will be a help. He's a strong Union man, and he'll do everything necessary to hold it together." He turned to Alex. "We have weak sisters in the South. They don't want to secede, but we'll manage to convince them. After all, it's a paper secession—Alex, it'll never happen in reality. Nullification worked in 1832; Congress backed down on their stand on tariffs. Doesn't that make you think we have hope now?"

Alex stood up. "I hope you are correct. Now, let's go see if those dear ladies are still scrubbing."

CHAPTER 44

Matthew's plan worked. After digging the paddles free, they felled trees to use as levers and inched the *Awl* back into mid-stream. Wiping the perspiration from his brow, Alex came to the bank where Olivia and Crystal waited. "Would you ladies care for a cruise down the Ohio—as soon as we scrape a ton of mud off our boots?"

"Was there damage?" asked Olivia.

"Doesn't appear to be. We'll know as soon as we put power to the rudders. How about a piggyback ride before I clean my boots?"

"I'll clean your boots if you will deposit me on the deck—with more dignity than piggyback," Olivia promised. Alex took her up on her offer, using a lifeboat to bring Olivia out to the *Awl*. A short while later they were all heading back down the Ohio, the boat apparently free of damage.

The next morning the *Golden Awl* tied onto the wharf. "Home again," Alex said with a grin as he patted the bow.

"This did make me wish we could be on the river again," Olivia said wistfully.

"I'd like it, too. If Caleb comes before the end of the month, we could take a short trip."

Matthew and Crystal started up the hill together. Olivia watched them and asked, "What have you and Matthew been talking about—or is it a secret?"

"I don't think it is. Tristram has been pressuring Matt to return to the South. He's hit Matt right where it hurts—responsibility to the home acres."

"Does that thinking disturb you?"

"No, my obligation is to God first of all. You know that."

"I just wanted to hear you say so." He bent to nuzzle her neck and she whispered, "Alex, we're so happy I'm nearly afraid."

"Don't be; remember your dream—me, you, and God."

Finally she sighed and backed out of his arms. "Are you going to stay down here and tighten that paddle?"

"Yes. Matthew is going to return and help me. It will take most of the afternoon. I want to check the pistons, too."

———

It was a late November morning when Lucas Tristram returned to the Coopers'. For nearly an hour Crystal had been standing by the window facing the road, watching for Matthew. When Olivia came into the room. Crystal glanced at her and turned back to the window.

"Let me guess," Olivia said slowly. "You and Matthew have quarreled again. Crystal, it's obvious you two are having problems. Even Alex has noticed and asked. I think you need his counsel. I wish you would give me permission to tell my brother about Joseph." Crystal shook her head.

"Olivia, now isn't a good time to tell Matthew about Joseph. Besides, Joseph isn't the problem. It's this conflict about whether or not he should return home. You know Tristram is responsible for this upheaval."

"Don't blame Tristram," Olivia stated. "Matthew's too high-spirited to be content with the pace your life has taken on. I just wish you two had come with us this fall when we went down the Mississippi. A new pilot—Mike Clancy—made the trip possible." When Crystal didn't answer, Olivia added, "We had a fine time getting acquainted with him. He's a good pilot—has his commercial pilot license. It was disappointing to not have Caleb, but certainly Mike is the Lord's answer to the need for another pilot."

"I suppose it's my fault," Crystal admitted. "I don't like that boat any more than Amelia does. I think it's related to being nearly killed in the explosion." She sighed. "But I would have forced myself to go had I guessed the result would have been this."

She faced Olivia. "Matthew was so angry at me this morning. I can't remember how it started, but soon everything was wrong. You may think this ridiculous, but I sense the change in him began at the time of Lucas Tristram's visit. Matthew keeps talking about his responsibility to the South.

"At times I think I should quit fighting and just urge him to follow Tristram, but somehow I feel that man's ideas are so wrong." She stared at the floor. "Perhaps because of Joseph I understand in a different way." Her eyes begged for reassurance as she looked at Olivia.

"You are my dear sister-in-law; don't ever forget that. And please, about Matthew, be patient with him. Your marriage is the best thing that has ever happened to him."

Crystal watched Olivia walk to the hall tree and put on the heavy jacket hanging there. "Going out?"

"Alex is working down on the *Awl*. I thought I'd go help him and prepare his noon meal down there. We'll be back in several hours."

Crystal watched Olivia disappear out of sight. As she turned away from the window, a carriage came down the road. She eyed the smart rig as it stopped in front of the house. The driver, a gentleman dressed in white, jumped out, tied the horse to the hitching post, strode purposefully toward the house, and knocked on the door. "Lucas Tristram," she said in dismay.

Slowly she went to the door. Reluctantly she admitted him, nearly hating his confident air and assured smile.

"My dear," he hung his hat on the hall tree and followed her to the parlor. "Is Matthew at home?"

"No, and I have no idea when he will return."

"Well, I shall wait for a short period of time. Perhaps we can entertain each other. Tell me about your home. I know you've mentioned being from New Orleans. And what is your father's name?"

"Cabet is our family name," she snapped, getting to her feet. "Mr. Tristram, may I offer you coffee or tea?"

"Tea. I'll come help you prepare it."

"It isn't necessary. Perhaps you would like to read the newspaper.

Alex was deeply disappointed to read Lincoln lost his bid for the Senate." She hurried out of the room.

When she returned with the tea tray, he put down the newspaper and came to assist her. "That is an interesting article; however, I do not suffer along with Alex."

"What do you mean?

"Douglas is the hope of the South right now. We'll be anxious to see him contend for the presidency next election. He has the best interests of the South at heart."

"Is that so? I thought Buchanan came nearer being that man. Didn't he try to push the Lecompton Constitution on Kansas, and wouldn't that have forced slavery on the territory? I understand his actions caused Douglas a good deal of displeasure, which makes me wonder if Douglas is all bad. He must have some moral standard. I appreciate people who can forcefully take a stand for the right."

Tristram placed his cup on the tray and chuckled. "My dear, you will be a smashing hit in Washington."

"Will be? What are you referring to?"

"I've every intention of seeing your husband elected to Congress."

"Because you must stuff every possible seat with a man who is a willing slave to the South's interests, regardless of his own convictions in the matter?"

"For a person only one step removed from being a slave herself, you are remarkably well educated in politics—or perhaps you echo beautifully the voices clustered around you. My dear Crystal, you might as well resign yourself to being friends with me." His voice dropped, and as he hesitated, his eyes began to twinkle. "Because I can make you or break you according to my whim."

Crystal's face flushed. *He knows!* she thought. *Somehow, he's found out!*

"Right now I want your husband to leave this organization and return South," Tristram continued. "The sooner, the better." He got to his feet and picked up his gold-headed cane. "Have you seen Joseph recently? I find myself very intrigued with that relationship. I must bid you farewell. Tell Matthew I'll make it a point to visit the next time I'm in the area." He paused as he pulled on his gloves. "My dear Crystal, I can't believe that you lack the power to convince Matthew to return South. In fact, I suggest you do it, or I shall be forced to do so."

"And how do you intend to do that?"

"Never mind. We'll handle that situation when it arises. Right now I see you as an asset in Washington. That impression could change."

From her seat beside the fire, Crystal watched Lucas pick up his hat and let himself out the door. Her hands were trembling. Pushing them hard against the pit of her stomach, she fought for calmness. "Oh, Olivia, help me!" she murmured.

———

That evening in their bedroom, Olivia faced her husband and said, "Alex, I must beg you, talk sense into Matthew. He is tearing Crystal to pieces."

Alex pulled off his shirt and came to sit beside Olivia, "What do you mean by that?"

She shook her head. "I can't tell you. She's taken me into her confidence, and I'd give anything to break that confidence. In fact, this afternoon I begged for permission to tell you the whole story, and she wouldn't hear of it."

"Yet she expects me to help her?" He studied Olivia's face, ran his finger lightly down her jaw and said, "I don't know where to start. Matthew needs to make a commitment of his life to the Lord. He won't be straight in his thinking until he gets his thoughts from the right source, and that's the Lord Jesus.

"But in addition to that, we don't see eye to eye on the issue of slavery. I suspect he's moving closer to being in sympathy with the South. He knows how I feel, but I can't make him change his mind."

"Not even to save his marriage?"

"Dear wife, I think you are overwrought. Come to bed now, and see if a good night's sleep doesn't give you a better perspective."

———

The line of pink and purple asters marching beside the stone path leading to the Coopers' front door was a herald of approaching autumn. After a brief rain the air was soft and the sunshine bright. To Olivia, who was seated on the front steps, it seemed the whole world was waiting for that plunge toward autumn. Sadie came out and sat beside her. "Where has the summer gone? It's been a year since thee was married to Alex. Outrageous wedding it was, but guess it's good enough. Thee both seem happy."

Olivia squeezed her hand. "We are; oh, Sadie, I don't understand why I was so fearful."

"Better to settle the questions first, not later." She sighed heavily. In a moment she shaded her eyes and looked at Olivia. "Don't like to think of winter this early. Winter gets so common a body expects it forever. Only one thing worse, that's letting life get us down so we forget to expect a difference."

"The winter of the soul?" Sadie nodded. Slowly Olivia added, "I think that's what Crystal and Matthew have."

"I know. I've been talking to the Lord about it. There's not much else a person can do when they don't know where to begin." She looked at Olivia curiously and waited.

Amelia came out the door. "Is this a secret session or are you open to comment?"

"If you have a comment on the weather," Olivia said, smiling up at her. "Sadie's full of talk about winter of the soul."

"I guess that's what I have." Amelia dropped heavily on the step. "At least I'm out of sorts with my world."

"Is your world different than ours?" Olivia asked.

"Well it isn't so full of young love that it's nearly sickening. And you needn't look offended, Olivia. I'm talking about Matthew and Crystal. One minute they're at each other's throats, and then they're all lovely." She sighed heavily. "Keeps me up half the night."

"We could move thee to the other end of the hall," Sadie said delicately.

Alex walked up the hill and sat down beside Olivia as Amelia began to laugh. "I wasn't talking about their late-night activities. I meant worrying about them. But my situation, I don't regret."

"Leaving thy husband?" Sadie's eyebrows lifted. "That's what thee meant?"

"That, and all the rest." Her voice was harsh as she added, "I did what needed to be done."

"He was unfaithful?" Alex probed gently.

"No, I was." She paused and moved restlessly. "Unfaithfulness can't be undone. I know that, but I'm working at getting on with life." There was a bitter twist to her lips as she said, "Can't change the past."

"But it can be forgiven," Alex stated. "Amelia, several times we've talked this way. I can't understand why I sense this bitterness in you. Don't you want God's forgiveness?"

"Of course, and I'm working at getting it."

"You mean all this—" The sweep of his hand indicated the boat and the house. "I've seen you working for these people until you were ready to drop. Are you telling me it's an attempt to gain God's favor?"

For a moment she hesitated. "Of course. Being sinful doesn't mean I'm unfit to do this."

"Well, certainly not. But work for God's kingdom comes *after* we accept God's salvation. Are you doing this under the impression that you're winning favor with God? Earning your place in the Kingdom of God?"

Watching Amelia, Olivia began to see the fatigue etched on her face. "Of course. Do you think I'd do this for myself—taking care of the slaves, sittin' with sick people, caring for children—just for the fun of it?"

"But for salvation?"

She got to her feet. "I tried the other way—down on my face crying out for forgiveness. It doesn't work. This is the only other thing I know to do."

"What is there in your life that is making you believe the great Creator God is unwilling to give you the same kind of forgiveness He has given each one of us?"

Slowly Amelia got up off the step. "Guess I need to think about that for a while."

That night the people came. Olivia and Alex were in the kitchen when they heard the knock and Amos' response. With a quick glance at her, Alex walked rapidly down the hall with Olivia following.

There were three men, a woman, and a small child. Alex faced them and asked, "Did I hear you ask for me?"

The timid man with the hat in his hands said, "Yes, suh. De man tell me to ask for Mister Alexander Duncan. He tole me you would see that we got into Canada?"

Olivia stepped forward and Alex blocked her way. "Help you

into Canada. Sorry, but you have the wrong information. I won't help you into Canada. I suggest you move on. The constable would be inclined to help you more quickly than I."

There was a muttered protest from the man. For a moment the group of people looked at each other, and then turned and silently filed out.

"Alex!" Olivia turned to look at her husband. "What—"

He touched her lips. "Did you notice? They had my name. And, did they look like the usual people?"

She shook her head. "I'm not certain what you mean."

"That man was wearing a black suit—old, most certainly, but there wasn't a sign of dust on it. Now, you know as well as I do, that the people don't stop to change their clothing before they pound on the door."

Olivia nodded. "They arrive looking frightened nearly to death." She threw her arms around him. "It was a trap, wasn't it?"

He nodded. "I've been expecting this since the advent of Lucas Tristram on our doorstep. Didn't any of you wonder what information he had besides my name?"

And only then did Olivia notice Crystal hanging on the bannister as if she couldn't stand alone.

CHAPTER 45

When she heard the knock at the front door, Crystal was in her bedroom, alone in the house. Hastily wrapping a robe around herself, she crossed the hall to the alcove. Pushing open the casement window, she saw Lucas Tristram.

Trying to appear cordial, she called, "You want Matthew?"

"Is he at home?"

"He's in the pasture with Amos. If you care to wait, be seated in the parlor; he should be back in a few minutes. I'll be down shortly."

She shut the window and returned to her room to finish dressing. As she combed her hair, she fumed, "Of all people! I had nearly believed him gone forever. It's been nearly a year, why must he come to annoy us again?"

She heard a step on the stairs, a footfall outside her door. Looking around for her robe, she caught her breath as she heard him call, "Crystal, Mrs. Thomas, I wish to talk to you before Matthew comes back. I'll wait in this little sitting room."

She took a shaky breath. "Very well. I'll be out shortly."

With trembling hands, she removed the robe and hastily began to dress, pausing to peer out her window toward the pasture. She heard Matthew call, "Alex, I'll be with you in a moment. Need to get my tools."

With a sigh of relief, Crystal took up her frock. At that moment her bedroom door was flung open. Lucas rushed in. He stopped, and a curious grin swept across his face. She heard the front door and as she opened her mouth to shout, Lucas tore off his waistcoat and dashed across the room toward her.

"Sir!" her scream was only a gasp.

"Tristram!" Matthew surged through the door. "What is the meaning of this outrage? Crystal, cover yourself!"

Lucas turned with a grin. "Outrage? My friend, you won't call me out for the likes of her."

"What do you mean?" Matthew roared, his giant stride took him across the room. Seizing Lucas by his shirt front, he demanded. "Explain yourself."

"Explain myself? Surely! Ah, so this is the state of affairs. An innocent husband. Matthew, perhaps you had best ask your wife about Joseph. I thought you were fully aware of the taint."

Matthew turned toward Crystal. He was still grasping Lucas' shirt as he searched her face, then he whirled. His one blow cracked through the room. Crystal watched the man in white feebly trying to regain his balance as he tottered backward into the hall. She saw Alex's startled face on the stairs one moment before Matthew flung Lucas' coat through the door and kicked it closed.

"Matt!" Alex's frantic pounding brought Matthew around.

His voice was heavy and slow as he replied, "It's all right. I'm not going to so much as touch her. I only want to talk to her."

Alex's feet thumped down the stairs. They heard a moan. Matthew turned to her. "I should have guessed this was too good to last. Tell me about it. Who is Joseph?"

Crystal finally forced the words. "You know Joseph."

"The slave you freed? What about him?"

"He is my father."

The rage melted out of Matthew's eyes and she watched the loathing grow. He studied her face, her exposed shoulders. "You've tricked me. Lucas knew; only I was in the dark! Nigger! Nothing but a dirty—" He wheeled, and before he walked from the room, he picked up her mirror and slammed it to the floor. With a twisted smile he watched her cringe and shrink against the wall.

From the foot of the stairs, Alex watched Matthew come down.

Each slow step seemed to jar his whole body. He stopped at the foot of the stairs. "Where did he go?"

"You didn't do much damage. He managed to get into his buggy by himself. I expect him to make it safely back to the hotel. Want to talk?"

Matthew shook his head and walked out the door.

Olivia came into the house. "What's wrong with Matthew? He didn't answer when I spoke to him."

"I think we have a problem." Alex lifted his head and glanced toward the stairs. "Maybe you should see if you can do something for Crystal."

Olivia hesitated. "What happened?"

"I don't know. But I do know Tristram was upstairs, and Matthew came close to knocking him clear over the railing. Better go up."

"Oh, dear Lord," Olivia moaned. "I can guess. Matthew's found out about Joseph."

"What about Joseph?"

"He's her father." She turned and went upstairs as Alex stood there, stunned.

Still clad only in chemise and pantaloons, Crystal leaned against the window frame. Olivia stood beside her and together they watched Matthew walk slowly down the hill. His shoulders drooped, and each step was fumbled and uncertain. "Crystal, see that? He does love you."

Crystal sighed. Moving uneasily, she stepped over the shattered glass. Her voice was hollow and weak. "It's not that. He'll get over love in a hurry." She turned, and the expression in her wide brown eyes made Olivia's heart sink. "You were right, Olivia. Matthew is too Southern. From what I saw in his eyes I know it's over. Matthew will never be the husband of a nigger."

Olivia put her arms around the woman. Crystal's skin was chilled. She moved away from Olivia. Turning her head, she said, "Please, I must be alone." With one staggering step she moved to the bed and dropped across it.

Alex walked down to the boat. As he expected, Matthew sat in the cabin with his feet on the table. He looked up when Alex entered.

Alex sat down. "I know it looked bad but I don't think the circumstances were what you—"

Matthew got to his feet and, turning his back, he sat on the edge of the table. "Look, this is a heavy load. I don't want to discuss it."

"In your shoes, I wouldn't either. But Matt, there are some things you need to take into consideration right now. Tomorrow is too late. Sure, you're bitter. I expect this is the situation Olivia and Crystal have been talking about. She wouldn't tell me what the problem was, but I'd guessed something was shoving the two of you apart."

"That isn't it," he said impatiently. "Crystal didn't want me to have anything to do with Tristram."

"Today demonstrated a character trait she must have suspected."

Matthew turned. "Or her fear of being discovered. I wonder if she was trying to buy his silence?"

"Matt, that's as ugly as you can get."

"Tell me what other view is a man to have of a woman like Crystal? I'm not talking about unfaithfulness; I'm talking about her willingness to deceive me. If, in the name of love, that isn't as low as a woman can get, I don't understand life and love. Now I wonder how low she would sink to buy his silence."

Slowly Alex said, "Have you considered her side? It is obvious Crystal's come from a family where there was love and self-respect, where she was valued for who she was. Isn't that the way it should be? Why should we consider one race of people inferior to us because of the color of their skin?"

Matthew turned and thrust his hands into his pockets. With his shoulders hunched he growled, "Cut it out! Alex, you've been raised as I was. What did your folks have to say about niggers? Did they tell you how fine and noble they are, how much they are to be respected? My dad threatened to horsewhip me if I ever went close to the slave quarters, and I knew what he meant. Do you think I can drop those feelings in a moment? Give me space, man. I'd like to think differently, but right now there's no way."

Alex sat down and shook his head. "Matthew, I've got to apologize to you." His voice was heavy and Matthew's head came up. He studied Alex's face and sat down.

"I've neglected you. The others came around with their questions, and I thought that was the most important situation. I thought about the problems they would face crossing into Canada, learning how to be people instead of slaves. I threw myself into helping them understand the love God was holding out to them. Because I saw your scorn, and because you didn't want to discuss Jesus Christ and His message of salvation, I've failed you. Despite the fact the Lord kept nudging, I didn't think your need was as great or immediate. Matthew, I'm sorry and now it's too late to say the things I should have been saying all along."

"Like what?" His face was still and curious.

"That Christianity isn't just for the purpose of making it to heaven or a way to create workers to do His work. Matthew, Christianity is learning to live the way God intended from day one. It's a repeat of the original drama in the Garden, played with a new cast, and in the midst of an obstacle course. If you'd known that and what obstacles you'd run into, I'm certain you would have been easy to convince. Matt, I've a feeling I've lost my opportunity to have any influence in your life. But don't turn your back on the only decent way to live."

"Christianity? You forget how I've been raised. I know all I want to know, and I don't want to discuss it."

They sat in silence. Finally Alex sighed. "I came down to tell you I must leave."

"What's up?"

"A job. Want it? There's something going on in Oberlin, Ohio. Might have to intervene with the authorities."

Matthew sighed, "Might. Tell me about it."

"It would help if you'd take it. I want to go into Canada and look for Caleb. Can't quit worrying about him. Fortunately I know the general area where he intended to enter. I'm going to take Olivia with me."

"A honeymoon?" Matthew's lips twisted, and Alex turned away. "Hey fella, there's still such a thing as forgiveness between the two of you. It's hard, but not as difficult as this."

Matthew sighed and looked up at Alex. "Cut it out! It's easy for you to say all these things, but I've never been caught up in religion and all this other. Maybe that's making a difference now. Sure, I have sympathy for these people, but I wouldn't give my life for them. Right now I see nothing except just forgetting the whole affair—because you know that's what it was. Just an interlude that needs to be forgotten."

Alex waited. Finally he said, "There's food in here. Clancy won't arrive for another day or so. Stay here until you go. Want me to gather up your things—at the house?" Alex saw his nod. He clapped Matthew on the shoulder and left.

Olivia and Alex faced Crystal. Her voice was dull and low as she said, "There's simply nothing to be done. I made my mistake when I refused to tell Matthew before we were married. I must live with the consequences."

"I'll go talk to Matthew," Olivia said.

Crystal caught her arm. "Please! I still have my pride. I'd never live at ease with him unless he comes on his own."

"Olivia, leave your brother alone. Right now talk won't do any good. When he comes to his senses, he'll see how unfair this is. Until then, we're invading his privacy."

Turning, Alex bent over Crystal. "We love you, Crystal. Right now there seems to be no resolution of the problem, but you are our dear sister and we'll continue to pray that you and Matthew will be reunited." He paused and added, "Could we pray with you now?"

She shook her head. "I know what needs to be done, but I need time to think about it all."

In the morning, Crystal watched Matthew walk around the house to the barn. She watched him lead out the mare, and strap his bag behind the saddle. Without a backward glance, he mounted and rode away. *Time. It's called the healer. Knowing Matthew, it will take more than time. Oh, my darling, how could I have lived in a fool's paradise?*

"Crystal, may I come in?"

With a sigh, she said, "Yes, Olivia. I suppose you're here to remind me I didn't eat last night. I'll go down with you."

Olivia looked deep into her eyes and then held her close. "Come, you know it's best to get on with life, and we'll be here to help you."

They were all there to meet her—Amos looking gruff and embarrassed, Sadie with tears in her eyes, and Amelia looking merely curious. But later, it was Amelia who gave the advice she accepted.

A week had passed when Amelia faced her over the dishpan. Her statement was direct and weighty. "I made a mistake once. It's like Alex says. The worse the sin, the harder it is to find your way out of the forest. Time doesn't heal, it hinders. I've tried to go back the way I came, but I waited too long. It's like tossing a rock in the river—out of sight, and it's gone. Crystal, somehow you're going to have to be the one to take the step."

The next day Crystal watched Amos and Sadie preparing to go into town. "As long as you're going, may I ride in with you?"

Sadie looked surprised and Crystal said, "I must take one step out of the forest. I want to visit Joseph."

Amos cleared his throat. "Daughter, we'd be glad to take thee and fetch thee home, too."

Very little was said on the way into town, and when Crystal reached the blacksmith shop the burly smithy looked from her to Joseph and said, "Yer leg's been bothering you. Saw you limping around. Take an hour or so off; business is light right now."

"Hank, I'm obliged." Joseph led the way to his little house.

Again Joseph bustled around the hut, pulling a chair up, preparing tea. Finally he settled opposite her and asked, "Missy, is it going well with you?"

"Joseph, please don't call me Missy." The tears began. He knelt beside her, making soft sounds of sympathy. Finally he asked, "Would it help if you just told me about it?"

"I think you are the only one on this earth who will understand how I feel."

He sat down on his stool and lowered his head. "Might be. And Crystal, might it be nearly the same problem?"

"Might be."

"Would it help if I tell how it was with us?"

"Please."

"Your mother, Evangeline, was the only white woman I've ever known who looked at me like I was a man instead of a machine to carry drinks or chop sugar cane. When it started, I was a house slave. There were problems. I wanted to learn, and it seemed I was always poking into a book when I should have been working." His voice dropped and a pleasant smile softened his face.

As if suddenly recalling her presence, he looked up. "Evangeline took it upon herself to teach me to read. In those days, her daddy was a busy man, and her mama—well you know how she is, sickly. Evangeline was left to entertain herself. She knew I was eager to learn how to read and do sums. After her teacher left in the afternoon, we'd meet in the garden and have our school.

"I was caught once and took a beating for it. Seems that made the difference."

"What do you mean?"

"We began to love each other. In the beginning we tried to deny it. This went on for nearly a year before she became pregnant. She wanted me to run away with her. The temptation was nearly more than this colored man could take. I suppose I'd have weakened if they hadn't discovered she was expecting and sent her away to the convent for a time.

"She came back just before you were born. I never did see her again. I suppose she still thinks I don't love her." He looked up and Crystal saw his eyes were brimming with tears. She held out her arms.

Finally she was able to ask, "But you aren't bitter. Why?"

"Just the Lord. He's taken away the hurt and misery. This life isn't the end of it all. One of these days I'll get to heaven and me and my Evangeline will be able to sit down and talk about it without the hurt we had here."

Before she left he said, "Want to tell your old dad what's troubling you? Now don't you get too close, you'll get my dirt on you."

"Oh, Daddy!" Crystal sobbed, the name coming out unbidden. "I've been fighting all the ugly things for so long. It's taken ugliness and Matthew's leaving to make me face myself, and now I want to make this up to you."

Dabbing at the tears in her eyes, she came to him. He held her off, saying, "Now, don't you go fretting. I've already made up my mind I'm going to Canada. Alex and Olivia are taking me with them when they go. Alex promised they'd see me settled with the rest of the people. That pleases me fine. I've been lonesome for the friends I'd made on the trip. Fine people they are, and now I'll be content."

"You won't let me do anything for you?"

"It would make me the happiest person alive if you'd write me a letter once or twice a year."

"I will, and I'm going to knit a sweater for you."

"There now. The wagon's come for you. I'll have Alex give you the address to write to me."

Slowly she started for the door, hesitated, and turned quickly. He was standing there, the loneliest person she had ever seen. Quickly she dashed back and threw her arms around him. She saw the hunger in his eyes and kissed him. "Goodbye, Daddy," she whispered before she left the house.

————

At dinner the next evening Amelia said, "Well, friends, this is the last evening meal we'll have together. I'm leaving in the morning. I'm taking a boat ride clear across Missouri—back the way I came, only I'm going clear on to the gold fields in the Rocky Mountains. When you hear about a woman making her fortune in the mines, you'll know it's me."

Olivia exclaimed, "Amelia! Are you certain that's what you want to do? It's so different than the way you've been—"

Amelia looked at Alex. "You told me I was doing it all wrong. I started thinking about it all. Why waste my time doing something that's not going to get me what I've been working for? Decided I might as well enjoy life. I'm going to live it up, just like I started out to do."

"Amelia!" Alex winced. "I'm sorry—this is just exactly the opposite of what I wanted you to do."

"You were trying to get me to do something, huh? Alex, you are the dearest man alive. Don't you ever let a woman tell you otherwise. But I don't think you'll make it as a preacher. You were supposed to give an altar call after you told me I was doing it all wrong, and before setting me straight."

She got to her feet and blew Alex a kiss. "Now, I've baked a dried peach pie for you all while you were gone today. We're celebrating. And dearie—" She ran around the table and embraced Crystal. "If you decide to come out Denver way, look me up. Might be I can find an interesting job for you to do. If nothing else, I'll hire you to cook in my kitchen."

"I thought you were going to dig gold," Alex said.

"More likely I'll run a house."

"A boardinghouse?" Sadie brightened. "Why, that's a good idea." Amelia's jaw dropped.

————

When Alex came into the bedroom and closed the door, Olivia turned to look at him. "Why are you leaning against the door, and why are you grinning like that?"

"Because my dear, this is all crazy. We're going to escape. I've been trying to shuffle people like pawns, and I think God must be laughing at my foolish efforts. Maybe He was the one who said first that you can lead a horse to water, but you can't make him drink."

"Oh, Alex, you are discouraged. Well, at least I turned out well."

"That didn't have anything to do with me. God got to you before I did."

"Alex, be serious."

"I am. We're leaving, too. It's all arranged. We're taking Joseph to Canada to find Caleb and his friends. Also, I hope to bring Caleb and Bertie back with us. In addition, Clancy is heading out, down the Mississippi. It was his idea."

"You trust him with the precious *Golden Awl*!"

"It's God's boat, not mine." He paused, "Now wife, come kiss me, since you haven't all day."

She turned to him and snuggled her head against his chest.

"Olivia, everything has gone wrong in the past several weeks. Lincoln lost the Senate seat, and we live in a state of unrest that's tugging at the seams of the whole country. And you—"

"Alex, you were the one who reminded me last time. I'll remind you now. Remember the dream? Me, you, and God. Does it still seem like a good combination?"

He sat down on the edge of the bed and pulled her onto his lap. "Olivia, you are like walking through green pastures."

"And you are my well-watered vine. Alex, Crystal told me about Joseph's philosophy. Life here is only for a short time, and then there's all eternity. The fairy tales say the prince and princess lived happily ever after. Maybe that's the only way to look at it. The ever after, even if some of the present isn't happy."

"I've been wanting to say that. But I've been fearful for you if—"

She placed her fingers over his lips. "Alex, I know. I faced that with fear and trembling before I asked you to marry me. It's settled. We'll enjoy today and live happily ever after."

"The prince and his princess."

"More or less. Our life may not be easy, but it will count for something. You, me, and God. We'll obey, and He'll take care of the rest."

Alex laughed and kissed her. "To Canada, then?"

"To Canada," Olivia replied. "And wherever else He leads."